AFLOAT

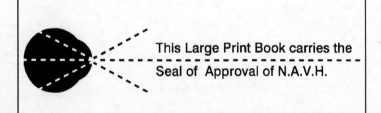

This Large Print Book carries the
Seal of Approval of N.A.V.H.

AFLOAT

ERIN HEALY

THORNDIKE PRESS

A part of Gale, Cengage Learning

GALE
CENGAGE Learning·

Detroit • New York • San Francisco • New Haven, Conn • Waterville, Maine • London

GALE
CENGAGE Learning®

Thorndike Press® Large Print Christian Mystery
The text of this Large Print edition is unabridged.
Other aspects of the book may vary from the original edition.
Set in 16 pt. Plantin.

LIBRARY OF CONGRESS CATALOGING-IN-PUBLICATION DATA

Healy, Erin M.
    Afloat / by Erin Healy. — Large Print edition.
        pages cm. — (Thorndike Press Large Print Christian Mystery)
    ISBN 978-1-4104-5899-5 (hardcover) — ISBN 1-4104-5899-7 (hardcover)
    1. Large type books. I. Title.
    PS3608.E245A69 2013
    813'.6—dc23   2013016890

Published in 2013 by arrangement with Thomas Nelson, Inc.

Printed in Mexico
1 2 3 4 5 6 7 17 16 15 14 13

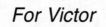

For Victor

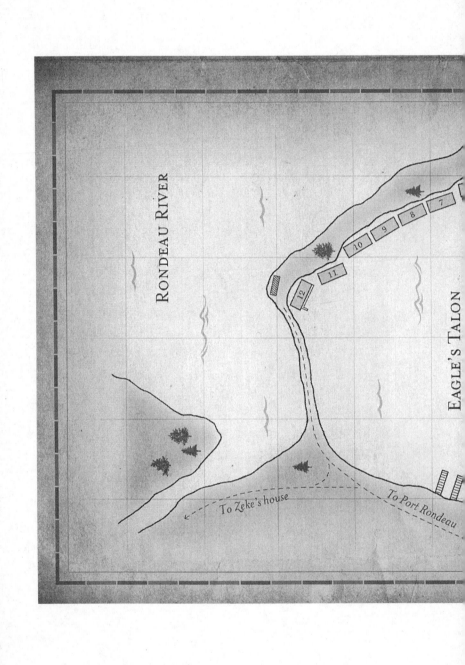

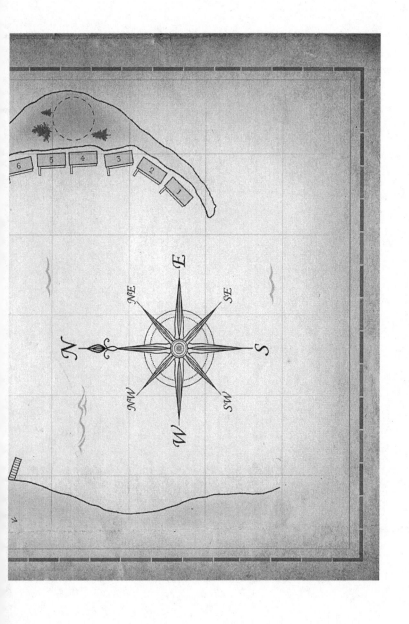

1

The wet suit and the water are black, and after the man slips into both, he seems to vanish from the world. He has come on a starless night to avoid being seen, to hide a few containers where they won't be found. He will be underpaid for this task by his anonymous employer, but times are hard so he takes what he can get.

He has gone into the water between his bobbing boat and twelve shadowy structures that float. They are gathered under the weak moon in a semicircle like disciples awaiting their teacher. But he is not the one they wish for. As instructed he will secure his packages under the second unit, which is squat and unfinished. Which will never be finished.

The silky surface between him and building 2 reflects the sky's silver stars. For a moment, before he lowers the diving mask, he is distracted by the glittering scene. The understanding gives him a jolt: because it *is* a starless night, and these are not reflections. They are sardine-sized creatures flashing with their own energy, flickering randomly, tricking his eyes.

He lets go of the boat and reaches out to touch one, expecting it to dart away. It flares instead, flaming like a struck match though fully submerged, and sends a tingling shock through the palm of his hand. He jerks back. The flame dies. With the thumb of his other hand he tries to rub the sting away.

The pain won't die. Nor will his sudden certainty that more secrets than his are hidden in this place.

He would turn back, if not for the money.

He dives into darkness to do his work, avoiding contact with the silver things, and as he swims they fade away. Fear hurries him along. He needs to be gone before the sun rises, before everything concealed comes to light.

2

If he had been looking at the day from a different point of view, Vance Nolan might have figured out the problem while there was still time to act. But when he first sensed that something was wrong, his instinct told him to search for the usual suspects: Equipment that might malfunction. Procedures that might be short-cut. Materials that might be shoddy.

So it was nearly noon before Vance realized that the thing bothering him was not any of these. Instead, it was an absence, a noise stripped away from the world, something like not being able to hear the sound of his own breathing.

He couldn't hear the birds.

Vance stood at the tip of Eagle's Talon, a long peninsula that hooked the wide Rondeau River like a bird snatching a fish. Feathery black willows spread shade across the land and housed plenty of feathered creatures, as did the tall grass-like leaves of the flowering river bulrushes. Most days Vance could hear the calls of terns and gulls and other waterbirds over the clattering human noises that rose from his construction site. But hammers, drills, nail guns, air compressors, trucks, and jocular workers had never drowned out the world as they did on this brilliant July day.

On the inside of the claw-like strip of land was a cove almost half a mile across, sparkling with summer sun. On the outside of the land's curve, the river was a swift highway that promised to transport a man to utopia if only he had a boat. Apparently the birds had set off for paradise already.

Vance removed his white hard hat so the light breeze could cool his head, then brushed shore dust off his short beard with his other hand. From this vantage, facing north, he could see the entire construction project going on inside the crescent of the cove. Before the first day of fall, the neighborhood that had been translated from his mind onto paper and then into a model would finally become a full-scale reality — though not exactly as he'd originally envisioned.

He looked north toward the top of the cove, where the long, skinny boom of a truck-mounted pump formed a towering arc nearly forty feet over the water. It scraped the sky's belly and then turned downward to deliver wet concrete to the surface of an unusual foundation. Constructed of sealed foam blocks, the platform was designed to float.

Here at Eagle's Talon, Vance built homes on water.

Technically, they were condominiums. Elite living spaces for wealthy owners, eight units in each of the twelve buildings, ninety-six units total. To Vance, though, they were the first step toward his real goal, which was to build beautiful amphibious homes for the poor. Until Tony Dean had scuttled Vance's plans, that's what these unusual units were supposed to be.

In spite of this, every day Vance stood here at the tip of the peninsula and reminded himself that all work was worth doing well.

On the day the birds fell silent, Vance's construction crew was assembling prefabricated aluminum walls on the cured foundations of buildings 1 through 6. A sub-contracted pump company had spent the week pouring the foundations of buildings 7 through 11. Building 11, the final pour, would be finished within a few hours. It would cure within a few days. Building 12, the model, had been completed in the spring and already had residents in four of its eight units.

On the shoreline behind 11, the rough-terrain concrete-pump truck was braced on extended outriggers between the water and the earth. Behind the truck, a concrete mixer continuously fed wet concrete into the pump via a chute. And on the floating platform, the pump operator guided the boom with a remote control while a laborer pointed the hose where he wanted the concrete to go. The truck's rack-and-pinion slewing system made a whirring sound as the operator directed it to shift.

The only detail out of the ordinary that day was the presence of a fifteen-year-old kid, the pump operator's son, who was permitted to sit in the truck's cab while his father worked down on the foundation. Vance wouldn't have allowed the kid on the site at all, and he had questioned his presence in the truck, but the operator assured him it wasn't against company policy.

Vance didn't really care. Too many things could go wrong at a work site like this, and all of it was his responsibility — especially the things that went wrong. So he had asked the subcontractor's foreman, Drew Baxter, to send the kid home. As this would have sidetracked the operator and delayed the day's work, Baxter refused and blew him off with a grin that made Vance feel uneasy.

It wasn't long afterward, while Vance watched this operation from the peninsula's southern point, that he noticed a small brown bird performing aerial stunts around the highest point of the concrete pump's boom. The silent bird made one, two, three loops and then plummeted toward the surface of the river, pulled out of its dive at the last possible second, and shot away, scratching the glassy water with the tips of its feathers.

That was the moment when the birds' silence commanded Vance's attention.

Vance reseated his hard hat, then peeled off his outer work shirt and left the tip of the peninsula. The summer heat had crept up on him. It caused the skin at the nape of his neck and under his beard to itch.

He began to walk back toward the pump-truck operation. At building 2, a young apprentice named Andy was bent over a drill, securing the wall to a floor joist. Andy was just out of high school but demonstrated the reliability and skill of someone who'd been doing this kind of work for much longer. Vance planned to keep tabs on him. The crucifix Andy wore around his neck dangled away from his body as he worked, then slapped his chest when he straightened up to wave a greeting.

Vance passed buildings 3 and 4, scanning the riverside bank for the gulls that usually insisted on being heard even when they hid. The lush vegetation looked just as it had yesterday. There was no sign of damage to the reedy nesting areas. But neither was there any sign of waterfowl.

Somewhere near building 7, Vance wondered if he should take the birds' silence as a clue to call it quits early. Sometimes the wildlife were prophets of disaster. There was another reason why the layer of silence sounded eerie to him, a troubling reason from an obscure corner of his memory that he didn't want to examine too closely.

When he reached building 8, the ground at Vance's feet vibrated as if someone had dropped a heavy load just yards away.

A mechanical groan raised shouts from the concrete crew at building 11. Vance dropped his overshirt in the dust and started running before his mind had completely registered the problem, though his eyes spotted it right away: one of the pump truck's forward outriggers was sinking into the water, and already the rear axles had given up their share of the vehicle's weight.

16

The truck tipped at a catawampus angle, pulled over by the weight of its long, arcing boom.

"Clear out!"

His command was unnecessary. The men on the foundation were already scrabbling off the floating platform and onto solid ground. Others backed off the area like ripples of water fleeing a tossed stone. The rubber hose thrashing at the end of the pump hit a man in the head and spit wet concrete into the cove as the boom swung away. And at the back of the pump truck, the concrete mixer's chute groaned and twisted and then snapped off.

On the sloping bank, the foreman, Baxter, seemed to have no head for crisis. Lips parted, eyes frowning, he was watching the truck fall as if it were an illusion and he was trying to sort out how the trick was done.

Someone was shouting and waving his arms as if to indicate the operator should swing the boom in the opposite direction. The operator seemed to have forgotten the boom entirely and was shouting about his kid in the tilting cab. Wet concrete sucked at his work boots and held him back from his son.

Within seconds Vance reached the truck. It was tipping swiftly, but he jumped onto the stainless step before it was too far off the ground, then transferred his weight to the wheel guard so he had space to open the door. The boy had been tossed off his seat toward the starboard side of the windshield. He dangled by the steering wheel with one arm and scrabbled to get his feet under him. A clipboard slid along the dash, clattered against a bracketed fire extinguisher, and then tumbled out the open window on the other side.

Vance yanked the door open. He braced himself, one boot on the driver's seat and one on the truck's frame, and leaned back against the heavy door as he extended his hand to the boy. They clapped a strong grip on each other's wrists.

The pair remained on the listing thirty-ton truck for no more than three seconds.

In the first instant, Vance looked past the kid's shoulder and out through the open window, which was almost touching the water. He saw the white paper of the clipboard fluttering like a fishtail as it sank to depths that hadn't existed when the truck was stabilized such a short time ago. A massive hole gaped under the forward right outrigger where solid ground had been just hours earlier. Beneath the surface of the water, mud was falling away from the bank like an avalanche. The paper was swallowed by swirling sediment.

In the next second, as he heaved the boy out of the cab, Vance lifted his eyes and realized that the plummeting boom would shear the bedroom balconies clean off the face of building 12.

In the third second they leaped. Vance turned in the air. And as they dropped behind the falling truck, he saw a person step out onto the nearest third-floor balcony.

The long blond hair belonged to Danielle Clement. Danielle, the young single mom of five-year-old Simeon. Danielle, who had caught Vance's eye and occupied a bright room in his mind since the day he'd met her at Tony Dean's office two years ago.

Danielle, who should have been at work.

She turned her back to the looming catastrophe as she reached for her sliding glass door.

Little Simeon was at her side.

Vance forced every remaining bit of breath out of his taxed lungs. "Danielle!" he shouted.

He saw her turn toward his warning, and then the hard ground struck the bottom of his feet and punished every bone in his legs and back, and the upended heavy equipment blocked his view of the worst tragedy ever to occur on his watch.

3

Danielle Clement arrived at Eagle's Talon only minutes before the blow hit her balcony, because a prospective buyer was expected that afternoon and it was Danielle's job to greet him.

There was no better place to live than on the water. At Eagle's Talon, all problems bobbed away on the current. The breezes lifted burdens off her shoulders, and the chuckling water rocked her mind into easy dreams. Two years ago, after her husband's unexpected death, Danielle never thought that such a peaceful place or frame of mind could be hers. But here she was.

Of course, the unit at Eagle's Talon where she and Simeon lived wasn't truly hers. It was Tony Dean's, provided to her by his unique brand of kindness, which she'd experienced for the first time one month to the day after her husband died. Tony found her paying respects at Danny's grave and apologized for the intrusion. He had done business with Danny, Tony said. She apologized for not recalling his name. At the time her world was a blur, and Tony seemed to understand. He had heard through the grapevine that she was looking for work, and he needed an executive assistant. Would she consider applying?

Danielle didn't have to say that she and Danny, in their late twenties, had considered life insurance a waste of cash, that Danny's death had put her behind on the mortgage, or that she was desperate to find an income that would support her and her son. Tony spared her that humiliation. He said only that he had thought well of Danny and would like to help her and Simeon in any way he could.

She accepted his offer with gratitude and a healthy amount of fear. She believed men as generous and as wealthy as Tony expected returns on their investments, and for months she kept her guard up. He was a successful businessman, a land developer with political aspirations, a man who demanded as much of others as he demanded of himself. But in the office she found him to be a respectable professional, and out of the office he was a perfect companion.

He took her and Simeon to dinner weekly.

He invited her to join him for public business functions and local political events. He gave her frequent raises and occasional bonuses that always exceeded her credit card and house payments. He paid for Simeon to play soccer and showered him with toys at Christmas and birthdays. And after two years of this, not once did Tony make a demand that wasn't strictly related to her job.

Danielle found it easy to be his friend, but she didn't love him, except in the way she might love a good book. In the beginning she worried often about what she would do if his interest in her ever evolved into something romantic. He was fond of pretty women but uninterested in marriage, and he asked her once if she thought that would work against him when the time came for him to run for office. She said it wouldn't, and he liked her answer, and that was the moment when relief replaced Danielle's wariness.

This easy state of things lasted until the day Tony told her he had set aside one of the Eagle's Talon condominiums for her and Simeon. She protested with her heart and her hopes in her throat. She had admired the project since the day she had first seen the blueprints spread across Tony's desk.

She couldn't afford such a spectacular place, not even on Tony's generosity. So when he explained that he had a job for her to do there, and the unit would be paid for, Danielle had a hard time containing her amazement. She could stay until the job ended, he said, or she could live there as long as she desired. In either case, she would pay nothing. He suggested she sell her house and put the tiny equity away for Simeon's college fund.

Danielle responded by throwing her arms around Tony's neck and whispering her thanks into his hair. He laughed, and her gratitude became a kiss.

Her own spontaneity shocked her. She withdrew, mortified for having crossed personal and professional boundaries.

"I'm sorry. That will never —"

He silenced her apology with a kiss of his own, changing in an instant everything about their relationship except the thing that mattered most: Danielle did not love Tony the way a lover ought to.

But she didn't dare say so. Pretending to love him was a very small price to pay for her son's financial security. An insignificant price. Only a fool would decline generosity like Tony's. In time, she told herself, she would grow to love him for real. He was a good man. He cared for her. Only memories of Danny held her heart back. She just needed time, and because Tony wasn't the marrying type, she had plenty of that.

So Danielle was still emotionally breathless when Tony installed her and her son at Eagle's Talon and instructed her to pose as an art broker who occasionally traveled but did most of her work from home. Her job was to "sell" units to prospective buyers, speaking to them as an enthusiastic resident. He furnished her unit to suit the part, saying, *It's not a deception, it's an operation.*

A little more pretending, Danielle thought. But when it turned out that she loved the job and was good at it, she minded the deceit less and less.

Whenever a Realtor or investor announced an intention to view the models, Danielle found a way to cross their paths and express just how delighted she was to live here — and there was no lying in that claim at all. Prospective male buyers gave Danielle the attentiveness reserved for half-clad supermodels who sold cars, though she dressed modestly and could navigate any conversation, even on subjects that were way over her head, for as long as the other party wanted to engage. Prospective female buyers seemed to find her adventurous and

enviable, living in such cutting-edge architecture. And parents had unending questions about her confidence in the unit's
safety — how did she manage with a five-
year-old, surrounded by all this water?

Danielle had an answer for every query
and a witty reply for every observation. And
depending on what best suited each situation, Simeon might be at Tony's corporate
child care facilities, or playing with their
neighbor's young son, or tagging along with
Danielle. She was the perfect chameleon,
any prospective buyer's ideal prospective
neighbor.

At her urging, Tony agreed to keep their
budding relationship a secret. "We don't
want anyone to think my love for this place
is artificial," she said. "Because it's not."

She thought he took her excuse at face
value.

With Simeon holding her hand, Danielle
walked up the peninsula from the parking
area in front of building 4, keeping to the
temporary pedestrian walkway constructed
on the east side, then reached building 12
by crossing the canopy-covered footbridge
between the peninsula's bank and the front
door. Simeon jumped his way across and
the bridge thundered under their feet.

She hated the name "building 12," which was better suited for an industrial complex than this gorgeous, environmentally friendly living space. One of her projects, though Tony didn't know it yet, was to think up a more suitable name for each of the structures by the time they were complete. Her neighbor Ferti had already dubbed building 12 the Unsinkable Molly Brown, a label that tempted fate too much for Danielle to like it.

The condominiums were unlike any she had seen, except in *Architectural Digest* and electronic photographs manipulated until their true beauty became artificial. Her job required her to grasp the notable details of the architecture, because she was often asked to explain it. Mammoth steel posts like stilts set deep into the riverbed prevented the buoyant foundation from floating away. Thick steel collars secured it to the posts and allowed the platform to rise and fall with the water's naturally fluctuating levels. In truth, Danielle hardly ever noticed the subtle movements.

The buildings themselves were an assembly of broad windows and prefabricated aluminum walls, the kind one might find in restaurants' walk-in refrigerators. These minimized waste and maximized energy efficiency. But the real feat of Vance Nolan's groundbreaking design, Danielle thought, was the way the silver walls shimmered throughout the day with all the colors of the water and the sun.

She pulled the glass door open for Simeon, and together they entered the residents' common area. Recycled steel beams rather than traditional load-bearing walls supported the upper levels. Aluminum room dividers were used in the open floor plan, creating artful boundaries between the fireplace area, a reading nook, a game room, and a kitchen and bar. Everything but the aluminum walls and the spare blue-green decor was white.

Natural light and a million-dollar view of the cove poured in through the west-facing windows, where oversize glass doors led out to a narrow patio and floating dock. Inside, on either side of the patio access, white staircases rose across the bright windows to the north and south floors. The steps were wide and bordered by thick glass rather than a traditional balustrade that would have blocked the view.

Danielle and Simeon took the south stairs to their unit. They ambled down the second-floor hall, where Ferti lived alone in the first unit and Mirah lived with her family in the second. The building's fourth resident, the retired police officer Jonesy Daly, lived in the only occupied unit on the north side. "The man's side," he liked to tease. At the end of the hall, another flight of stairs took them to the third floor. This staircase was enclosed, and though it seemed small and uninspired, it preserved the condos' private views of the river.

On the third floor, the unit opposite Danielle's was still empty, but she thought that the married attorneys who had stopped to see it last week might make an offer soon.

Two minutes before the concrete-pump truck collapsed, Danielle placed her purse on the kitchen counter and drank in the view. Each time she entered her third-floor unit she took a deep, contented breath. Her condo, like all the others, was long and narrow, a looking glass between the river on the east and the cove on the west. At both ends she had unobstructed views of water. Skylights, bright cork flooring, stainless steel appliances, and cabinets built from sustainable bamboo invited the rippling sunshine to linger.

Behind her, a handsome seating arrangement faced a flat-screen TV and the latest gaming devices, with additional seating in front of the river-view window, where she and Simeon often watched the construction crews moving around on the isthmus, and the boats in the distant channels. The Rondeau River was part of the massive Mississippi River system. Swift and nearly a mile wide at its broadest point, it was one of the many tributaries that watered the Midwest and delivered its cargoes to Port Rondeau, St. Louis, and beyond. Near Eagle's Talon, recreational sailboats were as common on the water as gulls in the summertime, and in the distance, the barges and tows in the shipping lanes stayed busy year-round.

Her kitchen and dining area overlooked the more restful cove side, a vast pool of liquid peace. Half a mile away, the opposite shoreline seemed a world apart. It sloped upward to an infrequently traveled two-lane highway that followed the river's curves. Busy people preferred the straighter routes of the inland freeways, which weren't visible from Eagle's Talon. The city of Port Rondeau was also hidden by the river's bend. Danielle liked to spend most of her time on this side of her home — particularly on the balcony outside her bedroom.

After dropping her briefcase on the floor, she withdrew a paper from her purse and reviewed her notes about the buyer she was to meet that afternoon.

Ranier Smith: late thirties, sculptor, divorcé with custody of his son — which was why Simeon was with her for the encounter. The fact that Mr. Smith was an artist worried Danielle a bit. Tony had given her the art-broker persona precisely because starving artists didn't fit the economic profile of the Eagle's Talon buyer. If he wasn't starving, Ranier Smith might prove to be Danielle's first real challenge.

"Can we go outside?" Simeon asked her as she settled onto a barstool.

"Just the bedroom balcony for now."

"But can we swim? Pleeeeaase?"

"Later, kiddo. In an hour or two. Go put away your stuff."

Until the construction was complete, it was necessary to keep Simeon indoors. On a summer day as gorgeous as this one, that was like keeping him in prison.

Danielle kicked off her snug shoes, shrugged out of her linen blazer, and decided not to keep Simeon tied down for any longer than necessary. After their "chance" meeting with Ranier, she would take Simeon up the road and across the isthmus to the cove's western shore, where they could wade and forage for the most perfect pebbles. She would invite Mirah, who had two children and was married to a surgeon,

31

to come. Ferti, a retired fashion designer whose wedding dresses were worn by celebrities, might even want to tag along.

But then Danielle had a better idea. Maybe it would be best to time their outing so that she could chat up the area's recreational features to Ranier. She'd have to change out of this pantsuit. She wondered how old the man's son was.

As she weighed this option Simeon burst out of the hall that separated the bedrooms from the living area. He held a Matchbox truck in one fist and a shining blue-and-silver pinwheel in the other. He launched himself like a long-jumper and hit the floor at Danielle's feet with a thundering boom that seemed to make the tall building shudder. The pinwheel started spinning.

"Careful! You'll sink us!" She was teasing, though in truth the vibration at her feet seemed wrong. It was out of proportion with what a forty-pound, five-year-old body could create. And it wasn't the gentle bob that the structure sometimes made on its steel stabilizing posts.

Simeon threw his head back and laughed with his mouth gaping open, pleased to have impressed his mother. "We're unsinkable!" he crowed. Ferti's influence, no doubt.

The floor shuddered once more, a half-second echo, and this time even Simeon looked surprised. Then his wide eyes crinkled into laughter again. Sometimes his happiness did more for Danielle than water ever could. When he was this bright, she knew she didn't actually need a home on the water to be happy. All she needed was a good life for her boy.

The kind of life Tony Dean could provide.

They went into the hall and through the master bedroom to reach the balcony. She pulled the cord that parted the curtains, opened the door for Simeon, then activated the wall-mounted motion detector that would alert her if Simeon so much as gripped the balcony rail while her back was turned. The infrared alarm system was a standard feature in every unit.

When the red light flashed twice, Danielle followed her son through the sliding door and onto the balcony. Afternoon light caught Simeon's pinwheel as the wind whirled it around. She turned back to close the screen door.

Someone shouted her name.

She looked toward the cry, toward the work site where crews were pouring concrete onto the pad that would become building 11. She saw the long metal arm of one of the construction trucks coming down on her roof like an ax.

She put her hands over her head and doubled over to shield her son.

The boom of the pump truck hit the roof like a mallet on a kettledrum, resonating with a low vibration that went straight through Danielle's stomach. The floor of the balcony dipped as the entire building took the impact, and her feet shifted for balance. Simeon's Matchbox truck clattered to the deck.

A sleek rain gutter popped loose of its screws and bounced off the back of her head before tumbling down into the cove.

The deadly mechanical arm of the pump truck began to slide off the roof before Danielle had caught her balance. It obstructed her sliding door before she could take Simeon into her arms. She saw their fate in a breath: that machine's next move would be to slice the balcony into the water.

Danielle snatched up her little boy. He threw his monkey-long limbs around her waist and neck. She hugged him tightly and fled the danger. She had room for only two short steps. Then her left foot hit the seat of a patio chair. Her right foot grabbed the skinny balcony rail.

She kept going, pedaling air in the clear blue sky.

4

Zeke Hammond learned of the accident in a vision. When it came to him he was resting outside on his deck, which stood on stilts above a creek that fed the Rondeau River, north of Eagle's Talon. A weather-beaten stairway led downward from deck to dock, where an aluminum rowboat thumped against the pilings.

The old redwood platform was low enough that he could fish from it when the trout were running and high enough to taunt floods in the rainy season, when the banks sometimes overflowed. The day of the accident was neither a fishing day nor a flooding day, but a fair-weather day good for doing nothing. The high back of an Ad-irondack chair supported his head and a footrest elevated his tender ankles, which were getting wobblier than they used to be.

"Zeke the Greek is getting old," he said to his pit bull. The gentle dog, who consistently proved that he was undeserving of his breed's poor reputation, slept stretched out across the redwood boards at the foot of the chair. "Good thing I've got you to take care of me, Ziggy."

The name had been bestowed upon the pooch by a neighbor who thought the dog, like the cartoon-strip character, had an unfortunate nose.

"Besides," she had said, " 'Zeke and Ziggy' has a ring to it."

In Zeke's opinion, a seeing-eye dog needed all the heightened senses he could get, to compensate for his owner's loss. So the fact that Ziggy had a large snout was a perk — though it was not the reason Zeke had picked him.

Landscaping had been Zeke's passion and his career until a crane that was transporting a railroad tie to a steep bank snapped its chain and deposited the tie on Zeke's head. In the crisis that followed, Zeke told God that in exchange for having to give up his passion, his livelihood, his work as a search-and-rescue volunteer, *and* his eyes, he expected to receive something pretty spectacular in return.

He did get Ziggy, who qualified as a real gift. The wounded dog needed his own gentle guide through life's pain, and Zeke had a soft spot for troubled hearts, human and canine alike. But Zeke also received what he liked to call "second sight." By this he meant that he could now see people and their troubles in a way that his busier, sighted life had prevented. This gift had opened up a new and surprisingly fulfilling career as a life coach.

This was the simple explanation he gave to most people. To his closest circle of friends he gave a deeper explanation: on occasion he received visions from God. He didn't know if the visions came to him the same way they had come to the old prophet Isaiah, or to the apostle John, or to the mystic fathers of Christianity. He knew only that they came from God, because they always pointed the way to love and life rather than to hatred and death.

On the sunny day that Zeke and Ziggy rested on the redwood deck, the vision came to him like a great idea, a sudden moment of clarity and anticipation. It looked like this:

Zeke's friend Vance Nolan was standing with a small crowd of people in the bed of a pickup truck. The truck was made of coarse concrete and polished aluminum. Except for Vance, the people had no faces, but their jostling elbows, their shoving arms and grasping fingers — these movements looked like panic.

The gray hulk of a vehicle sat on top of a hill, its crest just large enough to hold the truck level. At the foot of the slope, a golden snake with long spikes on its back and at the tip of its tail came out from a hole and began to weave itself around the base. The serpent was of such a length that it encircled the hill and overlapped its own tail. It arched its neck and bared its fangs, and Zeke expected the spiny reptile to strike someone. Instead, it began to spew a flaming liquid, orange and viscous like molten lava, hot and deadly.

The destructive stuff ate away at the ground. Crumbling clods of dirt left great craters behind. As the threat rose, the hill became an island floating in a noxious puddle. And as the ground was eaten away, the island began to fall. The truck began to slip down the hillside backward, tailgate first.

In his Adirondack chair, a dimension away from this drama, Zeke reached out to prevent the truck from plunging. His fingers cut straight through the metal and stone as if he were the ghost and the truck were real.

Still, the vehicle jerked to a stop when a hand that didn't belong to Zeke grabbed the front bumper and snatched the truck back. The hand had a human shape but an alien appearance, its skin glowing as if blue neon flowed underneath the surface and forced silver light out the tips of its fingers. And although the hand was not disembodied, Zeke couldn't turn to see the body it belonged to. The vision would not allow it.

In the background, hanging in the blue sky, a robin hovered on a breeze, its red breast like a tiny lick of fire. It waited, its dusty gray wings outstretched, for something Zeke couldn't identify.

One of the faceless men jumped out of the truck bed and onto the roof of the cab. He was a chunky, graceless fellow who landed off balance and dented the roof when his large backside smacked it.

Zeke heard a voice say, *Vance must stand, and God will give him the lives of all who stay. These things must happen, but see to it that he is not afraid.*

Then the blue hand released the truck and it resumed its fall, and the man on the roof caught a few inches of air.

Zeke jerked upright in the chair. "Catch him," he said aloud.

Vance was already reaching out. The larger man seized Vance's hand as his body caught up with the truck again, coming down hard on the concrete hood. He began to tumble over the side, still holding Vance, dragging him over the cab as he twisted toward the fiery lava flow.

With the swift agility of an athlete, Vance got his feet in front of him and braced the heels of his boots in the joint where the windshield met the hood. The man's arm snapped taut. Vance strained against the guy's massive weight as he climbed back onto the hood, all knees and elbows and beefy limbs.

The truck splashed down.

The fool let go of Vance's hands and fell onto his belly.

And Vance, still opposing the great weight with every muscle, flipped over backward and off the far side of the truck.

Zeke's blindness returned before he knew Vance's fate. He wasn't sure if the thick splash he'd heard so vividly had come from the vision or from the creek below his deck. Ziggy nuzzled Zeke's hand and whined.

"Yes, that was a bad one," Zeke told him. "You see it too?"

Ziggy's thumping tail seemed to have synced itself with Zeke's heartbeat.

"Enrique!" Zeke called out. Enrique was Zeke's tenant, a shipyard welder who commuted across the Rondeau six days a week because Zeke's rent was half that of the local apartments. Zeke charged less than he might have to the men who lived in his home because he wanted them to be able to stay for whatever duration they truly needed: six weeks, six months, or in Vance's case, nearly eight years. Vance had moved on quite awhile ago, but he and Zeke, the student and the mentor, remained fast friends.

Enrique had been with him since the spring, when Zeke found him sleeping in a bus depot because a knee injury had ended his military career prematurely and he had nowhere to go. He loved hot sandwiches and apocalyptic movies. Right about now, if Zeke's sense of time was on target, the bulky man would be on the other side of Zeke's screen door in the kitchen, using the George Foreman grill to weld a grilled cheese while watching a History Channel documentary about Nostradamus and his predictions of the end of the world.

Within a few seconds the screen scraped in its track and Enrique said, "Yeah?"

Zeke smelled pastrami and rye. "You got time to float me down to Eagle's Talon?"

"Sure. Nice day for it."

"I need to see Vance."

"Gimme five minutes."

"Grab some jerky for Ziggy?"

"Got it."

The heavy sounds of Enrique wolfing down his lunch and shuffling through the kitchen, breathy and grunting, to collect what they'd need made Zeke think twice. What if Enrique's face, though Zeke had never seen it, belonged on the overweight body of the man who'd let go of Vance? The sandwiches were to blame for Enrique's post-discharge pudge. Since trying to stop smoking, Enrique ate more than he ought.

Zeke hesitated. But only for a moment.

If the man in the vision was Enrique after all, then maybe, just maybe, he was supposed to go.

5

Vance was running. He couldn't see Danielle. The pump truck was still tipping as the earth fell away. Pebbles tumbled down the slopes of the dry bank, chasing the underwater hole.

He kept clear of the collapsing vehicle and beat a path between it and the cement mixer. Its mangled chute had deposited a gray lump of wet concrete onto the unpaved road. Vance hurdled it, then vaulted a barrier and took the shortest route to building 12. A footbridge spanned the water between the bank and the condos. He hit it at full speed. It vibrated with the weight of his pounding boots and felt flimsy under his urgency. His hard hat, which somehow had stayed seated while hauling that kid out of the truck, finally flew off his head and clattered over the guardrail.

At the bottom of the ramp he turned sharply to the right and chased a narrow walk around the perimeter of the building. In his mind he reached the water and found Danielle and Simeon already dead. Knocked unconscious by debris, then drowned.

In reality, when he reached the floating dock, he still couldn't see them at all. Vance looked up. The pump truck's boom hovered over the balcony beneath Danielle's, where it had come to rest.

Vance sprinted for the end of the dock. Out in the water, just a few feet beyond the bobbing wreckage that had been Danielle's balcony, a head broke the surface, gasping. First Simeon's, then Danielle's, pushing up under him. Simeon's mouth gaped for air but couldn't get any. Danielle was blinded by her own hair. She got her hands under the boy's armpits and held him high while she tried to keep herself afloat. Her mouth and nose went under briefly, but her arms kept her son in the oxygen.

Vance dived into the cove, regretting his heavy work boots and the unaffordable seconds it would have cost to unlace them. He kicked hard as he swam, keeping his head above the cool water, which was impossible to see through.

He thought he reached Danielle quickly, though time had become a strange abstraction. She was sputtering and calmly ordering Simeon to breathe while the panic of not being able to made the child thrash in the grip of her white fingers. She seemed to be trying to lay him down on top of the water, the way a person might attempt CPR on dry land. A conscious but breathless Simeon fought her and clung to her at the same time. He'd yanked a fistful of blond strands loose from her head. They tangled in his fingers. Black tracks of mascara cupped Danielle's lower lids and made her eyes seem haunted.

She didn't acknowledge Vance's approach. She didn't cry for help. But when his last long-armed stroke brought him within reach, she handed Simeon over as if she trusted him to know what to do.

In his hands, Simeon stopped thrashing. Vance's palms seemed larger than they had been, or the boy seemed smaller. He turned Simeon chest down into the cradle of his left hand, his legs straddling Vance's arm. The child, old as he was, balanced there like a baby. Vance's legs felt unnaturally strong, treading hard enough to lift his chest out of the cove. With his right hand he struck Simeon on the back.

Nothing happened. For a second he feared he'd hit too hard, that he'd stunned the boy's muscles. Then he worried he hadn't hit hard enough. That he'd have to hit again and risk breaking a bone or knocking the kid out.

He hesitated, then raised his hand a second time. But before he dropped it Simeon retched and gave up all the water he'd swallowed, then began to cough.

"That's my man," Vance said, rotating Danielle's son and pulling him toward his chest.

Danielle's silence was broken by a sob. She faltered in the water. Vance caught her arm while Simeon hacked, clinging to Vance's neck.

"He's okay," Vance told her.

"I know." Her voice was steady but her face was a wad of distress.

"Are you hurt?"

She shook her head. He held on to her and started kicking toward shore. His boots were like lead now, and he felt a small ache that promised future pain in his knees and back where he'd taken the impact of jumping off that truck.

An ambulance and fire crew sounded their arrival and hurried across the isthmus, lights flashing.

Simeon held tight to Vance and took deep breaths. He looked around the cove like he wasn't sure how he'd come to be in it. His sudden calm was shock, Vance thought. But when Simeon's eyes landed on his mother, one corner of his mouth turned up.

"Did you see them?" Simeon asked. Maybe Danielle didn't hear — her eyes were lifted to the missing balcony on her bedroom wall. Simeon turned to Vance and repeated himself. "Did you see them?"

Them? He must mean the emergency vehicles.

"Sure did," Vance said. Simeon's smile expanded and his eyes widened.

The dock was only thirty or forty feet off, but Danielle sagged as if it were miles away. It struck Vance then that if they'd been knocked straight down into the water, they would have fallen much closer to the building.

"Did you jump?" he asked her.

"Without thinking," she said. A shudder shook her shoulders as she lowered her eyes to her son, who was grinning like this was a water park. "I'm thinking about it now."

She pulled away from Vance's grasp. Still holding Simeon, Vance moved toward the dock in a sort of sidestroke. The height of that balcony was overwhelming from this point of view. Underneath Danielle's mangled screen door, obstructed by the tilting boom, there wasn't even a ledge left to stand on. The corner of a curtain fluttered out and brushed the top of the boom.

He admired Danielle's courage. The feeling was a magnified version of what he had experienced the first time he saw her, which in the first five seconds was a straightforward, hot-blooded appreciation of the way she rested her pen against her full lips while she pondered a problem. When he had been formally introduced to her half a minute later, the emotion was complicated by the picture of Simeon on her desk, the wedding ring on her left hand, and the way Tony Dean referred to her as "the sex appeal of this operation."

The crass remark, spoken in front of Danielle as if she were nothing more than a paid advertisement, had triggered all of Vance's protective instincts. He opened his mouth to object to the characterization, but she shook Vance's hand firmly and beat him to it.

"Actually, my salary requirements for that job title are out of Tony's reach." She winked at Tony, and Vance doubted she needed anyone's protection at all.

She was a married woman, and he checked his attraction to her. Still, he hated that she worked for someone who respected her so little.

A cool ripple of water washed up Vance's neck as he lowered his eyes and took in the scene at building 11. The incomplete foundation looked like a sinking ship. Two of its corners jutted out of the water. Whatever had opened up underneath the pump truck must have dislodged one or more of the support posts and dragged the pad down. The pump truck's front left outrigger had hooked the top of the platform, and it was hard to tell if the outrigger had rocked and pinned the foundation, or if the foundation had prevented the truck from sinking completely.

Freshly poured concrete slid like thick oatmeal down the sloping surface and into the cove.

The truck's cab was fully submerged now. The sprawling rear outriggers gave the whole vehicle the look of a diving frog. The long hydraulic boom, still resting against the facade of building 12, dangled over the water like a forgotten fishing pole.

It took only minutes for Danielle to reach the dock, which was when Vance noticed that Tony Dean had arrived and was extending a hand to help her up the ladder. She reached out with her left hand and — maybe because Vance had so recently learned to notice things that weren't there

— he saw that her wedding ring was missing. Danielle's husband was a stranger to Vance, and he had wondered what it meant when she and Simeon moved to Eagle's Talon without him.

Tony pulled her in and tilted his head close to hers, turned her toward him with a light touch on her elbow, and said something Vance couldn't hear. Danielle nodded, and the worry lines in Tony's forehead relaxed a bit. He kept hold of her fingers, though Danielle took a step away from him as if the bits of algae spotting her wet clothes might contaminate his. The businessman cut a *GQ* figure in a high-end suit and glossy Italian shoes. His SUV, as spotless and glistening as his wingtips, was parked up on the isthmus. It was way too much car for Vance's taste, flashing its custom gold paint.

The narrow shoulder of the road where Tony had parked offered a front-row view of the collapsed balcony, the fallen pump truck, the tilting foundation, the oozing concrete. Another man, lean and dark-skinned and dressed to complement the expensive car, leaned back against the front grill. He raised his phone and snapped a picture. Whether the man was a partner, investor, buyer, or broker, his presence was bad news.

Tony's concerned attention to Danielle became a frown over Vance as he and the boy reached the ladder.

"Fine day for a disaster," Tony said, glancing back at the picture taker. "Who do I get to blame for it?"

Vance ignored the question. Tony would force him to answer it soon enough, but probably not in front of Danielle. Her complexion had faded to match her pale waterlogged blouse, and she was staring up at her missing balcony, shivering. She pulled her hand out of Tony's. Vance climbed out of the cove with Simeon still clinging, river water raining off their joints.

"I'll build you a new one," Vance said to Danielle. Her eyebrows came together in a question as she reached for Simeon. "Another balcony," Vance said. Simeon was in no hurry to leave his arms, and she diverted her attention to peeling her son away. A chill rushed in where Simeon's warmth had been.

Vance smiled uneasily, wondering if he'd have to build her an entirely new home so soon after she'd moved into it. Building 12 showed no sign of any damage beyond the balcony amputation. But he worried about what the mud and water hid. If the steel

51

posts that secured the building had been destabilized by the shifting river bottom, they might overpower the structure's buoyancy and drag the condominiums down.

Tony resumed his interrogation of Vance, but the questions bounced off him. His attention had gone to a small brown bird like the one that had looped the arm of the pump truck moments before the collapse. It landed on a post at the top of the dock and eyed Vance without making a peep.

6

"Didn't you see them?" Simeon asked his mother as the paramedic put a stethoscope against his heart. They were up on the road, on the bumper of the fire truck, under a blue sky whose intense beauty had faded a little. Danielle had the uneasy feeling of being disconnected from the moment, of being a witness rather than a participant in the events of the last hour.

The wool blanket hugging her son slipped off one shoulder. She pulled it up and around him again. He shrugged out of it and she let it go, sensing that some things she used to think were important wouldn't be after this day. His hair was a half-dried pile of stiff straw.

"Mom, did you see the *workers?"*

"I've seen a lot of workers today."

"I mean the ones under the water," Simeon said.

The remark coincided with a breeze skimming the top of the water. The temperature of her wet clothes dropped.

"Did someone fall in?" She asked this of the paramedic, who might have information.

Simeon threw his head back and laughed. "That's silly! *We* fell in! Remember, Mom?"

"Yeah, I remember." Danielle took a deep breath, relieved to be standing here listening to this incredible sound of her son's happiness. "Someone *else,*" she clarified. "Did anyone else go into the water?"

The man shook his head. "Not that I know of. Everyone's accounted for."

She couldn't believe she'd jumped. She might never be able to stand on a balcony again. She would ask Vance to replace the hole in her bedroom wall with a window. Or a board to block the memories.

She hadn't thanked him. How could she have failed to do that? Shock had zapped her good manners, she thought. He'd forgive her. Vance Nolan was a decent man who asked thoughtful questions about her work and her interests while he waited for meetings with Tony. And he was nice to Simeon. But she had avoided him since moving into building 12, which was when she realized that their professional acquaintance was extremely one-sided. She knew less about him than he probably knew about her, and now, as her relationship with Tony took on new and awkward dimensions, it seemed a bad time to inquire. What did he think about how she could afford such an expensive home, or why Tony might have provided it for her?

Why did she care what he thought?

While the paramedic examined Simeon, Danielle looked around for Vance. Instead, she saw Ferti striding toward her with a fuchsia-colored throw draped over one arm. A bright yellow scarf encircled her smooth brown head, its triangle point caught up in the breeze like a boat's sail. The woman's tall form seemed erect enough to take on the world. Or at least a disaster at home. She unfurled the blanket as she approached Danielle.

"First I see you take a swan dive off the third floor, and now I see you out here dripping like one unlucky cat." She threw it over Danielle's shivering shoulders and pulled the coverlet around her. Ferti shot a disapproving glare at the paramedic. "You only carry one blanket with you at a time?"

"I told him I didn't need one," Danielle said.

"Like you don't need air to breathe," Ferti scolded. She leaned over Simeon and smoothed his hair. "Went cliff diving, did you?"

"He's a fish," the paramedic said to Danielle as he stood. "Swallowed some water but his lungs sound clear now. I don't see any cause for concern." Danielle nodded, and the man left them to go back to his ambulance, where someone covered in a hazy film of concrete was being treated for a cut on his forehead.

"What happened to him?" Danielle pointed to the one with blood on his face.

"He was holding the hose when the truck went over. Knocked off his hat and smacked him on the head. The thing looked like a whip."

"Did you see it?"

"No, I wasn't paying attention until that crane walloped us. There I am, holding on to my kitchen counter for dear life, and then you two drop past my window. Hope I never see anything like that again," Ferti said.

"It's amazing no one else was hurt."

"That's the truth." She shook her head slowly and stroked Simeon's tangled hair with her long, strong fingers. "I thought Molly Brown was going to go down after all."

"It can't fall," Simeon said. "The workers are holding up the poles."

"Are they, now?" Ferti smiled at him.

"They're keeping them from falling over," Simeon said.

Danielle said, "Honey, what are you talking about?"

"I *said,* the workers under the water. I keep telling you."

"But no one was in the water."

"But I *saw* them."

Danielle was sure Simeon saw something, the conjuring of a frightened imagination. But it didn't seem the time to correct him. Or even to express disbelief. She looked at Ferti for help.

"You must have Superman eyes to be able to see through that murky water," Ferti tried.

Simeon shook his head. "The workers were all lit up. Like the alien guys in that movie."

"What movie?" Danielle said.

"Mmm, *The Abyss.*"

"*The Abyss*!" Danielle said. "When did you watch *The Abyss*?"

Simeon said, "Laith and Haji were watching it."

Mirah's boys. Mirah looked after Simeon from time to time when the kids wanted to play or when buyers made late appointments to see the condominiums.

"I doubt baby Haji was watching. And Laith is much older than you," Danielle scolded, though how could Simeon have avoided seeing whatever Mirah permitted?

"Oh, it's harmless," Ferti said.

"He hasn't seen any of the Superman movies yet either," Danielle defended.

"We flew off that balcony like Superman, Mom."

Ferti winked at Simeon. "Don't have to see a movie to know who he is, do you?"

"Like this!" Simeon lifted his arms over his head and jumped off the back of the truck, then went after a rock that had caught his attention.

"Don't worry so much," Ferti advised Danielle. "There's underwater workers holding up our home! You can put that to work for you, Mom."

"Vance said he saw them too," Simeon said after fetching his stone, as if that would settle the question. For the moment, it did. First Danielle would thank Vance for saving her son's life, and then she would politely ask him not to do anything that would confuse fantasy and reality in Simeon's mind. He was at a tender age where it was important he knew the difference.

A trail of interesting rocks led Simeon away from them. Danielle watched him

show a fistful of his finds to a kindly interested firefighter. The moment doused her
with sudden and soul-sinking dread, the
kind that settles in when the mind finally
delivers all of its facts to the emotional
centers. If Vance had not helped her, would
that firefighter right now be bent over Simeon's dead body, covering her little boy with
a sheet?

"You're pale as that concrete, Danielle,"
Ferti murmured. "You tell your mind to stay
put. Right here, right now."

Danielle couldn't speak. She could only
nod. Was there any more terrifying job in
the world than being a parent? She had
devoted the last two years to sheltering Simeon from pain. By age three he'd suffered
enough, losing his father. But today she'd
failed him. Now she was in debt to Vance,
perhaps in the same way she was in debt to
Tony. It was not good for the single mother
of a young son to be in debt to anyone,
especially men, whether they loved her or
not.

"Vance saved his life," Danielle said.

Ferti's grunt sounded like disagreement.
Danielle looked at her, questioning.

"*You* saved your boy's life," Ferti insisted.
"Don't give that man credit due to you."

"What a crazy thing to say!"

"Isn't. You got Simeon out of danger, you kept him above the water. I saw that much. You had it, Danielle."

"He was choking." The thought of it cinched her own throat.

"You would've had that too, if you'd had to go it alone. Look, you'd fret over your son less if you gave your own competence a pat on the back once in a while." The women stood shoulder to shoulder, facing the scene of the accident. Vance was with the crews pressed in around the frog-legged truck, leaning over the murky water as if trying to see what had swallowed the cab.

"Even if I agreed with you, that's no reason to be ungrateful."

"Did I say anything about being ungrateful?"

Danielle would have accused Ferti of smooth-talking if the approach of Jonesy Daly hadn't closed her mouth. The retired police officer seemed too young not to be working, a fact that prompted him to give a self-conscious explanation to all he met. He left the force early for health reasons, he said again and again. He had a tricky heart that one year up and decided not to pass the required annual physical. His dangerously high weight — the effect of that serious heart condition, not the cause of it, he claimed — put his appearance in his mid-fifties, though he insisted he was only forty-three.

Jonesy was Eagle's Talon's first owner, set up in his unit before the last aluminum panel had been installed. Tony had little to say about his business transactions with the man, which Danielle thought might have something to do with questionable financing. How else could an unemployed forty-something police officer with a pocket-draining medical condition be the first to afford Eagle's Talon?

She made it a principle to avoid asking questions she didn't want to answer herself.

By the time Jonesy reached the ladies he was breathless. "You good?" he asked Danielle.

She nodded at him, thinking that he was the one who might need medical attention.

"Don't you worry about me," Ferti said wryly. "But thanks for asking."

"I know better than to ask you, Miss Ferti." Jonesy wiped his brow. "You'd take a bite outta any hand extended in your direction."

Ferti gaped at him. "Have I ever? No sir. Where on earth would you get such an idea?"

Their playful banter took the cold edge

61

off Danielle's distress. Already she felt warmed by a sense that the world was its normal self again. At a distance, Simeon unearthed a green bottle cap and lifted it so Danielle could see.

"I have my sources," Jonesy said, and he nodded at the executives standing at a short distance from Vance's crew.

Ferti looked their way, shifted her weight, and crossed her arms. "For heaven's sake. What's he doing here?"

"Who?" Danielle asked.

Three men in expensive tailored suits and fine leather shoes stood atop the bank, observing the accident from a distance: Tony, who took in the scene with both hands shoved deep in his pants pockets; Carver Lewis, an elegant investor who favored soft leather ivy caps and made Danielle think of jazz entertainers from the forties; and a third man she didn't recognize, who also appeared to have enough money to buy power. His flashy silver cuff links attracted the sun and her attention. The sight of this stranger stirred up a vague recall at the back of her mind. She should know him, she thought, but she couldn't pull up a name or a context that fit.

"Which one do you mean?" Danielle repeated.

Ferti seemed reluctant to answer Danielle's question.

"The weasel," Ferti said.

"Who?"

"Tony Dean. Makes me think of a weasel. All that slick hair. Not even a hot shower could penetrate those styling lotions."

Jonesy's belly laugh caused a crew member fifty yards away to turn around and look.

"She doesn't give a fig about that man or his hair," Jonesy said. "Only Carver Lewis can fluster this woman."

"You hush, son," Ferti ordered. "No one here is flustered."

As if he knew they were speaking of him, Carver nodded at Ferti and lifted his cap in greeting. He had a wide smile, a friendly, fatherly, life-is-fine-by-me grin that Danielle found herself staring at. She'd seen it before, many times, and it never failed to catch her eye as a sign of rare goodwill toward the world. Ferti harrumphed and turned her back on him.

"You come let me know if they're gonna make us leave or anything," she ordered Danielle. "Until then, I'll take Simeon's word that we got aliens keeping Molly right side up."

As she left them Jonesy called out, "There's no need to hide, Miss Ferti," and her sandals slapped the footbridge as if she wished it were his head.

Jonesy turned to Danielle. "What's this about aliens?"

"Something Simeon saw in a movie," was all she said.

Jonesy nodded and lifted a hand to shade his eyes from the sun. "You tell Tony that you can't stay in conditions like these. He ought to put you up somewhere while they sort it out. Somewhere with five stars attached to it."

"My balcony's gone, but I don't think the damage is any worse than that," Danielle said.

Jonesy shrugged. "Does it matter? Tony's good for it. You tell him he doesn't take care of you, he'll have to answer to me."

Danielle smiled at his kind concern. "He listens to you, does he?"

He winked at her. "I have ways to make him listen."

"And would you do the same for Ferti and Mirah?"

Another shrug. "What can I say to those women? Mirah won't do a thing her husband doesn't tell her to do. And you know Ferti wouldn't ask for help if she was drowning in the river."

"So I'm uniquely unable to look out for

myself, am I?"

"I don't know." Jonesy's humor gave way to something Danielle couldn't name. He crossed his arms and looked away. "Are you?"

The question made Danielle uncomfortable, and she couldn't escape the impression that Ferti and he might have been talking about her behind her back before they came out here to check on her.

"Do you know the other man with them?" she asked Jonesy.

"With who?"

"With Tony and Carver. There."

Jonesy squinted and frowned at the same time that Vance, saying something to one of his companions and pointing at something he saw beneath the surface, took a step into the water.

He went down fast. Danielle caught her breath as the two men nearest him snatched him back. Mud encased his leg up to his knee. When he found his footing again, he clapped his buddies on their backs and laughed it off. Jonesy's attention had been caught by Vance's plight too.

"There's a story in the news about a sinkhole that opened up in Wyoming this morning," Jonesy observed. "A sulfuric pit three times as big as the record. Think it's connected to what's going on here?"

She shook her head. Wyoming was hundreds of miles away. It was a ridiculous idea.

But Danielle was recalling the sensation of Vance's grip on her arm, holding her above the water while he also held her son. If there was a sinkhole about to swallow them, she believed he could lift them out of it. His clothes were still as wet as hers. She found herself staring at the thickness of his arms.

"I don't see anyone else," Jonesy was saying. "Just Tony and Carver."

Danielle blinked back into the present. The man with the silver cuff links had vanished.

A cloud had covered the sun, and others were gathering upriver. Simeon was tugging on Danielle's fingers.

"You don't have to be afraid, Mom."

"Hmm?"

"Don't be afraid."

"Afraid of what?" His words heightened her worry.

"Of anything. The worker holding up our house said we don't have to be afraid."

You can put this to work for you, Ferti had said.

She squeezed Simeon's hand and smiled at him. "That's good advice," she said. "I'm not afraid of anything, are you?"

"You're so silly, Mom. You know I'm not."

7

Zeke urged Ziggy down to the dock. Apart from feeding and sheltering his dog, this was the only occasion on which the blind man assisted his big-snouted guide. Until Ziggy, Zeke had never known a canine with an abiding fear of water. As far as most people with disabilities were concerned, the odd trait disqualified Ziggy for service, though the phobia was hardly his fault. His previous owner had, in a manic rage, attempted to drown him. The poor dog, doubly maligned by his trauma and prejudice against his breed, wasn't even available for service when Zeke learned of him. But when he did, nothing could stop him from taking on a partner who might need as much help as he gave.

Time and repeated good experiences, Zeke hoped, would rid the dog of his hydrophobia. He had been hoping this for several years.

At the edge of the dock, Ziggy sat and leaned against Zeke's leg, trembling but loyal. Water might make him quake and possibly lose his breakfast, but so far it had never derailed him from his duties.

Zeke located the rope that tied off the boat, then held on to the rough wood post and lowered himself into the vessel to wait for Enrique and the beef jerky. The boat had an outboard motor that they'd use for the return trip, but it would be unnecessary for the downstream journey unless circumstances required them to hurry. Zeke sensed by a mild temperature drop and a light breeze that a thin curtain of clouds had come down between the stream and the sun.

Abandoned on the dock, Ziggy whined.

"What would you do if I fell in?" he asked the dog. He asked the question every time, and Ziggy's only answer was to pant nervously.

Enrique's sandwich-loving body made the steps groan as he descended.

"Something up with Vance today?" he asked.

"Gonna find out," Zeke said. His mind was only half on Ziggy's phobia. The other half was on the voice of the vision — more specifically, on the words. *Vance must stand, and God will give him the lives of all who stay.*

69

These things must happen, but see to it that he is not afraid.

They were familiar words, but he wasn't sure why.

Ziggy's quick breathing leveled out. He must have caught a whiff of the jerky Enrique brought. It smacked the floor of the boat. Zeke grabbed hold of the sides just before Ziggy leaped in, found the beef snack, and snapped it up and swallowed with limited chewing. By the time the dog realized where he was, Enrique had unmoored, stepped in, and pushed off. Ziggy hacked once, as if surprised to have fallen for the old trick yet again.

"Did you hear about the quakes in Montana this morning?" Enrique asked. He smelled faintly of forbidden cigarettes.

"Montana? Not exactly earthquake country, is it?"

"You don't think the Rocky Mountains are earthquake country? Funny. There are three thousand earthquakes in Yellowstone every year."

"That many? Who knew? How serious was this one?"

"Seven point six, bigger than the Hebgen Lake quake back in 1959. And right on top of our country's biggest sleeping supervolcano."

"But it's not an active volcano."

"How do you define active?" Enrique challenged.

"How many thousands of years ago since it last spewed?"

"Who cares, if it could go off again in our lifetime."

Zeke didn't have an answer. This topic of conversation wasn't at the leading edge of his interests.

Ziggy turned circles in a space that was barely accommodating for a dog his size. His shifting weight rocked the boat. Zeke examined himself for anxiety and considered that the vision had upset him on a deep level. He was worried about Vance, and he'd heard that dogs could sense such disturbances in humans, sometimes even when a person wasn't conscious of it.

Enrique said, "I saw this movie once where the whole coast of California just broke off and fell into the ocean like a melting iceberg. *Crack!* And then cars exploding, people falling into the flaming crust of the earth. It was pretty cool."

"Hollywood likes its special effects," Zeke said.

"But an earthquake like that could happen, you know. And if it happened in Yellowstone . . ." Enrique whistled. "That place sits on a bulging pocket of magma. It's like the infected appendix of the Northern Hemisphere."

These things must happen, but see to it that he is not afraid.

"Well, I don't know the statistical chances of it actually bursting," Zeke said. "Especially not if there's ten or so quakes a day there already."

"Fifty-five quakes per day around the world, my friend. Twenty thousand a year, and a huge chunk of them right in our backyard. I mean, wrap your mind around that. The earth is a bag of microwave popcorn."

That might have been a cute way of putting it if fewer Pacific Islands had been decimated in the past decade or two. For some reason this caused Zeke to think of Vance's hill-turned-island falling into the water, the earth at its base cast away.

"Then I'd say the chances of California falling into the ocean are pretty small," Zeke said.

"It's better to expect the worst."

"Why?"

"Gotta be ready," Enrique said. Water trickled onto the surface of the stream as he lifted his oars out and rotated them noisily in the oarlocks. His rowing was uncharacteristically uneven today, Zeke thought.

"You okay?" he asked.

"Huh?"

"Your rhythm is off."

"Nothing's wrong with my rhythm. Maybe you have an inner-ear thing going on."

Zeke was pretty sure he didn't. He scratched Ziggy's ears. "Well, I'm all for preparation, but I can think of a dozen things I'd rather do than wait for disaster to strike."

"In the past eight years the world has exceeded the average number of major earthquakes every year. I'm talking about the ones around seven or eight points. More big ones happening than before."

"So what does that mean?"

"That's the thing! The scientists say it means nothing. That the average is just an average, and across time, the average holds, they say. I have my own theories."

"Such as?" Zeke probed.

"The government knows something we don't. They know it's coming, the Big One. The mother of all earthquakes. The disaster that ends the world. But what good will it do to tell us?"

Here, Zeke felt as far away from catastrophe as a man could get.

"You shouldn't rely on Hollywood for

your facts, 'Rique."

A puff of disdain escaped Enrique's lips. "I'm relying on my own wits."

Ziggy finally lay down on top of Zeke's feet. Zeke ran a hand down the dog's neck.

"I'm not saying you're wrong, Enrique. I mean, the Bible —"

"Your Bible."

"— says there will be more earthquakes than usual in the end."

"All kinds of religious texts have stuff to say about earthquakes. It's unscientific, prehistoric tripe."

"I was suggesting the Bible might support your theory that something major could happen soon."

"I don't care if it does or doesn't. Besides, that's not what you were doing."

"What was I doing?"

"Going religious on me. I respect you, man, but you've got to stop going religious on me."

Zeke laughed. "Comes with the territory. I told you before you moved in. I wasted years not speaking up about what I believe."

"Wish I'd lived with you then," Enrique muttered.

"No you don't. If I was quiet you wouldn't know who to talk to about what *you* believe."

After an amicable silence Enrique conceded. "Fair enough."

It was a friendly exchange accompanied by water caressing the underside of the boat. Zeke found himself thinking about how differently people saw the world and the events that shaped it. One man's suffering was cause for cynicism; another's — like Vance's — was cause for hope. That was one mystery he'd never unravel before he died.

"Ask you a question?" he said to Enrique.

"Sure."

"Why are you so excited for everything to end?"

"Can't say I'm excited. Except if it's true a big bang started the world, I wouldn't mind seeing the big bang that ends it."

"What's the fascination, then?"

Zeke waited for Enrique to give him a real answer. The usually cheerful birds seemed quiet today.

"In all the history of the world," Enrique eventually said, "how many of us ever really get the chance to do something heroic? I like to think I might make the evening news for lifting a car off a dying man or something."

An image of Enrique crouched beside a battered car formed in Zeke's mind. An old man lay pinned under the rear wheel. Enrique strained to lift it, broke out in a sweat, groaned and grimaced and cursed. In his efforts he stepped on the old man's outstretched arm and didn't seem to notice what he'd done. And then he gave up. Pounded on the roof of the car and kicked a dent in the door.

Zeke shook his head of the insight. He didn't always get those right. "When the whole world's on fire, no one's even going to be around to put your name in a police report."

Enrique huffed. He lifted his oars out of the stream, and Zeke felt droplets of water sink into his pants.

"Then tell me why *God*, if he's actually a conscious force like you think, would put us through that. Why wouldn't he just sort us all out with a magic hat and send us all to our proper houses and be done with it?"

"Maybe so we know beyond a shadow of a doubt that when we're rescued, he's the one doing the rescuing."

"Death isn't a rescue. That's nuts."

Zeke shook his head. "But no one really knows what happens in that moment when we die. Maybe it's the most amazing, thrilling rescue of the soul."

The sounds of the oars cutting and dragging were like breathing.

Enrique's voice was less defensive when he said, "I'm more inclined to think that some of us will dodge the end. A few lucky ones. There's always survivors."

"Only the highest-paid actors get to survive global annihilation," Zeke said.

Enrique chuckled.

8

The on-site manager's trailer, Vance's trailer, was blue and gray, like water meeting a cloudy horizon. They were the colors of his waterlogged jeans and shirt, accented by the thick black mud that encased his leg. He threw open the door and went inside to make a call and change his clothes before Tony started an inquisition.

The man needed a scapegoat to present to his investors, especially the one who was documenting the incident with his cell phone. Carver Something, Vance thought his name was. He hated the financial dog-and-pony shows he was required to attend, and he had trouble remembering names. It would be difficult to put a positive spin on a negative eyewitness account, but if it could be done, Tony would do it.

Accidents and injuries came with a construction worker's territory. Vance had witnessed enough of them to confirm that there was something out of the ordinary about today's disaster: the lack of a clear cause. In most cases blame was easy to place. Investigations were routine, but generally the truth wasn't hard to uncover within the first hour of an incident. This one would take longer. Whatever the problem was, it was big, deep, and potentially destabilizing.

Vance placed a call to the civil engineer who had originally assessed the site. He had to settle for leaving an urgent message.

At the back of the trailer, Vance got out of his boots and threw his sopping socks into the only empty corner. There was a shelf here, a board balanced on brackets high on the wall. An empty, dusty brown whiskey bottle sat on top of it. Vance had long ago reduced the bottle's black label to a stubborn cloudy sticker by picking at it, deep in thought.

He stood in his bare feet and reached up to take the bottle off the shelf. How many people might have died inside or beneath that truck, under that water, down in that hole? How many crew members might lose their jobs if Tony was too impatient to wait for the truth?

There was a time when Vance had looked into such bottles for answers to the unanswerable questions, the way some people looked into philosophy or psychology or theology or astrology or refrigerators or shopping malls or crystal balls. He'd invested in countless bottles, bottomless bottles, looking for the answers. This was merely the first one, which he kept because it had belonged to his father.

His incredible, strong, indomitable father, who couldn't be saved and wasn't strong enough to save himself.

Standing under the bookshelf, Vance shook the bottle gently and heard inside the whispery rattle of a slip of paper that he couldn't see through the opaque glass. It was the original label, which he'd soberly separated from the bottle more than a decade ago. He'd succeeded in peeling off a section large enough on which to write, *What you're looking for isn't in here.*

On days like today it was important to be reminded. And though he'd been sober for more than ten years, reminders weren't always enough to keep Vance from wanting a drink. Sometimes reminders just couldn't do the heavy lifting required to ease life's pounding troubles. But Jesus can!

Your promises are all I need, God, Vance prayed. *Just today, just now, they're enough.* It was a plea as much as a confession.

80

Please be enough.

It helped that he didn't keep any of this stuff hidden in a drawer or behind a blueprint somewhere.

"No one died today," Vance said aloud. "No one lost his job."

"Not yet, anyway."

Vance hadn't heard Tony enter. The water in his clothes had turned chilly in the air-conditioned trailer. The iciness, combined with the sudden passing of his urge for a sip of numbing, blinding fire, brought the moment into sharp focus.

The birds had stopped singing. The ground beneath the peninsula was falling. Perhaps the sky would be next.

His slick-haired boss was blocking the door, his smile artificial, his hands deep in trouser pockets.

"Did you drink that up or do you have any to spare?" Tony asked.

"You know I run a dry site." He lifted the empty bottle and tipped it back onto the top shelf.

"Not even a beer in a cooler somewhere?" Tony looked around without moving out of position.

Vance let him look. He peeled off his shirt and cast about for something to towel off with.

"That's too bad," Tony said. "So, you and me, no prying ears: what happened out there?"

"I just left a message at Beeson's office," Vance said. He found a clean enough rag on the back of his foreman's desk chair and blotted himself off.

"You need a civil engineer to tell you what you saw with your own eyes?"

"He can tell me why that shoreline looks different today than it did when he assessed it for us."

"You should hire a third party for that kind of inquiry," Tony said. "Beeson's got a reputation to protect."

"I trust him. But I'll get a second opinion. That means you'll have to wait longer than you want to for answers, though."

"Doesn't matter. I don't plan to wait. Not even for Beeson."

Vance had seen this coming, hadn't he? He reached for a dry cotton T-shirt lumped on top of a file cabinet.

Tony finally moved away from the door and went to Vance's desk. He tilted his head and studied the clutter scattered across the surface, reached out and pushed one piece of paper off another with the pads of his fingers.

"Give me your most likely scenario," Tony said.

"Sinkhole."

"Let's weigh the consequences of that option. If Mother Nature caused this accident, then Eagle's Talon has no future. If we have sinkholes, I have a piece of worthless property."

"Whatever caused this accident isn't a subjective thing."

"Sure it is. At this point it could be anything."

"I'm really only interested in the truth," Vance said.

"You're a nice guy, Vance. Truth is interesting to nice guys. But I'm a businessman. So give me your most likely scenario — and when I ask you for that, I'm asking for a name."

"You want a fall guy."

"I don't care what you call him —"

"Mother Nature, then."

Tony scowled. "I just want you to tell my partners and my buyers whatever it's going to take to secure their interests and protect ours until we can fix what's broken."

"I'm going to tell them I think we got a sinkhole, but it's impossible to say for sure until we get the engineers out here for a look."

Tony sighed and sat down in Vance's chair. He continued to examine the papers on the desk instead of looking Vance in the eye.

Vance said, "Avoid the lawsuit that these rich people are going to drop on you when they find out you put their lives and their investments at risk. Be frank with them."

"Not going to happen. Listen: if you say sinkhole *now,* all your men become unemployed. No telling how long they'll have to wait to resume their work. Those people living in building 12, they freak, they leave. All the contracts in place come undone. We have panic and chaos and all kinds of legal threats. But you give me an alternative scenario, you give me time. We have employed men and calm residents. And *then* we can say sinkhole — if that's even what it really is. After it's been filled in, shored up, whatever it is that has to be done to sinkholes to shut them down. Everyone has the truth, everyone is happy."

"Listen to you. Danielle's son almost died today."

"Come off your moral high horse, Vance. He didn't die. And I'm not asking you to lie, I'm only asking you to help me buy time for everyone."

Tony seemed to be looking for a particular

document on Vance's desk. He found it — a report bound between red plastic covers. He placed it in front of him and folded his hands atop the report like a salesman trying to close a deal. Vance recognized it as Beeson's original coastal-protection report.

"What do you think about that pump operator?" Tony said.

"Wallace?"

"Is that his name? He was distracted."

Was he? Who besides Wallace could really know? Vance recalled someone shouting commands over the operator's evident concern for his son, but that might be any father's reaction to a life-threatening situation, not the cause of it.

Tony continued, "His kid's in the cab, his truck starts to go down — if he didn't have that boy on his mind, he might have saved the truck."

"That's entirely different from saying he made the truck go over."

"Not so different, in the first hours of a tragedy."

"Tony, how do you think that even a singularly focused operator could have stopped thirty tons from doing what it wanted to do?"

"By swinging the boom away from the fall.

Turn it into a counterbalance. I've seen it work."

"The truck went down way too fast for that option. There was no warning, no time to correct."

"Then that will come out in the course of the investigation. Wallace will be absolved, reinstated, whatever is needed."

"I won't hang a man before he's —"

"What's it to you?" Tony asked. "Do you know him? No? Maybe he's not one of the good guys. Maybe this is poetic justice. The man doesn't even work for us, Vance. Let his own people deal with this problem. All you and I have to do is a little damage control. I have a very experienced PR department that can handle this for us."

Tony stood, holding the report, and started to flip through it. "Look, we can settle on a name right now, or we can tell a whole fleet of people that they're out of luck and out of work. Those are our choices."

"What if 12 goes down while everyone's sleeping tonight? Could you live with that?"

"It's not going down! It's a blasted *house-boat*. It *floats*."

"That's not how it works! If its supports become unstable they could drag it down, or at least put lives at risk. Didn't you even *look* at what happened to 11?"

"My financial risks in losing this entire development are much higher right now than the chances of that thing sinking."

Disgusted, Vance's mind turned away from argument. Instead, he tried to think of a way to get the few residents of 12 out of their homes without causing public chaos.

"You can't expect my cooperation," Vance said.

"You're not the only man I know who can build a floating house."

"Okay, well, you're not the only man I know who can employ me. And you're a fool to think that you can create your own version of the truth!"

"I've done it often enough."

Tony threw Beeson's report into a metal trash can sitting to the side of Vance's desk. The minor thunder was magnified by the enclosed space.

"Let me show you how it works, creating the truth," Tony said. He took a book of matches out of his breast pocket and folded the top back. "If you won't choose Wallace, I'll choose you."

"For the pump truck?"

"Yes. See, you should have heeded the engineer's warnings," Tony said.

He lit a match and tossed it into the trash can. Vance watched the pages catch. That was merely a copy of Beeson's report. It would be easy enough to get others.

"What warnings?" Vance asked. There wasn't a hint of sinkholes, and all of Beeson's recommendations had been implemented.

Tony said, "I'm sure Beeson will want to keep his slate clean. For the right price, I imagine he'd revise his original report to include unstable ground."

Vance held his tongue.

"The way I'll recall this conversation, if I must, is that you've just told me today's mishap was caused by a careless pump-truck operator. And I won't find out about the terrible sinkhole and your cover-up until it's far too late."

Tony headed toward the door as flames began to fill the metal can. The small trailer filled with the offensive smell of scorched plastic. He opened the door to a landscape that was much grayer than it had been when Vance entered. "If you'd like to prevent your career from ending this way, here's what I suggest: before the end of the day, you file a grievance with Wallace's company and talk his foreman into firing him. Then give me a quote for our press release about how all of this has been handled. This will buy me enough time to take care of whatever is lurking below before anyone's even worried about it. That's all you have to do, Vance."

Vance was hard at work on a different scenario.

Tony closed the door as the first raindrops smacked the top of Vance's trailer. Maybe the sky was going to come down on him after all.

9

The motion-sensor alarm that had been attached to the balcony was still shrieking
when Danielle and Simeon returned to their
third-floor condo. It was casting its blinking-
red warning across that gap and seeming to
say, *This is too great a temptation for a five-
year-old boy.*

She silenced the device and took stock of
the damage by poking her head out through
the opening. Someone had retrieved the
balcony platform from the water and hauled
it up onto the floating dock. Rain began to
dot the dock and tap the metal wreckage
with a minor tone. Beneath her feet was a
sheer drop to Ferti's once-identical balcony.
The brackets that had attached Danielle's
to the building were distended and straining at the screws. One had ripped out and
left a jagged scar.

Danielle drew a sharp breath and retreated
into her bedroom, listening for Simeon,

wishing she had a sixth sense that would give her his exact location at all times, from now through his young adulthood and possibly beyond. A maternal GPS. She heard Legos being poured out of a box in his bedroom and felt relieved.

The slider was jammed, firmly stuck in the half-open position it had been in after she and Simeon passed through. The only real danger was that passage about two feet wide where the curtain played a breezy peek-a-boo with the sky.

She needed a way to block it.

If Tony were here, he would pull his phone out of his breast pocket and summon someone to make the breach vanish. If Vance were here, he would assess the problem, leave, and return with materials to do the job. But both men were occupied with more urgent matters. She would have to figure out a temporary solution on her own.

The tall bamboo bookcase in her living room looked to be about the right size for a blockade. She guessed it to be about seven feet, high enough to prevent birds from getting in and children from getting out. While she quickly unloaded the case of its knick-knacks, she called Simeon away from his toys and put him in charge of the books.

"Make a path of books that leads to your

bed," she instructed. "Let's pretend those are the only safe place for you to step in the whole apartment."

"It's like the whole place is hot lava!"

"We've had an eruption, have we?"

"Like the one on Laith's TV!"

Danielle didn't want to know. "And you have bare feet."

"S'okay. I'll make a path for you too." Simeon threw down a paperback and balanced on it like a flamingo. He wobbled.

"Sorry, no books allowed in my room. But don't worry about me. I'm wearing my special fireproof shoes."

"If your toes start to melt, come find me. My bed's a lava-proof rescue boat!"

"I'll give you a shout if I need rescuing, 'kay? Right now I'm going to move this to block more lava from coming in. You should save your toys while you can."

Within minutes Simeon was safely occupied arranging and rearranging the stepping-stone books, making paths to his various toys and transporting them to the rescue-boat bed in his room.

When the case was empty, Danielle tilted it forward to rest on the matching coffee table between it and the sofa. With any luck, she wouldn't scratch up Tony's things. Then she took the flat sheet off her bed, folded it in half, and laid it on the floor where the case had been standing. When she righted the unit, it stood on top of the sheet. Picking up the linen tail, she was able to drag the bookshelf rather easily across the room and through the partitions that formed the narrow bedroom hallway.

The hall entry was open to the roof, and Danielle didn't even think about the bedroom door frames until the shelving unit was right in front of her door. It was too tall to go through.

Sidling around the bookcase, she grabbed the sides and pulled it toward her, tipping it onto its long end. It wasn't heavy, and the sheet underneath made it easy enough to push the unit into her room. But halfway through, the bookcase struck the end of her bed.

Danielle set the whole thing down and assessed the problem. The doorway and the position of the furniture didn't allow enough room for her to turn the case. And she wasn't far enough into the room to tilt the bookcase upright. Every angle and corner conspired against her. She needed someone inside the room to lift this thing up over the mattress. Or, lacking such a person, she would have to move the mattress.

"This is why I don't give myself much

credit for competence, Ferti," Danielle mumbled.

"Can I help?" Simeon asked from the other end of the hall.

"Stay in your room," Danielle snapped.

Her tone was sharper than she intended, and she turned around to apologize. But Simeon already had shrunk out of sight. She might have felt less guilty if he'd argued with her. She turned to go to him, to say she was sorry and explain what she was trying to do.

"Give you a hand?" someone said.

Surprised, Danielle pulled up and took a detour out of the hallway. On the other side of the main living space, a businessman stood at her front door, which tended to yawn if she didn't close it hard enough for the latch to fully engage.

The intrusion should have alarmed her. The man's football-player physique, which blocked her only exit, should have sent her memory banks into a review of every self-defense class she'd ever taken. Instead, her panic slept like a dog in the sun. He was familiar in a pleasant way. And a dreadful way. The thickness of his hair with the swirling curl at the crown, the way his ears stuck out just so, the slightly bowed legs — they could have belonged to her dead husband.

A buried grief thrust a fist through her heart. Because it wasn't Danny at all, of course, but the man who'd arrived with Tony and Carver.

"Will you let me help you?" he repeated.

How could he possibly know what she was trying to do? He couldn't see the hallway or bedroom from where he stood. As much as she needed help, she wasn't about to let a stranger into her bedroom.

"No. No thanks," she said. "I've got this."

"I guess you do. I'm Ranier Smith."

"Oh."

She had to think through the meaning of this. Ranier Smith — the prospective buyer she had been scheduled to meet earlier in a not-so-coincidental encounter. Why was he here, at her unit, instead of at one of the vacant condos with a real estate agent? And why had he come with Tony and Carver? And why had Tony given her this appointment if he'd planned to come himself? Her quick mind was sidelined.

She cautiously stepped out of the hallway and extended a hand.

"Danielle Clement."

She met his grip, noticing the brilliant silver cuff links. They were fashioned of strange silver pieces unlike any silver she had seen, coarse instead of polished, lumpy instead of smooth. They were the size of marbles and looked like balls of clipped threads, like something the seamstress Ferti might gather up off her studio floor.

"They're a rare type of native silver," he said, as if to explain them in terms she'd understand. Perhaps if she'd been a real art broker she would have. But she had no idea what native silver was, compared to the regular stuff. And she was embarrassed to have been caught staring.

He smelled like saltwater, out of place in this river setting. His hand was callused and dry. It was the hand of a laborer, and quite different from her late husband's. This hand reminded her of Vance's encircling her entire arm in his rough fingers, holding her out of the water.

"You're a sculptor?" she blurted without thinking. It was information from the file Tony had given to her. But he didn't seem surprised that she knew.

"What gave me away?"

Not the cuff links, for sure. She gestured to his hands.

Ranier nodded. "I work a lot with clay. Dries out my skin." He looked around at the art hanging on her walls, each piece properly displayed with just the right size frame on just the right size walls with just the right kind of spotlight. There were some bronze pieces on a table next to the entryway. Tony had initially put blown glass there until she insisted he replace it with something more childproof.

The man said, "And you're a mom."

This was not what she had expected his assessment to be. She quickly scanned the living room, but except for a few of the books on the floor, all evidence of Simeon was relegated to the bedroom.

He continued, "And an . . ."

"Art broker," she provided.

He regarded her with what seemed like wariness.

"I was going to say executive assistant."

His accurate guess changed the tone of their encounter. Danielle heard judgment in his tone, and suddenly she felt angry with Tony for not telling her everything she needed to know about Ranier Smith's arrival.

She took a step away from him and crossed her arms.

"Was there something you needed?" she asked.

"Yes, actually. I was asked to bring you a message."

"I thought you were . . . here to see the condos."

"Why would you think that?" he asked.

Why indeed?

"I, uh, saw you come in with Tony earlier."

"I actually came on my own, just to deliver a word."

A word?

The man reached into his breast pocket and pulled out a phone. He summoned the communication with several gentle taps of his forefinger on the screen. In a moment he began to read: "A message from the Living One who holds the keys of Death, to Danielle Clement, who will be judged."

What? Danielle forgot the bookcase, forgot the hole in her home that exposed her to the elements.

Ranier continued to read, "You say you are strong but you are weak. You say you can see but you are blind. You say you are rich but you have nothing to call your own, not even a white dress to cover your shame. What will come must happen, but you need not be afraid if you open your eyes to see. Strengthen yourself with genuine love. Invest yourself in true riches. Free yourself from selfishness. Then may you find mercy."

This man was no sculptor, no prospective buyer. He was a handsome, smooth-tongued freak. For a moment her thoughts were confused. She was offended. She was frightened. She was ticked off.

Ranier turned off his device and seemed to be waiting for her.

"What was that supposed to mean?"

"I think you know."

She didn't. Her mind was on *white dress* and *shame.* Whoever came up with that must know about her and Tony. But who would care? And who would dare accuse her of anything after all the losses she'd faced, and all she'd sacrificed to meet her son's needs? Weak! Blind! Poor!

"How could you? How could anyone . . . Why would you say something like that to me? You don't even know me."

"The Living One who —"

Danielle held up her hand. "Are you from a cult?"

"No, I come from God."

"Please leave."

"The Living God would like to free you from selfishness."

He was certifiable.

"Yes, well, the Living God isn't on my list of favorite people right now. What does he know about selfishness? He killed my husband and abandoned me to fend for myself."

"God didn't kill Danny. And he didn't abandon you."

Danielle balked. How did he know Danny's name? Had Tony mentioned it?

"Let me give you a tip on how to be more convincing, Mr. Smith: don't put *judgment* and *love* in the same sentence."

"This isn't judgment, Danielle. Not yet."

"Then what is it? The Living One who holds the keys to *death*? What's he doing with those?"

"I don't think you have heard the words correctly."

You are weak. You are blind. You have nothing to call your own. What was there to misunderstand?

"Danielle, you don't have much time."

"Go. Get out."

Ranier hardly seemed eager to escape her.

"I have a copy." He reached into his opposite breast pocket and this time emerged with a sealed white envelope, which he placed on the edge of the kitchen counter. She pretended not to notice.

Danielle decided not to say anything more. Keeping silent was, in her experience, the best way to get a person to leave. She could tolerate awkwardness longer than any person she had ever met.

Simeon arrived in the room by book, which carried him across the glossy cork floor like a surfboard. Danielle stepped between him and Ranier.

"Back to the lifeboat for a second, kiddo."

"It's not a lifeboat, it's a rescue — Hey!" Simeon had noticed Ranier. "How'd you get dry so fast? My hair's still wet."

Danielle didn't understand what her son was saying.

"It's a cool trick I know," Ranier said to her son. How could those same lips that had just judged her form a smile so affectionate, so like the boy's father? "Maybe I'll teach it to you."

"I'm supposed to stay in my room," Simeon announced, making Danielle suddenly feel small and ashamed and completely ineffective as a parent.

Simeon got off the book and walked around his mother, straight for Ranier. She reached out for his arm but he slipped through her fingers.

"If you're up here," Simeon asked, "who is holding up our house?"

All of Danielle's thoughts went to illogical explanations, impossible scenarios.

Ranier Smith lowered himself to one knee and put himself at Simeon's eye level. "Don't worry about that. For the next few days, this house is going to be the safest place you can be."

"Cool," Simeon said. "I like those." He

pointed to the shimmering cuff links, and Ranier allowed the boy to touch one. "They're weird."

"They're native silver," Ranier said. "Would you like to have one?"

"No," said Danielle.

Ranier slipped the expensive accessory out of the button hole.

"No," Danielle repeated.

Simeon took it from Ranier's fingers as if they were boys sharing jawbreakers. "Thanks. I gotta get back to my lava-proof rescue boat."

"Good idea."

The boy made crazy jumps across the lava and back to his books, saying "Ow! Ow! Ow!" with each leap. He held the cuff link high over his head in his left hand. Impossibly, it gave off light. It was an illusion caused by the weakening sun filtered through skylights, but the silver seemed to glow with its own radiance.

"I don't like people who won't respect my requests," Danielle said in low tones after Simeon was back in his room.

"Neither do I."

Ranier left her, pulling the front door closed behind him. Two seconds later she heard a puff of air in the outer hall, the shifting atmosphere of another door opening and closing somewhere else in the building. Her door latch, which had failed to catch, grazed the metal plate and glided wide open again, leaving her feeling dangerously exposed.

She went to it quickly, slammed the door hard, and locked it this time, threw the dead bolt. Then she rushed to her window that overlooked the peninsula. Hidden by the curtain and the rain pelting the glass at her living room window, Danielle could be certain that Ranier left her building. He did, in about the time it took him to descend the stairs to the main level. He crossed the canopy-covered gangway. He walked up the sloping shoreline onto higher ground.

She had the odd idea that Tony was behind the man's visit. But why? If he was, the crazy letter would make even less sense.

It seemed strange that Ranier didn't try to protect his expensive clothing from the wetness. He strode with an unnaturally erect posture down the peninsula at a diagonal, his open cuff protruding from his jacket sleeve. Then he stepped off the side of the road and went down the opposite embankment, his head up and his steps confident, until he disappeared and she could no longer see him. She waited.

Water began to ripple over the glass now,

an ocean of currents rather than a forest of drops. The once-golden afternoon was thick with grayness. This might be the storm that tested the integrity of the engineers' and the architects' work.

If Ranier had been a true buyer, standing with her under the shelter of an overhang as the rain came down, expressing this very concern, she would have had a dozen assurances about the soundness of the buildings' design. The floating foundations were not of the old bathtub design that might sink if a breach filled them. These were solid blocks of expanded polystyrene foam swathed in a tough polyethylene coating before being encased in concrete. The EPS foam was so light that it was unsinkable, and yet each cubic foot could buoy more than fifty pounds.

But Ranier was not a true buyer, he was a mystery. And he didn't reappear.

A fork of lightning drove itself into the horizon and, even at that great distance, warned her away from the glass.

Danielle's mind returned to the problem in her hallway, and she soothed her agitation with the decision to make room for the bookcase by moving the bed herself.

She turned her back to the window. She took long strides to the hallway but stopped when she saw, through the wide-open door of her bedroom, the bookshelf standing erect against the wall, blockading the damage.

10

Vance grabbed a slicker from a hook by the door and left the trailer a minute after Tony did.

If Vance had learned anything from his years as an alcoholic, it was that there was no avoiding the truth of a thing. A man could run from it for a while, pretend it didn't exist, even cleverly avoid it for a time, but eventually, if ignored long enough, truth would raise an ugly ruckus and demand an audience.

Vance's trailer stood at the top of the crescent-shaped peninsula, directly across from building 12, where a narrow quarter-mile isthmus connected the development to the mainland. For those not traveling by boat, it was the only way to or from Eagle's Talon. All trucks and contractors, buyers and investors, arrived via the one-lane blacktop road framed by a guardrail on both sides. At the mouth of the isthmus, coming or going, everyone had to pass the trailer.

Vance walked south, toward his crew. They had returned to their tasks, trying to hit the day's goals before the rain stopped them. He would send them home himself, though, and fetch a sheet of plywood to board up Danielle's exposed bedroom.

He passed a 4×4 parked behind the trailer and noticed Drew Baxter, the concrete-pumping foreman, slouching in the cab. Vance approached the heavy-duty truck, but Baxter didn't notice him. He was staring into the Rondeau River, perhaps wishing himself a world away from this bad day. Without his hard hat, Baxter's bald head seemed strangely vulnerable. Gravity pulled at his features tonight, tugging at the corners of his eyes especially. They looked defensive.

Vance tapped on the window and Baxter flinched, then rolled it down a crack.

"Waiting for a crane to fetch your pump truck?" Vance asked.

Baxter's face relaxed a bit, and he took the window all the way down. "If this rain keeps up they might tell me the slope's too muddy to get the job done today."

"Might be unstable even if it was desert dry."

Baxter sighed and ran a hand over his smooth-skinned head. He adjusted himself on the seat with the stiffness of a man who'd been in one position too long. But he was too tall and the cab too confined to give his long limbs a real stretch.

"Someone's going to be in hot water for this," Baxter said.

"Tony Dean wants me to pin it on you guys."

"What! Why? He doesn't even know what happened yet, does he? I mean, no one does! If that suit throws my men to the lions . . ." He stopped himself with a deep breath and took his tone down a few notches. "He's eyeing my operator? Wallace?"

"That's right."

Baxter shook his head and looked out at the river again. His rumpled shirt gave him the disheveled look of a man whose world was falling down. "No one who saw what happened today thinks Wallace is responsible."

"I have to agree."

"So why's he gonna waste his time?"

"Tony thinks he's buying time," Vance said. "Look, Wallace having his boy in the truck might create some pains for you. That's the issue Tony's going to bite down on. Get your stories in order fast. Do your reports tonight."

"You did your own safety inspection on top of ours," Baxter recalled. "We're on the same page, aren't we?"

"We are. I'll send a copy to you as soon as I wrap up here."

"What do you think went down today?"

"Hard to say. A sinkhole is my best guess."

Vance could see a thick vein running above Baxter's ear. Rain was running in streams down the interior of his cab and he wiped at them ineffectively. There was blood in the man's palm.

"You need a first-aid kit?" Vance asked, pointing to Baxter's hand.

"Nah. Just clipped it in all the commotion this afternoon." He rubbed at the injury with his thumb. "So someone'll probably get down there and have a look? Investigate?"

"Eventually."

The wetness on Baxter's hands turned grimy. He examined his fingers for several seconds before dragging them down the front of his jacket, leaving long brown streaks. "This is ridiculous. Isn't the first time Tony's heaped all his problems onto the backs of other men. Won't be the last. He put my brother out of business — underbid him, stole his best men for inflated paychecks."

"Ansel, right? Your brother?" Vance asked.

"You heard about that?"

"He came into Tony's office once while I was there. Gave him and Danielle an earful."

Baxter shrugged. "He gets animated when he's upset. I don't even go there with him." He gave Vance an insider's knowing glance. "Tony hasn't done right by you either, has he?"

"That's a story for another time."

"You don't talk about it, but everyone knows. No point in pretending. You know if Eagle's Talon wasn't your baby, I wouldn't be here at all." He smiled a little. "Couldn't even tell Ansel I took the job. He'd stop talking to me."

"And I appreciate it. I really do." Vance slapped the side of the truck. "That crane's not going to come out in this. Go on home. Pump truck'll be here tomorrow."

Baxter cleared his throat. "What can I do to help you?"

"Start talking about what happened. Don't shut up your crew. Can't have too much truth right now."

"Right. Nothing but the truth." Baxter resumed his ponderous study of the river and said, "As if Tony Dean ever cared about that."

The corner of Vance's eye caught a movement at a window in building 12, a large wall pane on the second floor that gave the person inside a river view. He couldn't say for sure, but he suspected the onlooker was Tony. Baxter almost looked exhausted enough to give the impression that he was off to fire Wallace, though it didn't really matter, not being a truthful impression.

"Look, I've got to go send some people home," Vance said.

"You do that," Baxter said. "But lookee here. There's my crane."

Across the cove, half a mile away, the lumbering form of a heavy-duty crane appeared on the two-lane highway that led to the isthmus turnoff. Water was already pooling atop the unpaved road under Vance's feet. Had it only been raining an hour? Vance walked backward, watching the crane's slow and rumbling trek. Baxter climbed out of his truck and dropped into a soupy puddle.

Driving a truck that size onto ground like this would be like dropping a dinosaur into a tar pit.

"Try to catch him before he gets to the turnoff," Vance called out. "Once he's on the isthmus, there's no turning that beast around."

"I'll call his dispatch."

Vance bent his head into the downpour and jogged off to relieve his crew. If they moved quickly enough, they might get home before that beast of a crane blocked their only way out.

Zeke had lived on the water for ten years before he was blinded and ten years since, and he never tired of traveling it. Their little tributary met the Rondeau River the way an on-ramp meets a highway, and the rowboat was sucked into the swift recreational lanes headed south. The rain came down on them all at once. Ziggy stayed in the bottom of the boat only because it was bobbing too vigorously for him to panic and stand. Zeke could smell the muskiness of the dog's wet coat.

"What happened to our great day?" Zeke's hair was already flat on the sides of his head.

"The gods heard you tempting fate, with all that end-of-the-world talk."

Zeke chuckled.

"Turn back?" Enrique asked.

"We're closer to Vance than home now. Let's aim for the north bank."

"No docks there."

"There's plenty of solid ground. And Vance's trailer is right there. But you're the captain of this vessel. If you want to try for the cove, I promise not to jump ship."

For one, Ziggy wouldn't be of any help if he did.

In addition to the completed docks that extended from Vance's floating foundations, there were three docks in the shelter of the cove's west bank, the calm waters where most boaters put in before heading to the river. Getting to any of these landings would add another half hour to forty-five minutes if the downpour didn't let up.

The current was strong against the bottom of the boat. The soles of Zeke's feet hummed. Enrique would have enough to do to hit the top of the peninsula's curve without getting swept around the bend.

At the mercy of Enrique's skill, Zeke let the man concentrate. This position was no less humbling now than it had been the day Zeke learned he'd never again direct anyone to place a sapling here or a shrub there. But after a decade, the loss of his physical independence pricked him less and less. His need to rely on others from time to time had become a sort of spiritual discipline.

Still, he did his part to help. He talked to God silently so Enrique wouldn't be distracted by him going religious.

The welder decided to follow Zeke's

advice. He navigated the boat toward the north side of the peninsula. The current stroking the hull shifted direction, and the rain that had been slicing across Zeke's profile now came straight into his face.

The Rondeau was a wide river, nearly a mile across, and rowboats were wise not to drift too far from land into the stronger currents and boating lanes. Even taking this into account, Enrique got them to the beach in less time than Zeke anticipated. But he was young, strong, and fueled by plenty of sandwiches. Enrique lifted the oars out of their oarlocks and dropped the fiberglass blades against his seat. The boat scraped the river bottom and wobbled as he splashed out and dragged them in. Ziggy stayed put, trembling, until there was more earth than water under the boat. When the dog exited, Zeke knew it was safe for him to get out too.

Enrique unclamped the outboard motor from the transom, anticipating that they'd have to wait out the storm, and Zeke helped him turn the boat's shell on top of it.

"The slope's not bad here, but it's plenty wet," Enrique said as Zeke took hold of Ziggy's harness.

The ground under his feet was a mixture of coarse sand, low-lying nubs of shore grasses that could turn wobbly ankles, and smooth pebbles like greasy ball bearings in these wet conditions. Ziggy led the way haltingly, patient for Zeke to find solid footing.

About halfway up, a tiny landslide took Zeke down to one knee. Ziggy sat next to him, waiting while Zeke kept hold of the harness. On his other side, Zeke sensed Enrique bending to offer an elbow. Between dog and friend, Zeke got his old joints stable underneath him again and stood. With their help he scaled the final yards.

At the top of the hill the raindrops seemed thicker, heavier, like being pelted with peas rather than pins.

"Trailer's a few hundred yards," Enrique said. But his voice was some distance off, not right at Zeke's side, where his elbow was. This strangely disembodied elbow.

Startled, Zeke let go.

"Hello?" he said.

"I'm over here," Enrique called.

"Who helped me?" Zeke said.

"What?" It sounded like he was headed back toward Zeke. "You okay?"

Zeke waved his free hand about, but the elbow was gone.

"Was someone just here?"

"Just us crazy dudes."

"You see Vance?"

"Not yet. They'll know at the trailer, if he's not there himself. This way."

Mud sucked at Zeke's shoes. "This storm wasn't forecast, was it? What time is it?"

"About four."

"The air feels later."

"It's warm enough. For a summer storm."

"I mean the atmosphere. Something night-time about it. Dusky."

"Well, it looks like four o'clock to me." Enrique's volume fluctuated, as if he was looking around. "Four o'clock with rain." He stopped. He whistled.

Whether it was an expression of admiration or disbelief, Zeke couldn't tell. "What?" he asked.

"Pump truck's in the cove, cab first. I'd like to see them get that one out."

A rush of fear came over Zeke's body. There in his mind was Vance, standing in the falling pickup truck, surrounded by death.

"Are they working on it?"

"Not anymore."

"You're going to have to paint a clearer picture for me."

It took Enrique so long to answer that Zeke began to wonder if he'd spotted something unspeakable. When he did find his voice, it seemed dazed.

"Truck in the water, rescue crane on the bank, up to its axles in mud. The isthmus road is completely blocked. Looks like they're trying to rescue the rescuer."

"You okay?"

"Yeah, why?"

"I need to find Vance."

"Is he expecting you?"

"No."

"Ten to one he's too busy right now for a social call."

"It's not exactly social."

"Tell me again why you needed to see him?" Enrique's voice was fully directed at Zeke now, and it bore a quality he'd never heard in his friend's tone before. It was such a foreign layer that Zeke didn't know what to call it. He waited for some insight into Enrique's question. Didn't get any.

"It appears he's on unstable ground," Zeke said.

"Who told you this was happening?"

"No one. Like I said, I didn't even know for sure anything was wrong."

Enrique's silence felt like an accusation.

11

Most of the men had left the peninsula before the remnant were cut off.

After Vance told them to wrap things up, the crews stowed their tools and secured their equipment and piled into their cars and trucks to escape. Their quick and steady exit held the rescue crane at bay more effectively than Baxter was able to. Disbelieving that conditions would be so bad after just a little rainfall, and unwilling to surrender the costs of a return trip, the crane operator drove onto the isthmus road as soon as a pause in traffic allowed.

The men who hadn't made it off by then were forced to yield. They called their homes to check in. They exhaled cigarette smoke through cracked windows, they turned up their radios, they tipped their heads back onto headrests and closed their eyes. And they sat in the mucky turnaround to wait, and wait, on the incoming crane, which became encumbered by mud the moment its rear wheels left the paved road of the isthmus. It blocked their passage like a clot in an artery.

To them, it was a momentary inconvenience. To Vance, it was an unsettling déjà vu with clear parallels to the Defining Moment of his youth, which he had never expected to survive, much less relive. The memory of that particular stretch of days during his fifteenth year ate up his other thoughts. Getting his men off Eagle's Talon as quickly as possible became an intuitive emotional priority.

He had retrieved a plywood sheet for Danielle by this point, but taking it to her would have to wait. His assistant manager, Marcus, was standing with Baxter at the top of the trailer steps watching the fiasco when Vance arrived.

"Stubborn bull," Baxter said of the crane driver.

Marcus nodded at the board. "Can I do something for ya?"

"Kick that crane back across the cove," Vance said.

Marcus grinned and crossed his thick arms. "Just say when."

The crane driver put the gears of the stranded crane in park, then opened his door to step down.

"You're not going to leave it here," Vance shouted over the rain. He approached the open door and stood where the man would have landed.

"Where the blazes do you think I ought to put it?" the driver yelled back. "And how?"

"Right there." Vance gestured to the shoulder, fifty feet away in front of building 12, not far from where it would have to be to get the pump truck out of the cove.

"Unless you're Superman and can lift this baby, she's not going anywhere."

"My men need to get home."

"It's a little rain!" the man shouted down. His position above Vance gave him a stooped, intimidating posture.

"Baxter told you it was more than that before you made the last turn," Vance said.

"Well, they can wait it out like the rest of us."

"It's up to you, if you want to pay their hourly wages while they sit here." Vance was not a man quick to impatience, but today that fearful childhood memory ate away at his tolerance for foolishness. "No? Then let's move it."

"Why don't we just call you crazy and take a vote."

Vance nodded and pulled out his cell

phone. "Why don't we?" He dialed the company number printed on the open door, then put the phone to his ear and stared down the driver while the line at the other end rang. "I'll poll your boss first. Maybe he'll let me do your job for you, if you don't want to."

The man told Vance where he should go but climbed back into his cab. "If she gets damaged it'll be on your head," the driver said.

Vance disconnected the call and turned away, and nearly collided with Marcus, who looked ready to kick anything Vance asked him to.

"You don't know how to operate one of those things, do you?"

"Not a clue," Vance admitted. "Let's get all hands on deck to help this guy."

Marcus trekked down the peninsula to wave men out of their idling cars and instruct them to join the effort. One of the crew supervisors, Sam, was first to respond. The former soldier was known by the guys as Slogan Sam, both for his love of snarky T-shirts and his brusque but fair manner. Today he wore a red T-shirt that ordered those who could read it to get out of his way. The back suggested that those same people should pick up the pace.

Sam had the idea of throwing down a makeshift road of peastones in front of the monstrous crane. Vance agreed, and spontaneous teams were formed under the thickening sky. Sam and Marcus gathered others to transport the small pebbles from a pile recently delivered to the turnaround. Together with Vance and Baxter, a group threw shovels and gravel and levers and sweat into helping the driver free the wheels from the depressions that trapped them. Young Andy brought a couple of steel scraps to use as wedges under the wheels.

Rain dripped from their noses and chins. It flattened hair and clothing and clung to everyone's physical flaws. It coated their thick-skinned natures in a high gloss.

There would be no backtracking for this monster now that it had left the paved road. There would be no three-point turns in this muck, no driving in reverse down a slick and bending balance beam a quarter mile long. Moving forward was the smaller risk, so the driver was forced to take it. He was a bottomless geyser of curses and frustration that tested Vance's eagerness to help.

From within the cab the operator maneuvered the crane and the gears to shift the vehicle's weight in their favor. Forward, back. Forward, back. It was a tedious effort that was unlikely to work until, suddenly, it did.

An hour after their endeavors began, the men cheered as the truck advanced out of the hollows. The gravel held it off the mud and delivered the vehicle to the narrow shoulder, where the ground held firm under a layer of peastones. Vance swiped the rain and sweat from his eyes and took a relieved breath.

Behind the truck, the Rondeau River sloshed over the top of the isthmus and poured down into the cove on the other side.

The water that glided over the road looked like liquid mercury, silver and deadly in the muted and fading daylight. Vance wasn't the only one to notice this spill. Marcus planted the blade of the shovel he'd been using into the soft ground by his boots and held on to the shaft.

"That happen much when it rains?" he asked Vance, though it had rained often since the project commenced.

"Not usually," Vance said.

It should have taken a week of steady rainfall, not these few hours, to bring water levels to that point. But the volume had increased so swiftly that the rippling waterway moved like an obese snake no longer able to take the bends gracefully. Gravity pulled the swollen river due south, straight across the isthmus and into the cove.

A burst of water hit the road with a spray Vance had only seen in photographs of the Hawaiian Islands.

Marcus whistled.

"What on earth?" Baxter said.

"Better move everyone out now," Vance said.

Marcus turned to climb into Vance's trailer, presumably to fetch car keys from his desk.

Vance followed him to retrieve his tool belt. "Andy riding with you again today?" he asked Marcus. The day laborer didn't have a car.

"Yeah. He took a wheelbarrow back to number 3," Marcus said.

"I've got to go board up that balcony in number 12," Vance said. "And maybe encourage the residents to find somewhere else to stay tonight."

"Andy and I'll stay until you get back. Make sure everyone gets off."

"When they go, you go. Don't wait for me. Tony's here, and I might have to outlast him if I have any hope of talking these people into leaving."

Marcus grunted. "He's gonna love that."

Vance nodded. His thoughts were already ahead of his movements. He was rehearsing arguments with Danielle, because she was the one he most wanted to go. He didn't analyze why. In his mind he convinced her — all of them — to leave, even though they lived in homes designed to withstand precisely this kind of event. Yes, *but.* The sinkhole under number 11 changed everything, he would say. Until they knew what really happened down there, no one should be sitting on poles sunk into pockets of air.

Danielle, look at what you and Simeon already escaped today. Please don't risk it. Do you have somewhere to go?

If she didn't, he'd take her to his own home. His dirty, cramped home that wasn't exactly set up for a family. No, that would be all wrong. He could call someone in his church. There were plenty of people there who could make a single mother feel safe and sheltered.

He was inside the trailer for maybe half a minute, and when he reemerged the line of cars was beginning to traverse the mud pits created by the crane at the mouth of the isthmus. There were maybe a dozen people waiting their turn to be jostled by the holes. Slogan Sam was bringing up the rear in his rattling pickup truck.

At the base of the trailer's metal stair, a bedraggled head turned toward the sound of Vance's boots stepping out. Zeke Hammond.

The sight of his mentor took Vance's anxiety down a notch, and a very strange thought popped into his mind: he *had* survived that terrible week of his life so many years ago, though not everyone had made it. Vance was a survivor standing among survivors, and so was Zeke.

The guide dog saw Vance and slapped his tail on the ground, splattering mud on the baggy pants of Zeke's stocky friend Enrique, who saluted Vance with unexpected good humor, considering he looked like he'd gone swimming fully dressed. Fingerless gloves covered his hands to protect them from the oars.

"Zeke!" Vance said. "Enrique, hi. What are — how'd you get here?"

"By the grace of God," Zeke said.

"That'd be a boat," Enrique clarified.

"You came by boat? In this?"

"It wasn't raining when we started."

"Go in" — Vance pointed to the trailer — "dry off. I need to board a window and I'll be back." He strapped on his leather tool belt and slipped a pair of gloves over his fingers before hefting the wet plywood in both hands.

"We'll help," Zeke said. Ziggy, sensing Zeke's change of posture, stood to follow Vance.

"Not much for you to do. It's in someone's unit. I don't even know if she'll let me in, all this mud. You should stay here."

"That's some mess to clean up." Enrique tilted his head toward the chaos at number 11. "What happened?"

"We don't know yet. Sinkhole maybe. Things are still too stirred up to tell."

"Anyone hurt?"

"We almost lost two boys. The pump operator's son and a five-year-old in number 12." Vance pointed at the arm of the pump truck, still resting against the side of Danielle's building.

Enrique frowned and looked in the other direction, down toward the bottom of Eagle's Talon. "There's kids here?"

"Well sure."

"But during construction?"

"Number 12's complete."

"That's not right. Shouldn't be any kids on a site."

Vance felt the same way, but what could be done about it right now?

"The five-year-old's a good boy. Sharp mother. He doesn't go past the barricades."

"Looks like that didn't matter today, did it?" There was more despair than accusation in his words.

"Everyone's okay," Vance said, perplexed about Enrique's uncharacteristic concern.

Another crest broke on the isthmus and the attention of all three men turned in the direction of the splash, which had doused an old Buick sedan. The driver slammed on the brakes and hydroplaned a few long inches.

"Truth, Vance," said Zeke. "Even though I can't see what you see, I've heard enough. I'd rather be on the water than in that tin box of yours right now."

The Buick resumed its progress, the driver's cautious foot causing the brake lights to blink.

Vance wavered. He'd survived three days trapped in a tin box of sorts, but it was merely a physical survival. The real trial of his fifteenth year, the real life-or-death battle, came afterward, when he had to get out of the box and face the judgment of the people who didn't understand what had happened inside — the people who thought that in any tragedy, there was always something that could have averted it. In the end, the tin box had saved his body but nearly destroyed his soul.

Vance supposed he'd rather be on the water than in a mobile trailer too.

"You think you're going to get to kick back on a white chaise lounge looking like that?" Vance kept his tone light.

"My skivvies are clean, if I must strip down."

Vance laughed for the first time since that morning.

"Okay," he said. "Come with me."

Enrique walked slightly ahead of them as they cut across the slow-moving line of cars.

"I might have misspoken," Zeke said. "It's not your trailer that worries me. It's more like I have a problem with this piece of land we're standing on."

"You have any idea what's going on here?" Vance kept his head down, shielding his eyes from the needling raindrops and guarding his steps.

"Not yet," Zeke said. "But I'll keep my eyes open."

12

In her kitchen, Danielle paced. Ranier's unopened white envelope kept catching the corner of her eye from the butcher block countertop. She had thrown the letter away. Then she had pulled it out of the trash. Then she had spent a silly amount of time concocting reasons why a judgmental message from God shouldn't mean anything to her.

It was because of that bookcase. A stranger had come into her home and done something tricky, and she could no longer trust her own beliefs about God and illusions and the flexibility of bamboo furniture in tight quarters. She wanted an explanation.

Simeon had given up his hot-lava game and was sitting on the living room floor in front of the wall-to-wall window. From here he had a front-row view of the drama involving the stuck rescue crane. He was making a construction-paper replica of the massive vehicle and had nearly exhausted her supply of clear tape. Scraps of gray and black paper littered the floor, and the contents of her craft box had been examined, scattered, and rejected in search of the perfect parts. The lid of a plastic strawberry box had been converted into a windshield, and she'd helped him cut off the ends of an empty paper-towel tube to make all the necessary wheels.

He had secured Ranier's cuff link to the top of his tennis shoe, slipping it between the Velcro closures. The light from the living room lamp kept catching it and shooting annoying flashes into Danielle's eyes.

She'd been distracted for several minutes when she realized he'd abandoned the paper truck and had tied a couple of the paper-towel cylinders together end-to-end with a long piece of string.

"What are you making now?" she asked, genuinely curious.

"Nunchakus."

"Nunchakus!" She took them from his outstretched hand and examined them. "What do you know about nunchakus?"

"Laith and Haji were watching —"

"Don't tell me," Danielle said, holding up one hand. How was it that Mirah's generous offers to look after Simeon from time to time could end up being an education in martial arts weaponry and who knew what else? Was it so hard for that woman to turn off the TV for a half hour, or to watch something tamer? "I'm not quite ready for you to learn Bruce Lee's tricks just yet."

"Who's Bruce Lee?"

A whiff of spicy cologne tickled Danielle's nose.

"A great fighter." The explanation didn't come from Danielle, but from a man standing behind her. Tony.

Does no one knock anymore? Had it been Ranier Smith lurking there, she might have cut him off at the knees with the weightless nunchakus.

"He was a great *actor,*" Danielle told her son, setting the empty paper-towel rolls on the floor next to him. He'd resumed his search for something that would form the crane's arm.

"His skills were no act," Tony contradicted.

Danielle's awareness of her rumpled state prevented her from making eye contact with Tony. Though she had changed clothes after she and Simeon were plunged into the cove, she had not combed out her hair or washed the sliding makeup off her face. And she had forgotten to put something down to protect the floors — Tony's floors — from their watery excursion. Light muddy prints exposed their movements through the condo. And the transported bookcase left a noticeable gap against a huge aluminum wall panel. The contents stacked on the sofas seemed haphazard and careless now that Tony stood here, looking at all of it without speaking.

He seemed untouched by the weather. He was dry and clean and smelled like cologne rather than wet earth when he bent down to kiss her. He did so as if her disheveled state were contagious, having no contact with any part of her but her lips. Quick and light.

Obligatory. It was because they were at Eagle's Talon, she decided. They hardly knew how to act as a couple in a place where their relationship was supposed to be secret.

"Have you recovered?" he asked.

"Yes," she said quickly.

"Is your son okay?"

It was a thoughtful question, a kind inquiry, that somehow caused her to feel as if the entire incident was related to some character flaw of hers — that if she didn't possess this flaw, whatever it was, *her son* wouldn't have suffered a near-drowning today. *Her son* wouldn't have been on that balcony at all, because maternal intuition would have warned her away from it.

"If I had a bottle of wine to offer you I'd have brought it up," he said. "I'll ask Jonesy. He'd give me one from his stash." The offer stunned her, so far was it from the kind of consolation she would have picked out for herself. What would she have picked, though? They had traveled such a short distance from professional to intimate that they'd had no time to build up a repertoire of comforts. He noticed her unresponsiveness.

"Should I tell him we need something stiffer?"

"Ranier Smith dropped by," she said, grabbing a tissue from the coffee table to swipe at the makeup under her eyes.

"Here?" He seemed genuinely surprised.

"That was the arrangement, wasn't it?"

"He canceled the appointment less than a half hour after you left the office."

Simeon stood to press his nose and hands against the window, the better to see what was going on below. From the corner of her eye, Danielle could see that the crane had moved.

"You could have let me know," she accused.

134

"I called. You didn't answer," he said. And it was at that moment that Danielle recalled leaving her cell phone in the car's hands-free bracket, so focused was she on juggling both Simeon and Ranier's file. Her fault again, blaming this man for a simple misunderstanding.

Tony went into her kitchen and opened her refrigerator door. Danielle turned to her purse for a comb to run through her hair, then sat down behind the kitchen counter while he rummaged through her things. His things.

"Why did he arrive with you?" she said. "Ranier Smith was standing with you and Carver Lewis after . . . before the rain."

Tony came out of the fridge with a box of restaurant leftovers that Danielle had planned to give to Simeon for supper.

"I missed lunch. Do you mind?"

She shook her head. She could give Simeon the frozen pizza that he liked, even though it was nutritionally worthless.

"Not the best day to be showing Carver around," he said. "But it was only the two of us. I can be glad of that, at least."

"I'm sure it was Ranier. There were two men besides you."

"Just one, Danielle." And his tone said, *Let's be done with this theory.* "You had a shock, don't forget."

"He was here."

"Then he came by his own steam." Tony finished off the leftovers in just a few bites and set the waxy brown box down on the counter right next to Ranier's envelope. The fork fell out and left red sauce on the surface. "Either way, I didn't see Mr. Smith. I suppose that doesn't bode well for my hopes in him, if he's a man who can't make up his mind. What did he think of the place?"

She had forgotten to ask.

"I don't think he intends to buy anything."

"Tell me all this mud wasn't here when he came by. Or that mess in your living room. Where's the bookshelf?"

"Hi, Tony!" Simeon made a sudden appearance at Danielle's knee as if he'd just noticed the man's arrival. He was holding up his truck, on which a rickety Popsicle-stick crane looked ready to come free of its tape at any second.

"Hi, Mr. Clement." Tony smiled down on Simeon's head.

Simeon giggled. "I'm not Mister, I'm Simeon!" This was a long-standing routine between them.

"Ah yes. You've grown so much that I mistook you for your father."

"He said we have the safest home around," Simeon announced.

Tony blinked. "Who?"

"Mr. Ranier. He said we have the safest house."

"Well then, he should have stayed here."

"He gave me this." Simeon lifted his foot above his waist so Tony could see the shiny cuff link attached to his shoe. The motion jostled the crane and it toppled off the truck.

"He did? It looks like it belongs to a pretty pricey set." Tony cast a questioning glance at Danielle. "If it were mine you would have had to pinch it from me."

"We shouldn't pinch people," Simeon scolded as he bent to pick up the sticks.

"That's exactly right, Mr. Clement. Nice truck there."

"I made it for you, but let me fix it first."

"I'd be honored," Tony said. Her son scooted back to his work zone.

"So the building is safe." Danielle turned her question into a statement for Simeon's sake but put a question mark in her expression for Tony.

"We'll know in the morning, won't we?"

A knock sounded on Danielle's front door. She leaned across her stool in order to see past Tony's broad shoulders and was surprised to find the door standing wide open. Vance Nolan waited there, holding a sheet of wood. He stood outside the boundaries of her space, waiting for her permission to come in. He was, today, the first man to ask her permission for anything.

"You have to push the door closed until it clicks," she said to Tony. "Maybe you could have someone fix that for me?"

"You know as well as I do who to ask."

As Danielle spun off the stool to greet Vance, she was finally able to name the emotion that comments like this repeatedly triggered in her, like knocking her ankle into the corner of the dishwasher every time it was open. It was shame, a constant reminder of how much he'd done for her and how little she had done to earn it. He didn't mean to, of course. Tony was never intentionally cruel. But for Danielle, who tried so hard to be in debt to no one, the suggestion that she might have asked for too much was hard to bear.

She collected herself quickly.

"Vance." She kept her voice low. "I was out of my mind earlier. I never even said thank you. I'm sorry."

"You're welcome," he said. There was kindness in his voice and nothing like offense or disappointment. "How's Simeon?"

Her son's voice belted out of the living

room: "I'm playing with nunchakus!"

Danielle caught herself smiling. "He's watching the crane drama."

"Entertainment at its best. I meant to come earlier," he said, pointing to the board. "I'll put this up over your slider for you."

She hesitated, because of the bookcase, and because she felt an irrational need to explain why Tony was there, eating in her kitchen out of a takeout box.

It seemed she should ask Vance to come in and take care of it for her, save Tony's valuable bookcase from the wind and rain, but she just couldn't.

"I know I'm covered in mud," he finally said. "I'll go clean up and come back."

"That's not —"

"Nolan!" Tony's greeting clapped right into Danielle's ear. "How did the contractor take the news?"

"Just like I hoped," Vance said.

"Good, good." Shoulder to shoulder, Danielle and Tony formed a solid barrier to the condo. If that was the message Tony wanted to communicate, Danielle found it hostile. She took a step backward, but not before she saw an understanding pass over Vance's face, a glance between Tony and Danielle that culminated in an uncomfortable pause.

He turned away from them to lean the plywood against the wall outside her door.

"I'm sorry you lost your ring in the fall," Vance said. He pulled a carpenter's pencil out of his tool belt.

"What ring?" Tony said. "Your wedding ring?"

"No," Danielle said. "It's safe. I don't — wasn't wearing it today." She hadn't worn it for a month. Not since she had moved in here. Which was the first day she'd taken it off since Danny's death.

Vance was writing something in the upper left corner of the wood. Numbers. The lead tip hovered for a moment. If Tony wasn't standing next to her with his arms smugly crossed, she might have said more. Vance completed what he was writing and pocketed the pencil.

"We've got quite a bit of the river coming over the isthmus. Now's the time to get ashore if you can."

Tony said, "I was just heading out."

"Do you have somewhere you can go, Danielle?"

She didn't think Vance had meant to include Tony at all.

"There's no need to send her and the boy out into this storm," Tony said.

Vance looked at him. "It'll only get worse

the longer they stay. I know you've been indoors. You might have missed that."

Danielle looked at her feet.

"I'm confident your work can stand up to it," Tony said.

"I don't know exactly how much damage this building has sustained, between the pump truck and whatever happened under number 11," Vance said, looking at Danielle. "We should take precautions."

The silence fell deeper and the rain smacking the front of the condos became louder in that moment. To stay was to thumb her nose at her hero; to go was to betray her provider. Her confidence in these buildings was nothing short of a public declaration on behalf of Tony's company. Still, she wondered why he didn't insist she move, no matter how small the potential danger.

She recalled that Tony once told her Vance was an alcoholic. Why that thought? Why now?

"I think we'll be fine here," she said to Vance.

"Please reconsider."

"We appreciate your concern," Tony said.

Vance continued to ignore him. "I wrote my number on the board. Call me if you need anything, Danielle, or if you change your mind."

She almost said she couldn't change her mind about needing to stay here, even if she wanted to, but then she realized he was talking about boarding up her exposed bedroom.

By the time she figured this out, he was walking away.

A burst of cool air rose up through the stairwell, followed by a shout from the second floor.

"Nolan!" The voice belonged to a man, breathless and running. Vance was already on the top stair. "Nolan!"

"What?" He started jogging downward.

"We've lost the trailer!"

Danielle raised her eyes to the east window, but she couldn't see what the man meant.

"Marcus and Andy" — Vance's feet pounded the stairs now as he took two at a time, plunging for the lower level, and Danielle's ears registered only the end of the explanation — "in it!"

Tony said, "A little rain on a river and everyone loses their minds," but there was nervousness behind his words.

Simeon tugged his mom's hand. She looked at him. He was holding up the paper-tube nunchakus, light brown on one side and a dark soggy brown on the other.

"These float in the bathtub. Can I use them in the cove?" he asked.

When had her son put water in the bathtub by himself, against every safety rule she had ever set for him? What was going on here?

The answer that popped into her mind was hardly the one she had been expecting. It was irrational. It was forceful. It was Ranier Smith looming over her, saying, *You don't have much time.*

It was Vance pleading with her to seek safety. Vance, always watching out for someone — right now, for two men she didn't even know.

It was every man for himself, wasn't it? Every woman, every mother. And she wasn't prepared to save her son's life, was she?

But she knew what she could do.

Danielle ran down the hall toward the stairs, shouting instructions to Tony and Simeon simultaneously: "Stay with him."

13

In the time it took Vance to carry the board up to Danielle's unit, the ties holding the world together began to snap. At the bottom of the stairs Ziggy barked at him once, and Zeke laid a hand on the dog's head. Enrique was already standing at the entrance, staring out at the destruction on the peninsula as if he were Lot's salty wife.

"Help us," Vance ordered as he hit the doors first. But he didn't wait for Enrique to follow, because he'd seen urgency: The footbridge, already elevated on the cove as the waters rose. River water, pouring in sheets down the bank. Enough water on the surface of the earth for Jesus and the devil to walk on. And the trailer lying on its side, doors down.

Once across the footbridge it took way too long to reach the trailer. It was Baxter who'd come in to get Vance, and he too was slogging through the uphill swamp, his bald white head spattered with brown splotches. The mud and racing water kept taking the ground out from under him. The dimness of dusk had overcome the sky even though it was still midafternoon.

Above them, Slogan Sam was already on the trailer's side, which had become its top when it flipped, pounding on one of the windows with his heavy boots. When the trailer shifted and knocked Sam off his feet, he turned onto his stomach and started hitting the glass with his bare hands. Vance reached for the hammer at his belt and managed to keep his footing.

The back of Sam's T-shirt accused Vance of lollygagging. *Pick up the pace!*

Baxter's 4×4, which had been parked right behind the trailer, was also relocated by the water. Its front fender had left a clear imprint in the thin wall of the trailer's backside. Baxter used the truck like a ladder and mounted the trailer in three bold leaps: bumper, hood, trailer. Vance followed him precisely but landed less successfully. The slick surface sloughed him off. He threw the hammer claw into the siding as if it were Mount Everest and he was sliding into a crevasse, and his fall stopped.

Baxter joined Sam in trying to break the glass, fists bouncing off. One of them might slice an artery if they actually went through it.

Now balanced on his knees, Vance pried his hammer out of the wall and glanced up, unprepared for the elevated view.

The isthmus no longer existed. The blacktop road, gone. The guardrails, gone. The cove, gone. The peaceful pool had become a roiling, angry current, a second river, a parallel twin to the Rondeau.

A vehicle bobbed in the violent waters, its four wheels pointing upward, pelted by stony raindrops that hit Vance's head too. It was impossible for him to tell who the car belonged to, or if anyone was inside.

"Back off!" Vance instructed as he crawled to the unyielding window.

Baxter and Sam saw the hammer and moved.

He'd removed the glove off his right hand to write on Danielle's plywood, and it was lost in the chaos now. In one bare-handed swing, Vance's blow shattered the glass and scattered it inside the trailer. The tool's slick shaft slipped out of Vance's grasp and followed the broken glass down. He quickly swept out the shards with his protected left hand and peered inside. The other men pressed close, blocking the precious little gray light.

"Marcus!" Vance shouted.

The trailer shifted under them all. Just an inch, not forward or backward or sideways, but up. Water was a weightlifter who tested the barbell and then dropped it to adjust his stance, his grip, before throwing all his effort into the challenge.

The trailer's tumble had knocked out the interior electricity, and though the sun had hours before setting, the grays were shades of charcoal within the trailer walls. The space still smelled of burnt plastic. Vance heard no evidence of shorted wires, no hissing or snapping or popping. He could see the general shapes of familiar things in unfamiliar locations: a swiveling desk chair's octopus legs, still spinning; a hulking metal desk thrown against the door, which was now the floor, which was taking on water; a pair of legs protruding from beneath it.

A groan caught Vance's ears. It came from somewhere other than the desk.

"Marcus!" he shouted. "Andy!"

Vance lifted himself off his belly and gripped the window frame. He pulled his feet up under him and then let them dangle into the cavern below as he prepared to swing down.

Baxter asked, "How're you gonna get back out?"

Sam said, "It's only ten feet."

The bigger question in Vance's mind was how he'd be able to get injured men out.

He lowered himself into the tipped room.

He hung by the window frame, sorting the relative darkness into meaning. There was nothing right about this place that he had stood in just a few minutes ago. A file cabinet that once stood by this window had shot straight to the other side of the trailer with nothing but a rack for coats and hats to block its way. It was upside down now, and one of the drawers had opened in that position. Papers that seemed overly white had made a heaping pyre too wet to be lit and too small to break his fall.

By swinging and extending his booted toe, Vance was able to transfer his body weight to the bottom side of the file cabinet.

The groan came a second time from the direction he faced, at the back of the trailer.

"Hold on," he said.

"Where?" The voice belonged to Andy.

The question didn't make sense, so Vance didn't answer. He was pretty sure he could get off the file cabinet and onto the wall that was now a floor. The trailer shifted.

The legs protruding from the desk next to the file cabinet didn't move. From this vantage Vance could see that enough water had seeped in to cover Marcus's head, pinned down by the desktop. Drowned, or killed instantly before the water arrived.

Vance hoped for the second scenario. He swallowed the pain of this sight and focused on Andy. "How bad are you hurt?"

"Not bad. Not bad." But his words sounded thick, like he was talking around cotton.

"Broken bones?"

"I don' thing."

"You don't think so?"

Andy didn't answer. The wall creaked under Vance's boots as he eased himself off the cabinet. He tossed a trash can out of his way. Aluminum cans and potato chip bags crinkled under his steps.

"Are you bleeding?"

"Is this river? Water."

"Did you hit your head?"

Vance's feet slipped into the joint where the wall and floor met. Now floor and wall.

"Where?"

The nonsensical words were troubling, but Vance was more concerned that Andy didn't seem to be making any effort to move. He couldn't help thinking about where this boy might be right now if he wasn't so fresh out of school, so new to independent adult life that he was still saving up to afford an inexpensive car and the very expensive insurance that all young men his age had to dish out.

But Vance knew it wouldn't have mattered if Andy had his own wheels, because he was the type of worker who made himself available until he wasn't needed anymore. This kind of crisis heaped on that kind of character was just plain unfair.

"I'm coming. I don't see you yet."

And in the next second he did see Andy's shadowy form, laid out on his side and still. His right arm was outstretched over his head, and his cheek rested on it. He had fallen onto the shelves where Vance kept that empty liquor bottle, onto a bracket ladder, where the height of each shelf could be adjusted. The narrow wood boards, which sat loose in their brackets, had flipped away. Vance leaned over the young man, wishing he had his flashlight.

"Hey, Andy."

"Glath," Andy whispered.

Vance put his left hand into the broken shards before he realized what Andy meant — *glass.* The heavy-duty glove stopped the chunky pieces from slicing him open. The shards were large and thick, the way a whiskey bottle broke when thrown down by a drunk.

"Let me have a look at you."

His eyes began to find sense in the din. All of Andy's limbs seemed straight, even relaxed. He didn't see any blood. But still, the kid didn't move.

"Did you hit your head?"

"Cloudy," Andy said, and Vance heard the wispy quality of his breath underneath the lisping, soft words. He feared a head injury.

"Is it hard for you to breathe?" he asked.

The kid grunted.

Andy's crucifix dangled sideways on its heavy chain, tugging at the neck of his T-shirt. The toes of Jesus pointed down, directing Vance's eyes toward the seriousness of Andy's situation. He was impaled on the bottommost bracket, freed of its shelf and converted into a knife that must have penetrated Andy's lung. Vance wondered if it had gone deep enough to hit the boy's heart.

Andy's bloody T-shirt bulged with the gathering water as Vance weighed the risks of pulling him off the bracket.

"Vance!" Sam shouted down from the window.

"With Andy," he called back.

"I'm coming down."

"No. I'll need your help from up there."

"Where's Marcus?"

Vance couldn't bring himself to shout the answer so close to the only survivor. "Just Andy," he said.

The drop in Sam's tone suggested that he understood. "Water's still rising, my friend."

Vance opened his mouth to call him down but was stopped by a worse revelation.

"Stay there," he said again. It wasn't the bracket in Andy's lungs that was going to kill him. It was the one above it, concealed by the pillowy position of Andy's right arm. Pointing upward at an angle torqued by Andy's body weight, the bracket sword had thrust itself through his cheek. Vance had seen the lengths of those brackets. He was the one who once arbitrarily set them at their various positions. The whole thing was inside Andy's head, and there would be no separating the two.

Andy seemed to focus on Vance. The lighting might not have been completely honest, but Vance thought Andy was trying to tell him he knew.

Andy took a short breath. "Scared," he said. Water that didn't belong to the river rimmed his eyes.

The unspeakable chaos outside the trailer seemed unimportant now. It was nothing more than a reminder of Vance's own mortality. He pushed the glass away, shifted from his unstable crouch, and settled onto his knees. They pressed into the leanness of Andy's young belly. So young. Vance lifted Andy's left hand and moved it to Andy's throat. Gently, he pressed the crucifix into the kid's palm, wrapping his own fingers around it all to hold hope together.

"You believe in Jesus, Andy?"

The kid couldn't move his head. His throat was nearly too swollen with blood to speak. But he managed, "Yes," clearer than any other word he'd spoken so far.

"Then you don't have to be afraid of anything. There is nothing for you to fear."

Andy closed his eyes.

"He's coming for you."

"Don' leave," Andy said.

"I won't. I won't."

Baxter called down from above. Vance's name came out of his mouth like a swooping roller coaster, going from low to high, shooting upward in warning: "Vaa-ance!"

A wave hit the side of the trailer before he had time to reply. It punched the wall, and Andy's body absorbed the jolt. His eyes opened and rolled, then fluttered closed again.

Vance began to recite a passage from Psalm 119. He had picked up the habit during his recovery from alcoholism. When the brain wanted a drink, it was useful to have scriptures at the ready. The time required to go to the Bible and open it and search for the right words often took longer than his will could endure.

As if to atone for all the verses he'd refused to memorize as a child, he'd started with the longest chapter of the Bible.

"Remember the word to Your servant, upon which You have caused me to hope," Vance whispered over Andy's head. He made the words a prayer. "This is my comfort in my affliction, for Your word has given me life."

Outside, Baxter was shouting for Vance to get out. The trailer began a slow, smooth spin.

Vance continued speaking the words he knew by heart and kept his promise to Andy as the trailer's steady rotation didn't stop. It seemed there was no barrier to catch them now, wherever it was they had been pushed — no man, no vehicle, no safety net, no isthmus. Nothing but a water slide into turbulent waters. Sam's and Baxter's boots thundered over Vance's voice as they ran to the back of the trailer and then leaped away.

"Forever, O Lord, Your word is settled in heaven." Even if Andy was no longer conscious, who knew what the spirit could hear? And Vance wondered if the verses might hold some comfort for him. "Your faithfulness endures to all generations; You established the earth, and it abides."

There were no insincere platitudes in Vance's words. There were no pat answers that could help a person feel better while he traveled to the next life. Vance *did* believe that there was nothing to fear, and much to hope for, in death.

But the fear of *dying* was a powerful force, and even strong men had to fight to hold on to belief.

As he knelt next to Andy in the dark, blind to the threats outside, fear crouched at Vance's spine and licked the hairs on the back of his neck. He spoke louder now, over the roar of the waters battering the rotating trailer.

"Unless Your law had been my delight, I would then have perished in my affliction," he said. "I will never forget Your precepts, for by them You have given me life. I am yours; save me; for I have sought Your precepts."

Save me.

Andy's life left him then, the one that would outlive this broken body. The real Andy, the eternal Andy, drifted through Vance. That was the only way Vance could think to describe it. An embrace that went right through him.

The trailer flipped over then like a rolling rock tumbler, tossing all of its contents until their rough essence was transformed into something shiny.

14

Danielle had seen Vance bolt out the front door of building 12 when she arrived at the bottom of the staircase, but she didn't plan to follow him. The common room held a few muddy people whose eyes were glued to Vance's back and whatever had demanded his presence on land. She doubted anyone noticed her as she passed through the doors on the opposite side of the building and stepped out onto the narrow patio.

Water sliced through her clothing for the second time that day. She was expecting the deluge, but the physical sensation of it was startling, as if she'd taken another harrowing plunge. Concrete-encased foam lay under the slender wood slats at her feet, but it didn't mask the sloshing strength of the rising water.

With her eyes downcast to avoid the poking raindrops, she took quick steps to the place where the wraparound patio met the dock that jutted out into the cove. Storage compartments that resembled a row of lockers stood here. There were eight, one for each unit in the building. Danielle's was stocked for show, though neither she nor Tony owned a boat. He liked his property fully furnished; practical usefulness was irrelevant. And so her locker contained docking ropes, a wet broom and squeegees, a first-aid kit, some fishing rods, deflated inner tubes, boat shoes, hats, and the objects of her desire: life vests.

She punched her key code into the numerical panel and opened the door. There were two vests, one for her and one for Simeon, tossed atop the piles of ropes and the boat shoes she would probably never wear. She took the stiff vests quickly and paused just long enough to consider whether anything else might be immediately useful. No. She pulled out, slammed the door shut. She would suggest Ferti, Mirah, and Jonesy do the same while they could.

The storage shed was a shield between her and the sideways rain. In the relative shelter she lifted her eyes and saw water gushing over the top of the isthmus. She felt just then the way she did upon waking after a deep sleep, when it took several seconds to recognize a familiar scene. *You are home.*

This is your bed. That is your door.

The isthmus had become a waterfall. At its base she saw what she thought was the tailgate of someone's pickup truck sticking up out of the cove. The water struck it and sprayed off.

You are home. This was your cove. That road was your only way out. That trailer no longer has a door.

She could see the trailer from where she stood, just above building 12 at the mouth of the road that had been washed away. Three men were beating on it with their fists and feet. One of them had a hammer. She thought it was Vance, but the light was unnaturally dim. Danielle squinted.

The rain shifted direction and came down into her eyes once more. She hurried back inside and crossed the common room toward the main entrance, which Vance had passed through minutes earlier. She clutched the life vests to her stomach and hurried to the adjacent windows.

She arrived in time to watch Vance — it *was* him — lower himself into the portable trailer. As the vehicle swallowed him, she startled when a man she had never seen before breezed right by her and hit the door running, bursting into the rain. He was about her age, a little on the chubby side,

159

the tails of his open cotton shirt sagging like wet moth wings.

"Enrique?" someone called out. But if that was the man's name, he didn't answer.

A dog appeared at her side. A service dog wearing a harness, and a blind man holding it. The animal's lovely brindle coat seemed out of sorts with its not-very-lovely pit bull face. She hadn't known pit bulls could be service dogs.

"This appears to be much worse than we originally thought," the man said. He had a head of thick sooty curls, gray at the temples, and a wide chin that he carried high, as if real sight could be found in courage rather than ability. His clothes sagged with the weight of water.

Danielle nodded.

The man said, "Tell me what you see."

"The road is gone. Just washed away. I can't believe it. And there's a trailer. On its side. It's got a huge dent."

"Vance went in," the man said.

She wondered how he knew. "Yes. There are two men on top, helping. A bald man and someone in a bright red T-shirt. And the man who just ran out. You called him Enrique?"

"I wish he had stayed in."

"He looks like he's not sure what to do. I

think there's a truck in the river. I mean the cove. But it's a river of its own now."

"They're gone now."

"Who?"

"The truck driver. And his passenger." He sighed and closed his eyes as though it was all plain as day right in front of him and he couldn't bear to look.

"How do you — ?"

"What else?" he asked at the same time the trailer shifted.

Danielle took a step forward and placed her fingertips on the glass. "It's moving. The trailer is sliding."

"I meant people, sweetheart. Who else is there?"

"No one — wait. Someone just came out of the crane, the one that got stuck. But he's on the far side. I can't see what — Oh!"

The sliding trailer began to spin in a slow turn toward the heavy crane. In her mind she urged the men on top of the flimsy box to jump off to safety, and then hated them for abandoning Vance when they did. There was no hope of them finding their feet when they landed. Enrique, who had rushed toward them to help, stopped abruptly at the sight of the traveling trailer. The crane driver, dodging the death trap, ran toward Vance's helpers. He collided with the bald guy and both slipped around on the glossy earth. They grabbed at each other's shirts to stay upright, but soon the pair glided like air-hockey pucks over the opposite bank. The man left behind lay still, his red shirt a splash of bloody color in the mud.

Enrique was backtracking, looking for a surefooted way back to 12's footbridge, when Danielle saw a swell of water rising behind the peninsula. She could see the crane man bobbing on the crest, clinging to the bald one as they both glided back onto the peninsula and then were carried south.

The swell caught the trailer like a feather on a puff of wind. As it traveled, it smacked the parked crane with such force that it bounced off, a resonating hollow gong, and made a nearly complete rotation in the reverse direction. It was dragging something on its belly, and it took Danielle several blinks to realize she was looking at the metal steps that once rose into the mobile office, now flattened like an aluminum can.

As the trailer came around, Enrique finally found the footbridge and lumbered back toward the entrance.

She described all this to the blind man.

Enrique returned only to make a quick departure to the public restroom. He barely looked at Danielle.

"Who else is there?" the man insisted. "Who else?"

"No one," she whispered.

"There *is*," he said. "You've seen him."

Danielle could see nothing but the solitary man in the red T-shirt who remained face-down in the mud, and the trailing mass of mangled steps catching his pant leg when it swooped by. It dragged him away.

The trailer completed its rotation as it hit the steep drop-off, the last bit of land between the development and the flooding cove that hadn't been overtaken by the Rondeau. The trailer went over it. The metal snag swung the man in its grip up over the top, a catapult arcing through the air that would not release its ammunition before it hit down. She heard his scream.

Danielle was out the door before he hit the water. The sound of the impact stole her breath, though she couldn't see it. A mortal smack, as if the water had been a pavement. He might be floating on white water, every bone in his body crushed, or trapped under the surface by the staircase that would not release him.

And the men inside the trailer — Vance, others — might have fared worse.

She ran along the front of building 12, needing only a burst of short strides to reach the rushing waters. Here, the floating condo seemed more like a clunky houseboat. She could feel the foundation rising and falling beneath her, rollicking inches of movement.

The river seemed angrier. The current swifter, the noise louder. The guardrails that had once prevented cars from slipping off the isthmus road had been peeled away. One section had popped off and lodged itself like a giant's javelin in the exterior wall just over Danielle's head. Metal piercing metal. The driving rain caused its long shaft to quiver. She tried to comprehend the force required to strip the metal ribbon off its posts and turn it into shrapnel. She considered the gap between the roof and the top of the broken road, where one end of guardrail sagged like a silver flag over the water.

There, at the top of the disintegrating land, right in the center of the waterfall's ledge, Ranier Smith was looking down on her. Feet planted slightly apart. Standing.

On what? Liquid foam lapped his legs and swirled around his knees, stuff that could flip a multiton trailer as easily as a toy boat. The trailer bobbed. A current steadied it.

Danielle held a life jacket in each fist, one for an adult, one for a child. She searched the water for the stranger who had been catapulted into it. Who was she to think she could help this man who might not even be conscious? She was nothing but a woman who needed frequent help saving herself. She needed help with everything, it seemed, from saving her son to saving her pride to saving her exotic cork floors. She resented her weakness right now. It might be the deciding factor in whether that poor man lived or died.

You say you are strong, but . . .

His body popped up to the surface of the water, his head thrown back and his arms spread wide to accept whatever fate was his. She shouted at him.

"Hey! Hey!"

He didn't answer.

"Swim this way!" she yelled. "Can you hear me?"

On his back, he had a chance. But he was much too far away for her to reach without jumping into the river. She thought of Simeon and didn't even waver in her decision to stay put.

A clang of metal on metal vibrated at her feet. She looked down and saw the trailer's flattened staircase ricochet off one of number 12's support poles.

She leaned over the catwalk rail as far as she dared and dangled her life jacket out over the water. Not even close. Already the man was gliding along the surface like a leaf in snowmelt, away from her.

"Grab it!" she ordered, and then she hurled the piece out over the scene, not even sure if the man was alive, or if she would come close to her target.

It hit him in the chest. She threw her head back, relieved. Then she refocused.

"Grab it!" she screamed again.

His left hand came up out of the water so slowly Danielle feared he'd lose his moment of opportunity. But then he placed it atop the float and held on.

"Now swim! Swim! Kick out of the current!" She grew angry at his inertia, which was, really, just an annoying reminder of her own powerlessness. Why couldn't she force a man to save his own life? "Fight it!"

He wouldn't. Couldn't. Did the reason matter? He spun away in a lazy dance that was going to kill him. Still holding on to the jacket, he slipped into the gray stew of water, clouds, and rain.

Danielle's throat felt hard and swollen. She paced on the narrow walkway, trapped by the frustration of having no means to help him, or Vance within that trailer.

Water poured into her eyes as if she stood under a shower, and Ranier appeared on the top of the trailer. Not there, then there. Fast as a blink. It was so hard to be certain of what she was seeing. But this was Ranier, she knew it, with a missing cuff link and a crisp suit that would not wilt in the downpour.

How'd you get dry so fast?

He bent over a narrow square opening, some kind of fan cover or vent, and dug his fingertips under the rim. With an effortless yank he pulled it off and cast it into the water.

Two hands appeared from inside, extended and grasping for the air. Danielle held her breath. Then a head appeared, and Ranier bent once more. She waited for him to grab the man's wrist and heave him to safety. Instead, Ranier touched the top of his head, placed his palm flat on the crown. Was he going to hold him down? But no, he stepped back and gave him room.

With just one jump Vance emerged from the guts of his battered office, lifting his own body through the space barely wide enough for his broad shoulders. But there was room between his elbows, and blood dripping down one arm into a glove that covered his left hand. He got his hips out onto the trailer roof and then pulled the rest of himself out.

Ranier stood behind him, watching.

"Help him!" Danielle ordered.

Vance lifted his head in her direction and squinted. Ranier pushed him off the roof.

Danielle gasped.

Vance went under a swell as the trailer picked up speed and rolled once more, taking Ranier down with it.

A terrible metallic groan came from over Danielle's head.

She ducked. Leaped aside. Felt the burst of displaced air huff into her ear as the weight of the guardrail javelin embedded in the side of number 12 finally dropped toward the water.

Vance surfaced. The rail plunged. And the two events happened less than a second and a foot apart. The water carried him straight into the barrier. She heard his breath leave him when he hit. But he clung to it by the armpits.

The rail at Danielle's end was only three or four feet over her head. She thought Vance might be able to come along it far enough to reach calm waters, where he could swim to safety.

He must have thought the same thing. She watched him lower himself back into the water and come up underneath the rail. He gripped it on each side and made efforts to swing his way along, a few inches at a time, the muscles in his arms sustaining both his body weight and the tug of the river. But his bare right hand kept losing hold of the slippery surface, and a cut in his left elbow looked deep.

"Use your shirt!" she yelled.

He paused. He nodded. He returned to where the current would hold his body against the fallen rail and peeled off his T-shirt. He threw the shirt over the top of the rail, wrapped the ends around his palms, and resumed. This time, the friction of the cloth kept him on track.

As Vance came toward her, she could see the undeniable proof that it was *his* strength, and not her own, that must be given the credit for saving Simeon just hours earlier. The physical perfection of his body filled her with a strange combination of yearning and inadequacy.

Her mother's voice accused her heart. *A good woman has all the resources her own family needs.* This was the mantra of Danielle's mother. *Don't ever put yourself in the position of having to rely on someone else.* Which was exactly what she had done in marrying Danny, which her mother had never forgiven. *Now look where you are,* she scolded Danielle when Danny passed and

Danielle didn't have her own source of income. *You should have listened to me.*

Danielle had responded by severing her relationship with her mother entirely. It was one way to heed the advice.

Vance came much farther up the tilting guardrail than Danielle had expected him to. He was fully out of the water now, his six-foot frame moving like a tight pendulum in short arcs as he progressed. She thought he might be reaching his limit. His face was a portrait of concentration and fatigue. His arms and chest were slick with water, and he spit raindrops from his lips with each effort-filled breath.

He stopped where he was and stretched his legs to their limit, trying to reach the coated railing at the walkway where she stood.

"If you let go, we can get you out of the water here," she told him.

He didn't let go. She felt mildly irritated.

"Drop," she said.

"Can't."

"Why not?"

He put his remaining energy into one last swing rather than into an answer. He lifted his heels and pulled up on the guardrail, then dropped his momentum toward her. A mighty swing. He let go. The shirt flipped straight down into the river, and in a blink Danielle saw the mangled scraps of metal — more guardrail? the trailer steps? a piece of construction equipment? — that had tangled in building 12's underwater structures. Anyone who fell on these wouldn't come out in one piece.

It looked like he might clear the barrier and land right next to her. Instead, the heels of his boots caught the rail hard, a jarring strike that could realign a man's bones. The impact sent a low and unsettling hum along the rail.

He might come forward, he might shoot backward. For a frozen moment, either outcome was equally likely. And then his hands moved an inch, and she knew he was going to fall away.

She reached up for him with both arms.

He grabbed her, wrists on wrists.

His weight was irresistible. He would pull her over with him.

Her ribs collided with the toes of his boots. Her hips crashed into the bar.

The snag was all he needed to correct his balance, and he was tipping forward again, over her head and into the wall behind her.

15

These were the sounds surrounding Zeke, who sat in the common room of building 12 on a deep sofa that might give him some trouble if he needed to rise from it quickly:

There were footsteps in a nearby stairwell, a rumbling descent, a rush of kids who hadn't spent their daily allotment of energy before being imprisoned by rain. The shouts were boisterous and boyish. Two unique voices, by Zeke's estimation. Neither one of them had reached adolescence.

There were footsteps in a farther stairwell, going up, light and soft, belonging to men who placed a high value on the quality of their imported shoes. These were Tony Dean's and Carver Lewis's shoes. Zeke was sure of it because Carver had introduced himself while waiting for Tony to join him. Carver's bright voice reminded Zeke of the sun, whose brilliance never changed even when foul weather covered it. They spoke of the rain, and then of singing in it, and then of Gene Kelly and Danny Kaye and Bing Crosby, and then of a beautiful woman named Ferti who lived upstairs, who had designed the wedding dress for one of Crosby's distant relatives, and who would one day design her own wedding dress when she was good and ready for sunshine. She was the kind of woman a man would gladly wait for his whole life, Carver said.

Zeke had asked Carver what he was doing down here when the woman he adored was right upstairs.

"She'll kick me right back down here to this sofa 'f I show my face uninvited." Carver chortled. "Sometimes a man's gotta wait. Keep doing the wooing, but wait."

And then he broke into a stage-worthy rendition of "Singin' in the Rain."

Tony Dean had interrupted Carver's theatrical declaration that he was "ready for love" and steered the man upstairs to the home of a fellow named Jonesy. "He's got enough food to feed all of Port Rondeau, and as much to drink. Are you thirsty? I'm thirsty."

Tony didn't acknowledge Zeke, even when Carver bowed out of their interlude more tactfully.

An alcove muffled the voices of the boys,

who were rifling for something in the closet that held cue sticks and Ping-Pong paddles and board games. Zeke had been on this floor several times while Vance was constructing it. It was a public room for the residents, a place to gather for social events, friendly competitions, billiards, movies, reflection, or food. The catering kitchen could be reserved for parties. Enrique had found a stack of bar towels there earlier, which Zeke had used for blotting Ziggy's sopping fur. Now they lay in a stinking heap on the floor.

"Found it!" one of the children shouted. "Race you!"

"Not yet," the other one said.

"Last one there's a rotten egg!"

"Wait."

And then the pounding of feet up the stairs again. Just one pair of feet this time.

There was the dripping of Enrique's wet clothes onto the saturated carpet under his chair. A soggy *plunk . . . plunk* that had cast a trance over Zeke's friend. In time, Enrique might have more to say about being the only able-bodied man who wasn't outside doing something useful.

There was the zippy click of Enrique fiddling with his cigarette lighter — flame up, flame down, flame up — but the absence of smoke told Zeke that the cigarettes had been left at home or drowned.

"I'm sure Vance will be okay," Zeke said to him.

"Do you think they're related?" Enrique asked. "Whatever happened under the water today, and this flood?" The question should have been brimming with his usual doomsday enthusiasm. Instead, he sounded hollowed out and worried.

"I can't see how," Zeke answered. "What makes you wonder?"

No answer but *zip click, zip click.*

Ziggy yawned and whined simultaneously.

There was the electric bounce of a television zapped into wakefulness by a remote control, then the clipped noise of channels changing and scripts being interrupted, one after the other. Someone might be searching for a weather report, someone Zeke had yet to meet. A woman maybe, reluctant to introduce herself to an old man and his dog and their morose companion.

The television offered up the falsetto happiness of a kids' program and hovered there. Zeke tuned it out and sank farther into the plushness of the sofa. He could feel Ziggy's chest rising and falling atop his shoes.

The wooden clack of balls knocking into each other on the pool table answered his question about the boy who had remained behind. Zeke's insight built a scene out of sounds: nine balls being dropped into a triangular rack, little hands pushing the rack around the green felt while the stripes and colors spun, slim fingers picking balls out and dropping them into the soft leather pockets, as many as would fit in each one. It must have been a very young boy at the pool table, perhaps the child of the invisible woman looking for a televised distraction.

After seven balls had been pocketed, the table fell silent. The TV sang on.

Zeke's thoughts turned to the meaning of this sudden storm, his disturbing vision of the gold snake, and the pump-truck accident that must have occurred around the same time that afternoon. Zeke ran the three events through his mental filters but didn't sift any new meaning from them. He added to this information the unidentified presence that had helped him up the slope, and a spiritual confidence that whoever — or whatever — had helped him remained outside to aid Vance and the others. He waited for sounds of their return.

A draft carrying the scent of wet earth crossed Zeke's nose, as from an open window or door.

Zip click, zip click.

Ziggy lifted his head from his paws and flicked an ear against Zeke's damp pants. The scent faded.

In the Bible, rain could bring a destructive flood or a fall-on-your-knees relief after seven years of drought. Water could drown an enemy horde or heal a man's leprosy. It could be turned to blood; it could be turned to wine. It harbored death and it delivered life.

Zeke wondered which category this present rain belonged to.

Ziggy stood and whined.

"What is it, boy?"

His pit bull nuzzled his arm, then waited for Zeke to extricate himself from the low sofa cushion. The dog led him to the wide door that opened onto the patio and dock at the back of the floating building.

"Let's go out the other side," Zeke said, giving the harness a directive tug. "That's not a poop deck, and you'd freeze up that close to the cove anyway."

Ziggy barked once and strained against his collar, a rebellious action that didn't feel at all like rebellion to Zeke.

"What?"

His mild-mannered dog jumped up on the door. His toenails clicked on the glass. He barked again and started to claw.

" 'Rique," Zeke called.

His friend made a slow return to the moment. "Yeah."

"Help me a sec?"

In the time it took Enrique to get up and cross the large room, Ziggy's whining reached a grating pitch.

"Yeah?"

"What's Ziggy fussing over?"

"Nothing. Rain's coming down harder than when we came in."

"You so eager to get wet again?" Zeke asked the dog.

Zeke pulled the door open and rain tapped on his shoes. Ziggy shot out.

"Tell me what he does." He expected nothing more than for Ziggy to hug the building and find a planter or deck chair to mark.

"He's running down the dock."

"Running? I have to drag him down docks."

"He's sniffing at the end. Circling." Enrique took it in, and Zeke pulled an explanation together at the same moment that he heard a splash.

"He jumped!" Enrique's exclamation was disbelief. "Ziggy just jumped in."

Zeke went after him, shuffling and spreading his hands, hating his blindness. These murderous waters were not the place for an animal to cure itself of fear. This rain was a Noah rain, Zeke thought as it cut right through his shirt. It was a death rain. Yes. Now that his dog had thrown himself in, he was sure of it.

Enrique grabbed him by the elbow and pulled him along the dock. Zeke's body took a reluctant, weighted posture. He didn't trust the human as easily as he trusted his animal.

Zeke could hear a thrashing. "Can you see him?"

"Yeah."

But Enrique didn't say more. He dropped to his knees and tugged Zeke down to his side. The thrashing sound had stilled. The raindrops smacked everything.

"Well?" Zeke snapped.

"He's down there." Down there, where concrete-pump trucks and serpentine devils sucked up the earth.

"Bring him up!"

"Should I go in?"

Zeke couldn't answer. Of course Enrique should go in and save the dog. Of course he should stay up here, where it was safe. Going into *this* water at *this* time was suicide for man and beast alike. Enrique remained on the dock next to him, both kneeling, waiting for the dog's irrational fear of water to be proven logical after all.

"Can you see Ziggy?"

"No."

Something thumped the bottom of the dock directly beneath where they were sitting.

Zeke sensed Enrique flatten onto his belly and reach into the space. The underwater slap struck again.

"There he is," Enrique muttered.

"Is he caught on something?"

"Dunno. He's gone again."

"He's still under the dock?"

It was an unanswerable question.

Enrique yelped, snatching his hand out of the water and jabbing Zeke with his elbow. He recovered from his shock fast enough, though, and scooted his waist to the lip of the wood planks.

"Hold my legs," he ordered. "There a kid down there."

Ziggy had gone in after someone?

The child formed in Zeke's mind. A little boy, holding a small wooden pool ball in each hand. "Is it a boy?" Zeke groped about and found Enrique's ankles. Lay down on them.

Enrique took a long draw of air and then plunged his head into the water. Zeke held

Enrique in place with the disturbing sensation that he was drowning his friend.

The ticking seconds raised his blood pressure until Enrique's body straightened like a board. "He's out of my reach. I'll go in. Get off." Zeke scrambled to help, no doubt giving Enrique a few bruises with his elbows. Where was Ziggy?

"Didn't you see the kid come out here?" Zeke couldn't hide his accusation.

"Am I his mom? I wasn't paying attention!"

"Where is his mother? She turned on the TV."

"The kid turned it on! It was just us in there, Zeke. It was just an accident!"

The water exploded and Zeke's ears picked out the familiar sound of Ziggy's panting.

"Oh no," Enrique said, and in Zeke's mind, the smiling kid holding the pool balls dropped them and fell into an unconscious heap.

"Keep holdin' that harness," he heard Enrique say.

Enrique grunted as he lifted the breathless kid out of the water and pressed him, dripping, into Zeke's chest. The boy didn't seem to be breathing, though his heartbeat knocked at the ear Zeke pressed into his narrow chest. Zeke knew CPR from his search-and-rescue days, and it came back to him like the memory of a childhood song. He didn't need sight for this.

As Zeke worked, Ziggy offered up a distraught *woof,* just now seeming to realize he was in a position he had been trying to avoid all his life, with no clue how to escape it. This was followed by a small amount of cursing from Enrique, who had trouble getting the frightened eighty-pound dog out of the water.

But soon everyone was out. Zeke had rolled the boy onto his side. Trembling, Ziggy belly-crawled closer, forcing himself between the man and the child. In this narrow space, the dog found his feet again. Zeke tried to push him out of the way, but the dog stubbornly stayed put.

He barked once, a sharp and forceful sound.

Zeke heard the boy heaving buckets of water onto the dock.

Ziggy's tail whapped Zeke's face while the kid coughed everything up and then finally found his breath again.

"Good boy," Zeke murmured. "Good boy." Zeke pulled the animal to his side, amazed to discover this unknown side of him.

Zeke put his hand on the boy's chest. The heart was strong. The lungs didn't rattle.

"Young man, what are you doing out here?"

"I wanted to see them again," he said. He coughed again.

"See who?"

"The workers."

"Everyone's gone home."

"They're still there," the boy said. "I want Mom to see."

"Where is she?"

"I dunno."

"Let's go find your parents," Enrique said.

"That was *neat,*" the boy said.

Zeke wasn't sure which part qualified. "I doubt they'll think so."

16

As the seriousness of their situation became clear, everyone who escaped the flood gathered on the public level of building 12. This wasn't an organized effort, but a simple human need that Vance understood. What they all sought right now was exactly what he had wished for the day his father died: hope. And the company of other survivors. Tucked in here, the tumultuous rain sounded more like a seashell's ocean call. The group's collective murmuring almost seemed louder than the unthinkable volume of rain.

Vance's own thoughts were loud enough to drown out the local TV anchorman, who was delivering breaking news to them from the wall above the bar in one corner of the room. The man's limited knowledge had become repetitive. The rain was heavy. The rain was unexpected. A shocking number of inches per hour. One source said six. Another eight. The disastrous effects were only now becoming known. There was only one cut from a weather camera that had been mounted on one of the wharf houses in Port Rondeau, in which the storm looked like an ocean-borne hurricane. This same piece looped again and again, because the camera had evidently been ripped off the side of the building and the broadcast crews were having trouble reaching their destinations. Viewers were urged to upload their own digital videos to the news channel's website, but obstacles hampered this effort too. Satellite interruptions. Connection failures.

Overflowing his barstool, the retired policeman Jonesy toggled to the national news whenever his thumb twitched. The larger world seemed unaware of their plight. Their anchors were covering a political sex scandal, casualties of the earthquake in Yellowstone, and the results of a study linking broccoli consumption to brain tumors.

"Give it up," Carver Lewis told Jonesy. He set his ivy cap on the bar and took control of the remote, returning their attention to the choppy local news.

Unbelievable, the anchorman kept repeating between temporary blue screens and flickering colored pixels. Their own satellite dish was taking a beating. *Unprecedented.*

Vance tuned him out.

Sitting in front of the fireplace hearth, which contained no fire tonight, he sat sideways in front of Danielle. She sat on a white leather ottoman and cupped his wounded elbow in her hand.

Danielle had ordered Simeon to stay within the confined space of the fireplace, sofas, and facing chairs. He and Mirah's son Laith, who looked to be about eight, played with Ziggy, tying bits of red yarn into the dog's harness. A quiet fury rippled over her eyebrows and made itself known in ferocious jabbing and wriggling of her tweezers under his skin.

"Twice in one day," she muttered under her breath. The peroxide she poured over the cut turned into a frothing mess that mirrored her own seething. Simeon's interest in the foam cast a shadow over the bowl that caught the bubbly pink drips. Vance had escaped the whiskey bottle shards at first, but when the trailer tumbled he landed right on top of the glass, and a piece like an arrowhead had buried itself deep in his arm.

"It's not your fault," Vance said.

"Not this time." Her eyes went to Tony, who was sitting at the bar with Carver and Jonesy, fiddling with a red bar towel and watching the news. "But that doesn't really

186

matter, does it?"

Danielle seemed to blame Tony for this accident, but it was Mirah who kept apologizing to Danielle for losing track of the boys. The pretty olive-skinned woman stroked the head of a sleeping infant snugged against her body by a colorful wrap. Mirah was a beauty, with hair that seemed too thick to gather up in one hand and wide brown eyes that needed no makeup to improve them. They were frightened eyes, though, darting about for the next problem that would be her responsibility to avert. She fluttered over the boys and repeated all of Danielle's remarks to them.

But Danielle accepted Mirah's apologies and continued to shoot scowls at Tony, who avoided her eyes.

Simeon set his yarn aside and concentrated on forcing the shank of a sparkling cuff link through an O-ring in Ziggy's harness. The piece of silver looked as if it had been lifted directly out of the earth. Fine strands like wires fashioned themselves in free-form knots and rippled with watery blue hues. He wondered if it had belonged to the boy's father.

Vance's bare shoulders were draped in a blanket that Danielle's neighbor Ferti had provided. It was an eye-assaulting yellow, like the head scarf that covered the woman's close-cropped hair. She reminded Vance of the feminine version of a sculpture his father kept in his den at home during Vance's childhood: a lean African warrior with a spear as long as he was tall, head thrown back in a cry — of victory or mourning, Vance never had decided. Ferti had that duality too, stern and soft at the same time when she looked a person in the eye. Maybe a tad more stern, especially when she set that steady gaze on Carver.

"Plenty of blankets to go around," Ferti said, dropping a stack of them onto the floor next to the hearth. "I knew I'd be cold in my old age and started collecting 'em forty years ago."

"Cold by choice," Carver said from the bar for all to hear. He didn't take his eyes off the TV.

"I find blankets more comforting than people," Ferti shot back.

Carver laughed heartily at this, and the faces in the room all relaxed by degrees into something just a little less tense than they had been.

Ferti lowered herself onto a chair opposite the sofa that Zeke and Enrique shared. "It's a wonder you're the only one who really needs a doctor," she said to Vance. Ziggy sat obediently at Zeke's feet and didn't object to any of Simeon's attention, but the dog's posture was erect and alert. "This all could have been much, much worse."

How much worse does it get than death? Vance thought, but he acknowledged her with a nod. She couldn't have known — he didn't even know — how many people the rain had killed already.

Before Vance and Danielle had come in from the weather, he lay stretched out on the narrow walkway, his head throbbing, without any real sense of what he ought to do next. River water sloshed into his ears. His mind was still back in the trailer with Marcus and Andy while Danielle had wordlessly untangled herself from the heap formed by their bodies. He looked up at her rain-lashed face and felt no urgency to get off the ground. He felt like he'd split open his head, smacking into that aluminum wall while trying to avoid crushing her, but she was looking at his left arm, which he suddenly realized was flaming with hurt.

"Did you see the others?" he asked through gritted teeth.

"The man in the red shirt caught a life jacket," she said.

"Sam."

Her eyes lifted from Vance's injury and

glanced downstream. "Sam. He was pretty bad off. I don't know where he is."

"And Baxter?"

"Was he the crane driver?"

"No, the bald one."

"There was a wave. He and the man with the crane — it took both of them down the peninsula. I just don't know. A pickup truck flipped over . . ."

Vance closed his eyes. Strong Marcus. Young Andy. Slogan Sam. Baxter. And he didn't even know the crane operator's name. His thoughts were so tied up by disbelief that they might all be dead that he couldn't remember, now sitting with Danielle in front of the fireplace, exactly how he'd come to be here, unharmed except for this brown blade of glass.

"I don't think Ranier made it," Danielle said softly. Vance looked down on the top of her head. Her usually smooth honey-blond strands were clumped and tangled across her uneven part. He didn't know who Ranier was. At that moment, he didn't want to.

"I'm sorry," Vance said.

Of everyone here, only the retired policeman Jonesy had actually seen the isthmus disintegrate, but he had little to say about how many were on the road when it washed out. He was a bold and boisterous man, a lover of food and finery, but this catastrophe had diminished his spirit. He sat heavily at the bar apart from Tony and Carver, his ample body overflowing the slender barstool, staring at a glass of red wine.

Danielle's tweezers hit a nerve, and his entire body jerked away from her.

"Hold still."

He tried, by mentally reviewing what the group had been able to piece together so far:

Sometime after the trailer went over the isthmus waterfall, the small rowboat that had brought Enrique and Zeke to Eagle's Talon was carried by a monster wave up and over the peninsula. The little craft was hurtled like a rocket into Mirah's living room window. Mirah had been in her kitchen, hands covered in a marinade for lamb shanks, when the boat shattered the picture window and came to rest in the center of her expensive Arabian carpet. Her son Laith and Simeon were (Mirah thought) in the bathroom assembling a floating Bionicle empire, and baby Haji was in a swing on the other side of the kitchen bar, or they might have been showered with the glass.

She didn't learn until afterward that the

boys had sneaked out to raid the common room's game cabinet, and only one had returned.

Ferti had been at the sewing machine in her second bedroom, which was her workshop, fashioning a bridal veil for her granddaughter. The impact of the flying boat through her neighbor's window startled her into making a bad cut in the filmy tulle.

Tony and the investor Carver were breaking out beer in Jonesy's unit while they waited out the storm. Apparently Simeon had been with Tony for only a minute before being deposited at Mirah's. This revelation had brought the first angry flush to Danielle's face.

It was easier to chat about a surge that could put a boat through a window than the same surge that could kill men and children. But Vance watched the blood seeping up from his arm like a hot spring and couldn't get the image of Andy, dying, out of his head.

Scared.

Don' leave.

I am yours. Save me.

The voice of Vance's father mingled in his memory. *Save me.* Years ago, Vance had not been able to hear his father's cry at the critical hour. Now it haunted him daily.

He sighed.

"That hurts?" Danielle murmured.

"No." He couldn't explain. Didn't want to. Some losses cut too deeply.

"There's quite a bit of glass in here."

"Then it needs to come out."

Her tweezers were brutal, but her fingertips didn't hurt at all. He concentrated on their softness. She supported his arm under a lamp that she'd pulled close, and her warm breath flowed over his skin. His mind turned to the probability that she and Tony were having an affair, and then to curiosity about her husband and the wedding ring she no longer wore, and then to irritability with himself for being constantly attracted to this woman who simply was not available.

When she lifted her head and showed him the largest of the bloody brown shards she had extracted, he wondered if she would know what kind of bottle it had come from.

"Woooowwww," Simeon gushed.

"That's huuuuge," Laith agreed.

Even Ziggy craned his neck to look.

She dropped the glass onto some gauze. Her bandaging efforts were as clumsy as her tweezer skills. She used three butterflies over the big gash, pressing down the wrinkles, and left the other smaller cuts to patch themselves.

"You really need stitches," she said. "Mirah's husband —"

And then she stopped, because Mirah's husband wasn't there, and it seemed that this fact turned everyone's quiet thoughts to loved ones who weren't with them while the vacuous news anchor chattered over their heads.

Vance thought that Mirah's husband was a surgeon, which would line up with the fact that he'd only seen the man one time. He couldn't recall the doctor's name.

"I haven't been able to reach him," Mirah said.

"That hospital is a fortress," Ferti said. "I'm sure he's fine."

"Yes, it is safe," Mirah said, staring out the window for long seconds, fingering her baby's silky hair. She blinked and turned to Vance. "My husband will have a shirt your size," she said. "I should have thought of it sooner. I'll go get one for you."

"He won't mind?" Vance asked Mirah. He needed a shower, having been in the river twice today. His jeans were caked with mud inside and out.

Mirah waved him off. But then she hesitated and glanced at the boys.

"I've got them," Danielle said gently. She

shooed them away from the dog and over to the game room closet, urging them to play checkers. Laith pulled some kind of hand-held game out of his back pocket and Simeon clamored for a turn to use it.

Ferti pushed herself out of the chair. "I'll help, Mirah. Let's get what else you might need to stay with me tonight."

Danielle looked up at them. "I've got a key to the furnished model," she said. "You should stay there, Mirah. There's room for you and the boys."

The women hesitated at the base of the south stairs. Vance read their expression as surprise. Tony turned on the stool and shot a glare at Danielle, which could only be read as disapproval.

Vance saw Ferti catch their unspoken exchange. "How'd you get one of those, honey?" Her lips were pursed and her eyes were puzzling out a question in her own mind. Was it possible the women didn't know Danielle worked for Tony?

Danielle was ransacking the first-aid kit for another bandage, though he didn't think he needed one.

Mirah said, "Thank you, but I'd rather not be alone tonight."

"Maybe someone else can use the rooms," Danielle said. Ferti's brow was working but she let her question go unanswered.

Danielle's eyes flicked upward and met Vance's as if to say the model could be his, then tossed the unused bandage back in the kit as Mirah and Ferti went upstairs.

"Sometimes I just don't think," she muttered. She looked at the boys, who were hunched close over Laith's small game screen.

"Most of us don't from time to time," he said. "Or even most of the time." He meant to put her at ease, because of course he had no idea what she was talking about or whether she deserved her own judgment.

"My husband died two years ago," Danielle said out of the blue, changing Vance's perception of her in the space of a breath.

"I didn't know," he said.

"I know what she's going through right now, Mirah, waiting to hear if he's okay. All the what-ifs. I just wanted her not to worry about her home too, with the kids. It's good she'll be with Ferti."

He had dozens of questions, and there seemed to be no polite way to ask any of them.

The TV picture flickered again. Seconds later the lights in the common room blinked. The boys around the game table uttered a unified "Whoa!"

"Electricity," Enrique said to Zeke.

Vance said, "We're likely to lose power."

The observation roused Jonesy, who pried his large self off the barstool and lumbered toward the group at the fireplace, holding a half-empty bottle of wine in his right hand.

"Then I'd best fix us all something to eat while we can still cook," he said. "Anyone hungry?"

Vance shook his head.

But Jonesy continued, "I've got a mess of steaks sitting out on my counter upstairs. Was expecting a few buddies over tonight. If we're going to lose power, there's no point in letting those go to waste."

"I'll help you eat 'em," Tony said. "And if you've got peppers and jack cheese I'll help you make the best Philly cheesesteak sandwich you've ever eaten."

"I'll go get my kitchen then," Jonesy said. He set his bottle on a coffee table at Zeke's elbow and turned to the men who were still at the bar. "Carver, come help me if your stomach so leads."

"I always let my stomach lead," said Carver, though he was by far the thinnest man present.

Enrique, who probably knew how to make a Philly cheesesteak better than anything Tony had ever put in his mouth, showed no interest in food.

Carver and Jonesy made their way to the north stairwell while Tony stood and lifted his chin toward Danielle, a request that she join him. She pursed her lips together and made him wait by returning all the items to the first-aid kit with more concentration than the task required.

"You got a generator?" Zeke asked Vance.

"If it hasn't been drowned. It's somewhere near the bottom of the talon," Vance said. "I don't know exactly where."

Enrique pushed himself off the chair, animated by the prospect of doing something helpful. "We still have a little bit of daylight. I'll go search for it."

"It's not safe," Vance said. "We can live without electricity for a while, if it comes to that."

"Actually, we can't. Mirah's baby needs it," Danielle said. "He uses an apnea monitor at night."

"Doesn't she have a battery backup?" Tony said. He'd come to Danielle and extended a hand to draw her to her feet. She stayed seated when she answered him.

"It's good for a few hours," Danielle said. "But not for being stranded."

Vance sighed and tried to think where that generator would most likely be, considering the tasks of the day cut short by the weather. Even if they found the 150-pound behemoth, they'd need a truck to get it to building 12. He wasn't sure anyone's vehicle had survived the flood, or whether the dirt road was passable.

Danielle finally yielded to Tony's pull. She stood and let him take her hand and lead her away from the men who remained near the fireplace furniture. Tony kept hold of Danielle's fingers and rested his other hand on her waist.

Vance focused on the floor. His thoughts about the generator resumed, and then suddenly he was watching them again without realizing he'd looked up.

Tony whispered something into her hair that Vance couldn't hear. Whatever it was, her stiff shoulders relaxed and she nodded.

Enrique leaned forward in his seat. "We might be able to use the crane as a generator. For as long as the gas and the battery last. It will get us a few hours."

"That'll be a trick without the engine keys," Zeke said.

"Or cables," Vance added.

The news anchor chattered at his dwindling audience. The same footage of the flooded intersection filled the screen. Vance overheard Tony saying, ". . . harmless to let him play with his friend. But it won't happen again."

He kissed Danielle's forehead, which might have been a kind gesture, except it seemed insincere to Vance. Practiced. He wanted to know why Tony had withheld his apology until all the residents were out of the room.

He was reading his own desires into the scene.

The lights blinked again. "I'd like to risk it," Enrique said. "If we lose electric now the kid's backup might not make it until morning, and we'll be worse off than we are right now."

"I think the generator is probably at number 6," Vance said. "I can't say for sure, but that's my guess."

"Let's hope it's not all the way down at number 1," Tony said behind Vance. "Number 1 is probably six miles downriver by now."

The front door opened in a burst of wet wind and Drew Baxter stumbled in looking like a chocolate bunny, bringing half the river with him. He let out a whoop and sputtered, wiping his face and exposing fair skin.

"Baxter!" Rising, Vance took the blanket

off his shoulders and offered it. "You're a mess!"

"Back at you, Vance! You must have had your own guardian angel haul your butt out of that trailer. Tell me Sam's okay too?" Baxter passed the blanket over his head and rubbed it down his arms.

Vance shook his head.

"There was another man with you," Danielle said to Baxter.

"The crane driver." Baxter scowled. "Fool almost drowned me. He was like a wet cat, clawing me to keep his own head up."

"What happened?" Vance asked.

"I don't know, really. One second he's pushing me under, the next he's just gone and I hit a wall — a real wall. Number 6, I think. Can't be sure. Can you believe my truck is still up there? What kind of wave picks up a trailer and leaves a truck?"

Zeke broke into the conversation. "Vance and Enrique are heading back out that way in search of the generator. What would you say to that?"

"It's a fool's errand. There's no walking or driving out there right now."

"Did you see a generator down at 6?" Vance asked.

"No. But I wasn't looking for one, was I?"

In the silence that followed, Vance saw

201

Baxter's eyes light on Tony.

Baxter swiped the towel across the back of his neck and then unfurled it in Tony's direction. The snap of terry cloth released a small spatter of black goo on the white furniture between them. Ziggy's ears flickered toward the sound.

Tony crossed his arms and planted his feet slightly apart.

Danielle stepped toward Baxter. "Your hand is bleeding. Let me clean it."

Blood mingled with the mud caking Baxter's left palm. He wiped it on the towel.

"It's a scratch. Leave it."

Danielle backed off.

"Who's got a phone?" Vance asked. "Mine was in the trailer."

"I do." Tony lifted his up for all to see.

"Call 911," Vance ordered. "Maybe we can get someone out here to pick up Mirah and the baby."

"Already tried that."

"Try again."

Tony raised his eyebrows and didn't budge.

"Tell them we're missing at least two men," Vance added. "Sam, the crane operator. It's not too dark to start a search if we have the right equipment."

"No one will pick up," Tony insisted.

"Indulge me," Vance said.

With exaggerated gestures, Tony held up the phone for all to see, like a magician about to make it disappear. Then he went through precise motions of turning on the speaker phone and dialing the three numbers.

The line rang. And rang. And rang. Tony held his patronizing pose until Vance lost count and finally told him to end the call.

Danielle groaned and put her hands atop her head.

"Okay," Vance said. "We're going to lose power. We have to go. I just haven't figured out how."

Danielle touched Vance's arm.

"I have an idea," she said.

17

Danielle's suggestion that they use Enrique's boat was practical, if crazy. But they couldn't haul the generator back to building 12 by hand. If not for the chance that Mirah's infant would need it, might die without it, would they have gone out at all? Vance wondered.

Baxter's manner became as sour as the crane driver's when Vance asked him to go back out into the rain and help search. It was a three-man job, and Jonesy was too heavy and Carver was too brittle. "What, Tony too far above this work to pitch in?" Baxter huffed.

When Vance approached him, Tony refused on the grounds that he thought a search for the generator was ill advised. The baby's apnea monitor had a battery backup, he argued. Even if that failed, there were means to ensure the baby's continued breathing. Like waking the child at regular intervals. No point in risking so many lives when there were simple solutions.

Vance disagreed and, in the end, successfully appealed to Enrique's and Baxter's manhood. They had to at least try to get Mirah's baby what he needed. They didn't have to be reckless about it. They could turn back.

Wearing a fresh cotton shirt and a lightweight rain jacket given to him by Mirah, Vance helped Enrique and Baxter push the twelve-foot vessel back out of Mirah's living room through the shattered picture window. The boat fell, puncturing the footbridge's awning before wedging itself in the murky goo between the bank and the building. Enrique searched for the outboard motor that would have helped them navigate the strong currents. No sign of it. But one of the oars was reclining on Mirah's once-luxurious sofa.

Vance worked hard to convince himself the plan was reasonable. Outside, the mud had become so treacherous on land that the water was a safer place for them to be. While the Rondeau River created its own powerful current through the former cove, the twelve foundations of Eagle's Talon functioned like current-busting jetties. These plus the gentle curve of the peninsula sheltered the margins of the cove, enough that Vance believed they could row down and back safely, and without a struggle against the current. If they could find the other oar. Or better yet, the motor.

The afternoon light, already muted by the storm, was rapidly fading. They would be able to search for the generator quickly enough. It would take longer, perhaps too long, to load it onto the boat and return to safety upstream. Three men plus the heavy equipment would tax the boat's capacity, but Vance didn't see how they could manage it with only two people.

Slipping and sliding and pushing their boat through mud, the three men intended to bypass the pump-truck disaster and put out at the dockless platform of building 10. But on their way, Baxter noticed the missing oar protruding from the unset concrete of number 11's battered platform. The paddle's handle pointed at the sunken pump truck as if blaming the vehicle for all the abuse it had taken.

There'd be no getting it without climbing onto the sloping platform. To do that, they changed their plan and put the boat in the water on the south side of number 12, uncomfortably close to that sinking pump truck, which Vance hoped was stable. From their position on the water he had a clear line of sight all the way down to building 1. Contradicting Tony, all the structures but number 11 looked littered with flotsam but were secure. Their stabilizing poles were still erect. Those walls that had been put in place still stood.

Enrique directed them with his oar and, as soon as they were close enough for Vance to mount the tipping platform, Baxter grabbed the foundation's frame to stabilize the boat.

If not for the rain and flood, the angle wouldn't have been dangerously steep to climb, and the concrete would have been thick enough to walk on. But the moment Vance plunged his boot into the goopy mess and leaned far to grasp the oar, the mound began to slide. It took him to his stomach in a second and then dashed him against the outrigger that had pinned the foundation, cracking his elbow before sloughing him off. Enrique reached for him and missed. For the third time in a day, Vance dropped into the black river water. His heavy boots pulled him down.

The temperature felt unnaturally warm, and brightness penetrated his closed eyelids. He kicked toward the surface but seemed not to move. There was no friction of water against his face or arms, no ripples tickling his feet or legs. The liquid was a glove protecting him from any sensation at all. He opened his eyes and saw that his pant leg was snagged on the front fender of the drowned pump truck.

But this failed to explain what was happening.

He hovered in front of one of the long steel posts that held the foundations of these floating buildings steady in the water, securing them to the shore. A swarm of glowing fish darted around the pole, flashing blue and silver and giving off a spectacular brightness. They were so colorful, so unexpected in this freshwater river, so close to the surface, that for several seconds Vance didn't even see what they illuminated. He had never imagined fish such as these, a few dozen of them moving like a cyclone around the twisted pillar of metal.

The distressed, shredded post. It should have been ramrod straight. It should have been smooth-surfaced and so new that it was still shiny clean. But the steel had lost its shape, had folded down on itself as if melted in the forge. Huge holes in the sides of the cylinder, six feet in diameter, gave it the appearance of having exploded from the inside. Scrappy shards stuck out at angles.

One of the bright things stopped darting around and hovered in front of Vance's face, so bright he couldn't look at it directly. He lifted his hand to shield his eyes. The fish — he didn't know what else it could be — touched the center of his palm. The sensation was feathery and gentle and took away the tight need for air in the center of Vance's lungs.

Then the lights shot away from the damage, expanding like a starburst explosion of their own past his face. He jerked his head away and felt the water move this time as it grazed his ears. The fish arced over his shoulders and out into the water, then darted downward, down and down to the bottom of the cove some twenty feet below, becoming pollywogs of light with flickering tails.

Here, the river bottom sloped away from the shore steeply. Underneath their silvery glow, the silt clouded the floor like fog on a stage. By the light, Vance saw through the disturbance a tangled rope of wires, the broken-off corner of a metal box, and the reflective red plastic of an indicator light.

The glowing creatures spread out, moving like liquid silver toward the shore. The land didn't slope gently upward as it ought to have. The entire bank seemed to have caved into a black hole, and the pump truck floated above it, clinging by one outrigger to that unstable foundation.

Through the murky darkness Vance could see the steel poles of building 12. The silver blue lights were swimming in a tight school around the surface of the long stilts. If they had been damaged by an explosion, the swimming lights hid the bad news.

The fiberglass oar was still in Vance's fist. It was pulling him upward. He realized that he needed to take a breath.

In one kick he broke the surface of the water, and when the air filled his lungs, the idea of a bomb filled his brain.

Why? Who? When? Were there others?

Enrique was leaning over the boat with an outstretched hand.

"Okay, man?"

Vance handed over the oar and shook the water off his face.

"You were down awhile. Thought I'd have to go in after you."

He wasn't sure where to begin explaining. "Something snagged my pants."

"Ah. I thought something caught your eye."

"Right," Baxter said. "Because down there everything is bright as day."

Enrique scowled at Baxter, then helped to

heave Vance over the side of the boat. "Did you see something?" Vance asked.

Enrique busied his attention with fitting the second oar into the oarlock. "Just some kind of funky blue light. Probably just you getting unstuck," he said. "You got a light on your watch, don't you?" He pointed to Vance's wristband.

Vance's watch gave off a green light, but he didn't point that out. "Let's get this done," he said, pushing off.

Baxter had retrieved an asphalt lute that had been embedded with some force, perhaps by the same wave that had thrown the boat through Mirah's window, in an exposed piece of the foundation's EPS foam. The concrete-placing tool, which looked like an oversized squeegee with a five-foot handle, had an aluminum alloy blade that he could use to push the boat away from obstacles.

The men stopped at the foundation of each building, braced the boat against the temporary bumpers that would be removed after the docks were installed, then sent Vance up onto the slick platforms and into the partially erected structures. He searched in 10, 9, 8, and at 7 discouragement settled into his bones. His heart returned to Psalm 119. *My soul melts from heaviness; strengthen me according to Your word.*

He took a deep breath and forced exhaustion off his back. But it wasn't fatigue that pulled him down as much as his discovery that the pump-truck accident might have had a human cause.

"Turn back?" Enrique asked.

"Yes," Baxter grunted. Rain was sliding off his shining round head and he was scowling.

Vance looked back up the water toward building 12. He couldn't see any lights. The rain seemed to have leveled out, slowing down from pounding torrent to steady shower, but who was he to say it wouldn't surge again?

The rain needled his cheeks. He turned his head downward toward the river.

A silver flash blinked beneath the undulating water, down near the posts that held building 6's foundation firmly in place. A shot of fear gave Vance a jolt. Were the lights a warning of more disaster?

In his mind's ear he heard a voice. *Did you see them?*

It took him a second to recall that it was Simeon who had asked him this. When the silver flash darted beneath the boat again, Vance's fear slipped away, and he wondered if the boy had meant something other than emergency vehicles after all.

The glistening fish was headed toward building 5.

"Let's keep looking."

Enrique and Baxter pulled the boat out while Vance pushed off the dock with the lute. Building 6, and all those south of it, had completed docks. As they approached, the boat came round the end of the dock just as a swell arrived at the same location. They tipped, and Baxter threw his hand out. The tossing boat pinned his palm against the wood, and Vance heard the bones crack.

Baxter bellowed and dropped his oar. Enrique caught it before it was swept downstream. The boat bounced and all three men were momentarily airborne, then were seated again with loud smacks on their tailbones.

Already, the wrong decision.

Blinks of silver and blue like an army of arrows gathered around the boat, pointing downstream.

Baxter was gripping his hand to his chest and yowling. Vance quickly stabilized the boat.

Enrique was staring at the glowing lights just beneath the surface. He pulled the oars out of the water.

"Let's call it a night, huh?" Enrique said, twisting to face Vance. There was fear in his

213

expression.

Turn back. The thought was on its way from Vance's mind to his mouth when the lights shot out of the water at Enrique's back, arced in unison like a single dolphin, and then reentered the water. The high point of their dive lifted Vance's sight to the sloping bank that rose out of the cove between buildings 5 and 6. His eyes fixed on two shadows there, crouched in the space that the low light couldn't touch. The shadows were heads. The shapes were human.

"I see someone," Vance said, pointing.

Enrique faced forward again.

"I think I broke it." Baxter's eyes were pinched shut. His tone was offended that his injury hadn't earned Vance's attention.

"You see it?" Vance asked Enrique.

"I see something. You think that's people?"

"Two of them."

"Could just be scrap," Enrique said.

"Hang on, Baxter," he said. "We need to check this out, and then we'll get you back."

Baxter swore but was in no position to argue. The water beneath the boat flattened out for a precious moment of calm, and Vance pushed off.

Enrique pulled on the oars, eyes scanning the water, and Vance kept an eye on the

214

shadows, hoping they were neither an illusion nor dead men.

A swell smacked the side of the boat, turning the bow to a favorable angle toward the dock at number 5. Then a second wave hit the stern, coming up over Vance's back and dousing him once more.

The boat thumped up against the dock and Vance got out, tying off loosely while Enrique held it steady and Baxter groaned his misery. From up here Vance could see that the shadowy hulk between the buildings was still in the water, caught under the narrow, railed walkway that encircled all of the buildings. The silver lights he had seen near his boat now floated deep in the water beneath the form, lighting it with a pale blue glow. As Vance approached, the lights blinked out, returning the watery crevice between the buildings to its dim gray state.

Water poured off the gutters at the edge of both buildings, forming natural translucent walls that were difficult to see through. He slowed his jog to a walk, trying to sort out the shapes.

"Hey there!" he called out.

At the corner he plunged his head out through the runoff and got his first real glimpse of the man in the water. He was faced away from Vance, his armpit hanging over something that floated. An open life vest, snagged on the foundation. It held up his arm at an awkward angle and pinched his shoulder and cheek together. The other side of the man's face pressed up against the bottom of the walkway, rising and falling short distances with the water, tethered by a loose strap that ran behind his neck and disappeared under the platform.

White lettering on the back of the man's bright red shirt was obscured by the water, but Vance already knew what it said. *Pick up the pace!*

"Aw, Sam." Vance's sigh was heavy. He jumped the rails and cut through the falling runoff, then dropped himself into the water.

The place where Vance slipped in was warm like a bathtub. Like the spot where the wet concrete had dumped him. He held on to one of the rails near the bottom and touched Sam's shoulder. When he got no response, Vance let go of the walkway and treaded water while he looked for his friend's pulse. Though the light was poor here, he could see the bloody mess on the side of Sam's head.

The crew leader's mind was asleep but his heart was fully awake. His breathing was even and as steady as the heartbeat.

"Enrique, a little help?"

He didn't answer right away. "I . . . uh . . . best to stay here or we might lose the boat."

It was easier to free Sam from the life vest than to free the vest from whatever entrapped it. As much as Vance wanted to take that vest with him, he had to leave it behind.

With an arm supporting Sam on his back, and Sam's head tilted upward against Vance's shoulder, Vance pulled him back to the boat. Immediately he noticed the change in the water's temperature from bathtub cozy to lemonade cool. A shiver passed through him.

"Just one guy after all," Enrique said. "Is he alive?" He reached over the side of the boat to help Vance, but his eyes were darting across the surface of the water.

"Yeah. It's Sam, one of my crew leaders. Watch his head."

Though pained, Baxter joined the effort by using his weight to counterbalance Enrique's as he pulled and Vance pushed from below. It was sloppy work, getting the unconscious man into the wobbling craft. There was no room for him to lie down, so they propped him against Baxter, who kept Sam from tumbling out by encircling his shoulders with his one good arm. The boat sank dangerously low in the bouncing waters.

"This is better than a generator, finding this guy alive," Vance said.

Enrique directed Vance to man the second oar.

"Better for Sam," Baxter grunted.

"Shut up," Vance ordered.

Enrique pointed the boat back upstream. Vance synced his efforts. Leaning into his stroke and keeping his eyes on the water right around the boat, Enrique broke the tense silence. "I saw this movie once where the earth was being overrun by these aliens, and the last few survivors were holding out at a fortress, but they were running out of food. So one of them risks it all, you know, to sneak out past the enemy lines and find something, anything, that they can eat. And he's gone for three days, right? And they think for sure he's gone down. But then he comes back, dragging this huge load behind him, and he's jazzed, because even though he couldn't find any food, he has something better."

Enrique stopped here as if silence could hook the other men's interest. Neither of them took the bait. To the west, the sun finally vanished, and the temperature fell with it. Vance concentrated on pitting the weight of the boat against the force of the current, which seemed strong even in this calm margin of the cove.

"It's a dead alien," Enrique burst. "The guy hauls it into their camp and says, 'I figured out how to kill 'em.' And they're all like, 'Wow, this is way better than food, because whatever you brought back, well, we were only going to burn through that anyway. Now we can get out of here, wipe out these monsters, go build ourselves a walled city, and plant some vegetable gardens or something.' "

Vance wanted out of this rain. Out of this boat. Out of this eternally difficult day. His oar cut the water. He dragged the vessel through, keeping time with Enrique. Cut, drag. Cut, drag. Rain was driving into his eyes. *Revive me in Your righteousness. Let your mercies come also to me, O Lord.*

"And then" — and here Enrique broke into a laugh — "you know it's gonna be bad because there's only seven minutes left in the run time, and sure enough, this dead alien begins to decompose and when he does he releases this toxic gas into the atmosphere that kills them all in, like, seconds. Bam. End of the human race."

Baxter said through pain, "Thank you for that inspirational message."

Enrique's voice took on the impatient edge of a person whose passions had never been understood. "I'm just saying that sometimes what seems better isn't really in the end."

"If that's an argument not to rescue you when you're half drowned, I'll keep that in mind," Baxter said.

Vance's patience was spent. "Sam's not an alien. He isn't dead. He won't leak toxic fumes — which a generator could do, you know. Let's take a good thing at face value, okay?"

Three of the little silver fish-like lights flickered beneath the water on the side of the boat, and when Enrique noticed them his rowing rhythm was disrupted. Vance opened his mouth to ask whether Enrique had seen these lights before, but Enrique met his eyes.

He said, "That kind of thinking always leads to trouble."

18

Ziggy's warm and soft chest filled and emptied as the dog rested against Zeke's leg. The companionship of an animal was a strengthening force on a good day, but even more so in a crisis. On an intellectual level, Zeke acknowledged that God should be enough for a man. But at the same time he liked to imagine that the first dog God ever created was like this one, soft and understanding and almost as good as a woman.

Zeke was alone now, left behind by the men in the boat, and the women and children upstairs. The men in charge of the meal had brought their food down to the catering kitchen at the back of the room, and their boisterous sounds spilled out into the common area.

Zeke pushed the noise into the background. He thought of himself as a load-bearing wall, sitting there on the sofa with a critical role to play, though he didn't have anywhere to go. He sat there and prayed for everyone who was doing the dangerous work: Searching for generators. Minding children. Carving steaks. Prayer was dangerous work in its way, he supposed. But wasn't that what he had been led here to do?

"She's the most intelligent one here," someone said before settling on the sofa near Zeke. It was the voice of Vance's boss, an authoritative voice, but underneath the confidence, Zeke heard the anxious tone of someone with a lot to lose. Of course, this impression might have been informed by Vance's opinion of Tony, which he had shared with Zeke from time to time. "She's brilliant."

"Ziggy is a male," Zeke said.

"Who? Oh, the dog. I was talking about Danielle Clement. She's incredibly smart, don't you think?"

Zeke didn't believe that suggesting the men take a boat out on the water qualified as genius. The scent of bourbon rose from Tony's glass.

"But your dog's not too shabby either," Tony said. His laugh was rehearsed, designed for good timing. He smelled like money, a fragrance of woody pulp too green to burn, plus the mild grime of having been handled by hundreds of fingertips.

Tony's voice was aimed at Ziggy: "I owe you some thanks, furry friend, for paying attention to the boy when I dropped the ball. I owe both of you some thanks."

"That credit does belong to the dog, I have to admit."

"I'm Tony Dean."

Zeke extended his hand and Tony took it. "Zeke Hammond. I thought you were going to cook."

"They've kicked me out. Say I'm no good with a knife. Which is true enough. What brings you to Eagle's Talon?"

"Friend of Vance's. Came to watch him work."

"It's too bad your dog can't warn you to expect foul weather."

"Oh, I had plenty of warning."

"You did? How's that?"

"A long and honest life. There's foul weather of some kind or another to be had every day."

"A pessimist, are you?" Tony asked.

"Not at all. Hardship can improve a man. Speaking for myself."

"I agree that difficulty creates opportunities for a man to think about what's really important."

"Yes." Zeke tried to clarify his point. "The

trick is to act on what you think. And to act well."

"Exactly," Tony said. "It's like you read my mind. I've been thinking of marrying that brilliant woman Danielle, and the trick is going to be whether I might act on it."

"Not on whether she'd accept your proposal?" Zeke said wryly.

Tony's laughter grated on Zeke's ears. "I like you more and more! Have you ever married, Mr. Hammond?"

"Can't say I have."

"Was it because you didn't act on the opportunity?"

"I'm surprised you aren't more occupied by all the setbacks this day has brought you."

Ice made music in a glass as Tony emptied the contents into his mouth. Zeke heard the swallow, heard Tony's tongue take the last drops off his lips, along with the last of his probably practiced smile. There was no lightness in his answer. "Everything will be taken care of. There's an answer for every problem. Usually the answer involves money, and I have plenty of it."

"I see."

"Take Danielle, for example. She loves my money. It gives her security. Nothing to fear for her or her son."

Zeke thought it would be unfair to point out that her son had almost died twice today, and there was nothing Tony's money could do about it.

"Does she love you?"

"Of course. You can't separate a man from his money."

"And do you love her?"

"If I didn't, I wouldn't consider marrying her."

"Of course." Zeke thought his mimicry was lost on Tony.

"She makes an equitable contribution to our relationship, even though she has no money."

"You mean she makes you feel important?"

"No, no." But Tony didn't elaborate.

"What contributions does she make, then?"

"Beauty. Brains. She could sell a condo to Oprah, I believe. She is a very hard worker. She works very hard to please me." Tony paused before adding, "Why am I telling you all this?"

"I'm a spiritual director. I suppose it's a gift that inspires confidence."

"Yes, that must be it."

"But help me understand: what contribution would she make to a marriage that she doesn't already — what would you get that you don't already have from her?"

"Now *that,* Mr. Hammond, is the question, isn't it? The question every man should ask. The one that might keep most of us out of a marriage. My financial adviser would rather I stay single, you know."

"I think I haven't been clear. What I mean is, should I warn Danielle?"

"Ha ha! Of what? Of the fact that anyone who marries does it for selfish reasons? Go ahead: she and I are very like-minded on that point."

That kind of empty motivation was what made people today so cynical, Zeke thought.

Tony continued: "Already I have given her a secure life. It's what women want, you know. Why not want something in return? If I adopted her son, it would do very well for my public standing. Make me a family man, you know. There are people in my line of work who support my . . . aspirations, who find family men more trustworthy than, say, a man like you. No offense intended."

Zeke began to think of ways to excuse himself from the conversation. He moved to the edge of the sofa cushion. Ziggy brushed his nose against Zeke's hand and sat up.

"And I think, too, that marriage engenders its own brand of loyalty," Tony continued.

"Let's say a woman learned something . . . unpleasant about her husband. A wife might be more likely to forgive him than a girl-friend would, don't you think? If he'd done a proper job of caring for her? She might feel . . . more inclined to be understanding."

"If there is something about you that Danielle doesn't know and might not like, may I suggest you tell her *before* you marry?"

"Nothing kills a romance like honesty," Tony observed.

And what kept Zeke in his seat at that moment was his sense that it was the first completely honest thing Tony had said since sitting down. The blind man heard the worry in the words, the spontaneity, the irony.

"If she loves you," Zeke offered, "she'll forgive you before the wedding. And then you'll have nothing to fear."

Tony the politician reentered the conversation. "I have nothing to fear anyway."

Zeke had never before felt as if he were a priest and someone was confessing a crime that had yet to be committed. What was he to do with this impression devoid of facts?

Pray. He must pray.

Tony changed the subject with inappropriate cheerfulness. "Did you know that Fergi is a renowned designer of wedding dresses?"

Zeke was sure the woman's name was Ferti, and was only slightly less sure the woman's ancestors hailed from Africa, which, when put together, caused him to guess that the name was a derivation of the African queen Nefertiti. Instead of correcting Tony, though, Zeke thought it might be more fun to give Ferti herself the chance to do it.

"She designed the dress that the president's daughter wore in the Rose Garden last year, and also the dress for that film star — what was her name? The one who just married for the third time?"

Zeke shook his head. This was a conversation to be had between women. He had never understood the fuss over white dresses. Being a landscaper he was partial to the idea of an outdoor Eden-style wedding with the bride and groom wearing nothing at all. Unfortunately for him, he'd never met a woman with the same fantasy.

"Well, everyone in Hollywood wants her, but she's only making one dress a year anymore. One dress, for the right price. It would be a nice gift for a beauty like Danielle. How many men could give her *that*?"

At this point Zeke finally succeeded in detaching himself from the sound of Tony's voice. He rose and stretched out his legs and turned his thoughts to a prayer for Vance in the boat, and the men with him, but no words came to his mind. Instead, his mind's eye was crowded with the image of a gold snake lounging on a white sofa. A gold snake with a man's head, greasy slick, sipping bourbon.

In the common room's game alcove, Danielle taught Simeon how to play checkers. Her mind was on the clock, and her eyes were often on the panoramic windows that faced the cove. Vance, Enrique, and Baxter had been gone for two hours. The gray sky was black. The glass had become a mirror that reflected the interior lights. She began to worry that her idea of sending them out in a boat was proof of Tony's wavering opinion of her.

"It would've been best if you hadn't tried to help," he'd said of her chasing after Vance earlier and leaving Simeon with him. "They know what they're doing. In these situations it's best to stay out of the way."

So somehow it was her fault, what happened to her son, but in the same breath he'd apologized for giving in to Simeon's demands to play with Laith. His touch reassured her of his understanding and made her self-conscious of the others in the room. Though none of the residents was there, Vance's presence made her feel ashamed. What was she doing, pretending to love this man who didn't love her son the same way she did?

But that wasn't a fair accusation.

She found herself apologizing to Tony for putting him in a father's position when he was hardly a father, and it wasn't until after he left that her apology seemed all wrong.

"King me!" Simeon demanded. She crowned his red checker and rewarded him with a smile.

"You're a quick learner. I think you're winning."

"I am!"

Jonesy and Carver had cooked up an aromatic meal that failed to stir her appetite even when the spicy scents filled every nook of the huge room. Vance's friend Zeke joined her in passing on the food, saying he would wait for the others to return. Tony ate and continued to place unsuccessful calls to 911. Even his efforts to contact others on the mainland proved futile. Calls could not be completed or were dropped after a brief connection. Texts would not go out. Carver took a plate of food up to Ferti, instructing Tony to stand at the bottom of the stairs and prepare to catch him after Ferti booted him down.

While Ferti prepared her condo for Mirah's family, Mirah returned to contribute her marinated lamb and feed her elder son. Baby Haji was still swaddled against her heart.

Laith, who at age eight was routinely defeated at all games by older members of his extended family, was very interested in Simeon's novice skills and convinced Danielle to let them go head-to-head. Simeon eagerly accepted the challenge.

"Did you reach your husband?" Danielle asked Mirah in a discreet tone.

Mirah's worried eyes glanced at the boys. She said only, "I'll make a plate for Simeon too." She rubbed baby Haji's back.

The news coverage had expanded a bit to include sensationalist shock more than solid information, until Danielle finally asked the men to mute the TV and turn on the closed captioning for the children's sake.

"If it comes to it," she said to Mirah, "Ferti and I will take turns sitting up with Haji while you both sleep. He'll be okay."

Mirah's smile was thankful but weak.

Danielle took up watch at the window, straining her eyes for any sign of the men. She leaned her forehead against the glass and blocked the light with a cupped hand. The rapids churning in the cove turned her stomach. Her breath fogged the surface.

When the aluminum boat bearing four men instead of three appeared at the end of the dock, relief poured over her.

"They're back!" she shouted, and the conversations muted by rain and television skipped a beat. Danielle hurried for the double doors that led out to the dock. Zeke stood. Jonesy looked up at her from the stovetop grill behind the bar. Tony stayed seated, chewing his food.

She dashed outside before she remembered a jacket, which was when she realized that it wasn't relief that had overcome her. It was need. Need of the strength these men represented — no, for Vance's strength in particular. Trapped by water and darkness, she suddenly wanted his protective arms around her son, his steadying grip on her arm, his hands gasping her wrists while they held each other out of the torrent.

When the crisis was over, she told herself, she would have to analyze that desire for what it was (self-doubt, weakness) and put it in its place. All that she needed she could earn and Tony would provide as compensation.

Her fingers quivered with cold as she

helped Enrique tie off. He turned to help Vance with the unconscious man who lay in the bottom of the boat, the man in the red T-shirt who had clung to the life vest she'd tossed him.

"We still have power," she said to Vance in greeting. She meant to encourage, but it came out like a condemnation. *You failed to get the generator. I guess we'll make it anyway.* She saw its effect in Vance's tired eyes.

"It's great you found him." She smiled. Vance turned away.

"Help Baxter?" He pointed to the bald man, whose face was a wrinkled ball of pain. Baxter was gripping his own wrist and holding his rigid hand in a tight embrace around the unconscious man's shoulders.

After Vance got Sam out, Danielle offered Baxter her balance and tried not to take Vance's cold response personally. "What exactly have you guys been doing?" she asked Baxter.

"Nothing important, that's for sure."

Danielle supported Baxter's good arm and they hurried across the dock. When Baxter slipped, she lifted his elbow before he fell. The surprise jolt rid Danielle of any need she thought she had. Maybe she should take Ferti's advice and work harder to become more self-reliant. She could help a man as

easily as one could help her. A widow had
to make do, after all.

19

The power failed at 9:21, a moment documented by the catering kitchen's hardwired analog clock. The silence of the television discouraged conversation, as if everyone suddenly realized how little they knew about anything out there or anyone in here.

Mirah kept baby Haji swaddled against her chest, where she was in constant contact with his heartbeat and his breath. By becoming the living monitor he needed, she could save what little battery power they had for a more desperate time, she had said.

"We'll have to conserve water," Vance said, grateful for having showered just an hour before the electricity went out. "Don't run the taps. Don't flush the toilets if you can help it."

"Why?" Danielle wanted to know.

"If the pump stations at the reservoir have lost power too, that'll impact the water pressure. Draining our reserves here puts our water at risk of becoming contaminated. Especially with this flood. It's a perfect storm of bad news for the water supply."

"Seems to me the best thing to do is stock up now," Jonesy said, "before any of that happens."

Vance sighed and rubbed his eyes. "The best thing to do would have been to stock up before we lost electricity." But that was all the energy for persuasion he had left in him.

He lit the gas fireplace for light and for warmth. The chill of being wet all day was settling into his head.

"You're inviting disaster, you know," Enrique said from the dark shadows of an isolated corner. The little flame from his cigarette lighter flickered in and out. "Some wave's gonna break the gas line and send us all up in a fireball."

It wasn't likely, but nothing about the day so far had been. Vance stared into the flames. It was possible that someone might have premeditated damage to the gas supply lines as well. What could he do about it at this point?

"Do you know something I don't know, Enrique?" Vance asked halfheartedly. He didn't receive an answer.

"I'm not worried about no gas fumes,"

Carver said from the alcove filled with bookshelves and only a few books. "It's all of Jonesy's booze that'll go up if there's a lit match in the vicinity." His voice and his body were relaxed. He slouched in a chair as close to Ferti as she would allow — or wouldn't disallow — while she cleaned up the bloody blow to Sam's head. The man was still unconscious, though she had declared his injury to be "a scratch."

"Then you better help me drink it up," Jonesy said. "What'll it be, Carver?"

"He's had enough," Ferti muttered.

Carver lifted his head. "But I haven't had anything, sugar."

"And that's all you're gonna get. If you think I'm barely putting up with you now, you just try me on this. Go ahead, drink something. See what you get for it. And don't call me sugar."

"She says she doesn't love me," Carver said to Jonesy. "But you can see it's just an act."

Ferti shook her head as she bent over Sam. "I never met a man so drunk on himself."

He reseated his ivy cap over his eyes, grinning.

The building's wireless modem went out with the electricity, and devices with satellite reception lasted only slightly longer. Cell phones began to lose their signals somewhere around ten, though Tony claimed that his phone had intermittent reception, especially from the third floor. Using a flashlight app, he came and went from Danielle's unit several times an hour, trying to reach any of his numerous business associates. His preoccupation with the phone raised a brief conversation of how the devices might be recharged without electricity.

In the absence of any real solutions, Jonesy produced a battery-operated radio but failed to find a signal. The two boys persisted through the static long after the adults gave up, until Baxter, whose pain was a bit beyond the help of over-the-counter aids, yelled at them to shut it off. He was pacing out his agony in front of one of the windows.

When they didn't, Baxter barged in on their fun and hefted the radio in his good hand, then dashed it against the hard floor, where it shattered.

All of the adults stood up.

The boys ran to their mothers.

Baxter appeared to be more shocked than anyone. "I'm so sorry. I don't know what just happened. I'm sorry."

Danielle pulled Simeon to her side. "Mirah," she pleaded, "don't you have *any-*

thing that might help take the edge off his pain? Doesn't your husband keep something on hand —"

"No. He doesn't. What would we use it for? Even if he did, I couldn't give it out. I wouldn't. He'd lose his license."

"Give Baxter some of that booze Carver thinks he wants," Ferti told Jonesy.

"I don't drink," Baxter protested.

"You do now," Ferti told him. " 'Cause if you don't I'm gonna break a bottle over your head and put us out of your misery."

Jonesy uncapped a bottle of Scotch and poured some. Baxter took it. Enrique asked for a glass of his own.

Vance stayed silent, feeling the old familiar pull: the promise of peace in a bottle.

What you're looking for isn't in here.

Vance turned toward his friend Zeke, the man who'd first uttered those words to him. Man and dog sat like stones accustomed to darkness. They came to life when Vance took a seat next to Zeke. Ziggy nuzzled Vance's knuckles and was rewarded with a neck rub.

In the game room, the boys resumed their checkers match in more subdued tones. Danielle found three pillar candles and gave one to them, another to Ferti, and then left the last one near the food that had been spread out on the bar. Lacking refrigera-

tion, she covered the food with red towels.
Too restless to sit, she stood at the window
that faced the peninsula, alternately eying
her son and the rain.

Vance leaned in close to Zeke to talk as
privately as circumstances allowed, but his
eyes stayed on Danielle. He worried about
her. He was hoping Zeke might give him
some insights that he could convert into assurances.

"You knew we were going to lose the
trailer," Vance said.

"I didn't. I only knew that you were up
against some trouble today."

"You had a vision?"

"Just one. A few insights on other things."

"What can you tell me?"

"That we are in God's hands. That's about
all I know for sure. The rest is so hard to
say, son. I'm still sitting on what it all
means. I've seen silver and I've seen gold.
Gold is bad. Gold is the serpent."

A shiver passed over Vance; his attention
came fully to bear on Zeke's sightless eyes.

"What is silver?"

"I don't know yet."

"I saw silver lights tonight in the water,"
Vance said. They couldn't see it now, but it
was liquid they still could hear, could smell,
could sense rippling beneath their feet.

"Lights like fish swimming. They're how I found Sam."

"Ah. That's the life in it, then."

"In what?"

"In the vision. The ones from God always point to life, yes? We've talked about this before. But I wasn't sure. It was the silver — a silver hand, a silver ring on its finger."

Vance couldn't help looking at Danielle again.

"Listen," Zeke said. He described the vision to Vance, in which Vance and many people stood in the back of a plummeting pickup truck. "The voice that belonged to the silver hand said, 'Vance must stand, and God will give him the lives of all who stay. These things must happen, but see to it that he is not afraid.' "

"What does that mean? 'Give him the lives of all who stay'?"

"I've had some time to ponder that. You got a Bible here?"

"Washed away in the trailer."

"Well, then I can't confirm it right now. You recall the story of Paul's journey to Rome, when he was shipwrecked? It's in Acts. Late in the book."

"He advised the boat not to sail, but they did anyway."

"Yes, and they sailed right into disaster.

But an angel told Paul not to be afraid, that it was his destiny to get to Rome. And then he told Paul that the lives of all the men who stuck with him would be spared."

The weight of the day sat on Vance's chest. He sank back into the cushions and watched the firelight transform the aluminum room dividers into glimmering works of art.

"I don't see the connection to our situation. Except for the massive storm."

Zeke impersonated the TV news anchor. "It's an unprecedented disaster."

"But I don't think it's entirely natural." Vance told Zeke about the damaged posts.

"So we have a human factor in the equation," Zeke speculated.

"Maybe. Could one bomb have put such a huge hole in the earth?"

"There's always a human factor in every equation." Zeke was smiling.

Tony sauntered down the south stairwell with his illuminated phone shining downward at his feet. When he landed, he shut the light off.

"I'm working with my assistant to get a helicopter out here as soon as the weather permits," Tony announced to the room.

"This weather's not going to permit anytime soon," Zeke said.

"Where would you land a helicopter?" Enrique demanded to know. His words were sloppy with alcohol.

"Plenty of room in the turnaround."

"Not enough *ground* on the turnaround right now," Enrique scoffed.

"Not enough light either," Vance said.

"While we *wait* for daylight," Tony said as if they were all dense, "everyone else, shut off your phones."

Mirah objected. "My husband —"

"We don't know how long we'll need these to last," Tony said, "so we'll rotate through them, one at a time. How many do we have?"

Five, they quickly determined. Tony's, Ferti's, Mirah's, Jonesy's, and Carver's. Enough to last several days if necessary. Vance's had gone down in the trailer. They could only assume Sam's was lost. Enrique and Zeke had left theirs in the house, as they always did when they went out on the water. Baxter's was out in his truck, already low on juice.

Vance saw the logic of Tony's plan, but the demand sat uneasily with him. It was a demand for control, he decided.

A flash, a crack like a gunshot, an explosion of sparks — all three happened at once with a force that knocked Danielle away from the window. Atop the peninsula, tiny flames were flying off the crane, and shouts from Mirah and the kids soon morphed into awestruck *whooooaahhs* from the boys as they ran to see what had happened. The tiny hairs on Danielle's arms rippled with static.

The dog was whining.

"Lightning," Zeke said. "Anyone else's hair standing up?" He placed a steady hand on Ziggy's head.

Mirah was on her son's heels. With one hand sheltering her infant's head, she used the other to pull Laith away from the window. Vance appeared at Danielle's shoulder as smoky wisps emerged from under the crane's engine cover. The very air seemed to smolder.

Vance reached out to pull Simeon away.

"There goes the crane option," Jonesy muttered, speaking of the possibility of using the crane's battery. The announcement was followed by drunken laughter from Enrique.

"Will it catch fire?" Mirah asked.

If it did, they had nothing but rain to put it out.

"It's okay," Danielle said to Simeon.

"I know! Isn't it cool?"

"No," she scolded. Vance could see her hands shaking. "What if someone had been in there?"

"But, Mom, there wasn't. Look, the roof's on fire."

It wasn't the roof but the gangway awning that had lit. One of the flaming bits from the crane must have landed there, but why hadn't the rain put it out?

Vance and Tony had the same idea at the same time. Enrique lifted his glass as the pair grabbed up the wet jackets that had been dumped at the doors and ran outside, beating at the scorch that was spreading rapidly across the bottom of the awning.

"What's keeping it burning?" Tony shouted.

It couldn't be fuel or the entire peninsula would be aflame. Vance looked up the slope at the crane and the flames spitting out from the engine cover.

"Oil," he said.

"Great. Just great."

Standing on the footbridge under the widening hole of the canopy, Vance jumped up and grabbed the black edges, dug his fingernails into the fabric, and brought his entire body to bear on tearing the awning down. It worked. The men stomped at the flames until the oil was spent, then dumped the scrap into the water. The fire on the crane continued to burn.

"Let's pray it doesn't reach the gas tank,"

Vance said.

Tony put his hands on his hips. "Why don't we do a little fire dance while we're at it? Cast a spell. Call up our dead ancestors for protection against the curse of Eagle's Talon."

"You sound stressed, Tony."

The crane's blaze, strong but small and contained, cast a red glow on the side of Tony's face.

"This place isn't cursed," Vance said. "And prayer isn't superstition."

"Just a couple hours ago you were recommending I evacuate everyone. The whole place might be unstable, you said. Who knows what that pump truck stirred up down there where no one can see? And suddenly you want to stay put?"

"Our chance to leave has passed. Trying to leave now will get people killed."

"Says who? I'm going to make a plan to get us out of here. We need a plan." Tony turned his back on Vance and made for the doors. "Help me if you care."

Vance had nothing against making a plan. But he wouldn't facilitate recklessness. More than a dozen other men, women, and children would be affected.

The last time Vance was in a similar position, there had been only three people involved. And Vance had been overpowered. And the only thing to come out of that disaster was death.

Vance thought of Danielle and Simeon. Zeke and Ziggy. All the others ordained to be in this place at this time, trapped in a dark place.

He couldn't let it happen again.

20

Danielle stood apart from the others, watching Vance and Zeke tip their heads toward each other, talking in tones too low to be overheard. She felt like a spy, wondering about their conversation, wanting to be let in on it, as if they were making plans that would save them all and she might be a part of it. When Vance glanced up at her she didn't know whether to interpret his weary smile as an invitation to join them or as a friendly warning to mind her own business. She turned away to the windows overlooking the peninsula and wondered for the first time if her car was still parked down in the turnaround, or if it, too, had been washed away.

Water striped the glass and cut her view of the scorched crane into disconnected partitions. She hoped this building was as stable as Ranier had said it would be.

What had become of Ranier, after he

pushed Vance into the water? For that matter, what *was* he? The crazy idea struck her that he was a spirit who had delivered terrible messages to each person here, harbingers that no one was willing to talk about. And who could blame them, if they'd also been told that they were weak or selfish or prideful or a failure of one sort or another? She looked around the room at each soul, together but solitary in these lengthening hours, alone with private thoughts even in the company of friends. What would a . . . a being like Ranier say to a man like Tony? Or Vance?

It was fatigued thinking, dreamish thinking. She didn't even believe in spirits. But she recalled him standing firm in the waterfall current; she saw him pop up, desert dry, onto the top of Vance's trailer while it bobbed in the river; she saw her bookcase standing upright to cover the hole in her bedroom wall. And she didn't know what else to think.

Mirah, Ferti, and the boys had gone upstairs to sleep, though Danielle doubted Mirah would close her eyes. Tony had gone to Jonesy's for more drinks. Carver, free of Ferti's condescending eye, had joined them.

Simeon was flicking checkers off the board in that aimless kind of play that he started when he really ought to be sleeping. Danielle wanted to put Simeon into his own bed, but she didn't want to scale the stairs to a lonely home with a hole in its side. And she worried that Tony might make a late appearance at her condo, which was really his, and want to repeat his earlier apologies and assurances with actions rather than words.

Not tonight, not tonight.

"Tell me a story." When Simeon was tired, his wishes were commands.

"Let's find a book," she said softly. It was a good enough reason to go upstairs. Then she realized that Simeon hadn't asked the question of her. He wasn't even sitting next to her, where he'd been thirty seconds ago, transforming checkers into missiles. He had squeezed himself between Zeke and Vance on the sofa, and the gentle giant Ziggy laid his chin on Simeon's knees.

"What kind of stories do you like?" Vance asked.

"Superheroes!" said Simeon.

Danielle intervened. "Simeon, they're talking. I'm sorry," she said to the men.

"It's fine," said Vance.

"I'll read you a story upstairs."

"But I want him to *tell* me one."

"It's late."

"Really, I don't mind," Vance said. "I'm a

little out of practice, but I can come up with something. Superheroes, huh?"

"Like Ranier!" Simeon insisted.

"Who's Ranier?"

"He's a superhero!" Simeon said, and he raised fists above his head. "The guy you saw underwater."

Danielle didn't know what to say. Vance's lips parted in surprise for a second before he replied.

"Well, I don't know any stories about underwater superheroes. Is it okay if I tell you a different one?"

"Sure."

Danielle sat back down on the ottoman in front of the fireplace. The warmth stopped her from protesting further, though Vance's eyes sagged. He had to be more exhausted than she was.

"On a planet not very far away from here, and not all that long ago (but a little while before you were born), two brothers got into a fight. Their dad was away, so he wasn't around to settle their argument."

"Where was their mom?"

"Uh, their mom. Well, their mom thought it was good for them to work out their differences without her butting in right away."

Simeon accepted this explanation.

"Their dad was gone because he was the

leader of their village, and their people were in trouble, so he left the village to find help."

"What kind of trouble?"

"The village was located in a beautiful place where there was plenty of food and water and fun things to do. It was such a great place that their enemies wanted it. The enemies were spying on the village and making plans to take it. So the father left to ask friends in neighboring villages for help fighting them off."

"Couldn't he just call them?"

Vance shook his head. "No phones. But his boys were smart young men, and before he left, their dad gave each of them superpowers. The oldest brother — his name was Sol — he got the power to control the sun. He could warm a cold day, and he could help plants grow. He could also set dry fields on fire, or make his enemies so hot that they didn't have the energy to fight."

"I would make every day sunny," Simeon said. "What did the little brother get?"

"His name was Ren, and he got the power to control the rain."

"I'd want to be in charge of the sun."

"Well, Ren could do some pretty neat things with the rain. He could make the village clean. He could give pure water to thirsty people. He could make swimming holes just about anywhere!"

"I like to swim."

"Me too. So their dad left them in charge of the village, and he told them that they should stay there until he came back with help. He told them that they must stay together and help their people, and under no circumstances should they leave the village undefended. They must not lose faith, he said. Then as soon as night fell and the enemy couldn't see him, he took a horse and sneaked away through enemy lines.

"The very next morning the bad guys attacked, and the brothers defended their village. Sol brought fire from the sun to build a wall of flames on the hillside between the village and the enemy. When the flames burned out, Ren brought such a flood of rain that the earth couldn't soak it up, and it washed away all the men trying to scramble up the scorched land. Then Sol raised the sun to dry everything out, and Ren brought a light rain to clear the air of smoke and to fill the jugs with clean water. The sun came out again, and vegetables grew in the gardens and fruit dropped from the trees. They went on like this for days, and no enemy ever got near the village gates. Soon the bad guys began to give up.

"One day they didn't attack, and the older

brother, feeling pretty good about what they'd accomplished, became restless. He sat for hours facing west, wondering why his dad hadn't come back. Sol began to worry that the enemies might have gone after him, or that he was injured and needed help. At the end of the day, he announced to Ren that he was going to go in search of their father.

"And so their argument began. Ren reminded Sol that they were supposed to stay together. Sol said Ren should come with him. Ren refused. *Remember,* he said, *we're not supposed to leave the village. If we go, who will defend them?* Sol believed that the enemy was scared off and wouldn't try again for several days — enough time to find their father and bring him home.

" 'What if he needs us and we don't go find him?' Sol argued. 'Our people can't go on without him.'

" 'You have to obey his instructions,' Ren said. 'I won't go against his word.'

"Sol saddled a horse and tried to run away. Ren called down such rain that the ground became too muddy for the horse to keep his footing. The poor animal broke his leg and Sol could not continue. He fought back with such a blaze of sunshine that it dried the earth in an instant and blinded his brother. Ren was in such pain that he couldn't fight back. He lost consciousness, and when he came around, Sol was gone.

"In his brother's absence, Ren discovered he could no longer control the rain. Without the sun to balance it, the rain poured without letting up, and it soon drowned their fields of food and brought a terrible chill to the village. It became difficult to build fires out of wet wood. Many people got cold and sick. Ren developed a terrible fever and couldn't get out of bed. He had nightmares that prevented him from resting and began to believe in things that didn't exist.

"Sol fared no better. When he disobeyed his father and left the village, the sun beat down on him with terrible heat. He went through his water supply too quickly, and then he couldn't find a river or a well. They had all dried up. He thought of turning back, but he was too ashamed. He kept going. He didn't make it far before his horse collapsed, and Sol got a sunburn so severe that he couldn't even walk. And when rumors reached the enemy that the village had lost its leader *and* his sons, they threw a party and made plans to burn the village down."

Danielle murmured, "Vance. He's *five*."

Wide-eyed distress was distorting Simeon's face. Vance cleared his throat. "But this story has a happy ending. It's about superheroes, after all."

"The hero always wins," Simeon said.

"Right. And in this story, we have *two* of them, remember?"

Simeon grinned at him.

"Actually, Simeon, there are three in this story. The bad guys are completely outnumbered. There's another superhero I haven't told you about."

"Who?" he said. "Is it Ranier?"

"No." Vance winked at Danielle. "It was their mom."

Simeon blew a raspberry. "Girls can't be superheroes!"

"Sure they can."

"What's her power?"

"Wisdom."

"What's wisdom?"

"Special smarts. Don't you think your mom is smart?"

"Yeah, but she's not a superhero. This story is weird."

"The true ones usually are. Well, the mother of Sol and Ren, who had never lost hope that her husband would return, was quite angry to lose all three of the men she loved, so she made a plan to bring them back. She had to wait for just the right time, because if she argued with her sons while they were strong, they would only fight her. So she waited long enough for them to grow weak. But she couldn't wait too long, or what would happen?"

"The bad guys would take the village!"

"Exactly. But because she was wise, she knew exactly how long to wait. And so, at just the right time, before the enemies were too close, she got together a team of men to go rescue her son from the desert land he'd created for himself, and then she convinced the village healers to tend to Ren, though they blamed him for all the illness in the place."

"I don't think they were very good superheroes."

"Sometimes even superheroes don't get it right the first time. That's something you've got to remember if you plan on being a superhero when you grow up." He clapped a hand over Simeon's knee. "Got it?"

"Got it."

"So, at the very moment that Sol came back into the village — the very second his body passed through the gate on the stretcher the men had made for him — the rain stopped. And so did Ren's awful nightmares. His mind became as clear as the sky, and everyone who was cold became warm, and the sun painted the village with color again. And he brought a jug full of rainwater to his brother and poured it all over Sol's sunburned body, and the blisters and cracked skin became new again. Sol asked Ren to forgive him and Ren did, because he loved his brother so much.

"The sky became so bright with light that the enemies lurking in the surrounding forests were exposed. There were no shadows to hide them, and the brothers went out together, shoulder to shoulder and back to back, Sol with a blazing shield and Ren with a bolt of lightning, and they didn't leave a single bad guy standing."

Simeon's eyebrows were high in his hairline, and his chin was tucked all the way back to his throat.

"The end," Vance said.

Simeon's expression didn't change.

"You're hard to impress."

"They didn't even fly," Simeon said.

"Not all heroes fly."

"Do they get capes?"

"If you want it that way. I don't see why not."

"Do they do tricks?"

"I thought the rain and sun bits were pretty tricky, don't you?"

"Something should blow up."

Vance considered this. "Maybe I can work that into the ending."

Simeon nodded conservatively. "What about their dad?"

Vance broke eye contact with Simeon for the first time since beginning the telling. He pressed the fingertips of both hands against each other and studied them for a second. Then he looked up at the boy. "I'll have to tell you that part of the story another time. It's getting late, and I think your mom is ready for me to let you go."

"My dad died," Simeon said.

Vance leaned forward and put his face inches away from the boy's.

"Was he a superhero?"

"Totally. He could drive boats, and he saved lots of people."

"Then you and I have even more in common than I thought." Vance extended his right hand.

Simeon took Vance's fingers and pumped once. "Cool."

The look Vance offered Danielle over the top of Simeon's head seemed apologetic.

"You're quite a storyteller," she said as her son, finally satisfied, gave up the conversation and lost himself in rubbing Ziggy's ears and staring at the fire. She slipped off the ottoman and sat on the floor beside Simeon. There was enough room for her to sit there without intruding on Vance's space. The firelight cast her shadow across his tired frame.

At the other end of the sofa, Zeke snored.

"Did you make up that tall tale?" she asked.

"It's not entirely fiction, if that's what you mean."

That wasn't what she meant at all, but she was too surprised by his claim to think of another way of putting it.

"I'm sorry about your husband," he said.

No one had said that to her in quite a long time. Though her own sorrow had faded, it was still present, in a misty kind of way, and those words were like a welcome friend lifting the gauze curtain and peering into the room where she sometimes went alone to sit with her pain.

"I am too."

"What was his name?"

"Danny."

"I didn't mean for the story to bring up anything painful for Simeon."

"I don't think it did. He adjusted more quickly than I did. It's been a couple of years. It's getting easier."

"What makes it easier?" he asked.

"Staying busy. Finding my own strength."

He stretched his legs out in front of him and slouched on the sofa until he could rest his head on the cushion behind him.

"When my father died," he said, "I didn't have any strength at all. I just rolled over and quit."

"How old were you?"

"Fifteen."

"Tough age to lose your dad."

"I don't think there's an easy age."

"But you came through, right? Look at you: saving drowning kids, hauling yourself out of capsized trailers and swollen rivers, going fishing for dead men."

His grunt was a dubious laugh. "Whatever I've got didn't come from me."

"Then where do you get it?"

"From God. From faith in Jesus Christ." *Amen*

In her mind, the gauzy curtain of separation fell between them. She poked her mental finger into it, driving it into his chest on the other side, pushing him away.

"The God who takes good men before their time."

"It's confusing, isn't it?" It wasn't the defense she expected him to give. Vance's eyes on her were compassionate. He didn't make any effort to talk her out of her opinion of the God who was, apparently,

working out for him. She would have preferred an argument to pity. She shifted so
she didn't have to face him.

He let her go, turned his eyes upward
toward the ceiling. She stole a quick look at
him and regretted severing the conversation. He was only trying to tell her his story,
not her own. She was selfish, selfish.

Ranier's accusation stood before her like a
smug judge.

She wanted nothing more in that moment
than to prove him wrong.

"So what parts of your tale . . . aren't
true?" she asked.

He closed his eyes. She thought he hadn't
heard her. She decided not to repeat herself.

She missed Danny.

The gas fire let off a short hiss.

"The happy ending," he whispered. She
almost didn't hear it. "I made that up."

"Why? Is the reality too gruesome?"

"I don't know."

"What do you mean, you don't know?
How does the story really end?"

"It hasn't ended yet," he said. "But I'll let
you know."

The firelight softened the strong lines of
Vance's profile. With his eyes closed and his
body finally relaxed, he appeared vulnerable. He didn't explain. She couldn't ask.

They sat together, neither sleeping.
Sometime in the night, the rain stopped.

21

True darkness gave birth to nightmares that didn't go away upon waking. This one had started as a family excursion, a backwoods cross-country ski trek to a remote cabin, just Vance, Pete, and their father. On that post-holiday January weekend, the world belonged to them alone. At the hideaway they hunted deer, barbecued venison, read books, and moved around the one-room shack in the comfort of their own spare company.

In the evenings, by the light of an oil lamp that gave off greasy fumes, Vance read a biography of David Fisher and copied various perspectives of the architect's Dynamic Towers into his sketchbook, which was filled with efforts to mimic his idols. Frank Lloyd Wright's Fallingwater, the Dubai Marina, and Frank Gehry's floppy Lou Ruvo Center took up most of the pages. Pete slouched on the sofa over his electronic notepad, toggling among NASDAQ, the *Wall Street Journal,* the beginnings of an undergraduate thesis that he claimed would get him into the Harvard Business School, even though his freshman year of college didn't begin until the fall, and a fourth site that Vance believed had nothing to do with his intellectual acumen.

Eventually, when their father tired of his own book, he brought out the poker chips and a brown bottle of Jim Beam, his one modest indulgence, coaxing his sons away from their solitary pursuits. They were lured by the stakes: the cot by the fireplace went to the winner, extra chores to the loser.

Pete was the loser the night before they packed up to head home. Vance wondered for years if Pete's soreness about this defeat explained any part of what happened after.

They skied out on a Sunday morning, intending to beat a blizzard that was rolling in earlier than expected. Their father towed a sled carrying the buck they'd felled, and even then, Vance had trouble keeping up with his pace.

The sky was still blue over the hills of virgin snow when they reached their truck at the trailhead. The only marks in the white ground were the ski tracks they'd made three days earlier and rabbit prints in a ruler-straight line from one tree to another. A breeze that felt like springtime pushed puffs of fluffy snow out of the towering evergreens' fingers and dotted Vance's yellow-tinted goggles. He felt irritated that an incorrect forecast might have cut off their adventure prematurely. He said to Pete that it would have been better to be stranded out here than stuck in a stuffy high school classroom, and Pete agreed with him. It might have been the last time they agreed on anything.

The snow started falling an hour later, while they were still on the tipsy dirt roads of the high country. The fierce winds were crouched behind the ridge and sprang out at them like a mountain lion as they came around an exposed bend.

"There she is," their father had said of the weather. Snow clouds riding the back of the wind came up behind the trees without further introduction, dimming the sun like lights going down in a theater. The speed with which the blizzard came up was startling to the brothers, but their father showed no concern for it, having traveled the mountain roads in wintertime often throughout his life.

He drove them down from the rugged peaks safely and didn't find trouble until their truck flattened out on the valley floor, where winds tangled with each other, dropping snow and then lifting it into the air again, tossing it into ten- and twelve-foot drifts against the foothills. Dad pulled over twice when the swirling storm became a white blind across the windshield.

After the second time, when they had a fleeting view of the county road that turned off to the south, toward home, the truck would not rise out of the slush. All four wheels became mired in snow and ice, spinning against the slick surfaces even with the four-wheel drive engaged. Snow already was piled up to the bottom of the wheel wells. They tried to rock the truck out but only dug themselves deeper. They tried digging but didn't have anything to put in front of the wheels for traction. Pete and Vance climbed into the truck bed with the dead buck and their cross-country ski gear. The protective tarp that wrapped the venison was white with snow, and ice was piling in the corners. They jumped and slipped and jumped some more, trying to bounce the vehicle out while Dad floored the gas.

After twenty minutes of this Pete fumbled his way back into the cab, and Vance dropped onto the jump seat by going through the rear window. His sweat was freezing into a thin sheet of ice under his bangs. He took off his knit cap, breathless, and sat sideways behind his father's seat. Dad joined them, shutting out the icy wind with a slam of the door.

"We could walk it," Pete suggested.

"Better to wait it out," said Dad.

"It's only two miles more to the junction. We've got the skis."

"Might as well be two hundred in this. Take one step away from this truck and you won't be able to find your way back to it."

"I hate not doing anything," Pete huffed, putting a foot up on the dash.

"Who says that waiting isn't doing something?" their father said.

The silence the three men sat in now lacked the restfulness of their tiny cabin.

"How long?" Vance asked.

"Long as it takes," Dad said.

Snow jammed the tailpipe like a rag and would fill their shelter with deadly gas if they ran the engine too long. Pete said they were more likely to die from gas produced by Vance, and Vance accused him of trying to divert attention from his own contributions to the sour air.

They started in an optimistic cycle of Dad clearing away drifts from the back of the four-wheel drive, scooping out the tailpipe with a stick, then running the engine and heater for fifteen minutes or so with the windows cracked. Within a couple of hours the effort to keep the car warm seemed pointless, though they tried to preserve a sacred space around the truck with their one small emergency shovel, a squat thing with a two-foot shaft and a nine-inch-wide metal blade. They scooped snow away from the truck at regular intervals. The exercise was a bit like breaking out of prison with a spoon. They brought sleeping bags, food, and water from the truck bed into the cab. They spent precious minutes scanning the radio stations for weather reports but picked up only static. They took turns doing the work outside as it became more difficult to stand up under the windy blasts. Visibility dropped to inches, and the precipitation became heavier and wetter. Sometimes the battered truck rocked like a cradle.

It was a great story in the making, Vance thought. He'd probably miss school on Monday after all. Their father told stories and Pete made up goofy lyrics to old camp songs. *One hundred snow-flakes are froze in my nose, one hundred snowflakes are froze. If one of them should happen to thaw, ninety-nine snowflakes will shout out, "That blows!"* Vance ate an apple for lunch and, inspired by the core, sketched a design for a modern skyscraper. He ate a bag of chips for supper and read his book on David Fisher as long as the light lasted without once feeling anxious about their situation.

As the daytime temperatures dropped, he pulled his bag up over his head and cinched the tie around his nose and mouth. He didn't think he'd be able to sleep without a place to stretch out his legs, and the very expectation seemed to hold real rest at arm's length. He got stuck in a shallow doze, aware from time to short time of a door opening and a frigid gust elbowing its way into the cab. He heard the low tones of his father and brother talking to each other but didn't catch their conversation, wasn't interested in it, took a careless and meandering mental walk away from it.

When Vance woke, the air of the cab was black except for the huffing clouds of breath pulsing in front of his father's and brother's mouths. The digital clock on the dash was too faint to read. The midnight hours were heavy and thicker than he'd expected them to be. His right foot was tingling, and when he shifted to free whatever nerves he had pinched, he kicked his father's seat.

Dad gasped and was awake.

"Sorry," Vance mumbled.

270

"What time is it?"

His father was closer to the clock than he was. Vance turned his face to the back window and worked his shoulder into a tolerable position.

"Father in heaven," Dad whispered.

Vance lifted his chin. "What?"

"It's eight in the morning."

"Can't be."

"According to the clock."

Vance wormed his own hand out of the sleeping bag and punched the light button on the side of his wristwatch. By the green glow, the truth was plain as the darkness encasing them: while they slept, the snow had hemmed them in and blocked the daylight.

Vance stayed silent, expecting his father to have answers. Pete stirred.

"Pete, where's the shovel?" Dad asked.

After a few groggy seconds, Pete pushed the shovel at his feet over to his dad's side of the floor for another routine round of cleanup. He came fully awake when Dad started the engine.

"What are you doing?"

Dad punched on the dome lights, and when Vance's eyes stopped squinting, he could see the surprise in Pete's eyes and wondered if the anxiety was as obvious in his own.

The engine was on only long enough for Dad to roll down the window. The snow on the outside kept its shape as a glistening pebbled wall that looked like shattered safety glass. By the dim light of the cab, Dad started chipping away at it with the narrow shovel, which was almost too big for the task, showering the driver's seat with ice that melted quickly under his body heat.

As Dad made progress, the heaping became lighter and less wet. He was standing on the seat, leaning up into the vertical tunnel he'd created, when he reached the surface. Morning light turned the snow tube a pale blue-green. A howl of chill wind dropped straight down into the cab. Vance sank into his bag like a cowering turtle.

Standing on the door's window frame, Dad's waist was finally level with the new surface of the earth. He stood there for a dreadful minute before coming back in, his face red and wind-bitten and contrasting with his bright blue snow bibs.

"It looks like there's a break in the storm," he announced.

"You mean there's more coming?" Pete said.

"Hard to say. But for now, this valley is under a clear sky."

Dad handed the shovel over the seat to Vance. Pete leaned away from the blade as it passed by his head. "Vance, I want you to dig into the back and get my skis. I put them right on top yesterday, right in front of your window."

"Did you know this was going to happen?" Pete asked.

"I hoped it wouldn't."

Vance felt clumsy working in the tight space, with nowhere to put the snow but on the truck's bench seat. Much of it fell off the shovel and littered the back. Dad and Pete scooped it into a plastic bread bag and toted it out the tunnel, but the progress was sloppy and took a long time.

"Where are you going?" Vance asked.

"I'm going to make a run for the junction," Dad said. He opened the glove box and pulled out a compass.

"I'm coming too," Pete said.

"You boys stay here, stay together. Where's the survival kit?"

"Back here," Vance said. The red plastic box was stowed under the second jump seat. He hesitated, not sure whether to go after his father's skis first or the kit.

"We'll both come with you," Pete said.

"No. The truck's sheltered. You can stretch our food and water for three more days if

I'm not dipping into it."

Vance felt guilty for his indulgence of the chips the night before.

"We don't really need each other's help to sit around," Pete argued. "But what if something happens to you?"

"Nothing's going to happen to me. C'mon, Vance. Let's have those skis."

When Vance found the first ski tip, he put the shovel down and pried the ski out, feeding the great length of it toward his father and out the front door before it had fully come in the rear window. Dad stood it up on the door, the front end poking up into the sky.

"You'd think that in this day and age meteorologists would be smarter," Pete complained. Vance thought he was trying to sound like their dad.

"They're not the problem," Dad said. "The real stinker is that in this day and age we think we know more than we really do. It doesn't hurt to be reminded now and then how little we actually control."

The second ski was easier to get through, but as Dad pulled it forward, Vance's jacket caught on the toe clip and pulled him off his unbalanced knees. He fell into the front seats and snapped the ribbon-wide ski in two.

"Nice move," Pete said.

"You come do it," Vance retorted.

"Just get another one," Dad instructed. They were all the same size and, for the situation, interchangeable.

By the time a complete pair stood in the tunnel with their poles, Vance's fingers were burning with cold. His gloves were wet and useless. He took them off and shoved his hands under his armpits to warm them, feeling uneasy about his dad's departure.

Pete shoved a water bottle and a bag of peanuts at their father, who tucked them into his jacket.

"Stay here, stay together," he repeated. "The minute you leave this truck I don't have any way of knowing where you are."

"If you're not back in a day I'm coming after you," Pete said.

Dad zipped himself all the way up to the neck and pulled his face muffler off the dash. "Are you a boy or a man, Pete?"

"C'mon, Dad. Really?"

"Prove it to me by doing the smart thing. The hard thing. Stay put." He pulled the muffler down over his nose and mouth. A wink at Vance was his only good-bye, then he climbed out of the truck.

Pete and Vance didn't say anything to each other while they listened to their father kick his boots into the toe clips and find his balance in the deep snow. The powder would make for tough progress. Pete sulked.

Vance clambered over the seat and hefted himself out of the cab with his numb hands. His father was already headed south, looking small like a lost blue jay in the snow-covered landscape, where the trees seemed to have no trunks and the county road had disappeared. He should have been gliding, skimming the top of the snow. Instead, his moves looked more like a shuffle. The shiver that passed through Vance was not from the cold.

The sky above him was a weak blue eye plagued with gray cataract clouds. They swirled in impatient turns at the edges of clarity, threatening to press in on anyone who dared to pass. Vance watched his father until the clouds swooped in behind him like a flock of vultures and the wind started shrieking again with hungry cries. Their terrible bird droppings of white snow came down thick this time, smearing the distinction between land and sky, and quickly filling in the tunnel that rose from the truck.

22

By morning Eagle's Talon was an island. The isthmus had been flattened to a mere riverbed, and the turbulent waterfall was reduced to a steady current because there was nothing left for water to fall over.

And what had become of the rest of the world? That was the question on Vance's mind as he stood on the end of number 12's dock, straining to see across the wide body of water that had once been a cove. Gray spirits of fog caressed the water, soothing it. The waterlogged air turned yellow daylight silver. It blocked his view of the mainland and of all the condominium units he'd built south of number 10. The foundation there remained in position on its supporting poles, though several inches higher than it had yesterday. Nearly a foot, Vance estimated.

Enrique's moored boat bumped against the end of the dock in a steady rhythm.

Danielle appeared at his side. "Mirah's going crazy. In her quiet way. The baby's getting cranky. She's waking him up constantly to be sure he's okay. And she still can't get through to her husband at the hospital."

"Not even on Tony's phone?"

"I guess not." Danielle put her hands on her hips.

"Has Tony said anything about his helicopter?" Vance asked.

"Only that it's still too foggy to fly."

"The pilots can't estimate when this will lift?"

"All I hear is Tony's side of the conversation. Which has involved a lot of huffing and puffing and getting mad about the weather." Danielle shook her head.

"We can't wait. Sam needs a hospital. It might already be too late for him."

"Is he still unconscious?"

He nodded.

"I guess we'll have to use the boat."

Vance agreed. "We should be able to cut across the current right here. Sam, Mirah, and her boys should be the first to go as soon as Enrique's ready to row."

"I'm afraid Enrique's not going to be good for much this morning," she said. "Ferti's pouring coffee down him at the moment,

278

but he's going slow."

Vance sighed. The choice Enrique made last night had been Vance's choice often enough in the past. "Then I'll take the first load."

She nodded. They stood side by side, both looking out over the water. "I don't like that you can't see the other side," she said. "A half a mile doesn't seem like it should be so far away, until you can't see it."

"It's a cove. Was a cove. The other side is hard to miss blindfolded."

"Unless the shoreline has been as radically transformed as that isthmus."

Vance had considered the possibility. "It'll take several trips to get everyone across."

"Baxter should go next," Danielle suggested. "It's pretty much a sure thing that his hand is broken. And Ferti. She has family. A couple of sisters and their daughters."

"You and Simeon should go before Ferti," he said. "She'd say the same thing."

Danielle looked away and cleared her throat. "I should wait with Tony. I'll tell Mirah the plan."

She turned to go back inside and bumped into Tony, whose hand was raised in front of his chest defensively as she crashed into him.

"Maybe you should run the plan by me

first," he said. "Seeing as you both work for me."

Tony regarded Vance as if he had been plotting a mutiny.

"I'm not your employee," Vance said. "Especially not in a situation like this."

Danielle took Tony's hand. "Vance's going to take Sam and Mirah's family —"

"Not Vance," Tony said, lifting his eyes. "I want you to stay here."

"Why?" Vance said.

"Because you know this building better than anyone else."

"What's there to know?"

"How to fix damages that still haven't made themselves known."

Tony's excuse floated around Vance like the mist, cold and not exactly transparent. He wondered if Tony was plotting his own escape.

"So you're going to take them across?" Vance asked.

"The captain must stay with his ship," Tony said.

This surprised Vance. "You want to be the last to go?"

"It's only right," Tony said. Vance supposed it was, though the gesture had a political aroma.

"Then who did you have in mind? Enrique's hung over. Sam's unconscious. Baxter's hand is no good."

"Jonesy already agreed," Tony said.

Jonesy. The overweight man whose heart condition forced him into early retirement. Vance tried to choose his words carefully. "His weight might be a problem. For the boat's capacity."

"He's strong." Tony wouldn't look him in the eye.

"His heart —" Danielle said.

"All the more reason to get him to safety soon."

"What about Carver?" she asked.

"Says he wants to wait."

"And I want a green chili burrito for breakfast," Vance said. "What any of us wants right now has nothing to do with it."

Tony shrugged. "Carver's not strong enough to row across a bathtub."

"Which is why I should take them. Or you. Really — *Jonesy*?"

Tony refused to respond.

The relative risk of sending Jonesy rather than Vance was so high that he had the crazy idea the former police detective had strong-armed Tony into sending him first. But Vance had nothing but a prejudicial history with Tony to support that notion.

Vance tried a different approach. "It's Enrique's boat. He's experienced with it. Let's wait for him to sober up."

"The longer we wait, the smaller our opportunity," Tony said. "So we're agreed: Jonesy, Mirah and her boys, Sam. They go first."

Danielle said again, "I'll tell Mirah," and this time Tony let her go.

Tony continued, "My helicopter can take four at a time. When things clear up, Carver, Baxter, Ferti, and Zeke will go first — the oldest and the injured. You, me, Danielle and the boy, and Enrique will go second. Everyone gets to the mainland safely. Do you have any problems with that?"

"Sounds like you don't expect Jonesy to make it back."

Tony turned to follow Danielle into the building. "With my plan, it won't matter if he does or doesn't."

"Maybe Carver would consider giving Danielle and Simeon his seat on the first flight," Vance said, lifting his eyes to the foggy sky. "Women and children."

Tony paused, turned. "I want them to stay with me. You understand."

"Why do I get the impression you want me to stay with you too?"

"Too many leaders in a crisis only leads to chaos."

Vance rolled his eyes.

"After this blows over," Tony said in a subdued tone, "we'll evaluate what's next, you and me. Who knows? This storm might be a sheep in wolf's clothing, Vance. The perfect cover for everything that went wrong here yesterday. Maybe no one has to lose his job after all."

Clearly, that wouldn't be for Vance to say.

Eagle's Talon had been Vance's idea before Tony Dean ever became involved in it, and it was at times like these that Vance wished there had been another way.

Inspired by the so-called floating architecture of flood-resistant seaside homes in the Netherlands and Japan, the original Eagle's Talon design team had envisioned a bohemian neighborhood that operated as a commune. They began to assemble amphibious houses on large, round pontoons, which gave them the look of houseboats mounted on rockets. Unfortunately, the homes were more artistic than structurally sound, and the vision was out of touch with financial realities. Halfway to completion, the effort was brought to a halt by the suicide of the project's brainchild.

When Vance first saw the forsaken, incomplete structures, his mind was captivated by the idea of these waterborne dwellings. With the exception of a six-year period when unrestrained alcoholism had put his skills into a catatonic state, he had been amassing his credentials as an architect and project manager since he was old enough to assemble Lincoln Logs and Erector Sets. The challenge of building on water excited his creative spirit.

Even more, his heart was held hostage by the daring squatters who had taken up residence in the deteriorating structures. These people had walls but no plumbing, blankets but no heat, curtains but no windows. Many of them had jobs, some of them had kids, and all of them had stories of hard times. They had resourcefulness on their side, though, and community that would have warmed the original builder's heart. They took care of each other.

Through them, Vance began to coax out an idea of building real homes for people who had none, in a place as stunning as this. Perhaps even on this very spot.

Vance began with the intention of buying the land. At the time Eagle's Talon was owned by the suicidal artist's grandchildren. They were a contentious bunch who'd regained some of their ancestor's wealth. They were united only by a common interest in "worthwhile risk." Vance quickly came to understand that this meant they put their investments into casinos, not neo-urban housing. If not for the state's laws against gambling, they would have transformed Eagle's Talon into a Little Las Vegas decades before Vance ever came along.

As it was, the family had encountered considerable trouble selling that "worthless" strip of land, no thanks to the projected costs of undoing what their grandfather had already done. If Vance wanted that land he could have it, they said. For the right price.

In terms of sentimental value, the peninsula turned out to be very nearly priceless.

Vance liked to think that if he and Pete had been on speaking terms, his financial whiz of a brother might have saved him from ever turning to Tony Dean. Pete had become extremely successful in the fourteen years since they'd last spoken. Sweating and stammering, fearing rejection far more than financial disappointment, Vance called and invited him to dinner.

Pete said, "I don't give handouts to people in exchange for a two-star dinner."

"It's not a handout. For me. Exactly," Vance said. And knowing right then that Pete would never have dinner with him, Vance gave him an elevator pitch about

Eagle's Talon. But fourteen years of blame crushed his confidence. He mangled his presentation.

"Good luck with your hobby," Pete said, and hung up.

Vance needed a philanthropist, but his proposal was quickly scorned within the small and tight community of Port Rondeau. His idea was reckless, he was told. An expensive project that couldn't be economically sustained or socially duplicated and most certainly would fail. It was so outlandish that his reputation began to precede him. Someone started a rumor that his alcoholism was still alive and well and tainting his common sense, and soon no one would even grant him an appointment.

The last one to meet with him, a fundraiser from Georgia, put Vance on a different path by suggesting Tony Dean.

"Tony Dean?" Vance was stunned by the suggestion. "The Port Rondeau developer?"

"The very one."

"But he's a businessman. A profiteer, even. And there's no money in an idea like mine."

"He's also a businessman with political aspirations. Everyone loves a businessman these days. He might catch your vision for reasons *you* haven't even thought of."

Within a week Vance understood. He was surprised when he prayed and felt no inner warning, no caution against requesting an appointment. Zeke encouraged him to pursue the lead. Vance was further surprised when Tony granted an appointment on the Georgian's referral. And he was shocked when the light in the developer's eyes became a fire.

They met in Tony's office, a striking building on the southern banks of the Rondeau River. Vance felt like a tarnished penny tucked into a tall stack of crisp new Benjamins.

"Yes," Tony said, "yes. It's a great idea. A social experiment."

"I don't think *experiment* is the best word to describe what —"

"Imagine a city free of its indigent population," Tony said, stunning Vance into silence. "Cities around the country might be delivered of their low-income eyesores, while the very populations that cause so much indigestion are relocated to rooms with a view! Imagine the masses, both relieved and envious!" The man laughed aloud. "But who would dare complain, if their streets are clean and they don't want the land for themselves?"

Vance cleared his throat. "Eagle's Talon is

probably going to be an atypical example of
—"

"This is America, Mr. Nolan," Tony had said, leaning toward him. "Anything can be duplicated."

"This peninsula isn't large enough to empty any city of people who need affordable housing. Twelve buildings, ninety-six sizable units —"

"You let me worry about that kind of detail," Tony said, and Vance was vaguely repulsed. The politician's motivations, though not entirely clear, were definitely nothing like Vance's.

Vance left the meeting wishing he had never described his plans to the man, but there was nothing he could do to prevent Tony from making a private offer to the owners of Eagle's Talon. Apparently his price was right, and in short order the peninsula was Tony's, and the development was Vance's.

Tony gave him access to an account bearing half of the venture's projected funding — Tony's own cash. Another quarter of the funds had already been committed by political associates and would be on deposit within ninety days. The remaining balance would be a breeze to drum up, Tony promised.

The night Vance got the green light, he spent more time than usual in prayer, unconvinced that Tony was an ideal partner. He stayed late at the one-room loft that was his first office, where he was the only full-time and sometimes-paid employee. The loft was on the stuffy upper floor of an old Port Rondeau wharf building. His Bible was open atop a stack of schematics on his drafting table, but he was no longer reading it. He was staring out the window, watching daylight fade and the river's blues intensify. The yellow light of the wharf lamps dangling from their posts was too weak to penetrate his dusky room.

"Is this what you want, God?"

The sound of God's voice was never audible to Vance. It was more of a cool sensation at the front of his mind. A clarity. Still, there were plenty of times when he wondered whether these impressions were from God or his own wishful thinking, and this was such a time. The thing that usually sorted it out for him was a sense of peace. In the presence of God, Vance's anxiety always faded away to nothing. In the presence of his own limited thoughts, his doubts festered and grew.

That night Vance slept and woke rested. He started the new work with perfect peace.

And quite a lot of enthusiasm.

That ended the day that Tony appeared on-site, when the project was well under way, and announced that he had changed his mind. He hadn't been able to secure the financial resources needed to complete the high-end, low-income housing, he announced without apology. To recoup his investment, he said, the buildings would be finished with luxury living in mind. He could sell them for a terrific profit. There was so little regret in his manner that Vance believed this might have been his plan from the very beginning.

Vance took the news by praying the 119th Psalm silently. *Remember the word to Your servant, upon which You have caused me to hope. This is my comfort in my affliction, for Your word has given me life.*

Vance's hopes lay in the bottom of his heart. He regarded them with a considerable amount of grief.

Within the hour Sam, Mirah, Jonesy, and the boys were in the boat, weighed so heavily in the water that there was only an inch between the river and the lip of the aluminum frame. Jonesy sat in the center out of necessity, looking far less confident with oars in his fists than he had been with a spatula and butcher knife. He was the only one not wearing a life jacket. There wasn't one large enough.

Mirah held her boys close. Jonesy faced Sam, who lay back on a pillow, still unaware of all the places his body had traveled in the past twelve hours, still ordering all who read the front of his T-shirt to *Get outta my way!*

Simeon had taken Ranier's cuff link back from Ziggy's harness and slipped it through the buttonhole of his jeans. Clinging to Danielle's hand, he leaned out toward the boat and gave a Matchbox car to Laith.

"You can borrow it until you get back," he said.

"You can watch one of my movies," Laith replied.

"Cool!"

"Take the current at an angle," Vance instructed Jonesy. "Don't try to cut straight across. You should hit the bank about a mile north of Port Rondeau. The bank's not too steep to get out there and climb up to the road."

Tony wore an artificial expression of concern. "I've texted my partner about bringing a car for Sam and Mirah," he said.

"It went through?" Jonesy asked, and his tone caught Vance's ear. It was condescension he heard.

"One can only hope." Tony's own remark was testy. "Have I ever let you down?"

"I expect the day to come." A sheen of sweat put a glow on Jonesy's brow. Humidity? Anxiety? Hypertension? Something else?

Tony gave him the name and number of his contact. "There should be someone on the road within the hour."

Jonesy said, "You all help yourselves to whatever I've got that you need, hear? Food, drink, blankets. Just in case — you know."

Mirah echoed him. "What's mine is yours." Everyone was nodding.

"I . . . uh . . . There's water up in my place. I filled some empty storage containers." Jonesy swiped at his brow and looked to Vance's reaction.

Vance sighed at this. Jonesy had just increased the likelihood that whatever might come out of their faucets now would be unfit to drink.

"You shouldn't have done that," he said.

Jonesy shrugged. "To me, some water seems better than no water."

"It would have been better if you'd just dipped your jugs in the river," Vance said. Which wasn't a half bad idea.

"Godspeed," Tony said. "We'll see you back here soon, Jonesy."

"Yup," Jonesy said.

Vance and Tony pushed the boat away from the dock. Tony didn't stay to watch them go. He and Carver went indoors while Vance watched in silence as the first refugees drifted into the fog's filmy hug.

Danielle and Simeon watched too.

As if mirroring Vance's deepest fears, the morning light found itself too weak to continue rising. It dimmed as the fog thickened and the burgeoning craft was swallowed.

23

The first rumbling passed through Eagle's Talon at two in the afternoon, six hours after Jonesy had gone. A low and monstrous growl passed through the earth like a warning, then silenced itself.

An hour later Simeon was sitting on Danielle's lap in the library alcove when the sun faded out so quickly that it became impossible to see the words of the picture book they were reading. Both of them looked up from the pages. It wasn't black outside the way Danielle would sometimes describe thick summer storm clouds. It was black like the-movie's-about-to-begin black, like stub-your-toe-on-the-furniture black, like bottom-of-the-Mariana-Trench black. It was black like a nightmare threatening to come night after night, the kind in which Danielle would try to run and not be able to move. Her pulse had increased as the light decreased, while she was doing nothing but sitting and watching.

This was a tangible darkness, blacker than the emotional pitch that had sucked up her heart after Danny's unexpected death.

In the center of the common area, someone turned the key in the gas fireplace. The firelight bounced off the glass-turned-mirror and cast a bleak shadow of anxiety over her usually bright son.

"Why is it so dark?" Simeon asked.

"I'm not sure. But don't worry, it'll be fine."

It would be fine. Everything had to turn out fine, one way or another, when the people involved in a problem applied themselves to solving it. This was the principle that had guided Danielle's life since the day Danny died. She wasn't the type of person who was energized by crisis; she didn't invite trouble into her life the way thrill-seekers or slackers did. On the contrary, she consciously avoided as many of life's obstacles as possible. All she had to do was work hard enough and stay three steps ahead of Simeon, shading his head from the sun with one hand and removing rocks from his path with the other.

But what was she supposed to do in a situation like this?

"Here! Use this." Simeon twisted Ranier's

cuff link out of his shirt's bottom buttonhole, which had been hidden by the book's covers, and held it up above the pages. Why was she surprised that the thing gave off enough light to see by?

They sat on the sofa where Slogan Sam had never regained consciousness. His absence and that of the others left a noticeable gap in the present gathering. Danielle most missed Laith, her son's only playmate. Enrique slept upstairs in the pristine model unit, where his post-hangover headache was sheltered from noise.

Baxter was pacing in the game room between the pool table and picture windows. Danielle had helped tape his bad hand to his good shoulder. It might have prevented further injury, but it did nothing to reduce the man's agitation. Zeke stood with him, occasionally speaking quiet words to him but mostly just being a calm presence. Baxter fidgeted with the black eight ball, turning it among his functioning fingers and occasionally rapping it against the glass of the blackened window. He muttered under his breath. The darkness set everyone on edge, but Danielle thought Baxter's restlessness was caused by whatever painkiller Ferti had found in Mirah's unit after her departure.

"At least this way Mirah won't be to

blame for anything," Ferti had said when she took the bottle of pills and a glass of water to Baxter. Her head was swathed in emerald green today, but the cheerful color couldn't hide the circles under her eyes. "They can arrest me if it comes to that. What on earth good does it do to deny a man what he needs, based on some law that really shouldn't apply in this situation?"

"It's like not being allowed to heal a man on the Sabbath," Carver had agreed.

"Not quite," Ferti shot back.

"Quite." His word had a bite that closed Ferti's own mouth. He tossed his ivy cap onto the bar and half sat, half leaned on a barstool, looking weighed down. But he softened his edge with that familiar, easy smile. "Both are about doing what's most loving for a fellow human being. But you wouldn't know anything about that, Ferti, would you?"

Danielle couldn't tell if he was being playful or prosecutorial. Ferti was speechless for the first time since Danielle had known her. And when Baxter's quaking fingers slopped his cup of water onto the sleeve of Ferti's dress, she let it drip onto the floor.

If anyone had noticed this odd exchange, they didn't seem to care about it. All but Simeon, who accepted his mother's words at face value, were muted by the incomprehensible afternoon scene. From where she sat, reading to her son, Danielle could see everyone. After medicating Baxter, Ferti busied herself with finding, arranging, and lighting more candles. Zeke and Ziggy returned to their place at the sofa. Carver eventually tired of Ferti's cold shoulder and joined Tony on the fireside chairs, legs crossed like they were having after-dinner drinks at a men's club — like there was nothing particularly terrible about their present situation. Vance's posture seemed more appropriate. He stood before the fireplace and looked into the flames, one hand braced against the mantel.

"Mom. Keep reading."

Danielle tipped the book toward the small glow of the odd cuff link and resumed her place. The rhyming story was one of Simeon's favorites. She'd read it so often that it was all but committed to memory. In any other situation she would have been able to read by rote while concentrating on something else entirely, like what she would make for dinner. But on this day, when the argument broke out and accusations started to escalate, her narrative flow was a little choppy.

"Did y'all know Ferti has a boat?" Carver said.

Tony lifted his face toward her, lips parted in surprise.

"What on earth?" Ferti's mouth fell open. "I do not."

"Title's in your name. Docked down in Port Rondeau. All you need to do is go get the key."

Ferti blinked and a light came into her eyes. "You didn't."

"Yes, ma'am, I did. Told you I would."

"After all these years?"

"I knew you'd come around one day."

("Mom," Simeon whined, "you're not paying attention.")

"Carver Lewis, I am not coming around. You had no business buying that boat *or* holding on to it. I didn't want it twenty-five years ago and I don't want it now. I don't need your boat —"

"Take a look at where we are right now, my love."

Tony leaned forward on his seat. "Does it matter whose boat it is? So long as we have a way to get it?"

"Now there's the pickle," Carver said. He laced his fingers together over his belly.

Baxter had stopped his pacing and approached the sofa to listen in. "Why doesn't

Ferti know she has a boat?" Baxter asked.

Carver said, "Why doesn't Ferti know she's as mortal as the rest of us and should accept a helping hand from time to time?"

"Your hand wanted to do more than help me," Ferti accused.

"Oh pooh, old girl. I never done anything but declare my love for you in a hundred languages, and you don't want to hear it. And I know as well as you do it ain't got nothing to do with me. No ma'am. It's all about you." Carver directed his explanation to Tony. "I bought this smart little cabin cruiser for Ferti —"

"Little! It's a yacht!"

("Mom! You *skipped* a page!")

Danielle turned back in Simeon's book and dropped the volume of her voice below the conversation she really wanted to hear.

"— back when she sold all she had to start up this dressmaking gig of hers for real. Sold her car, sold her house, would've sold her firstborn child if said child hadn't offered to feed her three squares a day."

"Your tales get taller by the year," Ferti said.

"She lived in a curtained-off loft of a downtown storefront for two years, when she could have lived in style on the water. All she had to do was accept the gift."

"I'm not the marrying type," Ferti huffed.

"There were no such strings attached to that boat, still aren't."

("No, it's *I can hold up TWO books,* not *these* books.")

"You should have sold that thing," Ferti said to Carver.

"You should have taken it."

"Didn't want to live on the water."

Carver's laughter was an explosion of mirth at Ferti's expense.

Danielle thought the conversation was absurd, the talk of luxuries and love while the world was covered in a black shroud. She realized she had completely stopped reading.

"Mom."

"Just wait a minute!" Danielle snapped, and the men glanced at her. She sighed and lowered her voice so only her son could hear. "Honey, I'm sorry. I need to listen right now. You look at this on your own for a few minutes."

Simeon pouted. She tried to move his small body off her lap, and he became inert. Dead weight. Irritated, she slipped out from under him before he was fully atop the seat cushion. He dramatically sagged to the floor. She let him stay there. He lifted the cuff link light to the pages he no longer wanted her to read.

Carver was saying, "Are you still too proud to accept my help?"

"Don't look at me," Ferti said. "You're the one with the key to the thing. You don't need my permission to do what you want to do."

Carver shook his head as if she'd missed the point.

"But do we have a way to go get the boat?" Tony asked this with the impatience of someone who'd asked the same question three or four times already.

No one responded. The firelight gave everyone something to focus on besides each other.

Ferti left the men and returned to Danielle and Simeon. She extended a hand to the little boy and said, "I was thinking you might like some Rice Krispie treats I made. Shall we fill you up with more milk and sugar than your mother might recommend?"

Simeon's muscles found strength again. He clapped the book closed and jumped up from the floor. "Yeah!"

"And I think Laith left a few of his toys behind, if you'd like to help me figure out what to do with them," she said.

"Okay."

"You fill me in on where this goes," Ferti

whispered to Danielle. "One woman to another. I want nothing more to do with it."

Danielle nodded. Simeon was already halfway up the flight of stairs, led by his bouncing jeweled light.

"Wait for an old lady," Ferti called out, and then she scooted after him.

Danielle joined the loose circle of men on the periphery while the lull in their ideas persisted.

"We could build a raft," Danielle said tentatively. She approached the group facing Tony, her eyes drawn to Vance's contemplative posture. "Out of my balcony. To get to Ferti's boat. Or whomever it belongs to."

Vance turned away from the fireplace and caught her eye. She couldn't interpret his look — not mocking, not surprised, but not supportive either.

Baxter kept his eyes on the restless eight ball turning in his fingers. Tony's gaze was comparatively admiring. He uncrossed his legs and leaned into the conversation. "That's not a bad idea. But maybe the dock would be a better candidate for a raft. Maybe we don't need a yacht if we have something big enough to carry all of us."

"You won't be able to navigate something that big," Vance said. "Not without some kind of motor."

"Okay, but Danielle's balcony would be the right size for — what? Three, four people? How many will it hold?"

Danielle said, "Maybe all of us if we cannibalize the exposed foam from number 11's foundation to support it." Danielle knew enough about the materials that kept Vance's buildings afloat to impress curious investors. The original seven-by-five-foot balcony floor had been reduced to something closer to six-by-four when it was snapped off the side of her home. She did a quick mental calculation and said, "I think we could salvage enough to support about twelve hundred pounds."

Vance was nodding. Reluctantly, she thought.

Tony clapped his hands onto his thighs. "Then we'll take as many people as want to help."

"Ferti and I will go," Carver said. "Forget what she says — she'll want to be the rescuer rather than the rescuee."

"I still think we should stay here for now," Vance said.

The room fell silent. Tony glared.

"We don't know what's happened to Ferti's boat. You've got a helicopter on its way, Tony, but it's not here yet. Why? Because it's not safe to fly, or because there's something going on out there that we don't even know about. How big is the power outage? What's this darkness all about? It doesn't seem the best time to put out in some jerry-rigged contraption."

"But now we need to consider that we don't have much water," Tony said.

"We have an entire river."

"Is it safe to drink in these circumstances?"

"Why wouldn't it be?"

The debate caused Danielle to blurt, "Ranier said that this building was the safest place we could be." She hadn't remembered his saying it until that very moment, and it came off her lips like a flash of confidence that was gone before she finished the sentence.

Carver said, "Who's Ranier?"

She cleared her throat. "The sculptor."

What was she supposed to say here?

She looked to Vance for help. "He was on the trailer with you."

Vance looked surprised. "When?"

"In the river."

Tony said, "Ranier Smith didn't get off the peninsula?"

"I don't think so."

Vance said, "I don't remember anyone."

"On top. He helped you out."

Vance was watching her closely. Zeke tilted an ear in the direction of her voice.

"I take it he went the way of our crane operator," Tony said. Danielle had no idea. "Not to speak ill of the dead, but he doesn't exactly sound like an authority on safety."

Zeke broke his long silence with an odd question. "What did this man look like?" he asked Danielle.

Tony laughed. "Why? Did you see him?"

"He looked like Danny," Danielle said. "My late husband. Tall, big ears. A little bowlegged. Expensive suit. And he smelled like saltwater. Like the ocean." For some reason this detail made her feel embarrassed. She should never have brought it up.

"Silver ring on his right hand?"

"Uh, yes. And these cuff links —"

"I'll be staying with Vance," Zeke said.

His logic made no sense to her.

Tony threw his hands up. "We can't just sit here."

"I guarantee you that those who stay with Vance won't be sitting around," Zeke said. "He's your man for this crisis."

Tony sighed impatiently.

"We've got some time," Vance argued. "We can continue stockpiling fresh water from the river, and there's enough food in Jonesy's place alone to last us a week."

"No refrigerator. The majority of it is already on its way to spoiling."

"Then we'll ration what we've got until we have to take more drastic measures."

Tony stood up to better argue eye to eye. Danielle had seen him in this mode dozens of times. "No matter how efficient we are, our resources here are finite! Over there, I have infinite resources. I have money, I have people, I have helicopters. I have the power to save, Vance. But not if we stay."

Carver was nodding at this good sense. The eight ball had stilled in Baxter's hand, and his shifting eyes were evaluating something beneath the surface of the men's argument.

"The truth is, you don't know if any of those things still exist," Vance said.

"Then I have to find out. That's what heroes do."

"Hero," Baxter scoffed. He lurked near Tony's chair. The concrete foreman was a head taller than the developer, but his stature was diminished by his slouch, his slinged hand, and his obvious reluctance to come within arm's reach of Tony's healthy fist.

"I think you're just making stuff up — I

don't think you have a real plan for us to get out of here. I think you knew Jonesy wouldn't come back. I think you knew your helicopter would be grounded. No, wait — I don't think you even *have* a helicopter."

"He does," Danielle said.

"Why would I lie?" Tony asked.

"Because that's what you do to get where you want to go. Isn't it? Isn't that what you were going to do to my crew — make up some story about how the whole pump-truck accident was my man's fault? And if that didn't work, you'd make sure Vance took the heat."

Tony looked at Vance.

"*He* didn't tell me," Baxter spat. "Jonesy did, you idiot. You really ought to keep better friends, Tony. The kind who can hold their tongues when they're throwing back the Scotch. Better yet, the kind who can't afford that stuff, who learn to enjoy a simple beer at the end of a hard day."

Baxter began to pace, and his volume rose.

"What story did you make up to justify giving Jonesy the first ticket outta here?" Baxter said.

"I don't know what you mean by that. But I haven't said anything to anyone here that isn't absolutely true." Tony spoke with a low cadence. The kind designed to convey authority and inspire confidence.

"The only thing absolutely true about you is that you are a user." Baxter pointed at Tony's chest, the eight ball still gripped tightly in his fingers. "You crawl over the backs of the honest folks and ruin them for your gains."

Danielle took a step forward. "Baxter, please. You don't know him."

"You don't either. Not if you're honest," Baxter said to her before returning to Tony. "You ruined my brother."

"He ruined himself, storming around town, barging into my office and threatening my staff." He gestured to Danielle, who had been on the receiving end of Ansel's tirades more than once. "No one respects a man like that." A small part of her had sympathized with Ansel then. He seemed more desperate than harmful. But now wasn't the time to contradict Tony. Baxter wasn't even listening.

"You spread lies about my truck operator. You're going to take everything from Vance, including credit for Eagle's Talon."

"I lead people through worthwhile risk," Tony said levelly.

"Your leadership is *worthless*."

"I dare you to say that when we're safely on the other side and I drop the charges against your employee who wrecked my floating foundation."

Baxter's fingers worked the ball, but he didn't have a retort for that. His silence was concession.

"I could use some of your professional savvy to construct the raft, since Vance isn't going to be of any help."

The silence in the room persisted until Baxter said, "I want to get out of here. That's the only reason I'll help."

"Good." Tony finally seemed to relax.

"But for the record, I don't trust you to keep us alive. And you shouldn't trust me either. I don't take abuse lying down."

24

Vance and his brother argued about plenty of things, but on the day they were stranded under the snow in their father's truck, they both believed they ought to keep their one escape route open. How else would they hear his shouts of return? Vance took inventory of their survival kit and found several strips of neon-pink cloth. The antenna was buried, so he had the idea of tying the little flags onto the end of one of the skis and erecting it above the truck.

Other items in the kit included a ball of twine, a role of baling wire, a twenty-five-foot nylon cord, a pocketknife, matches, a whistle, a windshield deicer and a (for now useless) scraper, first-aid supplies, a solar blanket, and hand warmers.

Next to this store-purchased survival kit, to which their dad had added a few things like batteries, a Maglite, short-handled screw-drivers, and pliers, was a homemade kit that Vance had contributed back when he was in junior high school. It was a three-gallon coffee can with three holes punched in the rim, a long piece of twine tied to each one of the holes, and a safety pin secured at the end of each string. Inside were a tin coffee cup, two books of matches, a squat pillar candle, plastic spoons, and several packets of dried soups, bouillon, and hot chocolate.

Vance emptied the can of these items and then filled it with snow, scooping it from the truck's rear window. He hung the icy can over the jump seat he had been sitting on by stabbing the roof's lining with the safety pins and bending them to close. That was the hardest part, frustrated by his cold, thick thumbs.

He placed the plastic can lid on the seat, set the candle in the middle of it, and lit the candle. The flame licked the bottom of the can.

Pete watched him, whether skeptical or impressed, Vance couldn't tell.

Mainly skeptical, Vance decided, when bursts of air coming down into the truck through the open window kept huffing out the flame.

"You're going to run out of matches," Pete said.

"Watch me and weep," Vance muttered.

He withdrew the solar blanket from the red survival kit and unfolded it. The lightweight Mylar crinkled and was large enough to form a curtain between the bench seat and the rear compartment. Without any help from Pete, Vance undid two of the large safety pins that held up the coffee can and made them do double duty, holding up the Mylar as well. It took ten minutes, but when he was done, Vance had a kitchen.

The candle flame stayed lit this time, and soon the sound of melting snow, breaking down and shifting in the can, punctuated the silence.

"I'll take some hot chocolate," said Pete.

It was tepid chocolate in the end, but for once Pete didn't complain.

The brothers stayed damp into the late afternoon, taking turns clearing out the tunnel that became more like an ice straw with their every pass through it. They gave up on the shovel and collected snow in the bread bag and the potato chip bag, scraping it in with fingers that were stiff and swollen red, then hauled it to the surface and dumped it out.

It was impossible to get warm in their wet clothes, and it was impossible to dry them.

Sometime around four, as the winter sun was falling with the temperatures, the snow stopped dropping and a wind kicked up. Vance tried to roll up the window, but Pete wouldn't allow it.

"How are we going to hear Dad?"

"It's dark, Pete. No one's coming tonight."

Pete was unrelenting. Vance couldn't stand the damp cold any longer. He stripped down to his shorts and wrapped up in his sleeping bag, which wasn't bone dry but was a huge improvement to his soaked shirts and pants. He cleared off the spare jump seat and loaded stuff onto the driver's seat. The back was confined and uncomfortable but more sheltered. This relief was better than food and water, and he quickly fell asleep.

He woke to an urgent need to pee.

Pete was sitting up in the front seat, staring at the white windshield. It was nine in the morning.

Vance reluctantly pulled on his clothes, which were crisp now, frozen to the stiffness of cardboard. Pete seemed to be as rigid as Vance's socks.

He put his hand on Pete's shoulder as he climbed out of the truck. "He'll come back."

Pete sighed and rubbed his forehead but didn't have anything to say.

The blowing snow had completely filled the tunnel during the night, but it was weightless and fluffy, and Vance quickly punched through it to the surface. The light reflecting off the snow stabbed his eyes. He lifted his arm to shield them. The sky was blue now, but the earth was alien, reshaped by drifts into a landscape Vance almost couldn't recognize. Evidence of his father's escape was erased. Whole trees were covered, forming new hills. Stripes streaked the powder where the wind had left tracks like a monstrous Saharan sidewinder. Their ski tilted toward the ground, pushed over. The pink strips of cloth he'd tied to the tips had been stripped away.

Vance replaced these with his knit cap, a bright Cardinals red. He tugged out a loose loop from the knit and wrapped it around the toe clip several times, so that even if the thread broke the cap should hold on, until it unraveled into a mess of yarn. Gusts punched at Vance's ears, making them ache. The cold seemed to blow right through him and his entire body rattled.

When he slipped back down into the truck, Pete was organizing the remains of their food, putting some of it on the dash and the rest into a boulder-gray backpack.

"Wh-what are you d-doing?" Vance chattered.

"Going after Dad."

"He said st-stay p-put."

"I know what he said."

Anger warmed Vance immediately. "You go t-take a look up there and then ch-change your mind. You won't even recognize the place."

"Okay." Pete slipped a hunting knife into the pack alongside some binoculars.

Vance rubbed his arms and dropped hard onto the driver's seat, as if that could block Pete, who had wrestling trophies lining the bookcase in his bedroom.

"Dad took the compass," he tried.

Pete shrugged, but he didn't look at Vance. "It's hard to get lost in two miles."

"You're so full of yourself. You won't even know when you've gone that far."

"Give it up, Vance. I know you just don't want to be alone."

"It'll be a relief not to be stuck with you."

"Too bad you broke your ski."

"It was *Dad's* ski."

"I wouldn't take you with me anyway," Pete said. He shoved the pack into the foot space and leaned over the jump seats, then slid the rear window open and fished for the remaining skis in the truck bed.

Vance couldn't decide whether he was angrier about Pete's abandonment or about his disregard for their father's orders. Nothing about Pete's leaving was good: If Dad was already on his way back, they'd get a boatload of what-for — Pete for leaving and Vance for not stopping him. And if something had happened to Dad, there would be nothing Pete could do about it.

Secretly, Vance was grateful that the sixth ski was busted, because he didn't want to be faced with the decision to go or stay. He didn't trust himself to make the right choice. He didn't even know what the right choice would be.

One of Pete's skis hissed across the truck's upholstery behind Vance's ear and poked its head out the open window.

"Please stay," Vance said.

Pete paused.

"If you go out there, all of us will be alone. And I don't care whether you think I'm being a baby or not. I'm just naming facts, and I'll bet you my Cal Ripkin baseball that there isn't a marine alive who'd tell you splitting up is a good idea."

The wind was blowing down into the cab again, slicing Vance's skin. It was Tuesday morning, nine thirty. Biology period. Vance had never wished more than he did now that he could be sitting on a stool staring at slides of mitochondria. The warmth of his anger faded to clammy anxiety. He couldn't stop the shivering.

"I don't really care what the Marine Corps says," Pete said.

"Then at least care about what Dad said."

Pete returned to his rummaging in the truck's bed. His boot came off the front seat, and Vance had to dodge it to avoid being kicked in the face. He shoved Pete's shin away.

"Ow!" Pete lashed back and caught Vance in the temple. "Cut me some slack."

"Knock it off."

Pete dropped back onto the seat, grinning at Vance. In one hand he held their father's poker kit, soggy in its zippered leather pouch, and in the other the barely tapped bottle of whiskey, which was purchased special for the hunting trip and would last the entire year at least.

"How about a little something to keep us warm?" Pete said.

Vance stayed silent, *sure* and *no way* each seeming to be the wrong answer. He wasn't quite sure how two ounces of bourbon heated a body. He had a much clearer idea of how it got fifteen-and nineteen-year-olds into trouble.

"And a fair way to settle the argument," Pete continued, holding up the poker kit. "Winner gets the skis."

It was a wager Vance couldn't turn down.
If he did, Pete would just walk over him and
out the window with his original plan.

"If I win the skis, you have to stay here,"
Vance said.

Pete dipped his head and raised the bottle,
and the game was on.

25

Tony immediately organized an effort to pool food and water in the downstairs kitchen. Danielle understood the practical reasons for this move. It would be easier to ration what they had if it was all in the same place, especially Mirah's and Jonesy's items. But she couldn't help thinking that Tony's real reason for controlling the food was, well, to be controlling.

He sent Vance, Carver, and Danielle to Jonesy's, claiming the glutton had more food and water than anyone else. He and Enrique went to Mirah's. Zeke bravely offered to help Ferti box up her kitchen. Baxter decided to start on the raft.

"I don't know how he's going to do that with his hand," Danielle whispered as she showed Zeke the way to Ferti's. Zeke didn't reply. "He needs help. Any chance you can talk Vance into changing his mind?"

"Nope."

Danielle sighed. "You're gutsy, offering to help Ms. Independent. You want me to stay just in case she turns on you?"

"Ten to one she'll let me stay because she thinks she's helping *me* out," Zeke said.

Ferti's condo smelled like the cologne Danielle's grandmother used to wear, a flowery scent that reminded her of Easter suppers and the scratchy pillowcases on her guest-room bed. Ferti's condo looked more like a workshop than a home. It was illuminated with numerous candles and strewn with projects in progress: willow baskets filled with skeins of yarn, overflowing shopping bags from a craft store in Port Rondeau, large sheets of matte board bearing sketches of brides in gowns, and vellum overlays of bold-line dress designs in various colors. A drafting table strewn with charcoal pencils and a spinning caddy of colored ink pens stood in a place of honor in front of the large window. The sofa was invisible under yards and yards of fabric. There was no television in the room, only a small dock for a music player.

Ferti and Simeon sat at the dining room table by the light of gold tapers playing Go Fish with cards that were sticking to Simeon's fingers. Marshmallow treats never made it all the way to a boy's stomach.

"We're here for your food," Danielle announced lightly, then she told Ferti the plan to collect food, build a raft, and try to reach her yacht. "And I brought you some help."

Ferti rose from her chair. "Anyone who wants to eat my food is welcome," she said. Danielle was amazed. "You goin' to help us, Simeon?"

"Can I have another Rice Krispie treat?"

"Simeon!" Danielle blushed.

"One for every box you carry," Ferti announced, moving toward the kitchen.

"Do I get some too, Ms. Ferti?" Zeke asked.

"Why, yes, please eat these all up before Carver comes back here to ogle them." She pulled out a plate and cut off a wedge of the lumpy, chewy bars.

"I don't think he's ogling your cooking, Ms. Ferti."

"Then polish these off so he won't be able to lie about it."

Danielle laughed and kissed the top of Simeon's head. "So what's your history with Carver?"

"No history. He's nothing but a stubborn old mule who doesn't know the meaning of 'I'm not interested.' "

"For twenty-five years?"

"I know! In some states it's criminal." She

handed the Rice Krispie bar to Zeke. "But he's not the creepy type. I think it's sweet."

"Honey, sweet can't fix life's problems. Only one who can do that is Yours Truly."

Danielle pondered this remark as she went to Jonesy's. It sounded right, but by the time she arrived she still didn't know if she agreed.

The police officer's unit was a mirror's reflection of her own. She lifted her flashlight toward the kitchen. Her light passed through the beam-bending shapes of plastic water jugs, filled to their brims with the water Jonesy had collected. Vance and Carver were bumping about on the other side of the long counter.

Weak rays from small battery-powered dome lights spilled out of the cabinets as the men emptied them. Danielle found two plastic shopping bags under the sink, but nothing else for carrying their stash.

"I'll go see if I can find more bags or boxes," she said.

In Jonesy's living room, she swept her flashlight beam over a classy leather sofa in antique blue. The design had the square angles and smooth look of the expensive Horchow brand. Its facing chairs were large, with deep seats, oak feet, and the same unusual color. She'd seen something similar to these while picking out furniture for the model unit. The armchairs alone retailed for three thousand dollars. The arrangement sat atop a tasteful area rug of rusts, turquoises, and browns.

Next to the sofa Danielle found a magazine basket with a handle. She emptied the contents onto the glass coffee table, which had a gorgeous wrought-iron base. Jonesy's love of food clearly extended to his reading pleasure. There were no sports rags or newsmagazines among the numerous copies of *Bon Appétit* and *Gourmet* and *Food & Wine*.

The focal point of the room was not the river view but an enormous flat-screen TV that took up most of one wall. On the opposite wall was a built-in wet bar complete with a wine rack and a ceiling-high glass-and-cherry cabinet, a small sink, cutting boards, and an ice chest. A glass bowl on the counter was filled with lighters and a package of cigarettes. In front of the bar were two cases of wine bottles that Jonesy must have recently purchased. She emptied these cardboard boxes as well and placed the bottles on the bar.

"He has a fine selection in there," Carver said to her from the kitchen.

Danielle was no aficionado.

She took the boxes and basket to the men,

then turned to the master bedroom, which was more elaborate than she expected, with silk sheets on the rumpled bed and a large telescope pointed at the sky. The room yielded a laundry basket and several pillowcases. The second bedroom was an office with an executive desk in the middle of the room. Her light revealed coordinating walnut bookcases, file cabinets, and console tables. Two wingback chairs faced the desk. A framed commendation and several photographs of Jonesy in uniform — weighing a fraction of his present bulk — graced the back wall, where he could see them from his desk.

In one of them he wore a business suit instead of his blues and was shaking the hand of Tony Dean, who held the gold shovel of Eagle's Talon's groundbreaking.

In the closet she found a large safe, a box of copy paper, and a file crate. These latter two were easily emptied and carried to the kitchen.

"Where's Carver?" she asked.

"He took the first load down."

"Without a light?"

"Found a little one in one of the drawers. Small enough for him to carry in his mouth."

After stacking jars of artichoke hearts and

pimentos into the crate, she held up a small cardboard box with a cellophane window in it. "What's this? Kwinoah? Q-u-i-n-o-a."

" 'Keen-wah,' I think. It's like a grain — a grass seed, actually. You can eat it like oatmeal."

Danielle wrinkled her face as Vance stepped up onto a footstool and strained to reach to the back of the pantry's top shelf. "I guess Jonesy is as tall as he is wide," he observed. "There's food all the way to the back up here."

"He could run for office."

"Why?"

"Because he's tall. Haven't you heard that height is a leading indicator of whether someone will be elected to public office?"

The steps creaked under Vance's boots. "Who says that?"

"Tony. I mean, not Tony — it was a study he read that he told me about. He's always worrying that he's not tall enough. He's planning to launch a campaign in the fall."

"Baxter's tall. That'll bust the theory wide open."

She smiled at that, then held up her carton. He dropped boxes of pasta and bags of jasmine rice into it.

"I think Ferti should run for president," he said.

Danielle laughed aloud. "She could probably do the job."

"You laugh more when you're not with him," Vance said, and the statement had the odd effect of putting a cork in her happiness.

"With who?" she dodged, though she knew what he meant.

"How long have you been together?"

It was hard for her to pinpoint the exact moment that had marked "together" for her and Tony. Was it the moment she'd kissed him, or had it started before that? "A few months."

He handed her some cereal boxes and she avoided his eyes.

"Why do you think that is?" he asked.

"Because it takes me awhile to commit to big decisions?" she said testily.

"I meant, why do you seem happier when you're not with him?"

Danielle was embarrassed by her misunderstanding. She felt flustered. "Maybe I'm just laughing because you're an odd guy who makes funny statements."

"I think it's because you know he's using you. Baxter's right about that much, you know."

Carver's footsteps in the entryway silenced the conversation and tamped down

Danielle's shock. She stood stupidly under the weight of her box for a long moment, then turned, looking for a place to set it.

"Here." Carver reached out to take it from her.

"I'll carry it down," she offered.

"You know Tony would sue me if I let you fall down those stairs in the dark," Carver said. "Stay here and load. We'll all live longer that way."

He spoke like a doting father. This was the only explanation Danielle could come up with for why his words didn't offend as Vance's had.

"Our man Enrique has sobered up and started a story," Carver announced as he cradled the box in his hands. "He says it was a bomb that took down the pump truck yesterday."

"A bomb!" Danielle exclaimed.

Vance stepped off the stool and leaned against the counter, frowning.

"And he says Baxter's the one who planted it," Carver finished.

"That's a terrible rumor to start without evidence," Vance said.

"Says he saw all the evidence he needed out on the boat with you last night."

"Did you see it?" Danielle asked Vance.

"I'm not sure what I saw."

"There isn't a sinkhole?"

"It looks like a sinkhole to me. But there might have been a bomb too."

"Why didn't you say anything?"

"Because nothing about it is clear."

"A bomb," Danielle repeated. "You think he suspects Baxter just because he and Tony got into it tonight?"

"I don't know," Carver said. "But if Baxter had a bomb on him tonight, we might all be goners now."

Danielle put the contents of a drawer into the magazine basket. Vance picked up her flashlight and the two wine boxes and went to the wet bar. She watched him open the liquor cabinet and whistle.

"This is quite an inventory."

He opened up a squat square bottle of something amber colored and began to pour it down the sink.

"What're you up to?" Carver demanded.

"You can't take this stuff with you," Vance said.

He needed to stay sober, Danielle thought. Nevertheless, the behavior was curious.

"It pains me to see that go down a drain," Carver persisted. "You got the money to pay him back?"

"He told us to help ourselves to whatever he had. I didn't hear him exclude these cabinets, did you?"

Danielle and Carver glanced at each other.

"Why don't you just come with us, away from this place?" Carver suggested.

"Actually, it's my plan to talk Enrique into staying with me," Vance said, "and I need him sober."

"Good luck on both points, then. You're going to need it."

Carver left them, and Danielle crossed her arms. "That was a cruel thing to say about Tony. What you said about him using me. You don't even know me."

"Baxter was right: Tony Dean uses people. It's truth, not cruelty." Vance rinsed the empty bottle and set it aside, then unscrewed the cap of another one and upended the bottle over the drain.

"You think I'm the kind of woman who'd let people use me?"

He shook his head. "I think you're the kind of woman who would leap from a third-story balcony to save her son's life."

"You say that like it's not a good thing."

"It's a dangerous, daring, life-giving thing. You're an amazing parent. I'm just not sure you look out for yourself."

The stench of the alcohol began to saturate the air around Danielle's head. If only he knew.

"Tony takes very good care of me." She didn't need to be defending him to Vance. "That's *hundreds* of dollars' worth," she said lamely, pointing to all the bottles. "What are you doing?"

"Have you ever known him to honestly, selflessly take care of anyone but himself? I don't trust him."

"And yet here you are, letting him write your paychecks."

"I was contractually bound before I figured this stuff out. But you're not. Are you?"

"If I am it's none of your business."

"I meant, please reconsider his plan to leave Eagle's Talon right now."

"No one's leaving yet. We're just building a raft. It might not even work."

Vance set the bottle on the cutting board and spent seconds staring at the label. Then he resumed his merciless raid of Jonesy's liquor. "Do you realize how many people know there's a group of us stranded out here? Everyone we work with, for starters. Ferti's nieces, Baxter's supervisors. The brother he keeps talking about. Everyone who knows Tony and you. If we stay, we can be found. If there's help to be had, it will come to us eventually."

"I can't bear to sit and wait," she said.

"Sometimes waiting is the most active,

wise, hopeful thing you can do."

"Danny used to say that," she whispered.

She sank onto the pricey sofa. In the shadows, her pain might be hidden from Vance's perceptive way of being. The sofa begged her to tip sideways and rest her head on a three-hundred-dollar pillow, where she could leave this place and go back to her happy past. The flashlight beam cut through the flow of liquor going down the drain and made a rippling pattern in the cabinet's beveled glass.

Vance stopped dumping and turned his back to the bar. He leaned back against it and gave her his full attention without shining a spotlight on her.

"He was a good, good man. He piloted boats for the Port Rondeau Emergency Services. Said the worst thing a lost person could do was wander around."

Vance nodded.

"All that time worrying about him dying on the job, giving his life for some adrenaline junkie who got in over his head, and he was killed in a car accident driving home from a meeting at church. A hit-and-run."

"I'm sorry."

"But we're not in that kind of situation, are we?" she challenged. "The kind where a person should hunker down in a cave and wait for the wind to change."

"What kind of situation do you think we're in?"

She shrugged. "A storm of the century. What do you think it is?"

He thought about it. "This blackness seems like something more. An opportunity to figure out what we believe while we still have time. How we're going to *be* with the people we're with. How we're going to take care of each other."

"You're talking like it's the end of the world."

"It was the end for all those people who died yesterday. Marcus, Andy, your friend Ranier — the people we can't even name. What if it is for us too? Doesn't it make you stop and think about what you really want? Are you chasing things you don't need? Have you settled for too little?"

"I'm more of a how-am-I-going-to-put-food-on-the-table-today kind of person."

"Then think about it this way: If you could have another family like the one you had with Danny, would you want it? Or would you make do with Tony?"

"That's out of line." She sprang off the sofa and knocked her knee on the coffee table. The blow knifed her nerves and took a certain number of style points off her objection. "You're just mad at him for pulling the rug out from under you when he couldn't pull together the funds for this place," she accused, rubbing her joint.

"No. Listen." He stepped away from the wet bar and touched her arm. It was enough to give her pause in the shadows between the faint lighting. "Tony Dean doesn't have anyone's welfare but his own in mind. Not yours, and not Simeon's."

"How would you know?"

"I know he's not capable of respecting a woman like you — and by that I mean a woman who has accomplished more in her life already than he ever will."

"That's silly."

"You've had a great marriage, and Simeon's a good kid. You've survived devastation without becoming a bitter person. Tony will never experience any of that."

"Well maybe that's why he's attracted —"

"He doesn't behave like a man in love. Can't you see what he's doing?"

Can't you see what I'm *doing*? She should walk out. Leave the condo. Right now.

"Exactly how should he behave, Vance? We're adults now, you know. We're not in high school anymore, all starry-eyed. I can't believe I'm having this conversation."

"If you were with me, I wouldn't hide our

relationship from anyone. Why do you have to keep yours a secret?"

Because I don't love him. Because I'm the user.

"This is a completely inappropriate conver—"

"He won't tell anyone because they would think the truth — that he's using you to do his dirty work."

"You don't understand."

"He didn't set you up here just so you and Simeon could live in a nice place, did he?"

The hot promise of furious tears burned the backs of her eyes. Her anger, she realized, came from shame.

"He didn't send Mirah and her boys away with Jonesy because he thought Jonesy was the best man for the job."

"You can't possibly know —"

"Danielle, *think.* Please, try to see Tony as he is, not as he's designed himself to look to everyone. Leaving Eagle's Talon is about what's in Tony's best interests, not yours."

She pulled her hand away. "The raft was my idea. We all want out of here."

"I'm afraid for your life. Let Tony risk his own. Stay here with me and let Tony come back for you on a boat that was actually made for the water."

"If you mean what you say, you should be begging everyone to stay." This would mean, of course, that when the catastrophe blew over, Vance would be out of a job and might also face the smear campaign of his life.

"I'm trying," Vance said. He picked up a sloshing golden bottle. "But the part about you deserving more than Tony can give you — that was just for you."

26

The whiskey was unbearable, like cough syrup that worked by burning away all the mucous that existed in a man's body, plus any living cells that had been touching it. Vance's sinuses flared, his eyes seemed to swell shut, and he almost tossed it up on the steering wheel. Pete laughed at him. He mimicked Vance's grimace, a bug-eyed old-man strain on his lower lip and neck that was as comical as it was inaccurate.

"People *like* this stuff?"

"Just wait," Pete said. The swig he took looked a bit more practiced, but his own nose wrinkled up.

"You've never tasted it in your life," Vance said. His eyes still watered.

"You'll never know," Pete said as he doled out the poker chips. They started with equal amounts, a family practice.

"Texas Hold'em?" Vance asked.

"Omaha," said Pete.

"It takes too long."

"You gotta be somewhere?"

"You'll cheat," Vance accused.

"How?"

"I don't know the rules as well," he said. "I'd rather play Hold'em."

"You can trust me," Pete said. He gave each of them four hole cards instead of two. "But if you don't, here." He handed over a folded pamphlet that had been tucked in the back cover of the poker pouch. Rules of the game for various versions. It was printed in microscopic single-spaced black print. Vance sighed and tossed it onto the dash.

He launched into the game with low expectations and no intention of lifting his glass again, but he was surprised to feel a pleasant burst of heat flower under his eyes and spread across his nose and cheekbones. It lasted for a few rounds before it started to fade. So quickly? He was still so cold that he had trouble holding his cards. He stole a look at Pete, who was setting up the betting blinds. His eyes flickered up over the top of his cards, then back down.

The second sip of whiskey Vance took wasn't as bad as the first, but it wasn't smooth. He thought letting the stuff roll across his tongue would save the back of his throat. Instead, it choked him up. His body refused to swallow for several disgusting seconds, until his mind won the argument and forced his tongue to do its job.

"I just don't see the appeal," Vance complained.

"You will."

Both brothers raised their stakes. The flush to Vance's cheeks had returned, weaker now but spreading toward his temples and creeping across his hairline.

Vance won the first round. He wasn't sure if it was a straight-up win or something Pete had allowed. But it gave him courage. Emboldened, he finished off his shot with a third sip, this one measured and aimed to hit his stomach before anything in his mouth or throat registered it. This effort was the most successful. He felt the icy breeze from the window at the back of his neck and was less annoyed by it now.

"See, it's not so bad," Pete said.

When Vance won the second round, Pete congratulated him by splashing another inch into the tin cup.

"Looks like we're going to be here for a while, if you keep this up."

Vance's good luck, combined with the bourbon, gave him confidence.

"You want to quit now?"

"No."

They started again.

"Dad's lived through stuff like this before," Vance said, thinking this was an opportunity to talk Pete out of his plans regardless of the game's outcome. "You should trust him."

"That doesn't mean he's always right."

"I didn't say that."

"Sure you did. What's wrong with you? When I was fifteen I had a master's degree in parental idiocy. When are you going to quit thinking he's perfect?"

"I just think that he's had more experience with some kinds of things."

"Dad's never been stranded in a blizzard."

"Neither have you."

"Then we both have equal chances of getting us out of here in one piece."

"Or of dying. We'll live longer if we do what he said."

"Pick your fate," Pete said. "Exposure out there or starvation in here. I hear freezing to death is like falling asleep. I'll take sleep for two hundred, please."

That made Vance grin. No one was going to die, really. That was the kind of thing that happened to other people. Stupid people. Not people who had a strong outdoorsman for a father and maps of the area and a truck stocked with winter survival gear, not to mention a frozen buck for eating. This was nothing more than an exercise in patience, he thought, and when it was over, they'd all groan and complain about how bad it was and maybe even make it sound just a little bit worse, to impress people. Especially the girls.

Vance continued to get warmer. If he closed off his throat to block his nose, the way he did when he took a dive into a pool, and only tipped in enough for one clean swallow, the liquor went down pretty easy. Each little sip moved the heat up into his head and from there down his spine along all his gajillions of nerve cells. But his toes and fingers weren't quite warm yet.

"Either way, I can only sit around and do nothing for so long," Pete said.

In an unexpected sort of way, Vance was able to sympathize with his brother. The edge of the disagreement had worn off, and he admitted to himself that it was pointless to argue about the merits of obeying one's father at their ages. Pete was a legal adult, old enough to make his own choices without getting stressed out over the consequences. Enviable, really. In the face of this, Vance's loyalty to his dad caused him some embarrassment. Insisting too hard that they do what Dad said felt childish, even while it also felt right.

"Someone will find us," Vance said.

"Dead or alive?" Pete asked.

The game continued, with Vance continuing to win and Pete congratulating him with whiskey. He drank the fiery stuff because it warmed him up, and for no other reason except that he had already won the skis and didn't have to concentrate much on his cards or whether Pete was abiding by the rules. One welcome side effect of the drink was that it put Pete in an agreeable mood. He resigned himself to staying put, broke out some Skippy, and ate it from the plastic jar by the spoonful.

"If I'm going to be stuck here with you, we might as well keep playing," he said.

"Might as well."

What else was there to do? Vance had finished his David Fisher biography yesterday and didn't feel at all interested in copying any of the pictures into his sketchbook. And the game kept his mind off worry for his father.

This, too, would be part of the hilarious story the three of them would be telling everyone soon. Hilarious because when Pete could shut down his self-righteous big-brother mode, he was actually pretty cool. He had a biting wit that could put a locker room full of guys on the floor, busting their sides. Every good joke Vance knew had first fallen from Pete's mouth.

Having abandoned his plans to take the remaining pair of skis, Pete shifted into his popular-jock gear, the one Vance had witnessed from a distance on the high school grounds. At school, Vance was so far beneath Pete's social radar that the two didn't even make eye contact unless there was an Extremely Urgent Reason to do so. Pete's definition of extremely urgent was pretty much limited to (a) Dad on his deathbed, (b) the world coming to an end, or (c) word that Alice Jenner was looking for a ride home.

Hidden from public view by the confines of their father's truck, Pete didn't seem to mind the presence of his kid brother. Vance was aware that brotherly love probably had nothing to do with Pete's sudden decision to treat him like a peer. He wasn't really sure why Pete usually wore two faces, and he didn't really care, except that he believed these rare moments together, one-on-one, reflected the more honest of Pete's personalities. Someday, when the necessary evil of high school was behind them both, Vance was sure that Pete would no longer be ashamed of their bond.

Vance's head felt heavy. He tipped it against the headrest and closed his eyes for a second, and a rare feeling of contentment centered itself behind his ribs. "You're not so bad when you're thinking straight," Vance said.

When Pete didn't say anything, Vance opened his eyes halfway, not far enough to interpret the look Pete was giving him with any kind of accuracy. It might have been worry. It might have been contempt.

"You should give up the act more often," Vance said.

"What act?" Pete looked away.

"The one where nothing can touch you."

"Nothing *can* touch me."

This made Vance chuckle. See? His brother was incredibly funny.

Vance reached out and poked Pete right in the center of his squishy cheek.

"Ow!"

"Touched you."

Pete didn't find *that* funny. And maybe it wasn't.

"Your call," Pete said, frowning at the community cards lined up on the bench between them.

"I raise you," Vance said as he put his cards down on top of the community pile, and then he thought that maybe it was the wrong time for that. Maybe he had put out his hand too early? Something was off with what he had done and he couldn't figure out what. Maybe he was just drunk, which he'd never been in his life, and this was how everything looked when a man was drunk: warm and soft and a little bit off.

Pete put his hand down on top of Vance's and said, "You again," then picked up everything for shuffling before Vance had a chance to get a good look at Pete's hand. This, too, seemed off. At the very least it was rude, but Vance supposed it didn't really matter.

Vance swept all of his chips into the growing pile at his feet. They fell, clattering and pouring over his shoes. How many was he up to now? He bent forward to count and banged his forehead on the steering wheel.

Pete laughed at him.

Vance started laughing too.

It was hard to catch his breath.

And then Vance passed out.

When he came around, he couldn't open his eyes right away. They seemed pasted shut. He lifted his heavy head and nausea forced it right back to where it had been resting, slouched against the driver's side door. The sensation of being dangerously close to tearing in two was immobilizing. There was an ice pick run straight though his head, he believed, from one temple to the other, pinning him to the armrest. Shifting at all would cause it to wiggle, to poke new holes and bleed him to death.

A loud groan brought Pete to mind. He wondered about the whiskey, and if Pete was feeling the effects also. It didn't seem like they'd had so much, but the specifics eluded him.

Vance moved his foot. The very least he could do, whatever the cost to himself might be, was find out if Pete was okay. His shoe connected with something hollow. The sound was unnaturally loud. It sent a low vibration through that spike in Vance's head and caused him to gag. The sense that it would be a very, very bad thing to lose his stomach inside the small space helped him to hold it down, but resisting his own body took all his limited concentration. He succeeded, exhausted.

He decided Pete could handle himself.

He rested.

A cool draft on his face brought him around the second time. Chilly nighttime air swept down the body-sized tunnel that reached up to the surface of the snowbound world. The truck cab was as black as it had been the morning the snow first encased them.

Vance's nausea had moved from his stomach to his head. The spike in his skull had been removed, leaving a dull ache behind. His foot was still on top of the hollow object, and it rolled when he shifted his legs. It was the empty whiskey bottle, and this time when it connected with the metal rim of the brake pedal, it sounded no more ominous than a spoon on a water glass.

He moved slowly, testing his limits, and found they had enlarged.

"That is wicked stuff," he said to Pete. "Never again, no matter how cold it is."

Pete didn't answer.

Vance lifted his hand and slid the dome light switch to the on position. The dull light was blinding, and he threw a hand over his eyes until it became bearable.

A blanket covered Vance's body.

The poker game had been returned to its zippered pouch.

The last pair of skis was gone.

So was Pete.

The Longest Night was an old movie based on a true story in which a girl was kidnapped and buried alive in a coffin for four days while her family searched for her.

Vance had seen it once on Pete's recommendation, because his big brother had a fascination with true-crime stories. He came to think of the hours that followed his discovery of Pete's betrayal as his own longest night.

The alcohol colored his perception of this event a little bit. He wasn't sure how much, but as he tried to review the facts, they no longer seemed to contain a clear truth. Was Pete bullheaded or brave? Was their father wise or a fool? Was Vance a good, obedient son or just a naive kid, a victim of older, smarter, more selfish men?

He no longer knew whether staying in the truck was the smart thing to do, but he had no way to escape it now, with one ski, no compass, and nothing but moonlight to guide him. He imagined Pete finding their father, the two clapping each other on the back with a relieved hug, then deciding it would be too much work to come back and fetch him too, seeing as he couldn't meet their efforts halfway. Or it was possible that they both were already dead, separated by miles of ice, and wouldn't be discovered until spring. He thought of how he might become a modern-day Ötzi the Iceman, preserved so well that scientists would speculate about his cause of death. Alcohol poisoning, they might say. Or despair, when they saw all the food still available for him to consume. The thought of food stirred up his putrid stomach.

Maybe he ought to write something down for the people who would find him, a kind of explanation.

He decided not to. The truth made him appear to be cowardly, and people liked stories about bold men whose every reckless effort succeeded. His reputation might be better off in the hands of people who didn't know anything about him. Strangers might reconstruct a story that put him in a more flattering light.

Someone might make a movie about him. A dark, independent film about the bleakness of dying alone, without hope, but nobly.

Vance sat in the cab as though already dead, staring at the truck's dash without seeing it, not noticing the cold. His thoughts returned to writing his own story, but a fiction this time. Something heroic and believable. Anger and shame and fear wrestled inside his heart with no clear winner. He wished the hollow bottle still had something in it to quiet the conflict.

He passed the hours writing mental drafts and tossing them away.

He didn't notice what time it was when

the dome light faded out. When the charcoal space inside the cab brightened to a flat gray, the dashboard clock was dead too. He recalled he was wearing a watch but didn't see the point of checking it.

The sound of a distant shout lifted his chin toward the tunnel at his open window. He could climb up for a look and probably find that the illusion of a human voice was a vulture's call.

The second shout sounded human indeed, but still it wasn't enough to rouse him.

In fact, he didn't even believe in his own rescue until dislodged snow fell onto his arms and a body in bright red snow pants dropped into the tunnel. There was just enough room for the man to brace the toes of his heavy boots on the open window frame and squat down for a look.

The man stuck a gloved hand into Vance's face.

"I'm Zeke Hammond," he said. "You look like you could use some help."

27

The leather sofa under Zeke's fingertips felt expensive and smelled new. He ran his palm over the agreeable surface.

Danielle had suggested he and Vance take Jonesy's condo for the night, and when she did, Zeke caught a mental image of her: with a brick in one hand and a trowel in the other, building a wall between herself and Vance.

"I don't think you're going to be Jonesy's favorite person when he comes back and finds what you've done to his bar," Zeke said to Vance. Vance's footsteps changed from padding to thumping as his boots left the large area rug and hit the cork flooring that ran the length of the condo. The liquor bottles he carried made dull clanking sounds as he placed more empty ones on the kitchen counter.

"That's a trouble for another time," Vance said.

"Don't trust yourself with the stuff?"

Vance didn't answer that question. "It looks like he has the means to replace it, anyway."

"Tony tells me the man is a smart investor."

"Yeah, well, Tony likes his investors."

Next to Zeke, Ziggy's tail whapped his leg. Spending the night on the second floor, that much higher off the water, was cause for the pooch to be happy.

"Enrique and I will dip some water out of the river in the morning," Vance said. "If the sun rises. No one even dared to go out on the dock in this pitch."

"Is he going to join us?"

"No. He says if he gets out of this thing alive he'll write a screenplay, and Tony's plan sounds better to him when it comes to that kind of thing."

"He's a confused kid. But that's okay. It'll take time for them to build a raft without your know-how, and I can work on him."

"Baxter's know-how will be all they need," Vance said.

"He's bent on leaving too?"

"The man's scared to death. He's got family and no way to reach them. Last thing he wants to do is stay here."

Vance poured himself a glass of water

from one of the containers on the counter. At least Zeke assumed it was water. Didn't smell like anything else.

"Did you tell Enrique about what I saw at 11, about the bomb?" Vance asked.

"I don't think I did." Zeke thought for a moment. "No, not that I remember."

"He's saying he saw the damage."

"Could the lights have been bright enough for him to see?"

"Maybe." Vance's voice was hesitant. "Yeah. I guess they could. But why not talk to me about it?"

"Well, if he knew who did it —"

"Baxter denies everything."

"Of course." Zeke wasn't surprised.

"See if Enrique might tell you more?"

"Okay."

Vance left the kitchen and joined Zeke at the coffee table, setting his glass in front of them. Air escaped the seat cushion as he sat.

"I'm oh for six, Zeke. I couldn't talk anyone into staying here." The pause that followed was familiar to Zeke, though he hadn't heard this particular brand of silence from Vance for years. It was the deafening scream of self-doubt.

"You're not a fool, Vance."

"It's impossible not to wonder if —"

"Don't go there, son."

"Pete wasted hours on me that day in the truck. Did all my begging him not to leave keep him from reaching Dad in time?"

"Why do you keep going back to that? Your father passed before you and your brother woke up that morning. No one but Pete disputes that fact."

"What if I'm wrong to urge everyone to stay?"

"Do you think you're wrong?"

Vance didn't answer right away. "Danielle said that this isn't the same situation as being lost, waiting for rescue. I keep thinking maybe she's right."

"No two situations are the same, Vance. Even if we were buried under an avalanche of snow right now, it wouldn't be the same situation because you're not the same person and Pete's not here."

Vance's boots tapped the coffee table as he rested the heels on the surface of the glass.

"How do I know what's the right thing to do?"

"The same way you have always known. You ask God. You wait. You listen for the wisdom that drowns out fear and brings peace to your heart. I think you've already done all this, haven't you?"

Vance sighed, as if mimicking the cushion.

"So I wait. But should I be helping them? If I help them build that raft, we could have it done in a few hours maybe. They could go tomorrow."

"And would that choice bring you peace?"

"I'd feel the way I do when a see a man walk out onto a high-rise girder without a safety harness."

"So for now at least, you know you're doing what you must do."

"Is it enough?"

"Is it enough? That's the question of a man who thinks that waiting is the weaker activity. But patience requires the strength of Hercules."

Vance rose from the chair and opened the window. Air steeped with moisture floated into the room. The air tickling Zeke's nose opened his senses to the scents of river water teeming with fish and summer algae. In his mind's eye, the smells became a visible breezy ribbon of blue and green.

And red.

There were red dots in the rippling watery colors. The specks passed by like fish in a stream and then, as he watched them carefully, began to rise out of the current and take wing. Silver-gray feathers opened up behind the crimson, and a whole flock of birds swooped over the water in a dramatic dive before turning as one and leaving him.

A single bird remained, hovering in front of Zeke's nose as if riding the winds of his breath. It was a common robin, so close that Zeke could see his own reflection in the bird's tiny eyes. He had seen this robin before, and when the ground seemed to fall away beneath Zeke's feet and he found himself floating in the air with the bird, looking down on the scene that had compelled him to come to this place, Zeke remembered: this was the robin that had floated above the vision of the of the silver-blue hand, and of the poisonous waters rising around a drowning truck on a drowning island.

"I know what you're waiting for," Zeke said.

"What?"

"The birds. You have to wait here until the birds return, see. Although there might be only one. I'm not clear about that."

"Like Noah, waiting for the dove."

"That's not the picture I got, but it works," Zeke said. "Is the darkness still there?"

"Like tar," Vance said. "But it's late now too. Almost ten, I think. Is this what it's like to be blind?"

"My blindness was crushing."

"This qualifies," Vance said.

"But I'd endure it all over again, knowing the outcome."

"Hmm. I'm not sure I'm ready to say that about my own stuff just yet."

Zeke chuckled. "I'd guess that's because your time hasn't come yet," he said. "So, you wait now. People will come around."

"I don't know. I'm not charismatic enough or something. I'm basing my decisions on my gut. On some vision you had."

"And on your past experiences."

"None of it goes very far with these folks."

Zeke wagged a finger in the direction of his friend. "You may not see yourself as the leader they need, but let me tell you: everything you need for this moment you already have, including the wisdom you've gained from your past. What happened to Pete when he left that truck?"

"He lost his foot to frostbite."

"Would he have lost it if he'd stayed?"

"Probably not. But he blamed me for that too."

"That's because you were a leader even then, son."

"I can't force anyone to do anything."

"No good leader ever ha—"

A shocking boom cut off the last of Zeke's

words. The space between the explosion and the vibration beneath his feet was no time at all.

"Did you see it?" Zeke asked.

"Upriver, a quick flash of light, and now nothing."

"No fire?"

There was a heavy pause while Vance had a look.

"If there's a fire, the flames can't penetrate this blackness."

"One of the boats in the shipping lanes," Zeke speculated.

"That's the general area."

"Yes. Did you feel it in your feet?"

"Danielle's little boy says we've got angels holding up this building. I sure hope he's right."

"Kids usually are."

An odd smell, something chemical and smoky, joined and then masked the more natural scents. It floated into Zeke's lungs like dread. Ziggy stood up and nosed Zeke's palm.

"Don't give up, Vance."

"How can I, with you to keep me on the straight and narrow?"

There was a second boom, louder and floor-shuddering and then fading back to peace.

"Don't give up on Danielle. Or Enrique. He needs a good, patient person like you in his life. All of them do."

Vance didn't answer, but Zeke envisioned his young friend standing before the open window, sheltered from the harm outside. And then the smoke blew in on silver wisps, scented like salt instead of fire. It looped itself protectively around Vance's head and chest — a spirit, a strength, an impenetrable armor. Zeke looked at this image the way he admired a finished landscape, a reality far more beautiful than the designs on paper.

And Zeke knew then that his job was done.

28

The day Zeke Hammond lost his sight was the day Vance got his life back. The day came almost six years after the landscaper saved Vance's body from the coffin of his father's truck. It was a day full of sunshine rather than snow, and tequila rather than whiskey.

Vance was renting a room from Zeke, who had taken to him in a paternal way that annoyed Vance no end, as if a man who'd never married and never had children of his own could appoint himself to be a father figure. But this was exactly what Zeke did, within twenty-four hours of learning that Vance's biological father was dead, frozen less than a hundred yards from the gas station he had been aiming for. Already a respected foster parent, Zeke Hammond applied for and was granted custody of the minor teenager.

At first Vance stayed because he had

nowhere else to go: no living grandparents, a mother who had surrendered her parental rights to him so long ago that he couldn't remember her face, aunts and uncles who shared Pete's stance on Vance's guilt. Pete blamed their father's death and his amputated foot and the sum total of his pain on Vance's childish refusal to let him go.

Vance blamed himself too. He had no desire to defend himself or ask anyone to take in someone who deserved to be cast out.

After he reached legal adulthood, Vance stayed with Zeke because the rent was cheap and because Zeke tolerated his behavior in a way no one else would. The high school dropout worked only to support his own intoxication, and tenderhearted Zeke would not throw him out even when he skipped a rent payment, and then several rent payments.

The day the railroad tie fell on Zeke's head, Vance had not paid the man for nearly nine months. He lounged on his basement futon, holding his tequila bottle up to the sunlight between swigs so that its refracted rays bounced around the room. At the moment the call came in, Vance was suspecting that his free ride might soon come to an end. There had been a fretting in Zeke's expression that didn't exist before, and a new reluctance to converse. Zeke's friends were probably advising him to force Vance into responsible adulthood.

There was no point in rushing it.

The phone rang four times and Vance let the answering machine pick up the call.

"Vance, this is Rod."

He tried to remember who Rod was. Couldn't. Didn't care.

"There's been an accident at the job site."

Right. Rod worked with Zeke.

An accident at Zeke's job site?

"Zeke's in the ER. I don't suppose you care, and I wouldn't even call you —"

Vance stilled on the futon. He did care. But hadn't he just *not* cared? This confused him.

"— but he's asking for you. If you're not completely wasted, do something for him for once in your life and get down here. And I swear, if you show up reeking of anything other than Coca-Cola, I'll be clearing your head in a toilet bowl."

Rod hung up.

What happened to Zeke? Vance's first response was to be angry at Rod for not saying. Anger felt good. He hadn't felt anything but irritation for quite some time now. He wondered if Zeke would die and he would lose his cheap digs.

Vance sat up. He leaned forward to put the long bottle of yellow tequila on the coffee table and just missed the surface. The bottle thunked onto the floor and slopped the stuff onto the carpet, which carried it straight into the soles of Vance's socks.

Something about the wet socks, something too deep in his heart to pull out, smothered Vance with the weight of his own self-contempt. Only a scum freeloader would be more worried about losing his crash pad than about the life of a friend. Zeke was a friend, after all. Maybe the only one Vance had, if he excluded his drinking buddies. Zeke was asking for him. Zeke, who had never asked *anything* of him, needed him now, and here Vance sat, in socks washed by tequila when they really needed a stiff detergent. His entire body needed a thorough scrubbing, inside and out, because Zeke Hammond needed him and Vance wasn't fit to set foot in a hospital. They would declare him unsanitary. Rod would wash him in a urinal.

Vance stayed on the sofa, staring at his half-empty bottle of anesthetic, hating himself.

Seven hours later Vance walked into the ER,

a little rumpled but clean. He'd managed a shower and a shave, and after a taxing search he found a clean shirt in the back of a dresser drawer. An iron in his quaking hands seemed like a bad idea, so he was wrinkled but combed. If his breath stank it was from three cups of strong coffee chased by Listerine. That last sip of tequila had been metabolized finally. His splitting head and his tacky skin confirmed it.

There was a bar one block down from the hospital. Vance planned a stop there just as soon as he was done here.

An ER nurse informed him that Zeke had been admitted and transferred to a room on the fifth floor. It bugged Vance that Rod hadn't called to tell him.

Vance hated elevators. They were death chambers, headline makers that very closely resembled the confined space of a truck cab under a six-foot snowdrift. But on that day, lacking alcohol in his blood, he felt like he weighed twice his usual mass and doubted he could climb five flights of stairs. He climbed into the metal box, punched the number 5, and closed his eyes. By the third floor he had slid down the wall to a squat that protected his stomach. On arriving, someone held the door open for him. Afterward, standing in the elevator alcove with his forehead pressed against the wall, it took him several minutes to reinvigorate his decision to see his landlord.

Down the hall, Zeke's door was closed all but an inch. Vance stood in front of it and stared at the wood. Should he knock? Barge in? Get a nurse's permission?

"You don't waste any time rushing to a dying man's side." The voice belonged to Zeke, altered by fatigue and the nearly closed door. But kindness carried it. Vance lowered his eyes and slipped inside.

Zeke's head was encased in gauze. His eyes were covered with a web of white. Vance sniffed his own shirt, confirmed it wasn't sending telltale odors up Zeke's nose. How had he known who stood in the hall? Vance glanced at the door, which floated back to its former position. Well, Zeke had a freakish way about him. Being sober just magnified Vance's impression of it.

"Hey," Vance said. He crammed his hands in his pockets, though he knew Zeke couldn't see his fingers quaking. He focused on breathing.

"You smell like a Laundromat. Not on account of me, I hope."

"Sorry." He didn't know what to say. What was a person supposed to say in a situation like this? *Bad day at work? Are you gonna make it? Why are your eyes covered up?*

"Don't make me do all the work here, Vance."

Vance cleared his throat. "You look like a near-death experience." Zeke's smile was forgiving and welcoming at the same time. "How bad is it?"

"It's end-of-my-career bad. Might-never-see-again bad. Trauma-that-I-don't-know-how-to-pronounce bad. But I'll live. Provided all my blood doesn't collect in my skull while I sleep tonight. The pretty nurses will be watching me closely for a while, which is more than most men can boast."

That whopper headache prevented any decent sentence from forming in Vance's mind.

"Rod called you?" Zeke asked.

Vance nodded, then when it occurred to him that a nod meant nothing to a man in a blindfold, he said, "Yeah. Why?"

"Because I thought I was going to die, and I told him I needed to talk to you. It could still happen, so let's get on with it."

Vance could name three or four people he would have guessed Zeke, on his deathbed, might call first. His own name was not on the list.

"Have a seat, Vance."

He did, his entire posture stooped toward the floor.

He shouldn't have come. If he had stayed with that tequila, everything would be better right now. This was one encounter he was already wanting to drown. His eyes locked onto a small chip in the corner of one of the floor tiles.

"Today I got a hundred-pound railroad tie dropped on my head, and do you know what ran through my mind while I had my face in the dirt?"

It was a rhetorical question, right?

"I was thinking, I failed that kid. Six years of opportunity gone like a wink."

"You've never done me wrong, Zeke." The truth of it put a rock in his throat.

"That isn't the same as doing you right. But I figure if I had to go stand in front of the pearly gates tonight, and St. Peter wanted to know why I didn't try to stop you from killing yourself with a bottle, your blood would be on my hands."

"Well, when it was my turn, I'd clear your name."

"The kid who was with me before you, Brian was his name. I pressed Brian too hard, trying to inspire him to a belief in God. I ran him off instead. Sometimes we overcompensate for our mistakes and err on the other side, see? As if we can find a universal answer to apply to every situation."

Vance didn't see.

"I hope you'll forgive me for worrying too much about repeating my mistakes."

Embarrassment was a too-tight turtleneck around Vance's throat. "I'm not in a position to hold back anything you need."

"That's right."

The room felt cold with awkwardness.

"I wasn't sure you'd come," Zeke eventually continued. "But I've had a few hours to rehearse what I'd say if you did. Are you ready for it?"

"Am I?"

"Well, I'm ready, so here we go: Your dad died for love, Vance. He put his life on the line because he loved you boys, and that kind of love is as close to God's love as any man can get, no matter what he thinks about religion. What are you dying for? Self-pity?"

The question rang loudly in Vance's ears.

"Your dad died so you could *make it,* not waste away in my basement nursing a bottle. You don't have the right to lay down your life for anything but love, Vance Nolan. Not for pain or regret or any absurd accusation your big brother might throw at you."

Vance didn't like the way Zeke named his agonies so glibly.

"I hope I live long enough to help you understand that your dad isn't the only man in this world who died for you. Jesus Christ hung on a cross and died a torturous death for you, and then he went to hell and back so you wouldn't have to go there at all. And he did it knowing you'd be sitting here in this room with me one day, hating yourself and hating him and not having a clue why your life is so full of so much hurt."

Vance's eyes burned. He didn't know where the tears came from. Anger, regret? Resentment that all his suffering might amount to little more in Zeke's mind than a Jesus conversation? He filled his cheeks with air and punched it out between his lips.

"But here's where I failed you: I haven't done my work to get the ground of your heart ready for that kind of seed, Vance. And that's why I hope you'll forgive me, and why I hope God will give me a bit longer on this earth to learn how to be bold. So today I just want to remind you that you are in debt to your father's love, not to your brother's condemnation. Do you hear me?"

Vance nodded. It didn't matter if Zeke couldn't see him do it. He didn't trust himself to speak. He had no idea how to repay that kind of debt, or why it mattered.

"I can't help but think that the railroad tie that fell on my noggin today was a divine opportunity — my second chance to show you that the point of this life is not to avoid hardship. In fact, I have a feeling that God's going to keep me alive just so I can prove it to you."

"That's crazy," Vance managed.

"Love is crazy, Vance. If we reasoned our way into love, no human being would ever risk it. Costs too much."

Vance wanted the spotlight off. "You just lost your eyes. Doesn't that mean you can't work? You can't . . . do much of anything."

"Want to help me learn?"

"No!"

"You think I should just do as you do? Roll over and die?"

"No." Vance sighed.

"Then let me live on my terms. Come along for the ride if you want, because I'm going to embrace this pain for your sake whether you'll let me or not. I'm going to show you that there's more to life than dodging pain."

"You are freaking me out."

"Good. Are you with me?"

Vance hesitated. The whole conversation was troubling. Embarrassing. Hopeful.

"You don't have the right to lay down your life for anything but love, Vance," Zeke said again.

"Okay."

Vance sat in the room for a long time, thinking about just leaving. About going home and packing up and finding a drinking buddy to take him in. But his thoughts never reached his hands or feet. He stayed there until the shifting sunlight crept across the narrow hospital window and finally laid its warm head on his chest.

"Good," Zeke murmured. "Good. Let's get started."

29

On the second morning after the deluge hit Eagle's Talon, Vance was awakened after only a few hours' sleep by sunlight straight through his eyelids.

He rolled off the top of Jonesy's bedspread and powered up his cell phone. The display declared it to be 3:47 a.m., though judging by the angle of the eastern light, it was somewhere around seven. Still no service. He checked the TV — still no power.

He stepped out onto the balcony overlooking the cove-turned-river. Down on the dock, in the hazy morning light, he could see the progress Baxter had made in fashioning a raft out of the balcony wreckage. Someone must have helped him. They had wrapped small blocks of the EPS foam in duct tape and attempted to fasten these to the bottom of the platform. The EPS wouldn't disintegrate in the water, but the tape would prevent it from falling apart if it was slashed or pierced. The raft might float, but it was too narrow to stay level. If even one person's weight tipped it, no amount of foam on the bottom would prevent it from going over. They needed a border to float it, a bumper that would keep the raft's weight centered.

Today, Vance was able to see the shoreline half a mile away. His eyes traced the most likely route Jonesy would have taken in the boat, though this was hard to judge. The current was steady but not rushing the way it had been when the others set off. There was no sign of a beached boat anywhere on either side of where Vance estimated their landing to be.

There were no vehicles driving on the distant road that followed the curve of the shore. No rescuers on the far cypress-dotted banks, assessing the situation of the stranded people. There were no sounds strong enough to outshout the waters of the Rondeau. No sirens or shouts, no generators or air compressors, no music or watercraft or children out for a summer swim.

There was no air traffic.

The silence was as heavy as wet snow.

In fact, something snow-like dusted the surface of the world, feathery light and nearly white. But it wasn't snow — couldn't be, in this July heat that was already climbing. It floated on the water without dissolving and gave it a greasy look. It looked like the ashes of a billion cigarettes.

Then Vance did see birds. Not the fowl that once lived on this peninsula-turned-island. Others now littered the wreckage of the broken isthmus. At the crumbled road their feathery bodies were fluffy tufts snagged on chunks of broken asphalt. Carried downriver by shifting currents, the carcasses had floated to the rocky places on the shoreline. Hundreds littered the cove. The stink of their early rot weighed down the oxygen.

But there was something else.

Water flowed easily over the barrier that used to be the isthmus. It was slow enough now for Vance to see a few high places under the water. He was evaluating whether there might be any way to cross the wet rubble on foot when the rising sun hit the water at a new angle. The light slid along the cove like a sprite, beating its wings and casting a shiny film of purple and green and gold across the surface of the water. Though the swirling color was mesmerizing to watch, like ink dropped on a wet paper, Vance's next thought was that it was also deadly.

Something unnatural saturated the water.

Something sprawling and toxic. Of the hundreds of boats and ships that traveled the lanes of the Rondeau in any given week, dozens of them carried hazardous waste from factories upstream to treatment plants downstream. If even one of these had been breached, the impact on the environment would be devastating.

He stepped back inside Jonesy's condo and slid the door shut, separating himself from the air until he might have a better idea what he was breathing.

There were two explosions on the river last night — two on the same boat? Or two boats, each facing unthinkable catastrophe? For now, there was no way of knowing.

Someone was rapping at the front door. Vance went out to open it and passed by Zeke, who had refused the bed and opted for the sofa. The smooth cork floor felt cool beneath his bare feet.

Tony stood in the hall in profile, facing the stairs. His slick style had begun to unravel, not only in his hair, which flopped down over his brow this morning, but also in a vague odor of stale clothing. Vance probably didn't smell like a summer flower himself.

He stood back from the door so Tony could come in. But the man stayed rooted in the hallway. The aluminum panels of the passageway reflected the white of his shirt from several different angles.

"Just wanted to touch base with you about Baxter," he said.

"What about him?"

"Is there any credibility to your friend's story about the bomb?"

"Enrique's? I haven't heard him tell it."

Tony tried to push his stray hair back into place but got no cooperation from it. "Do we have to do this, Vance? I'm tired. Tell me what you saw."

"A sinkhole. A mangled steel post. A broken device."

"So some*one* rather than some*thing* took down my foundation."

"How could I know, Tony?"

Tony closed his eyes and took a deep breath. Vance took a twisted pleasure in frustrating Tony's conversation, mainly because it seemed clear that he had already given Enrique's rumor credit for being wholly true.

"I only want to know your professional opinion: Does Baxter seem like the kind of person who would sabotage his own work to make a point?"

"The way I see it, Baxter isn't guilty of anything but a little panic, and maybe a temper tantrum in defense of his brother. What are you really asking me?"

"Why can't Baxter get this raft built? That's what I want to know — how hard can it be?"

"What, he was supposed to build it overnight?"

"It's *light.* We could go now. But the thing won't stay upright in the water."

Vance was surprised by this opportunity to prevent everyone from leaving Eagle's Talon. All he had to do was stay silent.

"You think he's intentionally messing up the raft?"

"The thought crossed my mind." Tony paced in the hall.

"Why would he do that? He wants off this place worse than anyone else."

"If you hate a man enough, you'll throw your own life away if you can take his with you. And Baxter thinks I'm the devil. How did he react, exactly, when you told him to fire his pump operator? Did you take responsibility for that or did you try to pin it on me?"

Vance held up his palm as if it could slow down Tony's runaway thoughts. "His hand is broken. He doesn't have all the right tools or materials. He's under a lot of pressure."

"You could fix this for us. You could get

this done."

Vance withdrew into his condo just as he saw Danielle ascending the stairs from the common area. "Tony," she called. "You have to come see this."

"You don't have the right to force us to stay," Tony said to Vance.

"I'm not forcing anyone to do anything."

"Tony!" Danielle repeated. Simeon's tousled head popped up next to his mom.

"When this is over, I'll make your life more miserable than it is now," Tony said.

"Right." Vance closed the door and felt like he was closing it on Danielle.

A new problem presented itself to Vance as plain as all the jugs lined up on the counter. There'd be no drinking the river water now.

"If the raft doesn't work, I'll divvy this up for everyone."

"Are we talking about the water?" Zeke was sitting upright now, probably wakened by Tony's questions.

"The river's contaminated."

Zeke nodded slowly. "I don't think Tony will be happy to delegate that job to you."

How many people would be stranded here at Eagle's Talon, and for how long? The unexpected need to defend Jonesy's precious supply propelled Vance though

Jonesy's apartment, starting in the bedroom, where he would have hidden a weapon if he owned one, then through the bathroom and into the office. He searched the closets, lifted the mattress, rifled through drawers, and unfolded linens. He groped the underside of desks and tables, he probed pillows, he peeked into lamp globes and floor vents.

In the office closet he found a safe about the size of a file cabinet. A large but straightforward digital pad controlled the keyless entry.

Vance went out to the living room where Zeke sat in a ray of light that he couldn't see pouring in through the east-facing window. "If you kept valuables behind a combination lock, where would you keep the combination?" Vance asked Zeke.

"In my head," Zeke said.

"Most of us write it down somewhere."

He took a turn around the room, trying to see things he hadn't noticed before. Personal mail, patterns in the wall art, order in the table's abstract centerpiece, a sculpture made of small glass blocks. He'd already ransacked the office's bookshelves, desk, files, and closet.

"People still like to use dates," Zeke observed. "Birthdays, anniversaries, divorces, retirements. They're easiest to recall.

Does that keypad have letters on it?"

"Just numbers."

"There you go."

"You're hilarious. What about a badge number?" Vance guessed.

"Vance. Sit."

Vance didn't sit. "I don't have much time to figure this out."

"True enough. You're not going to guess that combination in the time you've got."

So Vance sat. He took one of the wide chairs opposite his old friend. "And now I'm supposed to say, 'What do you mean by that, O Great One?' "

"I mean, Grasshopper, that I doubt your anxiety has anything to do with finding a weapon that probably isn't here."

"Who said anything about a weapon?"

"Don't you think if Jonesy had one he would have taken it with him?"

The man wouldn't necessarily have taken his entire arsenal. If he had a stockpile. Vance leaned back in the chair. "I'm not anxious."

"If you say so."

"But she won't listen to me. She won't stay."

"Are we onto the subject of Danielle now? I think I said something like that about you once, years before you came around."

"Danielle doesn't have years. She has maybe a few hours. She won't stay and I can't go. What am I supposed to do with that?"

Zeke crossed his hands over his stomach.

"Am I wrong about staying? I want to look out for her."

"Why?"

"Because Tony's a dog."

"Mmm." Which was Zeke's way of saying, *Wrong answer.* "Has God changed his mind since last night, or have you changed yours?"

Vance sighed. "I hate it when you do that."

Zeke lifted his brows. "I'm not the one doing anything."

Another knock at the door brought Vance off the chair.

He half expected to find Tony standing there with his allies, demanding he hand over the water that he hadn't had time to hide. Instead, he found Enrique, rumpled but recovered from his hangover of the day before, and Ferti, whose head was encased in a wide pink headband now.

"I hear you've got stuff to drink up here," Enrique said.

Vance opened the door wider. "I've got water."

"I don't mean water."

Vance hadn't actually dumped all the

liquor yet. He'd emptied two shelves before deciding to do the rest later, not realizing he wouldn't have a later. But this much was true: it didn't take any superpowers for a recovering alcoholic to anticipate the behavior of an active drinker in a crisis.

"Well, that's all I'm offering you."

Ferti pushed in past them both, saying to Enrique, "If he could predict our need for water, don't you think he could predict you too?"

"She's not admiring you," Enrique said. "The real reason she's come is because that raft is giving everyone fits."

Ferti snorted. "And the real reason you're here is because you expect that river to turn into a bed of pyroclastic fire."

"Anyone can see the ash. It's a volcano, I tell you."

"Right. And that rainstorm was a hurricane blown in off Lake Michigan. Where's the nearest volcano?" she challenged.

"Yellowstone," said Zeke.

Ferti's eyes widened. "Where the earthquake was?"

"Thank you," Enrique said to Zeke. "It's nice to know someone takes me seriously once in a while."

"I didn't say I believed it blew."

"But the earthquake was days ago." Ferti

said it like a hope.

"It's not that far a leap, is it? From earthquakes to eruptions?"

Vance should have felt relieved that these two were even here. Instead, his prevailing feeling was disappointment over how Enrique was handling his stress — by drowning it in alcohol, being argumentative, and accusing Baxter of something he probably didn't do.

"We thought we might sweet-talk you into helping remedy the problem," Ferti said to Vance.

"Sure. Come in. I'll listen. And then I'll try to sweet-talk you into staying with me here."

Ferti sighed. Enrique looked at the liquor bottles lined up on the wet bar. He fished in the glass bowl and pulled out a cigarette and a lighter.

Zeke rose from the sofa. "I do believe I'm ready for breakfast," he said. "Anyone care for a sandwich?"

30

Danielle's discovery might change everything for the better. That was her hope as she waited for Tony to finish speaking with Vance. She didn't hear what was said, but she sensed they weren't confessing their secret admiration for each other.

She made herself bright when Vance closed the door and Tony gave her his attention. "The raft is coming together."

"It's at a standstill," he said. "Baxter's about to give up."

"I think I can inspire him to try again." She reached out to take Tony's hand. "I want to show you something."

He withdrew from her touch and wiped his sleeve across his forehead. "I'm going to start losing support for this idea any second now. I have to get back to the raft."

"You really want to see this." She smiled at him, but his tone turned impatient.

"Just tell me."

Simeon was jumping up and down. "If he won't come see, can I tell?"

"He'll come." Danielle walked back down the stairs.

Tony did come, with his annoyance splashed across his face. They exchanged no more words as she led Tony from the north wing where Jonesy's unit was, across the common area, where the raft that wouldn't yet float was looking like a Dr. Seuss creation on the dock, and up to the third floor of the south wing.

Until just a few minutes earlier, the look and stench of the foul water that greeted her upon waking had stirred up Danielle's worry. It mixed with the disturbance of Vance's accusations about Tony and resulted in a kind of stress she hadn't experienced since the early days of life without Danny.

Tony had taken on a new manner since the storm. She supposed all of them had. His polished look was replaced by sweat stains and gray fingertips and grime across the legs of his pants. He had the look of man who applied more than just his mind to his work, and she found that attractive.

But she had trouble keeping her mind off Vance's poor opinion of him, because if Vance knew her own mixed motives, he would only think worse of her. She was upset with herself for letting Vance chew her ear.

She was more upset that she'd allowed herself to think, even for half a second, that Vance might be right about Tony's character.

"I set aside some sodas for you," Danielle said as they ascended the flight to the third floor. "They're not downstairs."

"What?" He stopped on the bottom stair and looked up at her. "Is that what you want to show me? Soda cans?"

She paused and looked down on him.

"No. Why are you ruining this by taking all your frustration out on me?"

He resumed his dreary climb without explanation or apology, and she waited at the top, already having second thoughts.

"Maybe you don't really care," she said.

"Don't start, Danielle. I'm tired. We're all tired."

"It's up here!" Simeon cried from the door opposite their own. "It's in the place next to us."

Simeon wiggled outside the closed door while Danielle unlocked it and pushed it open. She grabbed hold of Simeon's hand so Tony could enter the empty unit first.

She watched him step inside and then turn to face the living room. There, finally,

Tony gave her the smile she'd been hoping for.

A breeze cut into the room, an unpleasant chemical waft that came off the contaminated water. It was the strength of the odor that had drawn Danielle to investigate the unoccupied unit, and she discovered that the plate glass window that once showcased that amazing view of the Rondeau River had been shattered. Now the view was framed by glassy teeth. The picture window had been penetrated by Enrique's outboard motor. The massive wave that had sent the boat into Mirah's living room, directly beneath this one, must have catapulted the motor as well.

A fine dust of grayish flakes littered the floor by the broken glass.

Tony knelt by the motor. Reached out to touch it with his left hand. "*That* is the most beautiful sight I have seen all week."

"I thought you'd like it."

"I do, I do."

"It's smaller than I expected," she said.

"It's a wonder the window broke and the motor didn't."

"Can you attach something like that to the raft? Will it work?"

Tony stood and pulled Danielle toward him. "Everything I do works," he said, and he kissed her as if he were bestowing on her a coveted reward, which she supposed he was. Whatever it was about Tony's kiss that made her feel safe was, perhaps, the same quality that also made a man feel powerful.

"Mom, can I have a piece of this glass?"

"No!"

Tony gave her only enough space to see that Simeon had obeyed her before quickly closing the gap between them again.

She remained hyperaware of Simeon's eye on that tempting, shark-toothed window. She gently pushed away from Tony's undivided attention.

"You shouldn't worry so much," Tony said, making Danielle think of Ferti.

"I'm a mother."

"Yes, you are," he said, and she wasn't sure how to take it. A kiss shouldn't leave anyone exposed, least of all a child.

She stepped away from him. "Do you think this might change Vance's mind?"

"Maybe." His eyes were doubtful.

"Don't you want him and Zeke to come?"

"The more people I can get out of here, the better it will be for everyone."

"What do you mean?"

"Don't you think I feel responsible for this place, and for all the people who are stuck here?"

"Of course."

"Not to put too fine a point on it, but death doesn't reflect well on a man in my position. People have trouble forgiving leaders who've let others die on their watch."

"But it's not your fault if they go against your advice."

Tony regarded her as if finding valuable wisdom in these words. "No. No, it's not. You're right about that. But we're divided right now, and a house divided against itself cannot stand. You've heard that saying?"

She nodded.

"When people divide, and then people die, survivors create their own stories. Unique stories. Conflicting stories. In my case, not all stories will shed a nice light on me. Are you following me?"

She nodded again, feeling guilty of encouraging such stories by letting Vance tell them.

"I don't like it when I don't have control of my own story," he said.

"No one does."

Her agreement softened his expression.

"So I think you're right again," he said. "I think you are very wise, and we should try to pull everyone back together."

He slipped his hand behind her neck and kissed her once more, holding her to him through a sigh. Then longer still, until she became fully aware of Simeon racing a car across the kitchen floor.

She heard Vance say to her heart, *Can't you see what he's doing?*

He pulled away slowly, hardly pulling away at all, and breathed his next words over her mouth.

"I have a plan."

Tony released her finally, letting his fingers trace the top of her shoulder and wander slowly downward before coming to rest on her waist. A week ago she wouldn't have resisted the attention. But now, with Simeon — and somehow Vance — in the room with them, his touch embarrassed her.

"You inspire me." He took a satisfied breath and stepped away from her, smiling wide.

She looked away. "What's your plan?" she asked.

Tony braced his hands on his hips. "I'm going to prove that Baxter's frustration with the raft is just an act."

"How?"

"I'm going to fire him."

Part of Tony's plan, which Danielle didn't really understand, was to get Vance's help carrying the hundred-pound motor from the third floor down to the dock. He sent

Danielle to make the request, and she was surprised to find him deep in conversation with Ferti and Enrique, who looked guilty at being found in Jonesy's unit. After Danielle explained their need for Vance's help, a hopeful expression crossed Ferti's face.

Vance looked at her and said, "Maybe this is my chance to try to talk everyone out of this again."

Ferti shook her head, frowning. Vance ignored her and took Enrique to help him.

So Tony believed he could fire Baxter and reengage Vance, and Vance believed he could participate and win everyone to his side. Did the competition between men never end?

Danielle returned to the common rooms with Ferti and Simeon, who was complaining about being hungry. Danielle hardly noticed when Ferti offered to fetch him something to eat, though she must have said that would be fine. Her attention had landed on Tony and Baxter, who were standing apart from Carver on the dock, talking with their heads tipped toward each other.

Baxter didn't look angry over losing his job as raft designer. She sensed that Tony hadn't told her everything.

Tony saw her and came inside. "Is Vance

getting the motor?"

Danielle nodded.

"Ask Ferti if she'd get me something to drink?"

And then he went back out to the dock.

Vance and Enrique arrived just a few minutes later. The heavy motor waggled between them as they descended the stairs abreast. It looked smaller in their hands than it had on the floor of the apartment, and she had trouble envisioning how it would effectively push that balcony raft all the way across the cove. But she didn't know much about motors, after all.

"I'd like to see how he plans to attach it," Vance said, catching her eye and offering a peacemaking smile. She accepted it.

"First we'd better see if the thing is still alive," Enrique said. "Cost me two grand — it better be."

"A tidal wave can do a number on two grand," Vance responded, still looking at Danielle. She finally looked away. She thought he was speaking louder than he needed to, as if he wanted her to hear every word. "The motor's worthless in either case, if they can't float the raft."

Soon everyone had gathered on the dock to find out the answers to these questions for themselves. Their shoes left prints in the ashy flakes that coated the dock in a single, fine layer.

Danielle watched this activity from inside, urging Simeon to eat his PB and J and make the most of the daylight by looking at some books. After a few adjustments to whatever mechanical parts needed adjusting, Enrique declared the motor fit. And when it became clear that Tony wasn't sure how to connect the motor to the raft, everyone gathered round to offer an opinion of what might be done.

Everyone but Baxter. Danielle didn't notice he had slipped away until Simeon brought his crumb-lined plate to her and asked for another sandwich. No one else seemed to have noticed at all.

31

After Vance and the others went downstairs, Zeke felt his way around the kitchen for a bowl and one of the pitchers filled with water. Tucking the bowl under his arm, he carried the pitcher in one hand and held Ziggy's harness with the other. Together they went out to the balcony sheltered by morning shade. The cool temperature had a clarity in it that promised a bright if sour-smelling day — if the mysterious darkness didn't creep up on them again. He had felt that black sky on his skin, an unpleasant sensation like a greasy lotion, and hoped it wouldn't return.

In the confined space he oriented himself to a reclining chair and a square table topped with a slab of granite. He placed the bowl under the table and filled it with the water. Ziggy drank and drank, then took up his post at Zeke's side. Water dripping from his muzzle sprinkled the deck.

The sounds of absence, of people gone and electricity shut down, were pronounced this morning. But under the absence were the glub and splash of shifting water, the shush of oxygen passing through noses (Ziggy's large snout put out plenty of noise), and the underpinning whoosh of life, invisible like a seashore in a seashell.

These were the perfect conditions for prayer.

In such conditions Zeke's soul started out with words — *Our Father, who art in heaven* — and then slowly shifted through stages as he repeated and pondered the Lord's Prayer. When he did this, he regularly experienced a lightening of heart as the world fell away (*hallowed be Thy name*), a lightening of mind as he surrendered his own agenda (*Thy will be done*), a lightening of body as he entrusted it to God's care (*Give us this day our daily bread*), and a lightening of spirit (*forgive us, lead us, deliver us*) that he could only compare to sitting side-by-side with a dear friend who knew his flaws and didn't hold them against him.

But this morning the peace didn't come. He found it hard to get the world out of his mind. The thick air that wrapped itself around Zeke's ankles felt tight and threatening, as if it might pull him right down into the cove and drown him.

Sometimes a man had to insist on God's presence. He had to get his worldly body out of the way. Zeke pulled up his socks and adjusted his pants to ward off the chill, muttering to his body, "You comfy now, Zeke the Greek? You need a silk pillow? Let's get on with this."

He refocused and resumed his efforts to grab hold of God's hand.

"Thy kingdom come —"

I am coming. I am here.

Very rarely God spoke to him with such clarity that the voice seemed audible. And when he did, all distractions completely fell away, leaving Zeke standing in his own blindness on the pinnacle of a mountaintop, where all that remained was a space for his feet and a holy wind.

"Thy will be done —"

Even now, it is being accomplished.

"On earth as it is in heaven."

Soon there will be no distinction between the two. So soon.

"Today, Lord?" He surprised himself by asking it; he was not in the habit of pressing God to define mysteries. He didn't expect his Lord to answer.

For some. For you.

He wasn't sure what this meant, but he had a guess.

"Lord Jesus Christ, Son of the Living God, have mercy on me, a sinner. Thy will be done in me."

Zeke's contribution to the conversation stopped at this point. He sat in the companionship of God's presence and found it to be more significant than all his unanswered questions about what was happening at Eagle's Talon, and why, and when it would come to an end. He sat in peace and didn't think about time.

He heard the door of the apartment open, then close. The holy wind on the mountaintop disappeared, leaving Zeke on a simple balcony.

Ziggy's body shifted against the legs of Zeke's chair.

"Out here!" he called over his shoulder.

When no one answered, Ziggy whined.

"Enrique?"

He heard a stream of water hit the kitchen sink. A gurgle chased the splash down the drain.

Zeke sat forward in his chair and Ziggy stood.

The water flowed away and a pause followed it.

"Vance?"

A dull clunking of plastic containers ensued, a hurried motion of gathering them up and upending as many at one time as possible. There was jostling: of plastic pitchers, of metal pots, of glass bottles. The tone of the bumping bottles changed as their sides rattled against the basin and the contents flowed away. Zeke rose and took Ziggy's harness. He stepped off the balcony and into Jonesy's master bedroom.

"Who's there?" he demanded.

More water pouring out over the glugging jugs now, a flood of it.

An empty pitcher was cast to the floor. A thunk, a tumble, a hollow bounce. Ziggy barked at each noise.

Zeke emerged into the hall that led out of the bedrooms and into the living and dining areas.

"What are you doing?"

The person in the kitchen said, "Enrique and Ferti gave up so easily."

"Baxter?"

"We have to stick together if we're going to make it out of here alive. I can't do it by myself. We all have to help each other. But no one wants to take responsibility for anything."

This voice, this voice of authority that had given men confident instructions just a couple of days ago, was the voice of a frightened boy today. The terror that had struck this poor man had taken up permanent residence in his throat. Zeke placed a hand on Ziggy's head to silence the dog's frantic yelping. The animal quieted but maintained his tense stance.

"Baxter, think about what you're doing. We might need that. *You* might need that."

"If there's no water, there's no reason to stay."

"Some of us will stay no matter what."

"You shouldn't. You're being selfish!"

"Did Tony ask you to do this?"

"It's for the best. If you don't have water, you'll have to come. Vance will have to help us."

"Don't. Please take what you want and leave the rest."

"I don't need water. I need Vance. Don't you get it? I need his help to figure out that stupid floatie."

Thick gushes of water flooding the sink were punctuated by a dribbling from the counter to the floor.

"You should help me dump it. You should . . . not try to stop me."

"Down, Ziggy." The dog lay down, quivering. "Stay."

Zeke approached the kitchen.

"You ran your own business once," Baxter said. "You know what it means to lead. A successful crew can't have too many people barking orders. Just one person taking responsibility. It's why I'm going with Tony on this, don't you get it? I hate that man, what he did to my brother. But right here, right now, I know what's got to be done."

"I know you're scared," Zeke said. He reached out a hand toward Baxter's voice and bumped it on Baxter's elbow. The terror turned on him.

"I am not supposed to be here! I should be home with my wife and my kids. Right now I should be taking care of them, not talking people into helping me get there! We could have had the raft finished last night if Vance had helped out! He knows what we need to do to fix it. I know he does! Tony sees it too."

"The delay gave Danielle time to discover the motor."

"And what is that?" Baxter's accusations had become a fit of yelling. "One more problem to solve? One more hour spent figuring out if it will even work? Do you think it'll get dark again today, Zeke? Do you care? I do. And what devil will come on that darkness tonight?" Baxter's terror finally exposed the true depth of his fear:

"Oh, God, are people dying out there, like all those birds? That flood, those explosions! What's going on? I don't even know if my family's still alive." A sob cracked Baxter's composure.

Zeke felt embarrassed for the man, who had put so much confidence in his own ability to control the world. He lifted his hand to find the guidance of the counter and then took shuffling steps around Baxter's quaking form. His fingertips found one of the plastic water jugs and slipped around its handle.

Baxter's heavy hand prevented Zeke from lifting it off the counter. "Leave it." His throat was tight.

"Vance and I are committed to staying, no matter what Tony does."

"Why?"

"Because we feel it's what the Lord has instructed us to do."

"That's what you feel."

"Yes."

"The Lord speaks to you?"

"As I'm sure he speaks to you."

"What do you know about me?" The jug flew out of Zeke's hands, scraping the tops of his knuckles as Baxter knocked it away. Zeke heard it cut the air as it sailed to the floor, where it burst. "What do you know about God? And tell me, if you know so much, why do you think he might tell the two of us two entirely . . . *different* . . . THINGS?"

A pitcher of water crashed onto the tile and lost its lid, dousing Zeke's shoes and pants. That cold chill that was something more than water seized his wobbly ankles once more.

"What do any of us really know?" Baxter shouted, and a liquor bottle was smashed. Tiny shards of glass bouncing off the counter bit into the skin of Zeke's arms. He lifted his hands to ward off Baxter's flailing limbs, or to grab hold of them if he could. The tirade went on.

"I'll tell you what I know!"

The host of containers slid off the counter as if Baxter had swept them away.

"Baxter." Zeke landed on the man's forearm and seized it with both of his own hands. Baxter tried to wrench away. Zeke's fingers slid over the coarse hairs on Baxter's arm.

"I have to go, I have to get out of here!"

"Baxter, calm down." One more glass bottle teetered somewhere between counter and sink.

Baxter protested and grunted, and this time the bottle broke between Zeke's eyes.

■ ■ ■ ■

"Lord Jesus Christ, Son of the Living God, have mercy on me, a sinner."

Zeke completed his prayer and tried to open his eyes but had some trouble with it, maybe because it had been so long since he had closed his eyes to pray. After becoming blind it was no longer necessary to shut out any visual distractions except the ones that cropped up in his mind, so he couldn't remember what had compelled him to shut his lids in the first place.

It must have been the light. The brilliance that tried to spear his head was so sharp even now that he twisted his neck to avoid it. And yet it followed him.

"Zeke."

He didn't recognize the voice, but it entered his mind and brought the world in with it: the gentle *slap-slop* of water under his hips and shoulders, the heat of a hand that grasped his own, the scent of Ziggy's musky fur lying so close to his nose. And joy. A thrill caught behind his ribs and bounced there, anticipating, like a child at the gates of an amusement park.

"Zeke Hammond." The fingers that gripped his gave a gentle tug.

He succeeded in opening his eyes then, and the light rushed in, searing white and swallowing him up. He flinched, and the white was chased by pure and pulsing color. It tumbled over him, so overwhelming that he couldn't lift his head.

Someone else did this for him. Callused fingers slid under his neck and lifted him up out of the water with as much effort as it might take to pick up a leaf. His own heaviness seemed to fall away. Zeke began to laugh.

A man was smiling at him as if he fully appreciated whatever joke had just tickled Zeke. He supported Zeke's neck the way one might hold a newborn baby's. He wore a smart, crisp suit. His shirtsleeve was missing its cuff link.

"This time you see me," he said.

"I do," Zeke replied. "You were here when I first arrived. You helped me up the bank."

"I was. I did."

"I can *see.*"

The space around him was so vibrant, so sharp, that he couldn't remember any colors such as these in the world, and yet they were present in the simple kitchen of a food-loving bachelor, glistening with wetness as if it had been sprayed down with a hose.

"You've done well," the man said. He

tipped their foreheads together in a greeting that seemed at once too intimate for strangers but appropriate for the situation. "It's time to go."

The situation became clear the moment the man released Zeke's hand and neck, and Zeke rose not as if getting up off the floor but as if propelled up from the bottom of a pool to the shining surface above. And when he looked down to see what had happened, understanding came to him as quickly as his new sight.

The shell of himself remained on the floor. Its eyes were still open and blind. Its head was gashed and cradled by a pool of water and blood. Ziggy — whose poor nose truly looked even larger to the eyes than to the fingers — was stretched out in the shallows next to the old Zeke, but his eyes seemed to look straight at the new one.

Baxter was gone.

"Now that's something," Zeke said. "That pooch'll be all right?"

"He will," said his angelic companion.

"You stay with the boy, hear?" Zeke instructed his dog.

Ziggy blinked once and laid his head across the dead man's chest.

"What will happen to the others?" Zeke asked.

"That's not for me to say." He stretched out his arm to guide Zeke away.

"But you said that everyone who stayed with Vance would live. Did I misunderstand that bit?"

"No."

"Then why — ?" Zeke gestured to his earthly self.

"You are quite alive, aren't you?"

Zeke burst out laughing again.

32

Danielle's wristwatch said it was one o'clock when the darkness fell again like a funeral veil and drove them all indoors, away from the problem of the raft, which Vance hadn't helped to fix. But her watch differed from Tony's by forty-five minutes, and from Carver's by an hour twenty, and when this was discovered no one had anything else to say for a while. But she doubted it was the insanity of time that occupied their minds.

They learned about Zeke's death when Ziggy padded into the common room alone, tracking bloody paw prints down the white stairs. The dog found Simeon and lay down at his side, and Vance bolted upstairs, following the trail to tragedy.

Carver found Baxter in the model unit on the third floor, with broken glass in his good hand and blood on his clothing. He cowered in a corner, shaking and sobbing and babbling and saying it was an accident. His crime gave the men something to do. They created a kind of detention cell for him in the model, with Carver posting guard at the door to keep Baxter in, a claim that Danielle didn't believe. Where would the broken man go? It was more likely that Carver's aim was to keep the enraged Enrique out and prevent a second death.

There was a third reason for Baxter's isolation. By the flickering light of a candle, Tony told Danielle and Ferti that they and Simeon needed to be protected from Baxter's violence.

Ferti rolled her eyes. "Anyone in building 12 might have snapped the way that poor man did," she said. "Who's to say what a man's breaking point is? Or a woman's," she added under her breath. But today she let Carver rest a comforting hand on her shoulder.

Danielle felt less compassionate toward Baxter. After all, the rest of them were holding themselves together.

Ferti insisted on being allowed to tend to Baxter's injuries, deep cuts from the broken bottle. Tony accompanied her.

First, though, Danielle went with Ferti to the dressmaker's condo to help fetch muslin for binding Baxter's cuts, and a seventy-two-inch wedding dress bag, which they all hoped would be long enough to contain Zeke's body. Danielle wanted to take it to Vance herself.

Reluctantly, she asked Enrique to look after Simeon. A dead man was no sight for a five-year-old, and looking after him would give Enrique something to do besides stew over the death of his friend. Her real confidence was in the dog, though; Ziggy refused to leave the boy's side. She left them by the flickering fire, intending to be gone for only minutes.

On the second floor, Jonesy's door stood wide open, and the only light inside came from a still flashlight sitting on the kitchen counter, illuminating nothing in particular. It was aimed toward the living room, away from the kitchen. Danielle entered the tomb of a home. The rustling of the stiff bag draped over her arm was loud and intrusive.

"Vance?"

The sound of his body shifting position on a creaking chair came from somewhere near the dining area.

She passed through the flashlight beam and draped the bag over the back of a stool. She could see Vance's faint silhouette in one of the dining room chairs, one that offered a line of sight to the kitchen. It seemed insensitive to pick up the light and use it to her advantage, so she did without it. She found the table and slipped into the chair with its back to the heartbreaking scene.

Danielle slid her hands across the table and found his, covered them with her own. He lowered his head to his arms. His fine hair grazed the tops of her fingers.

The ticking of a clock she couldn't see boasted of keeping its own twisted time. The sound bent back on itself, reminding her of the long, blank seconds when she learned about Danny's death — empty moments that should have been filled with specific impressions. She had been cooking dinner in her own kitchen. She had been holding a papery purple onion that she didn't think to put down when the doorbell rang, and the onionskin broke and rolled out of her fingers as she opened the door to a somber police officer. After that was a gap of gray forgetfulness that lasted for hours, a collapse that had never reconstructed itself. She thought of it now as a forced walk into a new but empty life, as if she had just moved into a new but empty house, where she recognized nothing and was not given the option of living somewhere more familiar.

She wondered if this very moment would

become a part of Vance's own blank memories.

"I'm so sorry," she said.

An unexpected impression came over her that Jonesy was the officer who had knocked on her door. Probably because she was sitting in the man's home, with a dead body in his kitchen.

In time Vance lifted his head and turned his hands over so that her palms rested in his. He slipped one hand out and put it on top, sandwiching her fingers. She imagined that his face was pale and tired and disbelieving.

"I wish I'd known him better," she said.

"When I met Zeke, I was looking for a way to stop hurting." His sigh could have circled the world. "He loved me the way my dad couldn't — the way my brother wouldn't." Vance's words touched her heart like an ache.

Danielle wondered what heartaches framed his story. It seemed the wrong time to probe those old wounds while the latest one was so raw.

Vance said, "It sounds silly to put it that way."

"No, it doesn't."

He didn't say anything else for a long time. Silence had a way of stretching out the seconds. She waited, reluctant to bring Vance's attention to practical things, like how little time they had to take care of Zeke's remains with all the heat, all the water. It didn't take her long to decide to leave those matters to Tony, who had promised to come help as soon as Ferti was done cleaning up Baxter's hands.

Vance startled her by pushing his chair back from the table. "You shouldn't have to sit here. I'm sorry. Where's Simeon?"

"He's downstairs with Enrique. And Ziggy."

The flashlight flickered.

"I forgot about Ziggy," Vance said. He stood but kept hold of her hands, and so she rose with him though she had no intention of leaving right away. His fingers moved to her elbow, as if to guide her away from the horror of the black kitchen and back into the weak beam of the flashlight as soon as possible. She was reluctant to leave him here alone, though her mind kept flitting to Simeon.

"Ferti sent a bag," she said weakly. "For Zeke. It should be long enough. We have to —"

"I know."

"Tony said he'd come to help."

Vance placed his other hand lightly on her

shoulder and turned her away from her chair as if she didn't understand his intention to help her to the door. She stopped him by raising her free hand to his chest, and he took half a step back.

"Will you come with us now?" she asked.

"No."

"You won't even think about it?"

"This is where I have to be. If you stay I'll tell you the whole story. Stay, Danielle. I know I'm asking you to trust me. For Simeon's sake, if not for yours. Or mine."

Danielle's answer was not as swift as his. She wished she could see more than the outlines of his face. She wished she shared his conviction that staying was the wisest thing to do.

His fingers squeezed hers. "This building is stable. It's doing what I designed it to do. We have food, and Baxter didn't dump all the water. We have some time."

"Yes, we do — the raft still isn't working."

"It'll work eventually."

"And when it does, we go. We might go anyway. If we all sit just so, we might be able to keep it balanced."

"Danielle! Please. You have no idea what poison's in that water. The raft might flip over right in the center of the cove," he said.

The image of it sinking took center stage

in her mind. She resisted it.

"Doesn't the thought of putting Simeon on that raft make everything in you say no?"

It did.

"Wait here for Ferti's boat," he said. "Wait for them to come back and get you. Us."

She didn't want to tell him she feared that Ferti's boat hadn't survived the flooding, that there might not be any seaworthy boats left in Port Rondeau at all. Because if she was right, Tony wouldn't come back for Vance. The truth was, Tony might not come back for Vance even if he could.

Danielle wondered if she should stay here just to ensure that Tony came back for Vance.

She couldn't. She couldn't, because what if Tony decided that he didn't need to come back for her and Simeon either? What if the truth was that Tony's love for her wasn't any more real than her love for him?

"We can't stay here forever."

"I don't plan to," he said. "Only until it's clear to go."

"And what will clear look like?"

"A bird."

"Vance —"

"I know."

"Maybe it will look like a raft made out of foam and balconies."

"It doesn't."

"How do you know?"

"How I know doesn't matter if you can't trust me."

In some ways, it would be easy to stay with this man. It was his grief that tugged at her.

The flashlight blinked again and caught the corner of Danielle's eye. She glanced at it. She turned back and her cheek brushed the coarse hair of Vance's chin, which still bore the dampness of earlier tears.

He kissed her, and in the short beat of her heart before her logic objected, the kiss came to her like an invitation rather than a gift with strings attached, and it was impossible not to compare his lips to Tony's, and to find Tony lacking.

Or to compare Vance and Tony in every way, and find . . . that she was confused.

It was too late by then to prevent a bucket of unpleasant emotions from being upended over her head. She was betraying Tony, doubting herself, disrespecting Zeke's death and Vance's grief, and making way for more anxiety and guilt than she could handle in circumstances like these. She pulled away with more force than was necessary — because if she didn't forcefully separate she might go the other way entirely — and stumbled over the chair that was right behind her.

The flashlight died at the moment Vance caught her arm and steadied her. The chair hit the floor. The darkness was thick. His voice was contrite.

"Tell Enrique to build a stabilizing bumper out of the foam. At least a foot wide around the whole raft." He cleared his throat. "I'll help him if he needs it."

"Okay." She realized what he was giving her in those instructions: the freedom to leave in a raft that wouldn't flip over, even though he didn't want her to go.

"If you let me, I'd do everything in my power to protect you and Simeon."

"You couldn't protect Zeke."

He released her arm and withdrew of his own accord then. Her own cruelty shocked her. She had meant that there was only so much a human being could do in conditions like these — jump off a balcony, escape a tumbling trailer, row a boat to a dying man — and it wouldn't always be enough. No one could make any promises.

Not even Tony, she thought dimly as she groped her way out of the unit. Her salvation, and Simeon's, was entirely up to her.

When her hands found the open doorway, Vance's voice reached out to her, free of resentment but not of pain:

416

"Zeke didn't need protecting."

Vance helped put the raft to the test by building one like it. He applied Enrique's fury over Zeke's murder to the task of fetching an uninstalled prefab balcony platform from building 6. They retrieved it cautiously, this time going to the structure on foot, through a mangled mass of supplies and equipment strewn the length of the peninsula by the flood. Vance went first, high-stepping his way through the mud with only flashlights to penetrate the unnatural darkness. Together they found the stacked aluminum balconies in a protected corner of the lower floor and dragged one back behind them like a sled lashed to their wrists by canvas straps.

They didn't speak to each other except to communicate what was necessary to make the effort successful. But Vance spent a good portion of the treacherous hike having a mental argument with Zeke.

I shouldn't have told them what to do.

They'd leave with or without your help.

Not if they don't have a raft that floats. Both of Baxter's hands are worthless now. There's no more he can do.

You'd take advantage of his weakness?

I know how to fix it — I know how to tank it

too. I could force them to stay.

Don't you think the consequences of your interference would be worse than letting them go?

How? How!

You can't force a heart to accept a gift, Vance. Forcefulness is no different from selfishness.

But they'll die.

You don't know that. All you know is that the ones who stay with you will live.

So what happened to you, Zeke?

Vance's anger melted into an agonizing sadness. Over Zeke's death. Over the possibility that he'd never see Danielle or Simeon or Enrique again. Over the possibility that he was the fool, and that the sum total of his faith in God was a repulsive pile of misinformation.

He couldn't believe he'd kissed Danielle. He wasn't thinking of anything but what it would be like to be alone again, trapped in a metal box with the likely chance that no one would ever come for him. Loneliness was its own kind of hell. He didn't want it. He felt sick at the thought of her leaving, a selfish, desperate kind of sickness.

The sound of the balcony sliding through the muck at his heels was like a monster stalking him, licking its hungry lips.

Beside him, Enrique paused to catch his breath and hike up his sagging pants. His heavy belly poked out from beneath his three-day-old shirt. And the canvas strap in his hand was bloody across a blister in his palm that had opened up. Vance looked at the young man Zeke had taken under wing as if he'd never seen him before. Here was a guy who was probably like him in a lot of ways, because they were the type of guys that Zeke looked out for. But standing there with his perspective of Enrique limited to the circle of the weak flashlight beam, Vance understood that he knew almost nothing about Enrique's story.

"How are you holding up?" he asked.

Enrique sniffed once, nodded, cinched the straps around his wounded grip as if it were nothing, and leaned his overfed body back into the task.

Do you love these people, Vance?

Yes.

Then show them. Do what you can to help them stay alive, no matter what they choose.

They stopped at the tilting platform of number 11 to dig out more of the foam that was still exposed. They balanced these pieces on top of the balcony sleigh and then finished the journey.

"So," Vance said. "We can blame all this

on a volcano, huh?"

"Not *all*. Volcanoes don't make rain. But the darkness, the ash. Yeah. Betcha Yellowstone is one big pit right now."

"So why did it get light this morning? I don't get that."

"Weather patterns, Vance. The winds shift. Everything's messed up. Think about it."

It required more thought than Vance was willing to give.

Back at building 12, Vance worked swiftly with what few tools they had. He worked indoors, on the open floor of the common room. Enrique helped. Carver and Ferti took turns looking after Baxter upstairs. Tony and Danielle held lights. Simeon held his cuff link high and pretended it was a hammer, a screwdriver, a saw, a piece of floating foam.

Within a couple of hours Vance declared it seaworthy. It lacked the railing of the balcony raft Baxter had built, and the other one didn't have its stabilizing bumper yet, but otherwise the two were almost identical. He, Enrique, and Tony carried it outside and to the end of the dock. The plywood board that had been for Danielle's room, which Baxter had ultimately rejected for his raft, became a ramp that they would use to slide this into the water.

"I'll test it!" Simeon said. "Let me ride it!"

Danielle placed a hand on his shoulder. "This raft is for Mr. Zeke," she said gently.

Tony did the math to calculate the approximate total weight of all those who would be going with them whenever the sunlight returned: Danielle, Simeon, Ferti, Carver, Baxter, himself. The dog. They tried to approximate this weight by piling the raft with furniture. A mattress and box springs. Two bookcases tipped on their sides like bedrails. A set of dining chairs.

And atop it all, Zeke's body, wrapped loosely in a bolt of Ferti's stiff muslin, because the dress bag had been too small after all. They doused everything in three bottles of Jonesy's highest-proof whiskey.

"This is so medieval," Tony scoffed.

"You want to dig a grave in that mud with your bare hands?" Vance snapped. Their shovels had all been washed away.

"What if it washes up?" Danielle worried quietly, hating to ask.

"It's so small, the current could take this all the way to the Gulf."

"Wishful thinking," Tony muttered.

Maybe it was. If it happened that the raft was beached somewhere, maybe it would provide a clue to outsiders of all that had happened here at Eagle's Talon.

Carver and Ferti joined the group for this somber process. Vance watched with conflicted awareness that the respects paid to the dead were funded by self-interest. With the possible exception of Enrique, he wasn't sure that anyone here cared about Zeke's death as much as they cared about their own lives.

Could he blame them for that?

The men slid the death raft into the greasy cove, and a chair tumbled off the side, splashed, and sank. But after the first lopsided plunge, the platform leveled out and stayed afloat.

Everyone exhaled in unison.

Vance kept his eulogy in his heart as he leaned forward and set a match to Zeke's deathbed. And he ignored the others, whose silence morphed into relieved whispers and relaxed tones as Zeke floated away, a brilliant flame of glory against a black world of death.

33

Tony was waiting for Danielle in her unit when she went there with Simeon, desperate for a night's sleep in a bed, even if it didn't truly belong to her. Ziggy followed them — or rather, Simeon led the dog with falsetto praise and promises of food. Ranier's glowing cuff link dangled from Simeon's neck by a piece of yarn Ferti must have tied into a necklace for him.

"Do you like popcorn?" Simeon asked the pooch. "We have lots of popcorn."

The living room was lit by a strong battery-operated work lamp that someone had found when scrounging for raft materials. Tony was sitting on the sofa with his feet propped on the coffee table, eating an orange.

His presence here stirred up feelings of resentment, as if anyone who dared to eat an orange after such a day didn't deserve the presence of human company.

Danielle pulled a bag of ready-made popcorn out of her cabinet and gave it to Simeon, who trekked back to his bedroom with the dog in tow. Tony patted the cushion seat next to him. She sat, and when her son was out of earshot she said, "Should we consider waiting?"

Tony frowned at her. "For what? The raft is a huge success."

"The darkness falls earlier each day. Lasts longer. We might want to see if there's a pattern to it."

"The pattern is that it always falls earlier and lasts longer. So we should leave as soon as possible."

"What about the contamination? It might be toxic. It looks toxic."

"We've been out there working for a day, breathing it, and everyone's fine. And it didn't dissolve Zeke's raft. I think it's just some kind of oil. Harmless unless you're a fish."

"Or a bird."

"Good thing we're not birds."

Why did it take courage to speak her mind with this man?

"I've just been thinking that we have enough food to last a few days. If we're careful we can stretch the water that's left —"

"Don't be an idiot." Tony sat forward on

his seat. "You're scared. I get it. But you can't take risks from a point of weakness. It's deadly." He seemed to notice her stricken expression and softened his tone. "Don't you think Danny would have told you the same thing?"

Tony's resurrection of her late husband stunned Danielle almost as much as his characterization of her as an idiot. Tony almost never spoke of Danny because he didn't want to pain her. But now she wondered how well Tony had known Danny after all. In truth, she had been thinking that Danny might have found more to agree with in Vance's position, because it was more intuitive than rational. *There's only so much reason a man can live on,* Danny had been fond of saying. *When you're tethered to a boat and you're trying to guess which way the next wave is going to break over your bow, your gut will do you more good than your brain.*

But what was her gut compared to Tony's? Who was the wealthy businessman, the aspiring politician, the self-made leader? Who was the executive assistant, the single mother, the dependent?

Tony seemed to take her silence as acquiescence. He slid a white envelope off the table.

"I was hoping you could explain this to me," he said.

She recognized it immediately as the letter Ranier had left for her. "You're reading my mail?"

"Do you have something to hide in it?"

He'd opened her mail! She was angry about that. She didn't know if she'd ever been so angry with Tony about anything. She held her tongue and made herself sit still, as if nothing were out of place between them and never had been, never would be.

Tony withdrew the envelope's contents and unfolded the paper. It caught the light of the lamp and from where Danielle sat appeared to have a reflective silver quality. He read, " 'You say you are strong but you are weak. You say you can see but you are blind. You say you are rich but you have nothing to call your own, not even a white dress to cover your shame.' "

"I suppose you can agree with that much," she muttered.

" 'Free yourself from selfishness. Strengthen yourself with genuine love.' What does that mean? Did Vance write this? Is he working on you?"

"That would be a bad way to do it, don't you think?" she snapped.

"Are you seeing someone else, Danielle?"

"No!"

"And yet this is addressed to you, and signed, 'From the lover of your soul.' "

Well, Ranier had left out that part in his oral presentation, hadn't he? How could she explain what she didn't understand?

"That buyer of yours brought it. Ranier Smith. I have no idea what it's about. Though it crossed my mind that you were behind it."

Tony smirked at that idea and she couldn't fathom why.

"And what does this mean, at the bottom?" He pointed.

"What does what mean?"

"There are numbers here — 31421." He flashed the note to her. It was handwritten.

"No idea."

"Could it be a date?"

"It's meaningless."

"So you won't mind if I throw it away."

She didn't. But she did. Only because Tony had taken control of one of the very few things she might have a right to call her own. "Do what you want," she said.

He folded the paper and put it in the front pocket of his shirt. Not in the trash, but in that tucked-away place where he could reach in and snatch it back on a whim.

Their shoulders touched as they sat together. She found his proximity threatening rather than protective. The whole argument was wrong, wasn't it? It wasn't a fight for "them," for their bond, but for each one's own rights, each one's own ego. Because she didn't really have intimacy with him after all, did she? She only had needs that she thought he could meet.

"You and I are going to keep watch tonight while the others rest." Tony turned toward her and leaned in close to her face. *Keep watch over what?* she wondered. She had the most unwelcome thought that the two of them ought to be wary of each other, the way enemies circle a fire, face-to-face. He lifted his hand to the side of her throat and kissed her deeply. There was only one way this night was going to end, and for the first time since Danielle had agreed to share her bed with this man, she resented it. But she owed him.

Danielle woke at a black hour to the silence of emptiness. The sheets beside her were rumpled and cold. How long had Tony been gone? He had fallen asleep before she did, and only when she heard his even breathing had she surrendered to exhaustion herself.

There were no sounds but her own in the room now. She couldn't even hear the whispering of water through the gap in her wall until she held her breath and strained to listen. But there it was, along with the air that brushed the backside of the bookcase.

She exhaled and rose from her room to check on Simeon, grabbing the flashlight from her night table. He lay in his bed in a deep slumber. A faint blue glow from his precious cuff link escaped the spaces between his fingers. Ziggy stretched out to his muscular length alongside her boy. The dog opened his eyes when she looked in on the pair, then closed them again.

Danielle returned to her own room. Her bare feet glided over the cork floor the way her heart skimmed the surface of familiar thoughts. She had been using Tony for her own interests. She didn't know if the sex was his way of doing the same to her, but she couldn't point a finger at him tonight. All eyes were on her own guilt. Did she care about him? Yes — but not in the way a lover should. Her love for him wasn't pure, wasn't even real, was only a cover for everything she loved that he gave to her and her son.

All Danielle's irritability toward him dissolved.

"You have behaved no better," she said to herself. "Maybe even worse."

Danielle stood in the center of her bedroom thinking she might go look for him. She needed to tell the truth while there was still time for it to matter. She needed to apologize, to make a promise of repayment somehow, by some honest means.

The thought of doing such a thing filled her with dread. She didn't know if she could find the courage.

She set the flashlight down on an empty shelf in the bookcase and pried the furniture away from the wall so that she could put her face in the air. A tiny shock of static zapped the pads of her fingers, and she thought she'd picked up a splinter. But the case was smooth and her fingertips were fine, and with just a few small tugs she had enough space to lift the curtain out of the way and look out over the water.

She was surprised to see a moon, low on the horizon and twice its usual size, throwing white light like a runway across the waters and reflecting off the shining surfaces of Vance's aluminum buildings.

It was the first time she remembered thinking of them as Vance's.

The slippery stuff in the water caught the light too, and from her high vantage it looked like sparkling soapy ribbons rather than toxic waste. She thought she saw a flash of silver under the dock, but it didn't appear a second time, and her hope in see-ing it once more faded. Her eyes were strained and heavy with fatigue.

A crash and a cry jerked her eyes away from the beauty. The impact had a low metallic tone, an unimpressive gong; the shout was human, high-pitched and pained. And so brief — cut off, masked. On the third-floor balcony at the opposite end of the building, two figures struggled like shadow puppets.

There were two balconies between Danielle's unit and the one belonging to the model, but these were not enough to obstruct her view.

She knew immediately that the man against the rail was Baxter. His bald head was a tiny version of the big orb hanging over the cove, and his silhouette exagger-ated his skinniness, his height, the length of his limbs. He flailed defensively with only one arm.

Baxter's opponent was too masculine to be Ferti, too slender to be Enrique, too agile to be Carver. *Vance, no,* was her uncensored reaction — Vance, avenging the death of his friend.

One of his arms was fully extended in Baxter's face, elbow locked, muffling the yell that had caught her attention. His other arm delivered a breathtaking punch to the soft spot under Baxter's ribs, under the sling she had made for his broken hand.

Baxter doubled over. For a sliver of a second, the moonlight caught the attacker's face.

It was Tony, now stooping over Baxter's humiliated head, speaking words only for his ears. He was shirtless, covered only by his expensive slacks.

They stayed in this position long enough for Danielle to recover from her surprise. She thought she should intervene. Running all the way downstairs, across, and back up to the other side might take too long. Shouting might rouse people who just didn't need to know about this incident.

Before she chose, Baxter straightened his body with such swift force that Danielle heard the back of his skull meet Tony's jaw.

Both men staggered.

Baxter reached out to grip the rail for support. But now, the same hand that had broken a bottle over Zeke Hammond's face couldn't hold on to anything. Danielle thought he and Tony would both collapse.

Baxter went first, falling sideways in the direction of his useless, bandaged hand. He missed and sagged, catching the rail in his ribs. He kept rotating until he was folded in half again, belly on the bar, arm pinched against his chest. Danielle heard his low groan.

Tony stayed upright, catching himself against the sliding glass door.

They stayed frozen this way for painful seconds. Perhaps Baxter's blow had knocked sense into their situation. Maybe the next thing she heard would be the embarrassed laughter of two men who realized their foolishness.

She worried about the way Baxter's arm dangled, floppy and ill-shaped by the size of that balled-fist bandage that Ferti had applied.

Tony pushed off the door and stood free of its support. He took one steady step toward Baxter and touched him on the shoulder. Baxter lifted his head, then his neck slowly lost strength and let his head sag.

Tony bent and lifted the man by his ankles, then threw him over.

Danielle reached out a hand to stop his fall, so far away from her, so terribly close that she would never forget the sight: Baxter plummeting headfirst, his long body already in the sprawling formation of someone who had hit the ground. It took a gasp's time.

His head hit the rail of the second-floor balcony directly beneath his own. The collision redirected his fall by inches, just enough of them to bring his chin down on the dock and his body down on the water. There was a snapping of small bones before an otherworldly smack. She heard Baxter's life leave in a grunt; she saw death arrive on the shadow of a cloud passing in front of the moon. And then he slipped under the rippling diamond surface of the cove.

Her mouth was open, but no air came in and no sound came out, and when she lifted her eyes to judge Tony, she found herself leaning out into the air, and him watching her.

34

Vance was on the dock before first light, gripping the rail that surrounded the little makeshift raft. While he waited for the sun — half-hoping it wouldn't come — he prayed for each person who would leave the relative safety of this home he'd built. How had Tony Dean convinced them all to put their hopes in a balcony that wasn't even designed for the water?

His heart returned to Psalm 119: *I rise before the dawning of the morning, and cry for help; I hope in Your word . . . Hear my voice according to Your lovingkindness; O Lord, revive me according to Your justice. They draw near who follow after wickedness; they are far from Your law. You are near, O Lord.*

The sunlight arrived like a bird dragging fire on its tail feathers and setting the sky ablaze. It was a terrible beauty that shed light on the tainted water and warmed the sickening scent of more dead birds.

Vance reexamined the raft for soundness. He could think of nothing to improve it. In addition to the extra rails he'd assembled to enclose the surface and the foam floats, he'd built a transom bracket for the outboard motor from scrap and attached it to one of the balcony's short ends.

Ferti appeared with a bright purple beach tote slung over one arm. The bag burgeoned with food wrapped in plastic and matched the purple wrap that covered her short hair. She laid a hand on Vance's arm.

"How things change in a day. Including an old lady's mind."

Vance nodded. Death had a way of frightening people, though he had hoped that watching Zeke's body float away on the same kind of craft they planned to use might persuade them to stay.

She patted his elbow repeatedly. "I'm too old to take death lightly, you know. Gotta keep believing I can beat it for a long time to come."

"If you stick with Carver, he can probably teach you a few secrets."

"Now, Vance, I've never needed anybody to teach me anything, hear?"

There were no arguments left in him.

"But he's not a bad fellow, is he?" Ferti

said by way of tossing Vance a bone. "If we make it through this, maybe I'll reconsider. At the very least maybe I'll stop objecting to his stubbornness."

"It must take a lot of energy to keep that up."

"He's a tenacious one, that's for sure."

"I meant you, Ferti."

He wasn't looking at her when he said it. He was so tired now that he wasn't sure why he'd bothered to say anything at all. But Vance felt her eyes land on him, and it was too late to take it back. He noticed Carver come to stand behind her, either to offer assistance that would be rejected or to eavesdrop. Maybe both.

"Mm-hm, mm-hm. So what you mean is, I deserve a rest from my own stubbornness?"

"Maybe when it comes to people like Carver."

"Mm-hm." She transferred her heavy purple bag to her other arm, still holding him down with her eyes. "Well, when we get back here with my yacht, let's you and me have a chat about it. What do you say?"

His wilted smile was the best he had to offer. "It's a date."

Carver winked at him, and Vance lifted his chin in acknowledgment. Ferti spun around. "You going to accuse me of stubbornness too?"

"Not when I'm better at it than you," Carver said. He tipped his ivy cap at her, then reseated it low on his brow.

"Carry this," she ordered, and she thrust her bag out for him to take. He brightened as if she'd just asked him to marry her.

"With pleasure."

"So where did it happen, exactly?" Ferti asked Carver, and he shook his head. "Don't you try to protect me. I'm going to put Death in his place, remember? It helps to stare him down when you get the chance." She was looking up the dock toward the north end of the patio. "Do you know, Vance?"

He wasn't even sure what she was talking about.

"Then I'll just go figure it out for myself," she said, and she glided away on her flat-soled sandals, the purple fabric of her long skirt fluttering around her strong brown ankles.

Vance looked at Carver with a question in his eyes. Carver was shrugging into his suit jacket.

"She means Baxter," Carver said, looking up to the third-floor balcony. "Tony says he jumped last night. Went down and never came back up."

Vance felt the full burden of the weighed-down world at that moment. He raised his arms and clasped his fingers behind his head. If he'd thought to speak to Baxter, could he have prevented the man from taking his own life? It hadn't even occurred to him that Baxter might need some kind of comfort. He hadn't even had time to sort out his own feelings toward the man.

"Who was with him when it happened?"

"With him? No one. I set up camp with Enrique after Baxter fell asleep. I guess Tony discovered it a couple of hours ago — went to talk with him about whether he wanted to come with us or stay with you here. Left a note, I hear. I'm thinking Baxter already figured out that neither of his choices was good: on that raft with Enrique or alone with you in building 12."

Let my cry come before You, O Lord; give me understanding according to Your word.

"I'll look for Baxter's body," Vance said.

Carver set his mouth in a line and shook his head. Of course, as for Zeke, the river was the only suitable grave for a man in a location such as this.

Ferti was standing near the edge of the patio, studying a particular spot, then looking up to the balconies. From here, Vance thought he could see a smear of blood on the second-floor platform. He wouldn't have noticed it if he hadn't heard the news.

Enrique emerged from the building carrying a large bottle of something from Jonesy's bar. Tony came too with a plastic jug of water, dark circles cupping his eyes. Vance wondered where Danielle and Simeon were.

After Enrique got the outboard motor onto the platform, the four men lifted the heavy raft into the water. It dropped off the edge and splashed down, then bobbed like a buoy. Tony clapped his hands together and flashed a smile at everyone gathered.

"Excellent."

His enthusiasm was too much for the moment. Death crouched here on the dock and it lurked in the water. How many men dead? Did Tony even care?

Enrique climbed onto the raft and attached the motor to the transom. Everyone watched as if he were an illusionist about to perform a fine trick. But there were no surprises, and he secured the equipment quickly.

Vance turned his head. Danielle was standing beside him, and he hadn't noticed her arrival. Tony saw her at the same time and his smile vanished, which was when Vance realized that she was barefooted and empty-handed.

Tony squinted, though the sun was not shining on him. "Where's Simeon?"

"He's inside with the dog."

Danielle's voice lacked its usual strength, and Tony responded to it with more brusqueness than his polished political style usually allowed.

"Get him. It's time to go." He waved Carver onto the platform with Ferti's bag, and the old man found his sea legs easily.

"She feels right," Carver said. "C'mon now, Ferti. Let's show the kids how it's done."

"Danielle," Tony said when he saw that she hadn't moved. "I want to go. Now."

"Simeon and I are going to stay," she said. Her eyes went to the spot where Ferti had been looking for evidence of Baxter's demise, then darted away as if news of the man's death were a secret.

What had happened to change her mind? Tony didn't respond to Danielle's announcement. But he was frowning when he offered a hand to Ferti and helped her across the watery gap between dock and raft.

When Ferti was safely aboard, he came up the dock with the slow and measured steps of a man who was trying to choose his words carefully.

Vance's hope surged. He shifted his weight so that his right arm touched Danielle's shoulder. She didn't step away from him. And she preempted Tony's argument.

"I was thinking that a child and a dog on that raft could be dangerous for all of you. If we stay behind, everyone has a better chance. It's last minute, and I should have talked with you about it before now, but . . ." She gave way to his penetrating stare and looked down.

Tony licked his lips. "I know Baxter's suicide has really upset you."

The gentleness in his tone didn't match the sharpness of his eyes.

"It's terrible," Danielle murmured. She picked at a fingernail. "I guess it couldn't be helped. He was so upset."

The line of Tony's lips softened a bit. He touched her arm tentatively. "I'd rather you were with me."

Vance said, "She's right. The dog is terrified of the water, and he might cause trouble. And Simeon won't be separated from him."

"You'll come back for us, won't you?" Danielle lifted her head and looked Tony in the eye. "I don't have to worry that you'd leave us here?"

"No, no . . ." Tony was shaking his head.

"Because I only want what's best for everyone," she whispered. "Do you understand?" She waited for him to say something. He didn't. "Do you believe me?"

He nodded slowly before saying, "Of course I do." His attention lingered on her for a long time, and Vance wondered if he'd make one more attempt to convince her to go. But then he leaned forward and kissed her gently on the mouth, and that was his only good-bye.

Danielle's breath was a shudder as Tony walked the dock one more time, not looking back, confident and easy. He stepped onto the raft.

Vance took Danielle's hand, meaning to encourage her. She wrenched it away, then separated herself from him by two steps. Didn't matter. He was bursting with relief that she was right here, right now.

With his foot, Tony pushed the raft away from the dock.

Starting the outboard motor was a bit like starting a lawnmower. Enrique opened the choke and put the throttle in the on position. He gave the recoil starter a tug and the piston fired, then died.

Vance smelled gas.

Enrique pulled again. The piston fired

again and the engine turned over, and a flash of flame erupted from the motor.

The passengers flinched in unison and Enrique cursed. Vance ran to the end of the dock and snatched up the canvas strap they'd used to drag the prefab balcony. He tossed one end of it for Tony to catch, hoping to quickly reel them back in to the dock, but already the raft was too far out. Carver stripped off his suit coat and started beating it against the flames, causing the platform to pitch. Ferti lost her feet and landed hard on her hip.

Something had been damaged when the motor was cast through the window — a carburetor hose, a fuel strainer, a gas line, a regulator. It could have been anything, but surely Enrique had inspected the thing, put it in the water for a test? Vance had focused so hard on the raft that he didn't think of it.

It didn't matter now, though, because the real problem was not in the outboard motor but in the toxic waters surrounding them. There was just so much fuel there to keep the fire alive.

Carver's wild flailing threw a dripping petroleum flame across the surface of the water. Vance watched it plunge down not ten feet from the boat. Hot kissed cold with a sizzle that was swiftly followed by the *whoosh* of a small chemical explosion. There was a burst of orange light and an instant column of black smoke that pushed itself high above their heads. The dense smoke rose like bubbles beneath the surface of an ocean.

Whatever the flammable stuff was, the little raft was covered in the sheen of its residue. The foam wasn't flammable, and neither was the aluminum, but the ropes and straps and found scraps that held it all together — those were as good as candlewicks and kindling.

The captivated pause of everyone on the raft collapsed into an elbowing flurry of effort to get off before the fire spread. The chaos tipped the balcony precariously toward the dock side, and Ferti, already seated, slipped right under the horizontal rail that Vance had pieced together. The water jug and liquor bottle splashed down too.

Vance chased the raft. He ran back down the dock to the patio that spanned the front of building 12, then leaped over the rail that separated him from the pump-truck disaster of building 11, right into the thick water. He came up spitting and squinting, slippery with a chemical that might eat him alive if the fire didn't find him first. Ash dotted his arms and slid down his face.

His skin tingled but didn't burn as he free-stroked past the frog-legged truck, its cab still submerged in the cove, and then scrabbled out onto the ruined but dry spilled-oatmeal foundation. The dock for 11 hadn't been constructed yet, and the flowing water might bring the raft close enough for him to grab the rail and stabilize the platform while everyone climbed off.

But Carver had already left the raft. Dived in after Ferti, Vance presumed. He couldn't see either of them. Tony was clinging to the rails, mesmerized by the burning water. As the raft spun in uncertain circles on the current, Enrique caught sight of Vance and attempted to shift the float in his direction with his significant body weight.

The column of coal-black smoke had already doubled in height and reach. Blackness pushed against the windows and covered the balconies with a morbid drape. It shimmied underneath the foundation of building 12 and licked at the dock they'd all been standing on.

Vance could see that the raft's rail would miss his fingertips by inches. But if he moved up number 11's tilted foundation to a higher point, where the current passed beneath, Enrique might be able to jump up and grab Vance's hand.

Vance scaled the foundation a few more feet and threw himself down on his belly. He pushed himself out over the edge as far as he dared. "Enrique! Catch me!" There was no time to explain, only a hope that the man's wide-eyed reaction meant he saw Vance's intention. Enrique, taller than Tony, could grasp Vance's arm.

With only Tony to counterbalance his weight, Enrique placed his chunky knees on the raft's slim rail and reached up. Vance's arm was slick from the waste in the water. The heat from the motor fire seemed to melt his face. Enrique's grip slipped, recovered, and then seized upon Vance's shirtsleeve.

"Hold on," Vance grunted. "Use your feet."

He meant for Enrique to keep hold of the raft with his toes so he could drag it back to a place where he and Tony could climb out. Tony saw this and reached out for Enrique's leg. But the big man, clawing his way up Vance's arm like a wet cat, got his feet atop the rail, and when he pushed off he sent the raft spinning away against the current.

"No!" Vance shouted.

The *whoosh* of air fed the fire. It reached for Tony's clothing. He danced away from the flames.

"Tony!" Vance bellowed. "Get off of it! Swim!" Tony was deaf to all but the bubbling burn.

Everyone was stuck in his own predicament now, and there was nothing more Vance could do. The muscles and tendons of his arm screamed against Enrique's weight, so heavy that Vance couldn't shift to find a new position. The unfinished edge of the foundation cut across his pecs like a monster's bite. His hand was already going numb. He shouted his protest against the pain and the futility.

Where was Danielle? He twisted his neck toward number 12's dock, where the fire had punched fiery fists up through the wood. Flames pulsed in the spot where he'd left her standing.

"Danielle!" he bellowed. He didn't know if he could be heard over the crackling heat any more than he could see through the smoke that was roiling around the cove. The fire advanced, and then suddenly retreated, a living, shifting thing that was easily distracted. She didn't answer him.

Enrique swung on the end of Vance's slippery arm, too far down to raise himself up to catch the lip of the foundation.

"Let go," Vance ordered through clenched

teeth. "Swim it." At this point, Enrique could get himself out of this stew. There was enough for him to grab hold of here in the water, so close to land.

The command had the effect of a death sentence. Enrique became that much more frantic, clawing at Vance's skin as if he dangled over a precipice rather than a small body of water.

"I don't want to die," he whined.

"You won't."

Blood appeared on the surface of Vance's biceps. It made him think of Zeke's red snowsuit, so bright against the snow as he dropped into that tunnel to pull Vance out of his father's truck. He wondered what state Enrique had been in when Zeke decided to rescue him.

" 'Rique," Vance huffed. "I'm *with* you, but you gotta let go."

"Don't leave me."

The shirt across Vance's pecs felt gooey with more blood where the foundation sliced into his skin. He feared Enrique's weight might sever his arm from his body like a drumstick. And so he decided to fall into the cove with the frantic man, who might be taking perverse enjoyment in this scene if he were witnessing it in a movie theater. Vance twisted his right leg toward the edge of the foundation, then gripped the rim with the toe of his boot and pulled himself over, inch by scraping inch, until the balance tipped in Enrique's favor and they went down.

Vance tasted the greasy, bitter water on his lips and kept his eyes closed. Enrique slipped away, then found him again — clutching his clothes, tearing at his hair, dragging him down. His knee crashed into Vance's chest, and Vance gasped a choking mouthful of muck as Enrique reached over him.

He might have been reaching for the surface. It was impossible to say which direction that was as the men tumbled together, both gasping for survival.

Enrique's wading boot on Vance's shoulder drove him into a jagged metal surface that dragged across his cheek and tore at the tiny hairs of his close beard. The boot pulled away, and Vance braced a hand against the metal. He thought it was one of the foundation's steel posts that he touched. The water swirled around his skin and around the surface of the column. With his fingers he found the ragged edge that had scratched at him and quickly discerned that it was a gash in the post like a shark jaw full of metal teeth. And he could see in his memory the sight of that post that had been bombed and weakened.

He was running out of air. From here, he knew he could let the water lift him — he hoped not into a burning pool of chemicals.

He moved his blind hand carefully to avoid getting cut and put it right in the way of Enrique's boot. Why was he still here? The man's frantic kicking impaled Vance's finger on one of the spikey teeth. Vance freed himself, so angered by the pain that he hooked Enrique's ankle with his elbow like a wrestler. The boot was caught on the broken post, trapped by its own laces. There was no time to untangle the mess, and no need. As Enrique thrashed and Vance held on, his foot popped right out of the shoe. Enrique shot away, sending a ripple over Vance's face.

Vance followed him. Or tried to. His shirtsleeve had been caught between the boot's sole and the gouging spikes. He tried to slip out of the garment and found that his wrist was trapped in the cuff. The cuff's button, the boot's laces, the soft sole, the metal snags — his air-starved brain could make no sense of what was to blame or how to undo it.

Blast! How had Zeke managed to do anything without being able to see?

Vance's lungs and heart were pillaging his body for oxygen. There was simply none left to be found.

You don't have the right to die for anything but love. Zeke's words in his head had a calming effect, though Vance had never considered it might look like this.

He gave his arm a desperate yank. And another that tore something in the shirt, but not what he needed. And one more time.

And then he had nothing left.

35

Danielle shrieked when Enrique's clambering weight pulled Vance into the water. She still stood on the patio of building 12. The dock was already flaming up, and her shocked gasp caused her to start hacking on the black cloud that had begun to crowd her.

She lifted her eyes to the flaming waters. In a distant current, behind shifting pillars of smoke, Carver and Ferti floated downriver, neither of them fighting the flow. He held her head above the water, his slender arm thrown across her wide shoulders. Her eyes were closed, her head restful on his chest. His face was tipped up toward the sky like a praying man. And maybe that's what he had become. Maybe that's what they all would become before the day was out.

Danielle attempted one of her own.

God, help us make it through this. Alive.

It looked like the only one who stood a chance was Tony, standing on that raft, beating at the flames with Ferti's now-empty purple bag as the vessel moved downstream. He looked set to hit the dock at building 6 pretty squarely unless the current took him out again. Even if it did, he would have an easy swim if he got there before the flames did. She wondered why he hadn't jumped yet.

Danielle wasn't able to separate this image of him beating back the flames from the sight of him casting Baxter over the third-floor rail. It was the same violence. Because what would he have done if she hadn't bolted the door of her unit before he returned last night? What would he have done if he had seen her before she appeared at Vance's elbow and announced publicly that she wasn't leaving Eagle's Talon? Would he have told everyone that *she* had committed suicide too?

And what would he do when he returned to building 12 to find that they were the only ones left? Danielle. Simeon. Tony.

It might not be enough that she had protected his own departure and pretended she wanted him to come back for her. He had played right along with her, she thought. She believed they understood each other. *Let me go and I'll do the same for you.* But now they had returned to the unwritten page on which anything might happen. She looked again for Enrique, for Vance. Gone.

Simeon's cries reached her ears and a black cloud of smoke rushed her, and she hurried back into the house.

Inside, Simeon shrank in a corner of the game alcove where he would have had a clear view of his mom on the patio. His arm was slung around Ziggy's neck and he clutched Ranier's cuff link in his fist. His eyes were locked on the pillars of flame on the cove, swirling over the water like small cyclones. Danielle couldn't prevent him from seeing it all.

She knelt between her boy and the scene and took Simeon's face in her hands. They trembled. Her heart worked so hard that its frightened pace intruded on her breathing.

"Simeon, honey, look at me. Look at me."

He obeyed.

"Do you remember the workers? The silver workers you told me about? And the one who came to our home? Mr. Ranier?"

Simeon nodded.

"What did he tell you? Can you remember? I need you to help me remember what they all said."

In fact she recalled his exact words. Her

recall of Simeon's confidence in those words was vivid, and she would help him grab hold of it again. Because she could see now that this faith of her little boy was almost identical to the faith Vance had possessed when he warned them all not to leave. She needed that faith now. She needed at least one of them to grab hold of it. And of all of them, she had no doubt that Simeon was strongest.

"What did they say?" She shook his memory gently between her palms.

"That we don't have to be afraid."

"And Mr. Ranier said something else when he came to visit us. Right? You remember that?"

Simeon opened his palm and turned over Ranier's luminous silver cuff link with his thumb.

"Right. He gave that to you."

"He said our house was the safest place we could be."

"It is, Simeon. It is. We are going to be safe here, and we don't have to be afraid. Okay?"

"Our house will burn down."

The fact that it wouldn't came to Danielle like a break in the clouds. The relief this brought to her was so wholly unexpected that she even laughed. "Let me tell you a secret about this house, Simeon. The dock will burn, yes, and the awnings will too. Maybe even some little parts. But you know how this place is all shiny with metal? The metal won't burn, Simeon. The concrete foundation won't burn, the foam blocks inside of it won't burn."

"It won't?"

"We really are safest inside here." She smiled at him.

"Where is everyone?"

Her smile faltered. "Let's go upstairs. I need to do some things quickly. C'mon, Ziggy."

Ranier's cuff link bit into her hand when she reached out to help Simeon up.

"You've done a really great job taking care of that for Mr. Ranier. Do you think you can keep doing that until we see him again?"

Simeon nodded once more.

Danielle swept past the catering kitchen and snatched up as much of the remaining food as she and Simeon could carry. Then she rushed Simeon upstairs to Jonesy's unit, where what was left of Vance's water would be. Her own condo had been emptied of all but those sodas for Tony, and she worried that it would be filled with smoke that had fingered its way in through the gap in her bedroom wall.

Inside, she locked the door behind them and began a search for anything she could use to defend themselves against Tony's return. Surely a retired police officer like Jonesy would have some kind of weapon. Preferably a gun.

"Are you hungry?" she asked Simeon.

"Yeah."

"You can have some cereal," she said, handing him the box she'd tucked under her arm.

"Can Ziggy have some too?"

"Sure."

Danielle entered the bedroom hall and went into Jonesy's office. Her eyes burned. She'd done this before already, looking for containers to take Jonesy's food downstairs. She leaned against the side of the desk, her back to the door, defeated before she'd even begun. The closet door was open this time, the only thing she noticed that was different about the room. The tall safe still stood behind the door, bearing a digital keypad.

Simeon said something she couldn't hear from the kitchen.

"What?" she replied. If the safe were hers, and she had weapons, she'd keep them in there. But she had no idea what the combination code was.

Or why, when she ran her fingers over the

keypad as if she might just be able to pull a lucky guess out of her head, the words of Ranier's strange letter would come to mind.

What will come must happen, but you need not be afraid, if you open your eyes so you may see. Strengthen yourself with genuine love.

The letter was so offensive when he had read it, but not as terrible as when Tony had repeated it, mocking, using it as a reason to cast jealous suspicion over her and Vance. She wondered for the first time why Tony's reading of it had caused her to feel defensive of Ranier. She could think only of how similar the stranger was to her beloved Danny, who had loved her better than she had thought possible.

And then there was Tony, generous but motivated by something other than love. What was it? The desire to be loved? Or at least adored by people who might grant him power: the power to lead, the power to govern them.

She had given him that power over her without even feeling coerced, hadn't she? She had, so easily, given her safety to a man who threw another man over a balcony to his death.

Danielle wondered if Tony had somehow convinced Baxter to kill Zeke, if it wasn't the accident Baxter claimed it to be.

If that was the case, why hadn't Baxter just told everyone the truth? If he thought that protecting Tony would be protection for himself, Danielle had just fallen into the same pit. Tony would come back and kill her too.

All these thoughts came to Danielle in a flash. The voice of Tony challenging everything. Including: "And what is this?" Then pointing to the numbers underneath Ranier's words at the bottom of the letter.

The numbers didn't come to the front of Danielle's mind in a conscious way, but her fingers started working: 31421. Enter. She pushed the buttons without thinking and the digital panel clicked, then flashed a blinking green light. She was so surprised that she didn't open the door quickly enough, and the backup mechanism re-locked it.

She imagined Jonesy laughing at her. *Uniquely unable to open a safe, are you?*

A painful memory came to her on a burst of light: of Jonesy Daly, standing at the door of her house to tell her that Danny was dead, of that purple onion, rolling to a rest at the soles of his shiny shoes. How could she have forgotten his face?

Her fingers shook when she reentered the

combination code, but she opened the door in time. Already her mind was trying to piece the revelations together. Why had Ranier provided the combination to Jonesy's safe? Why had Jonesy never prodded her to recall that they'd met long before they became neighbors?

A gun case and an expandable file were the only items inside.

She reached for the gun case first. It was weighty and closed with durable latches that seemed to require their own key. But when she flipped them aside they yielded.

The weapon's velvety bed held nothing but an outline of the gun.

The file had an accordion bottom and was filled with about a dozen manila tricut folders. They were organized alphabetically according to what looked like the names of banks or investment funds. Just an orderly sleeve full of labels that meant nothing to her. Old case files, maybe?

She ran her fingertips over them.

Ryder & Howe, BCT Aggressive Growth Fund, SPC of America, Mutual Risk Management.

Clement, Danny.

The sight of her husband's name in the middle of a stack of corporations filled her with a peculiar dread. She withdrew the file and opened the cover, not sure what she expected to see. A formal police report? Grotesque photos of the accident that had taken her husband's life? She had never seen those, intentionally avoided them. But there was a photo at the top of the file of a car that was not her husband's. It was a car in a junkyard, smashed to a fraction of its original dimensions on the front passenger side. The custom gold paint was barely clinging to the car's buckled frame. Something about the paint made Danielle's fingers go cold.

She flipped to the accident report and saw Jonesy's badge number among the case file data: 31421.

In another photo there was a close-up of the vehicle ID number, and on the next page, a report from the department of motor vehicles identifying the VIN as belonging to one Tony Alexander Dean.

Jonesy had a photograph of Tony Dean's damaged car in a file bearing the date of her husband's deadly car accident. A hit-and-run. An unsolved crime. A case long cold.

It was not cold any longer. All her memories changed color under the hot lamp of truth: The way Tony had introduced himself to her as an acquaintance of Danny's. How

Jonesy had been able to afford an early retirement and lavish quarters in Tony's newest development. The true meaning of all the gifts and care Tony had tossed her way, like scraps to a pitied dog.

Tony, who had never loved anything more than his dream to someday hold a powerful office and the doting love of constituents, who had no shortage of blood money to cover up his crimes and save his name.

Danielle sagged and sat hard on the floor.

The Living God would like to free you from selfishness.

She heard the words as she'd never heard them before, as if Ranier were standing there next to her with his hand on her shoulder, reading the letter afresh and saying, *Not your selfishness, Danielle. Not yours. Tony's.*

There was a pounding at the front door. The noise set Ziggy to barking and Simeon to saying loudly, "I'm coming!"

"No!" Danielle yelled. She got to her feet like a newborn colt, scooping up the papers and photos as if they were her only link to reality, to truth. "Don't open it!"

She ran out of the small room, clipping her shoulder on the doorway as she exited.

"Simeon!"

But he had already pulled the door wide.

36

The water that slipped into Vance's lungs was smooth and metallic. It was liquid silver that belonged outside his body, all cold comfort. The river should have wrapped him like a mummy ready for the next life. Instead, it slipped down his throat in a quick second and raced to the ends of his airways, hopped right into his bloodstream, and attached itself to the last bubbles of oxygen there.

It lifted his chin. It expanded his lungs.

It raised his body a few inches in the water but failed to free him from the drowning snag of that exploded steel post. His arms floated like a puppet's on strings.

His fingertips nearly touched the small cluster of silver lights that had gathered round to shine their flickering bluish rays across his peaceful face. They seemed to watch him. And to wait.

At Jonesy's gawking doorway, Enrique stood in a grimy puddle, dripping like an oily swamp thing with only one shoe. Simeon squatted at his feet, shining that luminous cuff link onto one of the rainbow swirls in the water. Danielle saw the scrap of fabric sagging from his fist and immediately recognized it as a chunk of Vance's cotton shirt.

"Where is he?" she demanded. Simeon's surprised eyes turned to her angry tone.

The burly man broke down right there in the doorway. He mashed the cloth torn from Vance's back against his hair-plastered forehead and started sobbing. Simeon looked up at him. Danielle wished she could take back her tone, but she had seen him drag Vance down, and here was proof that he'd failed to bring Vance back up.

She couldn't ask what happened. Cupping Enrique's elbow, Danielle pulled him into the room so she could close and lock the door again.

The dead bolt clicked into place, locking out all ideas of how to distract Simeon from the news of more death. What was more riveting to a little boy than the sight of a sopping and sobbing grown man, massive

465

with grief?

Vance's fate bore down on her heart like the contents of Jonesy's safe. Like the hulking metal cabinet itself had pinned her beneath its unbearable weight. She leaned her forehead against the secured door.

"Mom?" Simeon touched her leg. She put her hand on his head.

"It's okay," she said to him.

"Mom, I can't find Ziggy," he said.

"It's okay," she repeated. The dog might have gone out when Enrique came in. Maybe he needed to. She'd sort it out later.

"But, Mom —"

"Later, Simeon! I'll have to find him later."

She pushed Enrique toward one of Jonesy's expensive sofas, likely bought with money Tony had paid him to stay silent about his role in Danny's death. It seemed right that they should be ruined now with toxic river water. Enrique sat heavily.

"Where's Tony?" she asked him, with more self-control this time.

He shook his head.

"Does that mean you don't know, or that something happened to him too?" The detachment in her own voice worried her a bit.

"Didn't see," he snuffled.

He couldn't even give her the tiniest morsel of information. Lifesaving information. His unhelpfulness — no, that was not the accurate opposite of *helpful,* but she couldn't put her finger on the right word — made her so angry that she stopped guarding her words. But she kept a lid on her volume.

"Vance is dead because of you, Enrique. Maybe Ferti and Carver too. Maybe Tony. How dare you come back here without knowing what happened to every single one of them?"

Enrique met her eyes then, and she saw the door to his emotions close. His tears evaporated; defensiveness slurped up his regret.

He said, "Surviving is its own kind of punishment, you know."

She had believed this once, briefly, after Danny died and she thought she couldn't keep going without him. But Simeon had needed her to, and his need was a privilege, not a punishment. Danielle looked at her son, who was standing bravely in the middle of the room without his dog, though his puckered chin and his frowning brows communicated his worry.

"Don't make a waste of Vance's life," she said.

Enrique pushed himself up off the sofa and snatched a lightweight blanket off the back of a facing armchair. He swiped it across his face, then slowly dried his fingers and lifted his eyes to Jonesy's liquor cabinet.

"Don't do that," she warned.

He ignored her, went directly to the sparkling glass shelves, and reached for a full and expensive-looking bottle off the top. The outside fires mingling with daylight and smoke cast a hellish glow over Enrique's defeated posture. The last thing she needed right now was the company of a drunk man. Enrique poured himself far more than should go into any one glass.

"That's not how to thank Vance for what he did for you," she said.

Enrique had lifted the glass to his lips. He hesitated for just one second, so that the golden liquid sloshed side-to-side, then threw back as much as his mouth could hold in one swallow.

"He should have had some of this before his last swim," Enrique muttered. And then he started to cry again, silently this time, except for the sniffling. He set down his glass and reached into the glass bowl holding the cigarettes.

Danielle made a move toward the bottle. Enrique saw her. He picked it up by the slim neck and hauled it off to the window, having grabbed only a cigarette lighter with his other hand.

"Bet you think you're pretty smart, changing your mind about getting on that raft at the last minute," he said, raising a shoulder to wipe off his cheek.

Simeon slipped his hand into one of Danielle's and she squeezed tight. In his other hand he held Ranier's silver cuff link.

Danielle's mind was already changing again, this time in the direction of leaving this room and going — maybe — to Ferti's, the only condo on the south side that wasn't exposed to the elements. There was the bookcase-blocked slider in her unit and the shattered windows in Mirah's and the one above it, where the boat and the motor went through. Even Ferti's place would be smoky.

Where were her spare keys to all the units? Still in the wood bowl on her kitchen counter, she thought, where they had sat on top of Ranier's white envelope for a time.

"Simeon, honey, go have a look in Detective Jonesy's office and see if you can find something to color with. Some pens and paper." She gently withdrew her hand from his grip and turned him toward the office. "It's okay."

"Can I use scissors?"

She nodded. Scissors were the least of her worries at this point.

"I'll make a sign we can put up to help us find Ziggy."

"Draw a really great picture of him."

As Simeon passed through the room, she went to Enrique's side and stared out the window with him. The fires continued to burn in smoky columns that rose up out of the water. Their flickering light and faint heat teased her eyes. She feared the coming darkness, feared how powerless it made them all. Everyone but Tony.

His helicopter never had arrived — she wondered what that meant. Perhaps Tony had never contacted his assistant. Perhaps Enrique was right about that volcano, and the rest of the world was also burning. She pushed back her own anxiety.

"You and I have a better chance of getting out alive if we work together. If you stay sober."

He shook his head. "No one's getting out." Then he swallowed another mouthful of whatever it was.

She put more courage than she felt into her voice. "Well, that's the talk of a coward."

"Yup. Vance wasted his life on me, that's for sure."

"Don't talk that way about him."

"I'm talking about me." He thunked the bottle against his chest so hard she feared it might crack in his hands. "I did this, you know," he announced.

"Maybe," she said. "I'd like to blame you, but the truth is I don't know how much you *should* know about outboard motors."

He shook his head, still staring out the window that overlooked the wide river. "I sank that pump truck."

It took Danielle a few long seconds to figure out what he meant, and then her thinking got stuck on what the sunken pump truck had to do with sunless days, and water on fire, and floods under houses made to float.

"Baxter hired me to bomb the posts, bring the platform down."

Danielle blinked and reached her hand out for the solid stability of a chair positioned by the window. "You said Baxter did that."

"Had to beat him to the punch. Who knows what he might have told Tony about me to avoid a payback for what he did to Zeke?"

Enrique's cheeks still glistened, from contaminated water and tears.

"I don't believe you," Danielle said. "All Baxter's men were working on 11. *He* was working on 11. He wouldn't risk his own life."

"I was supposed to do building 2. Got turned around. Accidentally wired the devices to number 11. Maybe that is why it's so hard for me to find work these days."

Danielle still couldn't see the logic. "Who in his right mind would destroy his own work so close to finishing it, but before being paid for it? What could Baxter possibly gain from doing that?"

"Don't know. Don't care. I needed the money, I got paid."

"Can you prove it was Baxter?"

"Who else would it be?"

That was not the response of a man who had any confidence in his own defense.

"Enrique, can you *prove* it?"

"Got a recording of his voice on my phone."

"You never met him?"

"Didn't have to. I knew his voice the first time he opened his mouth, so upset to see everything fail. Did you hear his rant against Tony? That was the clincher."

A picture of the truth was starting to form in Danielle's mind. She turned her back to the bleak scene on the water and stared at Enrique.

"I'm still not sure what went wrong," he

mused. "There was a bomb on all four posts, but only two went off. But it was so dark that night." He stared at the blood-stained gauze on his left hand, which she had helped him bind after he and Vance built the funeral pyre for Zeke. "Something in the water," he murmured. "I don't know. A cosmic fluke."

Divine intervention, Danielle thought. Because Vance had been here. Because Vance had the favor of the angels. Because Eagle's Talon was his baby and he was the best man ever to set foot on this island, even if he *was* an alcoholic.

She shook her head clear of crazy thoughts. Vance wasn't here any longer.

So why did she feel like Ranier was standing somewhere in the room, watching her?

"Drew Baxter didn't hire you," she murmured.

"Sure he did."

"It was his brother."

Enrique sniffed and shot a doubtful glance at Danielle.

"His brother," she continued. "Ansel Baxter — Drew talked about him, remember? Ansel is the one with the grudge. He's the one who made the real threats, who stormed around in Tony's offices when he could sneak by security. Have you ever met *him*? I

473

have, many times. Their voices are impossible to tell apart."

"Some brother, if he'll take out his own flesh and blood just to get revenge on Tony."

Danielle planted her hands on her hips. This man was so stupid, so careless, so ungrateful that she could never rely on him and no longer feared him. "Do you honestly think Baxter would have told his brother he was doing a job for Tony? Do you think you're the only one who's needed to take money where he could get it these days? At least Baxter earned his pay honestly."

Enrique drank directly from the bottle and grimaced.

"That makes you responsible for his death too," she said. "Unbelievable."

"Don't treat him like some martyr!" Enrique snapped. His medicinal breath surrounded her head. "Don't forget Baxter killed Zeke. You think I'm supposed to feel bad that he died of guilt?"

"Tony murdered Baxter," Danielle said, "because of your lies."

Enrique blinked.

Behind them, a door slammed and Enrique and Danielle spun away from the window. Tony, as soggy as Enrique, held up Danielle's keys on one finger and smiled at them.

"Actually," Tony said, "that's not the reason I killed him."

Enrique took another drink. "See?" he said to Danielle. "No one's getting out of here alive."

37

The snow under Vance's feet was familiar, if snow could be familiar in the way he was thinking of it. All snow was white and cold and fragile and crunchy, he supposed. But if it was true that no two snowflakes were exactly alike, how could he think that this particular mound on which he stood was exactly like one he had seen before, in another time and place? And how could the white landscape stretched out around him, all 360 degrees of it, be preserved in such infinite detail for nearly twenty years?

"Memory's tricky," someone said into his right ear. "Don't think about it too hard."

The voice didn't surprise Vance. It was as if it, too, had been an expected and inseparable part of the scenery. In fact, without turning his head to see, Vance knew exactly what his companion looked like: a tall man with curly hair and slightly bowed legs, broader in the shoulders than he, and dressed all wrong for a construction site, in an expensive suit with silver cuff links. Cuff link. One was missing.

He looked and saw that he was correct.

The man nodded. "I gave it to him because he's still just a child." This explanation made Vance immensely happy, though it hardly made any sense.

"Have I met you before?"

"I've been around."

"Danielle saw you," Vance said, remembering what she'd said about the man with him in the trailer.

"She needs far more than you do when it comes to that sort of thing."

"That sort of thing?"

"Angelic sorts."

"But I've never seen an angel. Before now."

"You never needed to. Before now. Your faith has always been large enough without that."

"Well, not always."

"Yes, Vance, even when you thought it had completely died."

The man bent down to scoop up a handful of snow, which he passed into Vance's cupped palms. The ball was unexpectedly warm, but it didn't melt.

"What is this place?" Vance asked. "I think

I've been here before."

"You have. Most recently" — and here the man looked at the place where a wristwatch would be, but he wasn't wearing a wristwatch — "three minutes ago."

"I've been here three minutes?"

"Not exactly, but that's the only way to explain it to you for now."

"Am I dead?"

"Do you feel dead?"

"No."

"There you have it."

"But the way we feel doesn't always tell us what's real," Vance pressed.

The man cocked his head to the side. "Sometimes true. Still, you're not dead. Yet."

Vance took a deep breath of the sharp air. Cleansing air, like the unpolluted, uncorrupted oxygen of the mountains where his father and brother and he used to visit. It cleared his head. He separated the snowball into pieces with his thumbs and let the flakes snow on his shoes.

"I like it here," he said.

"That's because this is what you were made for."

"I was made for snow?"

His companion laughed, an easy, comforting sound. "The snow isn't the point. Look

478

around."

The brightness of the crisp scene was more brilliant than any glare he'd known, and yet easy on his eyes. It was absolutely beautiful. He turned slowly, taking in the details of the snowscape, inhaling the perfection of it.

Vance had come nearly full circle when he saw the splash of stellar-jay blue in the snow. It stood out against the white like a jewel, too blue to be a rock and too solid to be a pond. It was the size of a man stretched out for a nap under the sun, and the sapphire color was as bright as his father's snow bibs had been all those years ago.

He had no doubt that he was looking at his father's body, lying within a hundred yards of a gas station, visible just beyond the trees.

As a teenager he had been spared this sight, though his imagination had reconstructed it countless times. The view was not at all what he had expected.

"Why isn't this the most terrible thing I've ever seen?" Vance said aloud.

"Because you're seeing what it really is — love in its purest form. You were made for love. You all were. Love and life."

"My father died."

"Your father lived. Saving you was more

important than saving himself. That kind of love can't die. See?"

The man lifted his arm and pointed beyond the blue form. His linkless cuff flapped in the wind like a white bird wing and sent a burst of air across Vance's eyes. He looked up and saw, moving away from them, a blue streak skimming the horizon. It glided like a weightless skier angling toward the setting sun.

Vance knew he was seeing his father, his living father, freed of his earthly weight. And as if his strength and speed were connected to his son's burdens by invisible strings, he pulled the weight of the world right off Vance's shoulders as he sped away.

"The day he left us, all the powder bogged down his skis," Vance remembered. "Look at him now. It's like he's not even touching the earth."

"He's not. Love is more buoyant than that foam you use to keep Eagle's Talon afloat."

Zeke Hammond had done what he could to relieve Vance of the guilt he clung to. But this sight of his father flying over unearthly snow stripped it all away: all the guilt, all the blame, all the what-ifs, all the fear.

Vance's chest was bursting with freedom. His smile was so wide it was hurting his jaw.

"Your love is the reason we came, Vance."

Vance turned his happiness to this stranger. "What?"

"To Eagle's Talon. You built it on love for your fellow human beings —"

"But Tony —"

"Can't change any of that, no matter how much effort he pours into saving his own skin."

For the first time since arriving here, Vance didn't understand. "And what did you come to do? So many people have died!"

"Remember," the man said with a sideways grin, "you're not dead yet."

"But Andy and Marcus! Zeke . . . Baxter . . . and what about Jonesy? Sam? Mirah and the boys? You'll forgive my saying that I don't think you've done such a great job keeping people alive."

"It's not for me to forgive you, and you hardly know what kind of job we've been doing."

"So where's Zeke?"

"He prefers the Garden to the snow. Not enough color here, he says."

For a moment Vance was speechless. Then he began to laugh.

"And where are the others?" he asked.

"I'm only told what you need to know."

"But they survived?"

"Those who have love always survive. Even if they die. And sometimes death gives other people a second chance."

"Like my father gave to me and Pete."

"Like you gave to Enrique," the man said.

"He made it?" Vance asked.

The man with him nodded. "Because of your great love."

This caused Vance to sputter. "I didn't love that man," he insisted. "I barely knew him."

"You were more concerned for saving his life than saving your own. Isn't that your father's love exactly?"

Was it? Vance didn't have an immediate answer. He couldn't take his eyes off that beautiful blue streak, which continued its trek toward the light without ever disappearing from view.

" 'Rique was a panicked fool, you know. There wasn't anything heroic about what I did for him. I meant to save myself too."

"Well, not even Christ welcomed death with open arms. Can't say I'd ever like to experience it. But the truth is that Enrique is worse than a fool, which has a strange way of making your love for him even more valuable."

"So why am I not dead yet?" Vance asked.

"Because this time you get to choose."

"Choose what?"

"Whether to go back."

In that moment, the last thing in the world Vance wanted to do was go back. "I'd rather ski with Dad," he said.

"If that's what you want."

"But what will happen to Danielle?"

"I don't know."

"Who's with her now?"

"Enrique. And Tony."

Vance took a deep breath. "Tony doesn't love her."

The angel said nothing.

"There's murder in Tony's heart," Vance said.

"Oh, he hasn't restricted it to his heart," said his companion.

The brilliance of the snow faded just a little in Vance's eyes. He watched his father gliding over a hill, always getting closer to the light but, somehow, never moving farther away.

"Is that all he's been doing since he got here?"

The man laughed a little. "Hardly. This is just a snapshot of eternity. For your benefit."

"If I go back, can I save Danielle?" he asked.

"From what?"

"From Tony."

"Ah. You mean from selfishness. I have no idea. That's entirely up to her."

"Then what can I do?"

"Love her the way your father loved you. The way Zeke loved you. The way you loved Enrique."

"I think I could do better than that. For her."

"Then why wouldn't you go?"

Putting it into words made the concern seem . . . cowardly.

"There's no one else to do it?"

Another shrug. "All I know for sure is there's no one else exactly like you."

"Will she die? Will I . . . die all over again?"

"Of course. Eventually. Those bodies of yours were never designed to be permanent."

"I mean . . . never mind."

Indecision wrestled within Vance. He wanted to stay in this perfect place, find his father and Zeke and all the other amazements he was so sure it contained. But he didn't want to leave Danielle and Simeon to Tony's whims. And he didn't want to die again.

Though maybe, now knowing what lay on the other side of dying, doing it again wouldn't be quite so frightening.

"Loving any human being always involves a little bit of dying." The snappily dressed man with the sloppy sleeve raised his eyebrows and cocked a half smile at Vance. "I hear it gets easier every time."

38

Tony was a shadow of his public persona, a diminished portrait of leadership. His entire personality sagged like his expensive clothes, now ruined, and his slick hair, now dragging down the sides of his face. Or it might have been that this was what he always had looked like, disheveled and deceitful, and Danielle was only now noticing.

"And so the fittest survive," he said, looking across the room at Enrique and pocketing Danielle's keys. Even his voice had changed, its charisma altered by disgust that someone like Enrique, so far beneath his estimation of himself, would be equally lucky. "I expected to be alone with my girl."

He took the same steps Enrique had taken to the liquor cabinet and selected his own bottle to nurse.

Danielle found it hard to look at him. The smooth sounds of Simeon cutting through paper with the usually off-limits scissors reached her from Jonesy's office. Danielle still feared what Tony might do to them, even with Enrique here.

Unless she made herself strong, she would be the weakest target.

So she summoned the boldness to speak.

"You and I won't ever be alone again, Tony."

Tony tapped the bottle against his thigh, regarding her with a look she couldn't decipher. She had never said anything to Tony but what she believed he wanted to hear, and in the second after the words left her mouth she braced herself for his fury, which until now she'd only seen let loose behind the backs of investors and partners who'd let him down.

But Tony took slow steps to her, then touched her gently on the arm. She tried not to recoil.

"I know you saw what happened to Baxter. I'm so sorry you had to see that, but I did it for you. I did it to protect you."

"What harm could that man possibly do to me?"

"He was a violent man."

"You sent him to kill Zeke," she said.

"No. I thought Baxter was faking his incompetence about the raft. I sent him to Zeke's to pour out their water — that's all.

487

If he was faking, if he wanted to sabotage our efforts to get off this place, he wouldn't have poured it out. It was just a test."

"Just a *test*? Zeke died! Baxter was really, truly a mess!"

"I should have told you everything. Forgive me, Danielle. I need you more than ever right now. We need each other. Please don't hate me."

Humility was not what she had expected. It unbalanced her. Against her better judgment, she looked at him. He leaned so close to her face, his eyes pleading and wet.

"If I could do it all over again, I would do it differently," he said. "I would write Baxter a handsome check and send him away, shelter you without the complications. But our options are just so limited here."

"Is that what you do when you make mistakes?" she whispered. "You just pay for them to go away?"

He withdrew by an inch.

"You buy your way into lives," she said. "Into hearts. Mine and my son's."

"I have money. What good is it if I keep it to myself? Everything I've done for you was because I wanted to."

"And did you give so much to Jonesy Daly out of the goodness of your heart?"

The lines of Tony's face hardened.

"You killed my husband, Tony. I know everything."

Tony's breath was sharp, pained as if he'd been accused of killing his own flesh and blood. "How did you — ? He *told* you? Baxter lied."

"Baxter knew about Danny?"

Tony's eyes widened as if she had slapped him. He didn't answer.

"What lie, Tony? Baxter didn't even speak to me. Is that what you meant by him hurting me? He knew about what you did to Danny, and you thought he would tell?"

Tony took a drink.

At the window, Enrique uttered a humorless laugh that sounded more like an animal grunt. And in the space of that noise, everything became clear to Danielle. She remembered Baxter saying that Jonesy told him about Tony's plans to blame the pump-truck accident on his operator.

"Jonesy told Baxter that you killed my husband. That you ran away and dumped your car and paid Jonesy to cover up the crime. He told Baxter in case he didn't make it back. Baxter knew."

"There was no *crime,* Danielle, there was just a terrible, senseless accident! Danny died instantly — you know that much. I couldn't bring him back. I couldn't do anything to change what happened."

"If it wasn't a crime, you turned it into one," she said.

"And why not? Unlike your husband, I still have a *life.*"

Danielle took a step toward him. "You have nothing but aspirations, Tony! You have a road to throw down over the bodies of people who stand in your way! A manslaughter charge would end your career. A hit-and-*run*?" She picked up the manila folder she had brought out from Jonesy's office and slapped it down on the glass coffee table in front of his feigned grief. It fell away the moment he looked at the contents. "Was Danny alive when you ran?"

"No!"

"Tell me the truth for once, Tony. Own your crimes!"

"I own them, Danielle. Don't judge me because I take responsibility in a way that you don't like."

"Is that what I am? Your obligation? A salve for your guilty conscience?"

He hung his head. In the weak sunlight that still resisted the darkness she noticed the strands of gray that he always so carefully hid.

"At first you were," he murmured. "You were Jonesy's terms — look after her, make sure she's taken care of. Falling in love with you wasn't part of the plan."

"You can see the trouble I have believing that."

"But you have to."

"Why?" she asked.

"Because you love me too."

She shook her head.

"I loved your lies, Tony. I loved my own needs, and I guess" — she faltered with a humbling realization — "I guess that makes me as selfish as you."

"Then we're perfect for each other after all."

"Did you send Jonesy away in that boat because you expected him not to make it to the other side?" She shook her head, both disbelieving that Tony would have done it and not surprised at all. "You *monster.*"

Tony slammed his hand down on the top of Jonesy's file. "Jonesy went first because he wanted to save his own skin. And I had to give him want he wanted, see, because of *this.*" He shook the file in her face. "He's the monster, Danielle. Not me. Do you know what it's like to have your sins held over your head like a guillotine? I could do some good in the world if all the self-righteous jerks who don't have the courage to lead weren't judge and jury to all of us who do!"

He grabbed hold of her arm and squeezed until the pinch pained her.

"You and Jonesy are one and the same," she said.

"And you're just like us, aren't you?" His breath, hot on her face, stank of days and nights and fitful sleep. "Of all people, you *have* to forgive me. You *will* forgive me, because you are good and beautiful and because I believe you do love Simeon, if no one else." A flicker of warning passed through his eyes. "Don't you see how much I need you?" he said.

She did see. She saw with disturbing clarity that Tony needed her to continue his deception and shield him from the consequences he'd buried under a mountain of money. He needed her to corroborate the story he planned to tell about all the tragedies that had taken place here, unspeakable events in which he never was the one to blame and occasionally was the hero.

She could never do it, of course. But unless she and Simeon got out of Eagle's Talon alive, it wouldn't matter.

"I see," she whispered. "I forgive you."

Tony released her arm and turned his back to the liquor cabinet, leaning back against the wet bar as if work were over and it was time to relax. "Good. That will make dealing with him slightly easier."

Danielle's eyes shot to Enrique, who had dropped onto a chair in front of the window. Water dripping from his body pooled at his feet. The liquor bottle was between his knees, and he fiddled with that cigarette lighter he had found on Jonesy's bar. He flicked the wheel with his thumb and held the flame aloft as long as he could stand the heat.

"What's one more body tossed into a mass grave?" Enrique asked no one in particular.

"At least yours would be fitting," Tony mused. "Seeing as how you actually committed a crime that would be punishable in court."

"You're referring to me bombing a post?" Enrique's flame petered out. "Please, send me to jail. Gimme a ride in that fancy helicopter of yours we've been waiting for." *Flick. Flick.* "That bird that you don't have, that you didn't call for, that will never come."

Tony crossed his ankles and his arms. "What makes you think I don't have a helicopter, Enrique?"

"If you had one, your pilot would have been here by now. On pain of death, right?"

Tony did have a helicopter, and an airplane as well, and three pilots on his payroll. Not sure where this confrontation might lead, Danielle took a step away from these two men, aiming to keep herself between them and her young son, no matter how the scales of power tipped in their favor. She did this by attending to the oily mess dribbled and puddling on the cork floors, forming a streaking path from the front door to the liquor cabinet to the chair where Enrique sat. She stepped over the rivulet toward the kitchen, thinking of Tony eyeing the mess with so much irritation the time she tracked in clean water.

She fetched a couple of kitchen towels and started at the front door, slowly sopping up what she could around the entryway. She used her shoes to push the stuff around, not wanting any of the unknown substance on her skin. Two bar towels were not going to get her very far.

"But what if my pilot is already dead?" Tony said. "What if the entire world has been flattened while we're all vacationing here at Eagle's Talon? What if we're the last survivors on the earth?"

Tony was grinning as if this theory were a joke worthy of the stage.

"Or," Enrique said, "what if you and I have finally arrived where we belong? What if this is the right kind of hell for two killers like us?"

Tony didn't answer and his smile weakened.

Enrique lifted his chin and looked at Tony for the first time. That cigarette lighter in his right hand lifted a pathetic flame too weak to illuminate Enrique's face, cast in shadows by the blaze outside.

Enrique said, "I think I don't want to be roommates with you."

He upended the liquor bottle into the oily swirls on the floor and held the flame in the stream of liquid. It ignited before it hit the ground. And when the alcoholic fire touched the toxic river water, the burn flashed all the way up to the ceiling.

Danielle saw both men duck away from the flare, but that was all. She was leaping into Jonesy's office, grabbing Simeon out of the office chair at the confetti-strewn desk, pulling her son to safety. There was no time for her to give commands or even for him to protest. She felt his body bump the corner of the desk as she pulled him out the door and dragged him into the hallway. The scissors still in his little fist clipped the wall with a metallic scratch. Her eyes were on the tiny gap of escape that she had just cleared away, not knowing five seconds ago just how much she'd need it.

It was blocked. Ziggy stood in the doorway, barking, and at his side stood Vance.

The sight of him was like being caught up from a free fall by a parachute. She cried out, so relieved, and pushed Simeon into his outstretched hands as he stepped into the room. He caught up her son and reached out to take her hand.

His eyes were not on her, though. She turned her head to see what he saw: a snake of fire twisting down the long and narrow space, and two human figures — one flailing and loud, trying to kick the flames off his feet, the other silent, a slouched and barely discernible form behind the curtain of fire.

"Get him out, get him out," Danielle ordered Vance, pushing on his chest and on her son's clinging body. "Get him out."

"Danielle —"

"I'm coming."

"There's no time."

"There is." The fire was burning the easy fuel first, the quick-burning drinks, the unknown substance that had been tracked in. The hungry beast hadn't yet tasted the food that would take more work to eat: the flame-retardant furniture, the hardwood cabinets and glass fixtures.

496

Her eyes were on Tony. His entire body was coated in fuel. He, like Enrique, was a candlewick that would soon be consumed. Enrique was beyond help. But the fiery tongues were devouring Tony's pant legs and he was begging her for help with unintelligible words.

Her own blind desperation had once led her to believe he was a good man, and she had taken advantage of it, lying to him about the state of her heart. Now that the truth blazed as bright and hot as the fire, she couldn't turn away from two facts: She wanted Tony Dean to die. But if she didn't try to save him, she would become exactly like him.

Only selflessness could free her from selfishness. There was no third option in this moment. Danielle went to him.

Tony had dodged the heart of the fire but couldn't get out of his soaked clothes. He had gone forward into the living room arrangement and now sat between a chair and the coffee table, thrashing his feet and beating on his legs with his own hands. His kicking lifted the glass top off the coffee table. It slid off and fell away. A ceramic bowl full of wooden apples crashed, and the decorative fruit rolled into the fire. Jonesy's incriminating file glided like a sled all the way into the kitchen. One of Tony's shirtsleeves lit up.

With the practiced moves of a mother who had undressed a wriggling boy for years, Danielle stooped behind Tony and yanked his shirt up and over his head against his light resistance.

"Let me help," she commanded, and the shirt came off. She cast it away as he returned to smacking at his own legs. Tony's body was still greasy and at risk. He kicked off his shoes, and Danielle overturned the coffee table's wrought-iron base into the fire. A sputtering splash of the toxins flew away from them into the kitchen. Then she did the same to the expensive Horchow settee that sat on one end of the area rug. She lifted the corner of the heavy carpet and folded it over Tony's legs while he screamed at her.

She pushed him over so that she could form a cone out of the carpet. And she beat at the weakening flames still snuffling at his feet and ankles until he withdrew himself from the narrow point, breathing hard and sweating. His socks and pants cuffs and skin were charred scraps. Tony fell back on the floor.

"Let's go," she said.

"Can't."

"Crawl."

He shook his head, groaning.

"Tony. You're not in pain. That will come later." She didn't know if it was true, she just needed him to move before the fire spread. Already it had climbed the lamps and consumed their shades in the corner of the room. The smoke was crawling along the ceiling, and the stench — the stench was unspeakable.

"It's just your feet. Get over it. Use your legs, your arms."

Tony lay there in the rug. She scooped him up by the armpits to drag him, but he was a slippery fish. She could get no traction on his skin. And he outweighed her.

"Tony. Please." She couldn't see what else to do for him. She could only see that fire, and her need to get out of it. "I don't know what else to do for you. I'm sorry."

Behind her another one of the blue leather sofas tipped over. Vance was there, clearing the last heavy piece of furniture off the area rug, then lifting the corner. Danielle grabbed the other corner. The carpet was so heavy, tacky on a nonskid slip beneath it. The fringe tickled her fingers, and the stiff nap of fibers refused to bend in her grip. Vance leaned, and the rug moved. Together, Danielle and Vance dragged Tony toward the door.

On their way out Danielle noticed that Vance was clean, dry, and in new clothes.

39

It might have been late or it might have been early. Vance had no way of knowing anymore. The darkness fell again, like a final word.

Against the backdrop of mostly empty bookcases in the lower level's common room, he watched Danielle nurse Tony's feet. The patient was cushioned on the sofa and Danielle sat on a footstool, illuminated by the pillar candles Ferti had supplied so long ago — or was it only a day? Vance felt rested and alert, and more fully alive than ever. Danielle looked exhausted and beautiful in her willingness to help Tony.

The fires on the water still smoldered, the size of rowboats rather than trees now. Vance believed the flames in Jonesy's unit would burn out, smothered by the confinement of the aluminum enclosure. He closed the windows, locked the doorknob, then pulled the door tightly shut to protect Simeon from his own curiosity.

Enrique's little fire may or may not have consumed all the food and water they had left, except for a few items they found in Mirah's and Ferti's units — some uncooked rice and split peas and soup mixes. These made Vance think of the powdered drink packet he had once mixed with melted snow in a tin can over a candle flame for his brother. But today there was plenty of fire and no drinkable water.

In the model unit they had found the orange pill bottle that had been Mirah's, then became Baxter's, and now would become Tony's. Three tablets rattled in the bottom of the bottle, enough to get him through the night. From Mirah's medicine cabinet they had taken burn ointment and rubbing alcohol, and in Ferti's condo they found more dress muslin, which they used for binding Tony's feet. Danielle's touch wasn't exactly gentle — Vance recalled her digging the glass out of his arm with those tweezers — but her movements were patient, even after Tony cursed her and then finally passed out from the shock and pain of the burns. She removed the burnt fibers of his clothing from his wounds and applied ointment to keep out infection. Vance thought the man was fortunate not to have anything worse than a blister above his knees.

He aided Danielle by wiping Tony's healthy skin clean with muslin soaked in the rubbing alcohol.

Simeon declared the pool table to be his super lava rescue boat, and Danielle encouraged this imagining. Ziggy jumped up onto the green felt and stretched out next to him. Danielle said the idea of the rescue boat was what finally coaxed Simeon to sleep, but Vance believed his peace came largely from the dog, who stayed.

Vance draped a blanket over Tony's cleansed torso. Danielle was coaxing a swath of muslin one more time around the man's foot.

"Thank you," Vance said to Danielle.

She glanced up at him from the corner of her eye as if to ask, *For what?*

"You stayed. With me. When everyone else tried to leave. Thank you."

She reached for a pair of scissors balanced on the arm of the sofa, and her fine blond hair fell forward like a veil between them.

She said, "I hate to tell you I stayed for entirely selfish reasons."

"You mean it wasn't because of my charisma and debate skills? My rugged good looks?"

A half smile broke into her expression of concentration on Tony's foot. She cut the tail of muslin lengthwise down the center so that it could be parted to encircle his arch and then tied off.

"Going forward," she said, "I'll stay just because you ask. No other reason needed." She pushed her hair behind her ear and looked at Tony's face, peaceful now that his mind had shut down and shut out the pain. "He looks kind, doesn't he? I just didn't realize . . ."

After a few seconds of her inability to finish that thought, Vance tried to deliver her from self-condemnation. "You just didn't realize — because you couldn't, you don't know the whole story — how much it would mean to me not to be left behind again."

She looked surprised. She opened her mouth to say something, hesitated, and Vance thought of kissing her perfect lips again, here by candlelight. But then he thought she changed her mind about what to say.

"Will you tell me your story?" she asked.

"I will, when you're rested."

"Including what happened today?" He saw her attention flicker toward his clothing.

Part of the wonder of Vance's return to

the land of the living was that he had shown up in the center of that lopsided foundation completely dry and free of the smoke that swirled around Eagle's Talon. His clothes were as neat as their first day home from the store, and without any of the injuries to his arms and chest that he'd received when Enrique pulled him under.

From Vance's point of view, losing Enrique was a true heartbreak. Maybe Enrique had expected the fire to take him as well as Tony; maybe he was just a drunken fool. Either way, the real tragedy was that Enrique never did grab hold of the hope Zeke had for him, the hope Vance was willing to resurrect.

"Enrique thought you'd died," she said.

Vance only nodded, but he wasn't even sure what he meant by that gesture — *Yes, that was a logical thing for Enrique to believe,* or *Yes, I thought I'd died too.*

There was nothing left for them to do for now, and the abrupt end of urgency felt like a roller coaster coming out of its final turn and into a hard brake. Danielle and he remained next to each other as if they had been breathless partners on the ride, their hair blown straight back.

Danielle let the silence stand. But she reached out and took his hand firmly, gripping hard as if she didn't want some unexpected drop to jerk him away from her.

"What are we going to do with him?" she finally asked, her eyes on Tony.

"Besides make sure his burns don't get infected?"

"I mean, should we lock him up? I think Jonesy has cuffs somewhere."

"Where would he go, even if he could walk?"

"I'm more worried he might try to hurt us."

Vance stood, keeping hold of her hand and aiming to pull her away from the ties that still tenuously held her to Tony, though they had gone slack. He could see it, though he suspected this present tugging had more to do with Baxter's and Enrique's deaths. She hadn't explained everything yet. She would, he suspected. They had time.

"We're four against one if you count Ziggy," Vance said, taking the scissors from her and placing them on a high bookshelf. "And Tony will sleep for a long time. Come here." He dragged a comfortable chair from the living room arrangement into the open space between Simeon and Tony. Then he gently pushed Danielle down into it. "You sleep too. I'll keep watch. I feel like I could run a marathon." She took his hand again, sandwiching his fingers in both her clinging palms.

"Please stay," she said, sinking into the cushions so that he had to stoop.

"I will. Let me go get —"

"Not until I'm asleep. Please."

Bending at this angle would quickly grow uncomfortable. He crouched in front of her and placed a hand on her knee.

Her head was already tilted back against the chair. "You saw everything before it happened," she said. "What would happen to people who didn't stay with you."

"No, Zeke was the one who could see. But I don't think it worked the way you mean. I don't think even he knew what he was asking people to avoid."

"But you believed him."

"Because I knew him. He was an easy man to trust."

"And to think I hardly knew the man I chose to trust."

Her hands seemed very small around his. He could have easily freed himself from them.

"I misjudged you," she said. "I misjudged everyone. I thought you were unreliable. I thought Zeke was nuts. And Tony . . ." Danielle sat up straight and came forward in the chair. "No! The police file!"

"What file?"

She closed her eyes, and Vance waited for her to explain.

"I left it in Jonesy's unit."

It wasn't the light that woke Danielle but Simeon's excited shouts, and the thumping air that knocked against the east windows.

The uncommon noise caused her to stir in the chair where she'd fallen asleep after hours of talking with Vance. He'd pulled a matching oversized chair over to face her, and by candlelight they propped their feet on each other's cushions and exchanged their stories. Danielle didn't remember exactly when she fell asleep — his near-death experience had jolted her to bright awareness for a long time, and his child-hood losses had broken her heart. But when she finally could stay awake no longer, she'd dreamed of being trapped in a truck under the snow with Vance, feeling protected and unafraid. In the truck of her dream Vance kept saying it didn't matter that the only evidence she had against Tony Dean for murder had been consumed by fire. He kept saying, "Love has already freed you," as if that was the only justice she needed.

Maybe it was. She dreamed he kissed her, and his kiss melted the snow away and freed her from the prison where she'd been stranded.

When she opened her eyes, the chair opposite hers was empty.

"Mom! Mom! A helicopter!"

Danielle seemed to be the last one to fully compute the meaning of the word. Vance was already standing at the double doors that led out to the cove-facing patio, which had been reduced to scraps of charred wood. He held on to Simeon's wrist with one hand, and in the other he gripped one of the bright red bar towels, which he waved over his head. Ziggy stood beside her son, his tail wagging to match Vance's arm.

The sofa that had held Tony was empty.

"Where's Tony?" she said aloud, but no one was listening.

Simeon was jumping up and down, screaming, and Ziggy was barking like a hunting dog before the helicopter was in view, even before it passed over the building from east to west, from river to cove, from death to life. The water smoldered with a gray haze like stage fog, and the air was thick with a chemical odor, but Danielle couldn't see anything burning.

The helicopter shot out over the roof and then turned south, flying low over the partially constructed buildings of Eagle's

Talon, searching. Sunlight blazing from the east bounced off of the aircraft's canopy and paint so that she couldn't make out the details. Danielle worried that the people on board would be more likely to be blinded than to catch sight of them.

"Is it Tony's?" she shouted at Vance, but her voice was lost in the noise.

At the bottom of the peninsula the helicopter began to bank toward the north, returning. The craft that turned toward them did not belong to Tony Dean, whose helicopter was as gold as his SUV and black as his heart. This one was red like the towel Vance clutched in his fist. Red like a robin's breast.

"Rescue looks like a bird," he said without looking at her.

The silver lettering that spelled out NO-LAN INDUSTRIES across the tail caught the rising sun and flashed like an acknowledgment.

Vance shielded his eyes though the view had no glare.

Danielle said, "I didn't know you had another company."

"I don't," he said, and when he lowered his arm she saw him surreptitiously wipe the corner of his eye on his sleeve. "That one belongs to my brother."

40

Tony Dean's mind was fighting its way through a fog of numbing drugs when he thought he heard Danielle say she had left Jonesy's file upstairs. He wasn't entirely clear about that, but the conversation that followed confirmed his first impression. Vance seemed to think the fire would have gobbled up the evidence by now. For Tony, the chance was too big a gamble. Soon enough, Vance or Danielle would go looking for it.

He would find it first and destroy it himself. And then he would finally be free of the handcuffs Jonesy had cinched around Tony's wallet and political career.

This was his plan, but his body's war against the agony of his feet, which seemed like they would crack and fall off his legs if he applied any pressure to them, held him down. He couldn't resist the pull of drugs and sleep. He couldn't outlast the soft tones of Vance's and Danielle's endless murmuring chatter. He couldn't tamp down his jealousy that raised his pain levels to shrieking levels. He fell back asleep.

But by the time his eyes snapped open to sunshine, furious dreams had reinvigorated him. The kid slept on the pool table. The dog beside him eyed Tony without lifting his head from his paws. Closer, Vance and Danielle slept like the dead in separate chairs. Danielle looked ragged, and Tony couldn't remember how he had ever seen anything more in her than an unwanted obligation. He didn't believe for a minute that she'd ever forgive him for being the one who ended Danny Clement's life.

Baxter's pill bottle was within reach. Tony threw one down his throat and decided against trying to kill them all. It was too complicated. Too much could go wrong in the attempt. Especially for a man who couldn't walk on his own two feet.

So instead he began a crawl. A slow, nonthreatening crawl that would not raise the dog alarm. He crawled across the floor to the bottom of the wide staircase, cringing every time his toes scraped the carpet. He crawled up the stairs, which were much harder on his knees but kept his toes free of the abrasive floor. He crawled down the hall

512

to Jonesy's unit, and once there, reached into his pocket for the keys he still had, which Danielle had never thought to take away from him.

He let himself into Jonesy's unit and locked the door behind him. The fire had guzzled up the alcohol and oil on the floor quickly, but then had wasted its time searching for fuel along the aluminum walls and fire-resistant flooring. It had burnt out before eating anything much at all.

Jonesy's file was still on the kitchen floor, peeking out from under the refrigerator. Tony retrieved it and then, breathless, rolled onto his back, exhausted by the effort. Then he began to laugh. Now, finally, he was in a position to negotiate.

But not until they woke up and figured out what he had done.

It was cause for celebration. Tony mustered the strength to crawl to the bar, then onto a chair that raised him up to the lowest bottle of liquor. He opened and drank, and laughed, and felt the effects quickly. Then he slipped back into the deep sleep his pain required.

Pete Nolan set his late-model Robinson down in the thick muck of the unpaved turnaround and disembarked as the rotating blades came to a rest. His prosthetic foot gave him a limp so slight that Vance might not have noticed if he didn't know the full story. Pete looked like his father — their father — with his quickly receding hairline and sun-lined face and narrow nose. He had the stoop of a man who'd spent many hours behind a computer, and there were fewer smile lines around his mouth, but except for these details Pete might have been mistaken for the man who skied away to save their lives sixteen years ago.

A ball cap cast a shadow over Pete's gaze, which seemed to have trouble meeting Vance's head-on. He shook Vance's hand and then held on, covering it with his other smooth-skinned palm and squeezing tight. He was short of words, and though Vance had enough overflowing his mind for both of them, he thought maybe they should go without for a while. Twice Pete opened his mouth to speak, and twice he failed to produce anything but what could be communicated by a tighter grip.

Vance rescued him. "I've never seen a prettier sight than that Robin of yours."

Pete glanced at the helicopter. "I figured my Apache would be overkill," he replied, which caused Vance to laugh. In truth,

Vance might have laughed for joy at anything Pete said, because the sound of his voice was so welcome to his ears. And besides, Pete was incredibly funny.

Pete followed Vance up to building 12 and removed his hat when he entered. The brothers made introductions to Danielle as if they'd been apart for a day rather than for a decade and a half, and immediately started fielding questions from Simeon about the red helicopter, the most important being:

"Will I get to ride in it?"

"I dropped by to recommend something along those lines," Pete said. Vance held a hand out to the sofa that remained in front of the cold fireplace. Pete sat down on the hearth.

Simeon turned his enthusiastic eyes to Danielle and nodded like a bobblehead. She winked at him. "Patience, hon."

Her son attached himself to Pete by sitting down on the floor directly in front of him. The dog did the same.

"This is Ziggy," Simeon said. "I like your metal foot."

"Do you now? I like it too." He extended his leg so Simeon could take a closer look. "Not so much at first, but it has its advantages."

"What's advantages?"

"I can bust down a door without breaking my toe."

Simeon's eyes widened.

"Maybe I'll have to work that into my superhero story," Vance said. "With an exploding shoe or something."

Simeon grunted. "Yeah."

"We lost power," Vance said. "What's going on out there?"

"How long ago?"

Vance and Danielle shrugged at each other. "It's hard to say. Three, four days."

Pete frowned. "Port Rondeau was hit Wednesday."

"Flooded?" Vance asked.

"Some say it brings to mind Hurricane Katrina back in oh-five."

For an hour the little group asked questions and Pete told them what had been happening in the days when they'd been cut off from information and all sense of time. A rash of earthquakes was blamed for causing the supervolcano under Yellowstone to begin to roil and spew ash for miles, occasionally blocking the sun.

"That's the cause of your periodic darkness," Pete said, and Vance wondered at the depth of its blackness.

"And the ashy stuff," Vance said to Danielle.

"It wasn't very much," she added.

"It's only just getting started. The winds are swirling. The Rocky Mountains have taken the biggest hit. Right now the Pacific is turning into a mud pit."

"Did you hear anything about what happened to poison the waters here?" Danielle asked.

"Only the most general idea. The high waters covered a sandbar in the middle of a heavily trafficked lane, and a tanker ran aground."

"What did they spill?"

"No one's saying. It seems no one has to yet. I tell you, communication in this neck of the woods is fragmented. Lots of power interruptions, a lot of people can't get phone reception. Everything's unraveling, Vance. It took me three days to get here from Boston."

"How did you know I'd be here?"

"I follow your career," Pete said. He fiddled with the bill of his cap, rolling it in his palm. For a while, the only sound in the room was the light bumping of Simeon kicking the underside of the coffee table. No one asked him to stop.

"I was as skeptical as everyone else when

you started," Pete said. "When you called about investing in this place, people were already talking. All the way up in Beantown."

"It's a small industry," Vance said.

"I was curious, I really was. I would have kept you on the phone longer if I wasn't such an" — Danielle's eyes shot a respectful but clear request over Simeon's head — "astronomical jerk," Pete chose.

"Things worked out," Vance said.

"If everyone knew how strong this place really was, Port Rondeau would have evacuated everyone here."

Vance guffawed.

"You know how to build a shelter, Vance. Which is more than I can say for myself."

"So you need to move in with me, huh?"

Pete cracked the first smile Vance had seen since they were separated.

"I need your forgiveness more than your house," Pete said.

"You have it," Vance said. "You can have both."

"I'm the baby brother here, the way I blew you off all these years."

Vance looked at his feet. "That's the past."

"Well, technically. But I hope you and I will have some time to work it out properly."

Vance marked these words as the moment

he knew he'd never again fear being left to survive alone.

"I don't know," he joked. "I don't play poker anymore."

"I play checkers!" Simeon piped up.

"A wise choice," Pete said to the boy. "If you pack up your checkerboard, I'll promise you a few rounds once we get settled again."

"Where?" Danielle asked. She seated herself next to Vance on the sofa. "If Yellowstone goes all the way, is anywhere safe?"

"We'll know when it happens. But for now, the farther east we can get, the better. Let's go back to Boston, take stock."

"Can you control the sun?" Simeon asked. "Because someone's been doing weird stuff with the sun and the rain, and if you and Vance are going to start working together again, maybe you can fix it, and we won't have another flood."

Pete looked to Vance for help.

Vance only smiled at him. "What are you thinking? Europe?"

"Too early to say. But a partner of mine has a large piece of property in Newfoundland. We're welcome there if it comes to that. Is it just you three?"

"And one more," Vance said. "If we can find him."

Beside him, Danielle shivered.

"Four should be no problem."

"Who's the partner?" Vance said. "He must be a pretty generous guy, if he's willing to take in strangers."

"I've known him for years, met him when he created a sculpture for the atrium of my New York office. Pure silver. I'll show you pictures. Extremely successful. You ever hear of an artist named Ranier Smith?"

41

Until that morning Danielle would have said she no longer cared about Tony, that he deserved whatever ill end might find him. But compassion overcame her. She wished their search for him had been fruitful, so that she might have had time to exchange forgiveness face-to-face, as Vance had with Pete. But they searched every inch of building 12, every closet and crevice except for Jonesy's unit, which remained steadfastly locked as they had left it the day before, and found no evidence of him.

Vance speculated that Tony had gone down to hide in one of the other buildings or made an attempt to swim the cove. Pete suggested they search for him from the air. But while they gathered a few items from the condominiums that might be salvaged for good use, Danielle stood outside Jonesy's door with her own theory. She had no trouble imagining Tony climbing those stairs, unlocking this door with her keys, which he might have held on to during his ordeal, then hiding here. It was the perfect place to protect his aspirations from all the terrible consequences of his own actions. Because certainly he knew that she wouldn't protect him the way he wanted her to.

But she thought they both could use a second chance.

She tried to call him out with promises of a new beginning — not with her, but with a changed world. She spoke loudly enough for him to hear, telling him about Pete's arrival. He must have heard the helicopter arrive, though he wasn't in a position to have seen it land. There was room for him in it, she said. There was room for him in Boston. At the very least they could get him to his connections in New England. If the portrait of the country was as desperate as Pete had painted it, there would be nothing for anyone to do but forgive their neighbors' wrongdoings and start over. Her thoughts turned briefly toward her mother, and Danielle wondered how hard it would be to seek her out. She had been in Arizona the last time they connected. If Yellowstone continued on its course, Danielle didn't have a lot of time. It was a devastating kind of grace, but maybe all new beginnings were.

"Please come out," she said. "Please come with us."

If he was there, he didn't respond. If he heard her pounding, he ignored it. And because Tony more than anyone else here would have been first in line for escape from Eagle's Talon, Danielle decided she had been wrong after all.

She hoped she was wrong.

You don't have a lot of time, Ranier had said to her. She would ask him about it next time she saw him. And between now and then, she had many other questions that she hoped Vance would be able to answer. She wanted to know everything he knew, especially about how to stay strong.

She took Simeon's hand in hers and together they followed the Nolan brothers out to the bright red helicopter. For her son, she would need all of her strength, and all of Vance's.

In the helicopter, Danielle sat in the back between Vance and Simeon, with Ziggy stretched out over their feet. The noise was immense, a rumbling that she felt all the way to the bottom of her stomach even with the headsets that covered their ears and made communication possible. Simeon pressed his face and hands to the small window that looked down over the Rondeau

River as the helicopter rose off the turn-around.

Eagle's Talon looked humble from the air. Vance's attention was on it as they passed down the length of the crescent-shaped land mass, which now looked more like a moon than a bird claw. It wasn't the right time, with everyone listening to all conversations, to ask what he was thinking or to tell him what was on her mind — namely, that Vance should be proud of what he had built, even though it would never be finished the way he once envisioned it. She would always remember the charred aluminum walls, the blackened docks, and broken glass windows as perfect, having done everything they were designed to do. In particular, to save lives.

His pinched brows paired with the relaxed line of his mouth conveyed both sadness and relief as he took a look at Eagle's Talon from a new point of view.

They stayed low in search of Tony. If he was hidden they might draw him out with their ruckus. But after two passes, Danielle knew that this too would prove a waste of time.

She took hold of Vance's hand and appreciated the strength of it. The calluses and scars and rough patches were consistent with everything that she admired about his character. He laced his fingers through hers and with a gentle tug and a finger pointed at the window, indicated that she should have a look at something.

Pete was turning around above the collapsed isthmus road, preparing to pass over the development one last time before continuing east. Vance made room for Danielle to lean into him so she could see.

Beneath them, the currents of grimy rainbow water had yielded to shifting shades of blue and gray. The river flowed as swiftly as ever, in as much a hurry as they were to head south. It seemed to Danielle that she could see the layers of water as if they belonged to a sapphire onion, translucent and milky and potent, with the darkest shades on the bottom and a glittering transparent film over the top. It was strangely lovely, marred only by a few burnt bits of unidentifiable flotsam.

Danielle turned to Vance, so close in the tight quarters that his nearness crowded her thoughts. But she successfully resisted the urge to throw her arms around his neck and kiss him, as she had once made the terrible mistake of doing with Tony in a moment of huge emotional relief. The problem wasn't that she didn't trust Vance. She did. This time, her trust in him was great enough to become respect, the two feelings so completely filling her head that there was no room at all for neediness or fear.

She locked eyes with him and didn't feel the least bit awkward about her boldness. Instead, she was content to see that the connection pushed aside the little bit of sadness in his eyes. He rewarded her with a smile.

"Your work was perfect," she mouthed.

He laughed and shook his head, as if she'd made a funny error. His nose caught a strand of her hair, and he pushed it behind her headset and said through the mic, "See the lights?" Then he pointed again at the window.

Danielle's heart was full when she leaned in for another look, with Vance's confident touch steady on the center of her back. This time when her eyes went to the water she saw them: flickering silver lights rushing up from the riverbed toward the surface. They looked like copies of Ranier Smith's native silver cuff links. Those toward the bottom seemed to be the size of eggs, but those closer to the surface were nearly the size of footballs. Their glow varied in intensity just as the water varied in shades of blue, and liquid caused the light to shift and made it seem to breathe. She thought there were twelve, but their fluctuating sizes and pulsating glow made them hard to count.

They came together as if magnetized into a formation that first resembled an arrow. But it lengthened into a V more similar to a gaggle of geese flying south for the winter, and then finally thickened and filled out one last time to a brilliant glowing, beating shape that was undeniably a set of wings, stretched out like a bird testing the wind before leaping.

A thunk that Danielle felt in the soles of her shoes made her look away from the window. There on the floor of the helicopter's cabin was Simeon's cuff link, which he had been carrying in the pocket of his shorts. There was a frayed hole in that pocket, as if the jewel had just popped out, and when Danielle stuck out her toe to kick the piece back toward Simeon, she couldn't. It gripped the floor so tightly that she couldn't budge it. The stubborn jewel was a powerful magnet stuck to the floor. Ziggy woofed at it once, then pawed at it a couple of times, then left it alone.

The light it gave off was the same silvery blue as before. The same bright illumination as the wings in the water. She had the crazy idea that it would punch a hole in the bottom of the helicopter and merge with the watery wings below. But it stayed anchored in place.

Did you see them? she remembered Simeon saying. What she was seeing now was the only thing he could have meant. Danielle was astonished. She recalled his recognition of Ranier the first time he showed up at her condo and glanced over her shoulder to look at her son. At his window, Simeon was waving to someone she couldn't see.

Surely these were his "workers," and Vance had been in on the secret for some time.

On the far bank, around a bend in the shoreline, Danielle spotted Enrique's boat, the one that had transported Jonesy, Sam, Mirah, and the boys. Someone had pulled it up high onto the shore and left the oars and the life jackets neatly arranged in the bottom. Their friends had made it this far, at least. She hoped Carver and Ferti might also have survived.

Vance saw the boat too and they shared a relieved sigh over it.

She took in an awe-filled breath just before the explosion sounded, a powerful boom far greater than the noise generated by the helicopter. Danielle flinched, but there was no fireball or landslide to explain the breathtaking sound, the crack of an iceberg falling into the ocean. For a moment she feared another volcano, another earthquake, another tanker run aground, all worse than their predecessors.

The pump truck's boom that was still braced against building 12 began a nails-on-a-chalkboard skid down the structure's face. The half-sunk truck resumed its descent into the cove, completing its dive, until the rear outriggers were swallowed too.

Pete slowed the helicopter, turning it to a low hover at the bottom of the peninsula. The silver wings that had taken shape beneath number 12 began to beat the water, gliding off like an elegant ray, through the cove and toward the open Rondeau River.

From up here, building 12 looked strangely small and fragile, about to be reduced to the fate of number 11, or to some early stage like the other ten foundations still floating on the cove.

She kept her eyes on it, and within seconds the face of building 12 began to tip toward the water. Though she couldn't see the forces at work underneath, she was able to imagine them, as only one thing could explain the unbelievable sight. In the front, the steel poles that kept the tall structure in position on the shoreline took a bow like a stage actor at the final curtain call. And as they bent forward and down, they held fast to the attached foundation. At the back of the building, the structure rose and groaned and strained, snapping away from the footbridge as if it were made of toothpicks. Finally, with a clap-of-thunder crack, the structure freed itself from the rear posts, which now protruded from the water at awful angles.

Danielle covered her mouth with her hand. Vance was shaking his head, riveted to the scene.

"There's no one to hold it up anymore," he said.

The metallic complaints of the building continued for long seconds and ended only when the glimmering facade of building 12 smacked the water. Glass windows shattered. Bits of concrete and foam littered the water as the weight of the building snapped its own foundation free of the broken posts. Then, like a secret compartment in a floor, the beautiful aluminum structure somersaulted and the lightweight foundation took its place on the top. Soon there was no sign of her home except the buoyant foam-and-concrete slab, its fractured steel supports protruding from the bottom, moseying down the river past its neighbors.

"That hurts," Pete said in low tones. But Danielle made out the words and bit her lip. Vance's expression was unreadable. She sandwiched his hand in hers.

Beneath the helicopter, the silver-blue wings emerged from the water like a living ice sculpture, dripping. They beat against the air and came up underneath the landing skids, bolstering the craft, so that Danielle could see only the wingtips out each window.

Pete raised his voice over the headsets. "No sign of your friend. Are you prepared to leave him behind?"

"He left us," Vance said. "It looks like the workers have packed up and punched the clock too."

"Who?" Pete said.

"He doesn't see it," Danielle mouthed to Vance. For some reason this made her want to giggle.

"The workers," shouted Simeon. "Now they're holding up our helicopter."

"Good. I'll take all the help I can get."

Vance said, "This Robin is now officially the safest place in the world that we can be, Pete."

"Is that so?" Pete angled the bird eastward and picked up speed. "Your word's good enough for me."

Vance tipped his head back against the cushion and closed his eyes, the picture of contentment. Pete's ready agreement with his brother gave Danielle's heart its own wings. She had been freed for this promising new beginning, rescued by the very definition of mercy. Rescued by Vance Nolan.

She stared at him, grinning, taking advantage of his restfulness. He deserved this reprieve, when others who believed in him could finally step in to share the load.

Sleep a bit, her heart urged him.

He squeezed her hand.

DISCUSSION QUESTIONS

1. In what physical things do you put your sense of safety (e.g., money, sound structures, good health)? How do you respond when these securities are threatened or stripped away from you?
2. In what circumstances do you feel like you really need a strong certainty that God is real? How does this compare to times when you can live comfortably with your doubts? What accounts for the difference? If you don't experience a shifting confidence, why do you think that is?
3. Natural disasters and accidents represent hardships that are far beyond a person's control. Compare the ways Tony, Danielle, Vance, and Zeke respond to the various uncontrollable events in their lives. Which behaviors do you admire? Which serve as a warning? How do these compare to the ways you typically react?
4. Zeke observes that suffering affects

people differently. "One man's suffering was cause for cynicism; another's was cause for hope." Do you agree? If so, what accounts for the different reactions of the human heart?

5. How would you characterize Vance's rescue of Enrique? Was it heroic, foolish, coincidental, or something else? What did you think when Ranier characterizes it as a loving act?

6. Ranier tells Vance that Danielle "needs far more than you do" when it comes to proof of the spiritual realm. What do you think of the fairness of this possibility, i.e., that God might not reveal himself to each of us equally, or even in similar ways?

7. The letter that Ranier brings to Danielle seems offensive at first, but her experiences gradually reveal the love it contains. Have you ever had a similar experience while reading the Bible? Explain.

8. What perspectives does *Afloat* offer about the true nature of life and death?

9. How do you react to Ranier's remark, "Loving any human being always involves a little bit of dying. I hear it gets easier every time"?

10. If given the choice, would you stay in heaven or return to earth? What factors —

what people — might influence that decision?

ACKNOWLEDGMENTS

This manuscript would not exist without the creative determination of Thomas Nelson's former fiction publisher Allen Arnold. Thanks for your trust and confidence, Allen. May God bless all the works of your hands in your new career.

This manuscript would not have taken the shape that it did without the thoughtful observations of my editor, Ami McConnell, who always seems to know the right thing to do and keeps my bellybutton gazing in check. Thank you, Ami, for so carefully tending my manuscript and our friendship.

LB Norton has worn the editor's glasses that I must remove from my own face while writing. Not only that, she has a brilliant sense of humor and an artist's touch. Without you, Anne, I'd be adrift on a sea of overstatement and melodrama. Thanks for rowing out to fetch me back.

It's never an agony to turn my books over

to the most skilled and capable Thomas
Nelson Fiction team. Daisy Hutton,
Amanda Bostic, Becky Monds, Jodi Hughes,
Kristen Vasgaard, Katie Bond, Ruthie Dean,
Laura Dickerson, and Kerri Potts, you
inspire my confidence again and again in
this Publishing Age of Excitement. I watch
in admiration. The future is bright.

Meredith Smith and Dan Raines of Creative Trust, Inc., have been wise advisers for
me in a time when it seems anything can
happen to a writer. (Nothing bad — it's all
good material.) Thank you for bestowing a
generous heap of your special smarts on me.

Leah Apineru of Impact Author Services
has saved my sanity more than once. Thank
you for doing and for learning all the things
I don't have the courage to tackle.

Vance's vision for the buildings of Eagle's
Talon was inspired by the works of architect
David Hertz, in particular his Panel House
of Venice Beach, California. Although the
Panel House stands on solid ground, its
prefabricated aluminum panels and narrow
footprint captured my imagination.

And I would be remiss not to thank the
entertaining members of Concretepump
ing.com, who answered my novice questions
with patience and a chorus of practical
wisdom. Q: "What are the emergency proce-

dures in the event that a pump truck desta-
bilizes?" A: "Get the (bleep) out of the way!"

ABOUT THE AUTHOR

Erin Healy is the best-selling co-author of *Burn* and *Kiss* (with Ted Dekker) and an award-winning editor for numerous best-selling authors. She has received wide acclaim for her novels *Never Let You Go* and *The Baker's Wife.* She and her family live in Colorado.

The employees of Thorndike Press hope you have enjoyed this Large Print book. All our Thorndike, Wheeler, and Kennebec Large Print titles are designed for easy reading, and all our books are made to last. Other Thorndike Press Large Print books are available at your library, through selected bookstores, or directly from us.

For information about titles, please call:
  (800) 223-1244

or visit our Web site at:
  http://gale.cengage.com/thorndike

To share your comments, please write:
  Publisher
  Thorndike Press
  10 Water St., Suite 310
  Waterville, ME 04901